DARK WATERS

OTHER BOOKS BY CHRIS GOFF

A Rant of Ravens

Death of a Songbird

A Nest in the Ashes

Death Takes a Gander

A Sacrifice of Buntings

DARK WATERS

A THRILLER

CHRIS GOFF

CROOKED LANE

NEW YORK

Published in the United States by Crooked Lane Books, an imprint of The Quick Brown Fox & Company LLC.

Crooked Lane Books and its logo are trademarks of The Quick Brown Fox & Company LLC.

The Library of Congress Cataloging-in-Publication Data is available upon request.

ISBN (hardcover): 978-1-62953-192-2
ISBN (paperback): 978-1-62953-372-8
e-ISBN: 978-1-62953-205-9

Cover/book design by Lori Palmer

Printed in the United States.

www.crookedlanebooks.com

Crooked Lane Books
2 Park Avenue, 10th Floor
New York, NY 10016

First Edition: September 2015

10 9 8 7 6 5 4 3 2 1

FOR DANIELLE, WHO TOOK ME TO
ISRAEL AND BECAME THE CATALYST.

Chapter 1

The smell of falafel hit Ben Taylor's nose the moment he opened the door. For the hundredth time, he cursed the preponderance of eating establishments around Zinah Dizengoff Square. The mingling of odors created a non-Kosher smell that oozed from the surrounding buildings and wafted up from the outdoor dining areas. The only respite came at sundown on Friday, when every business establishment in Tel Aviv closed for Shabbat.

"Luce, we need to get moving."

"I'm coming, Daddy."

His daughter sounded annoyed, but Taylor cut her some slack. It was tough being eleven. Especially since he had picked her up and set her down halfway around the world—without her mom and without her friends.

"We don't want to be late."

"I said, I'm cooooming!" Lucy dragged out her final word as she stomped through the bedroom doorway, tying up her blond hair with a ponytail band. "Have you seen my Coach bag?"

Translation, pink purse. Her mother had given it to her the day before they had left for Israel. Lucy carried it everywhere.

Taylor glanced around the sparsely furnished apartment. To his left, a small entertainment center faced a sofa littered with the remnants of yesterday's *New York Times*. Between the entertainment center and sofa, a rickety end table served as a catchall.

No purse.

Behind the sofa, a small, empty table and four metal chairs segued into a kitchen of miniature proportions.

"I don't see it, Luce." He glanced at his watch. "Six minutes until the fountain goes off. You either go without the purse or we miss the show."

Taylor figured that would get her moving. Lucy liked their daily routine—heading into the square, stopping to watch the fountain in all its glory, and then walking along Sharon Street to Alon, cutting through the residential neighborhoods, past the dusty school yard and down the block to the strip mall where Alena's office was tucked away in the basement. Following Lucy's treatment, they would saunter back, taking their time to window-shop. Taylor liked the bookstore. Lucy liked the Pizza Hut. Taylor figured it reminded her of home.

"I *need* my bag," she said.

"Did you check the bathroom?"

Lucy dashed down the hall and came back seconds later, flaunting the purse on her arm. Cropped blue jeans, black flip-flops, and coral-tipped toenails completed the "all-American kid next door" look. She struck a model's pose with her little-girl frame. "Ta da!"

"Come on," he said. "Let's move it."

She stepped around him, swishing back her ponytail, her white tank top riding up on her tanned stomach. Only her pale face and the dark circles under her eyes belied the picture of health. It frightened him.

Taylor keyed the deadbolt and led the way down two flights of stairs and through the garden bereft of chairs, benches, or plants. Across a wide expanse of gravel, the back door to the bar catercorner to the apartment complex stood ajar, propped open by a large, black, plastic trash can. Straight ahead was the back entrance to the apartment building offices.

He stuck to the sidewalk, skirting both doorways, and held open the garden gate. Heading across the street toward the square, Lucy edged closer.

On their first day in Tel Aviv, they'd learned that, in 1994, Dizengoff Square had been the site of a suicide bombing. A bus trundling down Dizengoff Street had passed underneath the elevated pedestrian square and exploded, killing twenty-two people and injuring forty-eight others. The story had terrified Lucy.

In Israel, suicide bombings were never a thing of the past. While they had gotten used to seeing soldiers with guns and being searched every time they entered the grocery store or mall, the military presence served as a constant reminder of the possibility for violence.

Now, starting up the rise toward the fountain, Lucy dogged Taylor's heels. He knew the gathering throng spooked her. She possessed a fear of crowded places—and teenagers—and Dizengoff Square served as a Mecca for Tel Aviv teens. Still, her love of the spectacle of the fountain trumped her anxiety.

The *Fire and Water Fountain* stood in the middle of the overpass. Created by Jewish artist Yaakov Agam, the fountain was more entertainment than art. Four times daily, it spun to a pulsing musical beat, flashing a variety of colors and spewing fire and water into the air. The display was listed in every guidebook and on every website as "among the top ten things to do in Tel Aviv."

Today the square seemed busier than usual. Young and old, Jewish and non-Jewish, soldiers and civilians crowded the walkways. People lined the waist-high walls and filled the benches that encircled the square, waiting for the show to begin.

Ahead of them, Taylor spotted their landlord, Ofer Federman, coming toward them. A tall man with close-cropped hair and dark glasses, he towered a head above the crowd. As always, he carried a bag full of crepes, purchased every day at 10:50 a.m. from the stand on the opposite side of the square.

"*Shalom aleichem*, Lucy. Ben."

"*Shalom,* Mr. Federman," Lucy answered, plastering herself to Taylor's side. He squeezed her shoulders and nodded to Federman as they passed.

"Look, Daddy, there's a seat." Lucy grabbed Taylor's hand and tugged him forward. One-half of a blue bench sat empty, the other half occupied by an olive-skinned man in a black, short-sleeved shirt, clutching a small computer.

As Lucy scooted onto the bench, the man glanced up at Taylor. "Together?" he asked, first in Hebrew, then in English.

"Yes," Taylor said. "But we're here every day, sometimes twice a day. I can stand."

"You may have it." The man's accent made him hard to understand, and he no longer looked at Taylor but at some point beyond. Taylor started to turn around, to see what captured the man's attention, when the man stood up.

"I insist," he said.

"It's okay, really," Taylor said, but the man hurried off.

Lucy scooted over and patted the bench beside her. "Front row seats."

Taylor smiled.

They spent the next five minutes watching the people filling the square. Lucy pressed up close to his side, and he draped his arm lightly around her shoulders. It was these moments he cherished most, the times when she seemed just like any other child.

A commotion beside them caused Taylor to turn. A computer clattered to the pavement. A man on a bench to their right clutched his throat. A tall man in sunglasses stood behind him, one arm snaked around the seated man's shoulders, one arm held out to the

4

side. Sunlight flashed off the blade of a knife in his hand. Blood gushed from the victim's throat.

Then a shot rang out.

A red circle bloomed on the assailant's forehead. His head snapped back. His arms flew up. The knife clattered to the concrete, and both men dropped to the ground.

Taylor reacted. Pulling Lucy to her feet, he pushed her forward, toward the cover of the fountain wall. A moment later, the fountain cranked into motion, its pulsing music and erupting fire whipping the crowd into a bigger frenzy. People screamed and ran for cover. A young mother pushing a baby carriage veered to the right, the carriage on two wheels. Someone knocked into Lucy, sending her sprawling onto the pavement.

"Lucy!" Taylor grabbed the back of her shirt.

She scrambled to her knees, her face bloodied. Grabbing her unzipped purse, she frantically scooped up its spilled contents—a cell phone she carried in case of emergency, lip gloss, and a small Hello Kitty wallet.

An Israeli soldier nearby shouldered his gun to return fire. When a bullet slammed into the sidewalk near his feet, near Lucy, the soldier jumped for cover.

"Move!" Taylor yanked his daughter up. He dragged her closer to the fountain and pushed her down behind the concrete wall. "Stay down!"

Hunching over his daughter, he put his body and the whirling fountain between her and the shooter. A third shot ricocheted off the edge of the fountain above his head. Was the sniper gunning for him?

Taylor pressed tighter the fountain wall, closer to Lucy. He knew he had taken a chance coming here, but what else could he have done? Lucy's life hung in the balance. He knew Alena would save her, just as long as he didn't get her killed first.

Chapter 2

Batya Ganani lowered her rifle and stared down at the square from her fourth-floor perch in disbelief. Her assignment had been to oversee the exchange and provide backup in the event of a double cross. Now Cline and another man were dead, and the contact had escaped with the USB drives. Colonel Brodsky wasn't going to be happy.

She replayed the scene in her mind. There had been no trouble with the exchange. The men had passed in the square and exchanged drives. No one seemed to notice or care. Both men carried tablets and stopped in the square to verify the exchanged information. Then Cline's contact had nodded, and another man had stepped forward and slit Cline's throat from behind. She had done the only thing she could do. She had put a bullet through the forehead of the accomplice. When she finally had a clean shot at the contact, the trajectory was low. The bullet clipped the wall of the fountain. She'd missed.

The sirens on the street grew louder, and she cursed her luck. Soon the building would be crawling with soldiers and police. It was time to go.

Picking up the rifle, she folded the sling close to the barrel and palmed the weapon near the trigger, holding it upright against her back. She only needed to get to the hotel's trash chute without the rifle being seen. She wore indistinguishable clothing—black pants, black shoes, a wig, and a black, short-sleeved T-shirt that showed off her cleavage. Experience told her that few men, or women, would notice anything else about her. A loose black jacket helped conceal the weapon.

The hallway of the hotel was deserted, the beige carpet and walls broken up by closed white doors. In case any residents peeked out of the peepholes of their doors, she kept her head down, the hair of the wig obscuring her face. She avoided the main elevators and exits and made her way to the end of the hall.

She stepped into the small service room, dropped the rifle into the trash chute, and made her way to the service stairs. By now, soldiers and police would have cordoned off the lobby. The stairs led to the kitchen and then to the basement, where the trash chute emptied. From there, a separate set of stairs led to the street.

She encountered no one as she made her way down from the fourth floor to the kitchen. The door creaked softly as she pushed it open.

"Who is there?" a young soldier demanded.

Ganani considered playing the frightened guest, but she couldn't risk being detained. Stepping into the kitchen, she flashed identification.

"*Yasam*," she said, the lie coming easy. She slapped her credential holder shut before the soldier could note the differences between it and the shield of the Israel Police Counter-Terror Unit.

"You don't dress like *Yasam*."

"We had a tip. I was placed here to appear like a guest." She did her best to sound annoyed, making it clear it was not his place to question her. "Why aren't these stairs being guarded?"

The soldier, all of eighteen, kept his eyes glued right where she wanted them. "I am guarding them."

"Then you need to be in the stairwell, *Turái.*" Private. She spoke gently, as if addressing a child. Ten years of added experience left her feeling generous.

The private glanced up at her face and then back at her breasts. "I was told to stay near the door."

"By whom?" As the seconds ticked by, her feelings of generosity waned.

"The *samál.*"

She drew a breath that made her breasts rise. "Go tell your sergeant there must be two people here—one by the door and one in the stairwell."

"I have orders not to leave."

Enough already. "What is your name, Private?"

The boy glanced up again.

"Tell me your name."

"I don't want any trouble."

"Then go tell your sergeant."

"Yes, ma'am." He saluted and turned on his heels.

Once he disappeared, Ganani wasted no time. The basement entrance was hidden behind a five-tiered metal cart covered with jars of pickles, olives, and jam. Pushing the cart out of the way, she tugged open the wooden door.

Kicking a baluster free of the railing, Ganani secured the door from the inside. Then, scrambling down the wooden steps, she retrieved her rifle from the mound of bagged trash beneath the chute, slung it across her back, and moved quickly across the dirt floor to the outside door.

More steps climbed to the street entrance that opened out onto a small concrete pad crowded with trash and recycling bins, nearly a block from the main entrance of the hotel. Her car was parked across the street directly in front. Looking through the dirty, barred window beside the door, Ganani could see three soldiers standing on the opposite sidewalk. These were not young men and would not be so easy to boss around. One of them leaned against her black Volvo C70.

Pressing her back to the exit, she drew a deep breath. It wouldn't be long before someone inside discovered the basement. From her position by the window, she could hear footsteps in the kitchen. Best to take her chances outside.

She was reaching for the door handle when a commotion in front of the hotel saved her. The young soldier who had refused to give her his name bolted into the street. From snatches of conversation, she ascertained that he had returned to the kitchen and found her gone. Now he sounded the alarm. Not to be left out of the action, the three soldiers near her car raced away behind him.

Ganani waited three counts and then slipped outside. She closed the door, jamming the handle with a trash cart from the outside, and moved swiftly to her car. Popping the trunk, she placed her rifle inside, along with her black wig, and shut the trunk. Sliding behind the wheel of her Volvo, she slipped on a pair of tortoiseshell sunglasses and pulled the car into the street. A policeman on the next corner gestured her into the far lane and waved her on. Two turns later, she reached Ben Yehuda Street and was free of the area.

Rolling down the car windows, Ganani let the breeze ruffle her hair and strip away some of her tension. There were still things to do. First she needed to call her boss. Then she needed to find Cline's contact.

Chapter 3

The dirt path ran perpendicular to the edge of the paved road. Packed hard from heavy use, it wound downhill through a valley of thorny bushes before forking uphill, skirting the town of Tūlkarm and ending at the workers' crossing at Taibeh. The stamped ground served as a testimony to the permeability of the border. It also served to convince Haddid that he was correct—peace was the only answer.

In just over a week, President Hadawi would meet with Israel's prime minister, America's secretary of state, and leaders from Gaza and the West Bank to try to broker a peace. To Haddid's way of thinking, only this could guarantee the future of Palestine. Without a peace agreement, Israel would continue its encroachment on the West Bank, Gaza, and the Golan Heights. Without a peace agreement, Palestine would eventually cease to exist.

He glanced around at the others making their way from the West Bank into Israel and imagined most of them believed the same thing. They were men and women who simply wanted to work and come home, put food on their tables, and spend time with their families. How sad that their voices could not rise above the noise of Hamas. Like the voices of the free world, only those who shouted loud enough were heard.

"Why so serious, Haddid?" asked Mansoor. "What are you thinking, my friend?"

Haddid had nearly forgotten his friend was beside him. The two of them had been close, like brothers, since grade school, yet he lacked the courage to tell Mansoor the truth. "I was wondering how Israel will survive when the wall is finished and the border sealed."

Mansoor threw back his head and laughed, his white teeth flashing against the deep brown of his skin. "Not to worry, Haddid. If they finish the wall, there will be a gate. Besides, once our mission is complete, Israel will have more to worry about than building a barrier to keep us out."

The mission. Haddid stared at the ground.

His friend had worked hard to bring him onboard, but in the end, it had been the unspoken threat to his family that had pushed him to join. Although Mansoor believed in Abdul Aleem Zuabi, the head of the Palestine Liberation Committee, or PLC, Haddid considered Zuabi just a well-spoken, middle-aged man who came from somewhere outside of Palestine. As a leader, he emerged after the latest intifada and wanted the eradication of the State of Israel for no better reason than hate.

His was an untenable position, thought Haddid. Israel was too strong. There were already too many dead.

Mansoor clutched Haddid's arm at the elbow, dipped his head, and spoke quietly into his ear. "We are to meet Najm and Muatab in Yaffa this afternoon. By now, they should have the information that Zuabi requires."

A wave of nausea tightened Haddid's stomach. He battled the urge to knock away Mansoor's bony hand. The chatter of the workers around them filled his ears, then the crossing appeared in front of them and all conversation ceased, as though tiptoeing silently across the border made them invisible.

The legal crossing into Israel was fewer than one hundred meters to the north, but few of the workers ever crossed there— only those with blue cards. At the official checkpoint, Israeli guards stopped and questioned all people entering or leaving the West Bank—mostly curious tourists, reporters, or Israeli occupiers. Most workers slipped across the invisible line under the watchful eye of the enemy. They were the illegal workers, happy to sweat in the jobs undesired by a group of people who, by virtue of religion, viewed themselves as superior. The Palestinians built Israeli houses, cleaned, cooked, and tended the gardens, and the Israelis paid them under the table. It was an arrangement that had existed for years. Usually they dispersed into the bowels of Israel without confrontation, yet, occasionally, like a pack of wolves, the soldiers would move in and scatter the workers like frightened gazelles. Separating the weakest, the soldiers would terrorize some poor soul who could not run so fast. The only difference between the soldiers and wolves were that the soldiers were not hungry, just bored. Today, they were simply too busy.

In Netanya, Haddid and Mansoor climbed aboard a bus bound for Tel Aviv. It was crowded and hot, and Haddid sat alone near the back. The windows were open, and he could smell the flowers of Ramat HaSharon, a city of wealthy Israelis who employed many illegal workers. The bus stopped there and emptied out. Mansoor moved back, sitting beside Haddid. Mansoor marveled at how modern the city was, but Haddid barely listened. All he wanted was to smell the sea.

Chapter 4

Raisa Jordan drank in the view from her office window. To the west, the blue waters of the Mediterranean stretched as far as her eye could see. Closer in, the waves lapped the expanse of sandy beach bordering the new high-rises, the Dolphinarium, and the ancient golden city of Yafo. She'd only been in her new post as assistant regional security officer, or ARSO, for two weeks, and already she loved Tel Aviv.

"Jordan." The RSO's voice crackled over the intercom. "My office. Now!"

From his tone, Jordan knew something was wrong. She headed for his office, her heels clacking on the black-and-white tiles of the hall. She entered without knocking.

"Check this out." Tom Daugherty gestured with the remote toward a TV mounted on the back wall of his office. "Can you believe this shit?"

Jordan frowned at the images. An amateur video flashed across the screen. It showed a Middle Eastern square, dust billowing in the wake of panic. The voice-over wasn't loud enough to drown out the screams. Most people were running or ducking for cover. A man and child had plastered themselves against the concrete wall that surrounded a fountain erupting in fire and water. To the right, two bodies lay on the ground. The photographer zoomed in.

"What's the newscaster saying?" Daugherty turned up the volume, as though decibels were synonymous with understanding.

Jordan was surprised he didn't speak Hebrew. She'd had to take a six-week immersion course in the language before being assigned to her post, and Daugherty had been here nearly two years. "There's been a shooting," she translated. "In Zinah Dizengoff Square. This feed is from a bystander's cell phone."

"How many dead?"

"She hasn't said. Soldiers returned fire and have surrounded the building where they believe the sniper is hiding."

"They have the shooter pinned down?"

"It's unclear." Jordan looked at Daugherty. With the secretary of state due to arrive in five days to oversee peace talks, the embassy was on maximum alert. "How far away is the square? Do we need to do something to protect the embassy?"

"No." His gaze never left the screen. "Dizengoff's two clicks away. The Marines are ready in the event of an attack."

Jordan nodded and turned her attention back to the video. The female newscaster spoke again.

"What's she saying now?"

"The shooting has stopped. Two confirmed dead."

"Then either the gunman is a very bad shot or he only wanted to kill certain people."

Jordan agreed.

The photographer zoomed in and showed a close-up of a soldier turning over one of the bodies. Blood seeped from a gash on his neck, making his white shirt look as if it were tie-dyed red.

"*That* doesn't look like a gunshot." Jordan took note of his clothes and the cut of his hair. "Is he an American?" The State Department had recently issued a traveler's warning. She looked to her RSO for direction. His face had gone slack.

"What is it, sir?"

14

"That's Steven Cline."

It took her a moment to process the name. "The ARSO I'm replacing? Isn't he supposed to be in Washington?"

Daugherty picked up the phone. "Patsy, get Ambassador Linwood on the line, stat!" Then he turned to Jordan. "You wanted your first assignment? Well, here it is. Get your butt out there and figure out why my former ARSO is lying dead on a street in Tel Aviv instead of at home with his family in D.C."

Chapter 5

Najm Tibi sat inside a cafe one block from Dizengoff Square and whispered a silent prayer to Allah that his own life had been spared. Muatab had not been so lucky, and Tibi grieved for his friend. They had accomplished the mission, but at what cost?

Moments after hearing the first shot, Tibi had yanked the USB drive with the plans out of the American's computer. He remembered staring down at his friend. Muatab never twitched. His eyes were open. Realizing there was nothing he could do, Tibi had turned to run, stumbled over the girl, and dropped the drives. Then, scooping them up, he had fled to safety nearby.

He patted the zippered compartment of his computer sleeve, where he'd transferred the drives once he was out of range and positive he hadn't been followed. Watching the drama unfold on the mounted television, his guilt over Muatab's death grew. How could he have known they were walking into an ambush?

The footage on the screen showed the shooting was over. Soldiers and police were gathering at the scene. He watched as the bodies were turned over. While gentle with the American, the soldiers flopped Muatab on the concrete like a fish on a rock. There was no more doubt. His friend was dead.

Anger festered in Tibi's belly as the Israelis in the bar reveled in Muatab's death. To them, Muatab was nothing more than a killer.

But to Tibi, he was a hero. The Palestinians would celebrate him as a martyr. As it was written in the Quran and ordained by Allah, "A soul for a soul." They would avenge his death. Tibi would see it was done.

The camera panned to a view of the Zinah Dizengoff Hotel. The newscaster reported that the shots were fired from a fourth-floor window. Tibi was sure the shooter was gone by now. But who was he, and how had he known about the exchange? No one at Tibi's workplace of work was smart enough to figure out that he had taken anything of importance. After all, he was just a maintenance worker. And Zuabi had only given him instructions that morning to meet the contact at Dizengoff Square. That meant the sniper had to be an Israeli or an American, either working with the contact or having tailed him to the square.

Tibi decided he had waited long enough. Paying for his coffee, he exited the bar and headed south, swept along in the wake of the crowd pressing toward Dizengoff Square. Before he could break off and move toward the bus stop, a soldier moved toward him.

"Hey, you!"

Tibi froze.

"What are you doing?"

As an Israeli Arab, Tibi knew he was someone on whom suspicion might fall. He didn't want to bring attention to where he was headed, so he pointed across the street to the post office, with its red-and-white sign and deer logo. "I am going to the Postal Authority."

"Then why are you lingering here?"

A surge of anger made him brave. He was a citizen of Israel, with the same rights as anyone else. "Because there is a crowd stopping here."

Those who only minutes ago fled in terror were now filtering back. Tibi understood why. What better place to relive a near-death experience than the crime scene? But this soldier focused on him. Not because of his presence, but because he was Arab.

The soldier waved his rifle. "Move along."

Even though he wanted to stand his ground, Tibi knew now was not the time to stand and fight. Turning away, he struck out toward the Postal Authority. He would go in and then out the back. In the end, all Tibi wanted to do was leave him with no memorable impression.

Chapter 6

Jordan parked the embassy vehicle on a side street near Zinah
Dizengoff Square behind a dozen other police and military
vehicles pulled up haphazardly to the curbs and counted twenty-
three Israeli soldiers blocking the perimeter of the square. Their
khaki green uniforms offset a long row of bright blue removable
metal fencing, creating a picket-like effect as they stood at attention, their guns ready. Even so, a large crowd had gathered. Workers from nearby office buildings had come out to gawk, along with
the hotel staff and the waiters and cooks from the restaurants lining the street. Along the sidewalks, parents boosted children onto
their shoulders. Tourists snapped photos. Everyone looked to see
what was happening near the fountain—everyone, that is, except
a solitary man who kept his head down and moved swiftly toward
the Postal Authority. Something about him struck her as off.

Jordan tracked his movements as she climbed out of her car.
At the entrance to the Postal Authority, the man looked up. Olive-
skinned, with dark hair and dark eyes, he appeared to be an Arab.
He held open the door for an elderly patron and then ducked
inside. When he didn't exit quickly, she chalked up her suspicion
to nerves.

She reached for her Kevlar vest—the one with "Federal Agent"
stamped on the back—and slipped it on over her shirt. Regulations

required she wear it, though from her perspective, it was like donning a bull's-eye. Her outfit screamed "American." There was already one dead agent. Why not make it two?

She checked her gun, making sure it was visible on her hip and holstered securely per the Defense Security Service—better known as DSS—agreement with the Israeli government. Attaching her ID to a lanyard, she slipped it over her head and reached back to gather her hair into a ponytail. Then, taking a deep, calming breath, she headed toward the barricades.

"Special Agent Jordan," she announced in Hebrew to one of the guards stationed at the edge of the square. She held up her badge. "Who's in charge here?"

A tall, thin man kneeling beside Cline's body signaled to the guard to let her through. He stood as she approached and extended a hand.

"Detective Noah Weizman, homicide division," he said, his English perfect. "Daugherty informed me that you were coming and would be following the investigation. It makes sense seeing as one of the victims is yours." He pointed to the body. "It was my understanding Cline was headed back to the United States soon."

"That's correct." She didn't add that Cline should have already been stateside. His transfer request had cited family reasons—that his mother was ill and he was needed at home. But a cursory check Jordan conducted less than a half-hour ago turned up that his mother was on an extended Italian vacation with his sister.

"What about the other man?" she asked. "The one who slit Cline's throat. Who is he?"

"No ID yet. We think he's Palestinian. We're running facial recognition. So far, no hit."

"What about the shooter? Did you catch him?"

Weizman shook his head. A dark curl settled on his forehead, accentuating his tan and the strong line of his nose. He pointed to the hotel. "Whoever she was, she set up on the fourth floor and managed to elude the soldiers."

She? Female terrorists weren't unheard of, but normally they carried out missions via suicide bombings or poisonings, not through sniper rounds. "How do you know it was a woman?"

"A young soldier stationed in the kitchen saw her. He claims she identified herself as working for the Israeli Police Counter-Terror Unit."

"Did he get a description?"

"He claims she had a nice set of tits. Oh, and black hair." Weizman shrugged as if to say, *it happens,* and then gestured toward the Palestinian's body. "The sniper's first shot brought him down."

"Only two victims?"

"Correct." Weizman scraped his fingers across the stubble that darkened his chin. "Any ideas on what your man was doing to get himself killed?"

Jordan shook her head. It seemed Cline had gone off the grid. During her fact-finding mission, she uncovered that he had notified the State Department in D.C. that he would be delayed in Israel by a week and had rescheduled his flight from Ben Gurion International Airport to Dulles. She had no idea why he had not informed their RSO.

Squatting beside the bodies, she studied the wounds and the blood spatter patterns. The wound at Cline's throat seemed the clear cause of death. An entrance wound in the Palestinian's forehead indicated he had died from a single-round shot from a high-powered rifle. No doubt there was a gaping hole in the back of his head.

Jordan stood. "Any witnesses?"

"Fifty or so. Those two were the closest." Weizman pointed toward a man and a young girl seated on the wall across from the fountain. "The man was almost killed by another shot. It's possible he was a target."

"How do you figure?"

"He told us. The last shot fired drilled the fountain right above his head. Maybe you'd like to speak to him. He's one of yours."

"One of ours?"

"An American." Weizman led the way across the square. When they reached the man and child, he introduced Jordan to the police officer standing guard. "This is my partner, Detective Gidon Lotner. Gidon, this is Special Agent Jordan."

She extended her hand to Lotner.

The short, stout man ignored the gesture and nodded curtly. "This is Judge Ben Taylor and his daughter, Lucy."

The judge seemed to be taking stock of the situation, though the young girl was clearly shaken. She huddled close to her father while he gently stroked her hair. The gesture touched Jordan at gut level, reminding her of her own father.

"Judge Taylor, I'm the assistant regional security officer assigned to the U.S. embassy. Whenever there are incidents in Tel Aviv involving Americans, I am sent out to investigate."

The father nodded, but the child look scared. Jordan dropped down to her eye level.

"How old are you?"

"Eleven."

"You must have been scared."

The child shrugged. Blood spatter spotted the front of her white tank top like brown freckles. She clung to her dad's hand and kept her eyes focused on the concrete. "I lost some of my stuff."

"But you and your dad are okay."

The judge, who was watching his daughter, said, "Can we do this later?"

Jordan shook her head. "It's better for us to get the information while it's fresh in your minds." She stood up, focusing on the present. "Judge Taylor, can you tell me why you're in Israel?"

"We're here because Lucy is sick."

Jordan studied the girl. When the child looked up, Jordan was struck by the depth of the circles etched under her chocolate-brown eyes.

"Go on."

"We're seeing a doctor here—Dr. Alena Petrenko." The judge's arm slipped around his daughter's shoulders, and he drew her closer to him. "It's making a difference."

Jordan noted an edge to his voice.

"Is your mother here?" she asked Lucy.

"My ex-wife is stateside," the judge said. "Lucy spends her summers with me."

Again, Jordan took note of his tone. Maybe he didn't get along with his ex-wife, or maybe it was something else. "What type of judge are you, Judge Taylor? State—"

"Federal."

That got her attention.

Jordan turned to Lucy. "Do you mind if I speak to your daddy alone?" She tipped her head at Detective Lotner, waiting for Lucy to respond. Lotner scowled. Lucy looked scared.

"It'll only be for a minute," Jordan said. "You can wait right there." She pointed to a bench farther away from the fountain and the dead bodies.

Lucy tightened her grip on her father's fingers.

He leaned over and whispered something in her ear. Reluctantly, she let go of his hand, moving toward the bench with Detective Lotner.

"Thank you," said Jordan, waiting for them to get out of earshot.

"Let's get this over with," the judge said, his voice commanding, like a man who was used to giving orders rather than taking them.

Hoping to put him at ease, Jordan sat on the edge of the wall beside him. "Judge Taylor, did you know either of the two men who died?"

"No."

"Do you know of any reason someone might want you dead?"

Taylor's eyes narrowed. "I'm a federal judge."

"Let me rephrase. Do you know of any reason someone *here* might want you dead?"

Taylor looked away. "I would never willingly put Lucy in danger."

"I'll take that as a yes." It was obvious that his daughter was his primary concern, so when he didn't respond, Jordan played the card. "I need an answer, Taylor, for her sake as much as yours. I need to know if someone here tried to kill you."

The judge drew a breath and exhaled loudly. "The last case I presided over involved two American children orphaned when their parents were killed on 9/11. Based on the conviction of a Palestinian named Mohammad Al Ahmed, their attorney asked for a court-ordered freeze of his U.S.-based investments until liability was determined. It essentially ties up U.S. funding of the Palestine Liberation Committee."

"And you complied?" It wasn't really a question. She knew about the case. She had been there for it, not to mention the fallout that brought her here.

Taylor nodded.

"Have you received any specific threats from the Palestinians?"

"No."

"So you thought it was safe to come here?" Again, it wasn't really a question, and Jordan had to work hard to keep the criticism out of her voice.

Taylor looked at Lucy. "I didn't have a choice."

"Judge Taylor, only a crazy person goes out and plays in the bully's backyard after handing down a verdict like that. You are aware that the Palestine Liberation Committee has a presence here? That there are people here who might see you as hampering their efforts by placing sanctions on their money?"

He turned his attention back to her. "I'm not stupid, Agent Jordan."

"No, you're not." But neither was she, and none of this added up. Jordan tried a different tack. "You're here because of Lucy, because she's sick? Why not see a doctor at home?"

"Because Alena Petrenko is the best in her field."

Jordan pushed herself up from the wall. "You're sure you didn't know either of these two men?"

"I've never seen either of them before."

It might make sense if Cline had been in the square to protect the judge. But Daugherty would have been the one who assigned him, and Daugherty thought he had already left for D.C. Plus, it didn't fit for the sniper to kill the Palestinian and then take a shot at Taylor. He had to be shooting at someone else.

"For what it's worth," Jordan said, "I don't think you were the target. I think you were just in the wrong place at the wrong time. Unfortunately, your face has been all over the news, and we need to get you out of here." She placed a hand on his shoulder. "I'll send someone with you to help pack up your things and make arrangements for you and your daughter to stay at the embassy until we can get you on a flight back to the U.S."

"No." He spoke sharply, and Lucy's head turned in their direction. He gestured to his daughter that things were okay. "We aren't leaving."

Jordan frowned. "Excuse me?"

"We need to stay."

"Look, I don't know what prompted you to come here in the first place, but now it's clear that the only reasonable thing for you to do is to go home."

"We can't," said Taylor. "Not yet. Besides, you said it yourself, no one was shooting at me."

Jordan heard the conviction in his voice, but it carried no logic.

"Judge Taylor, maybe you don't value your own life, but what about Lucy's? What about her life?" She gestured toward the girl, who was paying close attention.

"You're right. We probably would be safer at home. But it's for her sake that we have to stay."

Jordan could hear his desperation and see it in his eyes. "The doctor?"

"Lucy goes for treatments every day. That's where we were headed when . . ." His gaze shifted toward the bodies. "It doesn't matter what happened here. Finishing her treatments is more important. I'm not taking her home until they're done." He held up a hand and measured two inches of air. "We're this close, this close! We just need two more weeks."

Chapter 7

Haddid followed Mansoor and disembarked in Yaffa. The stone walls quickly engulfed them as they wound their way west, moving from one narrow passageway to another. Near the water, they turned south and threaded their way through the maze of tourists who had come to see Yaffa, the "Bride of the Sea."

Mansoor spat on the ground. *"Ignorant bastards."*

Haddid was twenty-eight, too young to remember Yaffa in the early days, before *al-Nakba*, the 1948 occupation. But his father had told him how, prior to the war, Yaffa had been a thriving seaport surrounded by citrus groves that scented the air. It was renowned throughout the world for its fish and oranges, and the people had prospered. The exports to Europe afforded fishermen and farmers the chance to live in magnificent houses lining the shore.

Now those same houses had been made into flats for rich Israelis or converted into restaurants, art galleries, and shops that catered to the throngs of visitors happy to erase the Palestinians from memory. Even the streets were given Hebrew names. Not one Arabic sign remained. History had been washed until there was nothing left.

All around them, the crumbling houses, their colorful plaster walls fading and cracking, were destined for destruction.

27

Haddid's stomach roiled as they tromped past *GivatHaZevel*, the rubbish mountain, where the remains of the demolished homes festered. Israel's intent had been to construct a knoll on which to build villas for wealthy Israelis. Instead, it ended with an unstable mountain—a mix of fetid water and crumbled asbestos. Here, iron gatherers worked, horses grazed, people were married, and children played. To view the sea, one had to climb *GivatHaZevel*.

Passing through the neighborhoods, Haddid eyed the laughing women uncovered in the sun, the playing children, and the old men lounging in the doorways, and he felt sorry. Like so many of mixed heritage, these people did not belong. Israel didn't embrace them. Neither did Palestine. They were a people to be tolerated and used, cast off into the ruins of a brighter yesterday and expendable at the end of the day.

Mansoor tipped his head at the entrance to Najm's apartment building. They climbed the stairs and knocked.

"Najm, it is Mansoor. Open the door."

Haddid heard someone moving inside. A shadow crossed the peephole and then the door swung inward.

"Mansoor." Najm held a beer in one hand. Mansoor swept through the door and gave Najm a hug.

"You remember Haddid."

Najm nodded and closed the door.

Haddid glanced around the apartment and noted how nicely Najm lived. His was a spacious apartment, and he had furnished it well. The floors were tiled in Arab fashion, but he had covered them with authentic Persian rugs. A sofa with two matching chairs faced a state-of-the-art entertainment center, complete with a plasma screen television and high-tech stereo system. Not many young Arabs enjoyed these kinds of possessions. Only those who dealt drugs, had power through family ties, or had brains lived like this.

Mansoor looked around. "Where is Muatab? Tell me, did we succeed?"

Najm's mouth twisted as though he felt pain. "I'm afraid I have some bad news."

Haddid felt a twist of fear. This did not bode well.

Najm told them how Muatab had killed the man from the State Department.

"That deserves a celebration," Mansoor said, again looking around. "So tell me, where is my brother?"

"He's dead."

"What?" Mansoor's expression froze, a mask of disbelief, fear of the truth, and pain.

Haddid placed a hand on his shoulder, while Najm told them about the shooting.

"It was over so fast. There was nothing I could do," he said. He started to reach out and then turned away instead, taking another slug of his beer.

"No!" Mansoor's grief spilled out in torrents.

First had been denial, then anger, then bargaining with Allah. Najm and Mansoor drank beer while Haddid drank soda, pressing the frosted bottle to his cheeks, dispelling the heat. As day turned to night, they talked of Muatab, reveling in his childhood feats. They spoke of honor and duty and sacrifice—and a pledge for revenge.

"Tell me Muatab's death was not wasted. Tell me you have the information for Zuabi."

"It's right here, Mansoor." Najm picked up the computer sleeve. He turned on the tablet and pulled two USB drives from the zippered pocket.

"You have verified it?"

"During the exchange at the square."

"Show me," Mansoor ordered.

Najm set the tablet on the ottoman and slipped a pink-tinged memory stick into the USB port on the back. Working the mouse, he struck a key on the keyboard. Mansoor leaned forward in anticipation. Najm took a swig from his bottle. Haddid remained rooted in his seat. The content only meant trouble if placed in the hands of men who wanted to derail the peace process, and Zuabi didn't want peace.

R and B music erupted from the computer, and the three men jumped. Najm spit beer everywhere.

"What the fuck?" He set his bottle down on the end table and tapped a few more keys.

Using both hands, Mansoor gestured at the computer. "What is this?"

"It should be what Zuabi wants," said Najm. "I verified it."

"Could it be on the other one?"

"No." Najm picked up the other USB drive and tossed it on top of his office ID badge in a bowl on the coffee table. "This one is the one with the plans. The one I was to give to the American. I put the information on it myself."

Music blared from the tablet speakers.

Najm turned back to the machine. "Let me try a different file." More music.

Mansoor raked his hands through his hair. "What is this?"

Najm leaned in close to the screen. "Every one is a song."

Mansoor pointed his finger at Najm. "You are a dead man." He yanked the memory stick from the computer and flung it against the wall. "Zuabi expects us to return with usable information."

"Maybe the music is code?" said Haddid.

Najm let go of the mouse. "No, the American gave me the documents." He slammed his fist down on the table. The bowl in the center jumped. "I tried to tell Zuabi to make the trade over the Internet."

"The American refused," Mansoor said. "He didn't trust our encryption technology to protect him."

Haddid nodded. "He thought it safer to do this the old-fashioned way."

"See how well that worked out." Najm's voice carried a note of bravado, but his hand shook when he lifted his beer. "Without the information, Zuabi has nothing. But we still have the plans Cline wanted. We still have something to trade."

"With who? The Israeli police?" Mansoor said.

"Were the USB drives ever out of your hands?" asked Haddid.

Without warning, Najm pulled up his feet and kicked away the ottoman. "After Muatab was shot, I had them both. As I was running, I stumbled into this girl. She spilled the contents of her purse."

"You think she has the drive?"

"It's a possibility."

Mansoor stopped pacing. "Where is this girl?"

"I don't know," Najm said. "But from something her father said, they often watch the fountain."

Haddid's hopes for an end to this mission faded. If they found the child, it would not end well for her. "But you don't know for certain that we'll find her."

"It is our best lead," Mansoor said. "Tomorrow, we will stake out the square. We will go and get what we came for. Muatab will not have died in vain."

Chapter 8

It was well into the night before they wrapped up the crime scene and arranged transport for Cline's body. Jordan headed home for a shower and something to eat. The next morning, she went in early and beat a straight line to Daugherty's office.

"Give me the rundown," he said.

She talked him through the scene and then laid out her concerns about the judge. "He won't come in."

"So let it go, Jordan. You did your job. You offered." Daugherty reached for the phone. "I'm more interested in knowing what Cline was doing out there. Bring me the answer to that question, and I'll give you a gold star."

Daugherty waved her off, and Jordan banged the door on her way out. Figuring out what Cline was doing in the square wasn't going to be easy.

Plopping herself down in her chair, she flipped on her computer, typed in her user name and password, and waited for the machine to load. At this point, she had four possible leads—Cline, the Palestinian who'd killed him, federal judge Benjamin Taylor, and the unknown shooter.

Detective Weizman was working on identifying the Palestinian and the shooter. On that front, his databases likely would prove more effective than hers. But, to cover her bases, she sent a picture of the dead Palestinian from her phone to her computer and started running it for facial recognition.

That done, she pulled up Steven Cline's State Department dossier. She had skimmed the report on Cline the day she was offered his job. Nothing had caught her eye at the time. Now, with him knee-deep in whatever was going down, she hoped maybe she'd find something she missed.

The records detailed a family man with a wife and two kids who would soon be sitting Shiva in Tel Aviv. A Jewish funeral traditionally occurred within twenty-four hours of death, and seldom more than seventy-two. In Cline's case, there would be some type of autopsy, and extended family would be given time to attend. Jordan figured it would be three days.

Focusing on the dossier, Jordan found that Cline—other than collecting a few parking tickets over the years—was as clean as you could get. A Stanford grad, he spoke both English and Hebrew, had studied Middle Eastern cultures in school, and had served at this Tel Aviv post for nine months before requesting an emergency transfer back to the states. Raised Jewish, he was the youngest of five from a family not known to be particularly pious, though he had spent one year in Israel between high school and college. Because of his DSS background check, the records were thorough, right down to his father's eye color and his mother's rosebud tattoo.

Jordan wondered what she was missing.

She pulled up his wife's record. Born Tamar Kaufmann, Cline's wife had attended a Jewish school in Chicago. She had met Cline during a study year in Israel shortly after their high school graduation. They had returned to the states, attended college, married, and had two kids—Hannah and Martin, ages two and four.

They'd been back in Israel less than a year. Then, one month ago, Cline had asked to be replaced. He claimed that his mother was ill and that he and Tamar needed to go back to the states to care for her. A lie. Instead, he'd arranged a leave of absence from his new post in Washington, D.C., and stayed. Why?

Digging a little deeper, Jordan discovered that Tamar Cline attended the Ida Crown Jewish Academy. Opened in 1942 as the Chicago Jewish Academy, it was conservative—ultraconservative—and ultrareligious.

Glancing at the clock, Jordan factored in the time difference and then placed a call to the school's administration offices. She found herself stonewalled by a chipper-sounding woman with strong nasal overtones who claimed she was unable to reveal information about any student, past or present. An official request could be made in writing.

Jordan hung up and put a call in to the DSS office in Chicago. The local field agent said he would dig around and call her back.

While she waited, Jordan skimmed the State Department files on Ben and Sarah Taylor. There was the same old information—where they were born, who their parents were, whether or not they liked broccoli, and when their divorce was finalized. But two interesting facts jumped out. One, Sarah Taylor was a junior senator from Colorado who served on the Senate Committee on Health, Education, Labor, and Pensions. Not a reason to go after her family, but interesting nevertheless. The other involved Judge Taylor's service record. He had done one tour as a Navy SEAL before heading back to school and the bench.

A Google search on the senator turned up a few recent articles. One pulled from the *Rocky Mountain News* archives revealed that Senator Sarah Taylor had been a key player in crafting Title IV of the Patriot Act, which paved the way for retroactively disallowing foreigners with ties to terrorist organizations entry into the United States. A reason for someone to go after her, but not for someone to target her ex-husband and daughter.

The second article, published in the *Denver Post*, chronicled the trial in which Judge Taylor had ruled to freeze the Palestine Liberation Committee's U.S.-based investments. That might have triggered an assassination attempt by the Palestinians. It had definitely triggered the incident in Denver.

Jordan knew all about the case. She'd been the one to flag the false passports identifying the terrorists who had holed up in the Lebanese consulate. Their target: the federal courthouse in downtown Denver. One of the terrorists died that night, along with the Lebanese consul's daughter. The other sat in a maximum security prison in Florence, Colorado, refusing to talk.

But the scene today had been different. The gunman—or woman, rather—in the square had put a bullet through the Palestinian's head before firing a shot that barely missed the judge. It made no sense for the shooter to play both sides of the fence.

Her phone rang, and she picked up. "Jordan."

"Dirk Walsh, Chicago DSS, here. I have the records on Cline's wife. What do you want to know?"

"Everything."

Jordan could hear him rustle pages. "Of note, it says here that her family is ultra-Orthodox and that she was *shomer negiah*." Observant of touch.

"Meaning she didn't have physical contact with any members of the opposite sex?"

"Affirmative. No holding hands, no hugging, no arms around her shoulders at the local movie theater."

"Is that normal?"

"Odd for most," said Walsh, "but common enough among ultra-Orthodox Jews. Especially ones raised in the West Ridge suburb of Chicago, locally referred to as the Golden Ghetto."

"If that's the case, why the notation in the file?"

Another page turned. Agent Walsh hummed into the phone and then said, "It seems Tamar ran into trouble with some of her fellow students." More pages crinkled. "She filed several reports stating that 'violations were made against her.'"

"What kind of 'violations'?" Jordan envisioned kids poking her, tapping her on the shoulder. Counting coup.

"It says that a group of boys trapped her in the stairwell between classes one day and took turns fondling her breasts. Shortly after that, her parents showed up with Rabbi Tiran Marzel. He demanded someone ensure her rights."

"Marzel? How do I know that name?" Jordan keyed the letters into the search tab on the browser.

"He has ties to a known terrorist group."

On cue, her computer pulled up a picture and several articles.

"Anything else I can do for you?" Walsh asked.

"Can you forward me a copy of your notes?"

"Will do."

Chapter 9

Ganani perched on the perimeter wall near the Dizengoff fountain and surveyed the crowd. Word about the shooting had moved through Tel Aviv like fire through a forest, and the sheer number of people gathered for the 6:00 p.m. show was as much of a spectacle as the fountain itself.

Odd how the hint of death held so much attraction. All that remained of yesterday's incident was a spot of blood on the concrete that had refused to be washed away, yet the people pointed and whispered.

Standing, Ganani stretched and moved so she had a better vantage point of where the body had fallen. She'd been hanging around the square, waiting for Cline's contact to show since early that morning, since an hour after Brodsky had called her and told her to get down to Dizengoff Square.

Through her government contacts, she knew that the police had not yet identified the dead accomplice and that nothing of any value had turned up at the scene. They had recovered a damaged tablet, but nothing on the hard drive had been retrievable. They had the accomplice's knife and were running his fingerprints through AFIS, the Automated Fingerprint Identification System. She thought the contact had made away with the information, but Brodsky heard through his informants that someone was making inquiries about what had been found at the scene and wanted to identify the American witnesses.

Ganani's stomach churned. It was a long shot, but if Cline's contact didn't have the USB drive and was looking for the Americans, he might return to the scene of the crime. For her sake, he had to show. She felt no remorse for the shooting, but locating Cline's contact was an imperative. Brodsky had made that clear. Without the plans the contact had intended to trade, the mission was over. If she failed to find him and secure the plans, she didn't know what her boss might do.

Closing her eyes, she listened to the voices of the people around her. By the time she was eight years old, she had known her destiny differed from those of her friends. Raised in Ramat HaSharon, a wealthy suburb of Tel Aviv, her father had worked for the Israeli government. He was an important man, a friend to those in the highest power. The year she turned ten, he had sent her away to school.

"Learn your languages," he'd told her. "They will come in handy."

Now, whenever she heard snatches of Arabic emanate from the crowd, she studied the faces. At last, she was rewarded. Three young Arabs were making their way onto the bridge. Cline's contact was the man in the lead.

The three men climbed the rise, Cline's contact moving with confidence. The other two men walked with more hesitancy, suggesting that they did not belong. Attractive and young, they drew attention. Women watched from hooded eyes.

Cline's contact made a beeline for a bench to her right with a three-hundred-sixty-degree view of the square. He appeared to be scanning the crowd, looking for something—or someone. He suddenly tensed and spoke softly to the others. Too softly for her to pick up his words.

Ganani tracked his gaze to an American man and a young girl exiting a small garden at the Dizengoff Apartments. It was the child who had been in the way of her shot. Why were these two foreigners of such interest to the Arabs?

Ganani snapped several pictures with her cell phone—one of the American and the child, several of the three men. The contact and one of his colleagues stayed in the shadows, but the tall one with them kept his eyes locked on the girl. The malevolence with which he regarded the child made Ganani's skin crawl.

The man and his daughter made their way into the square and sat on a nearby bench. The fountain revved up, and the crowd oohed and ahhed. The girl appeared mesmerized, clinging to a pink purse and her father for dear life. Her father kept a hawkish gaze on the crowd. Once the fountain spun to a finish, he placed a hand on his daughter's back and said something to her. The child nodded. The two rose and moved away in the opposite direction from where they had come.

Ganani expected the Arabs to tail the pair, but to her surprise, the men conferred.

The tall man gestured toward the apartment building on the west side of the square.

Ganani's gaze drew a straight line from the men to the window of the apartment offices. An old man sat behind a desk near the window facing the sidewalk. If what she thought was about to happen came to pass, the old man would meet God tonight.

The Arabs headed toward the apartment building, and Ganani pushed off the wall. Ignoring the appreciative glances she drew from the men around her, she adjusted the leather vest that covered her shoulder holster and gun and smoothed her black slacks. With her white T-shirt and wide-buckle belt cinched tightly around her waist, she looked like any of the young woman getting off work in this cosmopolitan city—minus the three-inch high-heeled boots. She wore black flats instead.

She tailed the men to the front of the apartment building. The men entered, and the tall Arab lowered the blinds. Unable to see and unwilling to draw too much attention, she walked past the apartment building. Then, making sure no one was watching, she slipped through the gate in the hedge into the garden and hurried around to the back.

The back door to the adjoining bar stood ajar, and Ganani paused. She watched for signs of people and heard only music blaring into the small courtyard. Cigarette smoke poured out of the open doorway and disappeared into the night sky like smoke drawn from a mouth to a nostril. A few apartment windows above the bar were lit up, but no one stood at the glass.

Once she was sure the garden was empty, she slipped along the pathway to the back door of the apartment office. Peering through a crack between the blinds and the edge of the window, Ganani could see that the tall Arab had backed the old man up against the wall. The Arab wanted the apartment number of the girl and her father.

The apartment manager finally spoke. Then, in one swift motion, the tall Arab slit his throat. The old man's eyes widened in horror. His mouth gaped open. Blood sprayed from his jugular, dotting the tall Arab's clothes and spattering across the surface of the desk. The Arab pulled back his supporting arm and dropped the corpse to the floor.

As the men inside came toward the back door, Ganani moved for cover. These men were quick to violence. Slowing her breathing, she slipped into the shadows behind an olive tree just as the door swung wide.

"The apartment is on the second floor," the tall man said, striding to the center of the concrete patio and pointing toward the stairs. "Najm, you keep watch. Haddid, come with me."

Neither of the men argued. The man called Najm, the smallest of the men and Cline's contact, took up a post at the bottom of a set of open stairs. A well-muscled Arab, the one called Haddid, followed the giant up two flights of stairs to an apartment on the right.

The tall Arab knocked.

Ganani prayed the father and daughter had left no one at home.

Chapter 10

Haddid glanced around as Mansoor pounded on the door, sensing someone watching. A resident of an adjacent apartment? A bar patron tucked into the shadows of the open doorway? Or was it Allah, as displeased with the senseless murder of the apartment manager as was Haddid? The manager was an old man. He did not need to die.

But there had been no stopping Mansoor. Haddid had not seen the knife, nor had he seen the murder coming. Worse, he had never before seen his friend unleash such violence. He knew Mansoor was enthralled with Zuabi, but this was a new level of dedication. One brought on by the death of his brother, Muatab, perhaps. Mansoor's seemed a vengeance as yet unfulfilled.

When no one answered the knock, Mansoor raised his boot and kicked open the door. "Look for the USB drive."

The two of them ransacked the living room—Haddid sifting through the contents of things on the tables, Mansoor sweeping everything onto the floor. He even slit the furniture, though, to Haddid, the idea of a child hiding the USB drive in the cushions seemed absurd.

Leaving Mansoor to his task, Haddid slipped through the doorway into the first bedroom. A child's room, the walls and furniture were white. A white bedspread draped to a black-and-white-tiled floor. The one personal touch was a gray stuffed rabbit nestled between the bed pillows. Near the door, a computer sat on a small white desk.

Haddid reached for the mouse and the screen lit up a picture of a young pop star. He wasn't sure which one—only that the boy pretended to play a guitar.

"What have you found?" demanded Mansoor.

"It's her computer."

"Is there a drive?"

Haddid shook his head. "It has a password."

Mansoor grabbed the computer and sent it smashing to the floor. *"Allah yela'an American kelbeh."* May the Lord curse the American bitch.

"She is only a child, Mansoor." The pain from Muatab's death was changing Mansoor, and the depth of his friend's anger stirred the fear lodged in Haddid's chest.

"She is an infidel."

Haddid bent down and picked up the computer. The screen wobbled on its hinges. "There was no need to break the computer."

Outside, sirens blared in the distance.

Tibi yelled up from the garden. "Let's go. Someone must have called the police."

Mansoor headed for the front door. Haddid set down the computer and started to follow when something small and silver in the trash caught his eye. The USB drive?

Haddid leaned down and grabbed the lip of the waste can. The sirens were getting closer. He pawed through the papers and tissue in the trash, but all he found were gum wrappers. Maybe his imagination was playing tricks on him and he hadn't really seen it. Or maybe Allah willed that it remain behind. Without the information on the device, Zuabi's plan would be ruined. A much safer alternative for his family and for all of Palestine than the endless war the plan's execution would bring about.

"Haddid!" Mansoor called out.

"Coming," Haddid set down the waste can. He would leave it. If the USB drive was there, let it end up on *GivatHaZevel*. One more piece of garbage on the rubbish hill.

Chapter 11

Ganani pressed herself against the scratchy trunk of the *zayit* tree, breathed in its sweet sulfur smell, and waited. Upon hearing the sirens, Cline's contact, the one named Najm, had called out to his friends. Now he paced back and forth at the base of the stairs, jumpy and nervous, startling at every noise. She focused on keeping her breath shallow and even and hoped that her dark outfit did not make too deep a shadow against the ash-gray of the tree.

Louder sirens on the street drew Najm around the corner. Someone must have discovered the old man's body.

Ganani debated scaling the garden wall, but then she would not have what she came for. It was clear Brodsky was right. The Arabs were still after the USB drive with the schedules—the one Cline was prepared to trade. She could only guess at the content. Or, for that matter, at what these men wanted with it. She only knew her boss wanted it back, along with the plans that the Arab was supposed to pass off.

At last, the men appeared on the landing. As they headed for the gate, Ganani considered her options. There was little she could do but follow them.

She waited for the three to exit the garden before she moved out of hiding. By the time she could follow, the police had converged on the apartment manager's office. Slipping into the bar through the propped-open back door, she pushed her way through the crowd on the dance floor to the front door. Once outside, she scanned the crowd for the tall Arab. She caught sight of them exiting the square on the other side.

Hurrying up the rise to the square, she crossed the road and tailed the three along Dizengoff Street. She kept a respectable distance and had to run to catch the ninety-two bus when they boarded, dropping into a seat near the front as they worked their way toward the back. The other passengers eyed the men with anger and distrust. Ganani relaxed into her seat while the other passengers, along with the soldier beside her, kept watch.

For their part, the men hung together. They spoke quietly to each other, avoided eye contact with everyone, and disembarked in Yafo.

Ganani waited until the three had moved away from the stop and then climbed off the bus before it rumbled away, slipping into the shadows of the buildings. Pressing her back tight to the stone, she relaxed only after the Arabs set out, seemingly unaware of her presence.

Tailing them was more dangerous here. The residents of Yafo were mostly Israeli Arabs, and although some dressed more Western, in her attire, she would stand out as a Jew. Unzipping the pocket of her vest, Ganani pulled out her paper-thin, black pashmina and shook open the fine wool. Draping the shawl over her head and neck, she crossed the ends in front of her, flipped them back over her shoulders, and zipped up her vest to hide the belt with its flashy buckle.

She kept pace with the men. Ahead of her, Najm strode with confidence. This was his part of town. The other two kept glancing around, forcing her to hug the buildings. They didn't belong here any more than she did.

She followed them to a four-story apartment building in the heart of al-Ajami. Here, men and women gathered in the streets to talk. She nodded to several of the women as she passed, keeping her hair and face hidden, careful not to meet the eyes of the men. When Cline's contact turned into the building, Ganani walked past.

Once she rounded the corner, she picked up her pace and ducked back into the alley. There were no people here. Trash littered the ground, and scrappy cats dug in the overflowing garbage. The scent of rotted meat mixed with the pungent smell of feces, and her stomach turned. Above her, small balconies faced the sea, but no one stood outside enjoying the last of the sunset. They couldn't have handled the stench.

Ganani watched the windows for a sign and was rewarded when the light came on in a third-story window. She backed up against the wall and forced herself to hold still for ten seconds before stepping out into the alley.

She studied her options. Each floor had three windows that cut relief into the plaster wall above her. Based on the placement of the alleyway door, she deduced that one of the smaller windows was off the stairwell. Another small window most likely serviced a bathroom. Then there were the double glass sliding doors off the balcony. That was the best entry point, but there was no way to reach the balcony from where she stood.

She examined the building, taking note of a series of thin ledges running at windowsill height along the rough-plastered building. Whether a visual detail or the marking of an addition, each ledge looked wide enough to traverse. It meant going inside, up three floors, and out a window.

The back door stood ajar. Ganani approached with caution. With no one in sight, she slipped inside and climbed the first flight of stairs.

On the second landing, she encountered a group of teenage boys. Keeping her head down, she ignored their comments about her tight pants and their questions about why she was unaccompanied.

"*Sharmuta*," they spat. Whore.

She paused on the third-floor landing and listened for sounds of the teenagers climbing the stairs behind her. Luckily for them, they didn't follow.

She could hear voices from inside Najm's apartment, but only garbled words. Ganani tried the door handle first. It was locked. Not surprising. Kicking the door open was her easiest access option. She could deal with the three men, but she feared the noise would attract the teenagers and with them the rest of the neighborhood. That might jeopardize the retrieval of the drives.

Crossing to the stairwell window, Ganani grabbed the handle and yanked upward. The window squealed and stuck as she tried to raise it.

She froze.

After a few moments, when no one came, she examined the window. Either something was blocking its track or it was rusted. A quick check of the track showed no obvious obstruction.

Reaching into her vest pocket, Ganani removed a tube of lip gloss, smeared it onto the track above the window as high as she could reach, and then climbed onto the windowsill to reach higher. Suddenly, voices mixed with those of the teenagers in the stairwell, and she scrambled down from the sill. A man and a woman passed by, and she pretended to be headed down.

Once the couple turned the corner to the fourth floor, Ganani grabbed the window handle and yanked upward. The window budged. She kept pumping it up and down. It was like rocking a car out of a sand hole, with the lip gloss working a little farther into the track with each motion.

It took a few moments, but eventually the window opened enough for her to squeeze through. She listened for signs of anyone on the stairs. Looking out, she checked the alley. Then, tying the pashmina securely around her neck, she slipped feet-first out of the window. Flipping onto her stomach, she searched the outside wall with her toes until her shoe caught an indentation. The ledge was at windowsill height, so she would need to climb before traversing.

The window frame provided the grip she needed, and she pulled herself up, using her toes for leverage. The ledge to her right was all of two inches wide. Centering her balance, she clung to the window with her left arm and reached up with her right to find a handhold. Her fingers brushed the rough plaster until she found a small indentation between the blocks.

Ganani inched her way toward the balcony that hung maybe three meters away. It seemed farther. The ledge crumbled under her feet with each step, not leaving much for her toes to grip. Fingerholds between the plaster-covered bricks became more and more difficult to find. She kept her eyes trained on the target and did her best to ignore the ground looming three stories below.

She was halfway to her destination when someone shut the window. Her heart rate quickened. A rush of white noise filled her ears like surf pounding inside a shell. Pressing forward into the plaster, she waited.

When no one raised an alarm, she drew a deep breath and started moving again. She felt relieved when her foot touched the balcony, but then the iron wobbled under her weight. A cursory inspection showed that one anchor had torn loose from the building.

Ganani cautiously lowered her weight onto the platform. The metal swayed and groaned beneath her. She caught her breath as someone came to the window.

The lighting played in her favor. The sun had set and the alley was dark, lit at only one end by a bare, low-watt bulb. Above her, she could see a man silhouetted in the glass. She heard the latch pop and the door opened a crack.

Ganani prepared to attack. Her position was not optimal, but the element of surprise was on her side. If he jumped back, she could follow. If he leaned out to confront her, she could throw him onto the road.

"Haddid." It was the tall man's voice. He sounded distant.

The door shut. But she didn't hear the man relock it.

Ganani edged her way closer to the sliding glass doors. The balcony swayed under her feet. Peering inside, she discovered the doors opened into a bedroom. A king-size bed was pushed up against the north wall and a Persian carpet covered the tile floor. A large piece of contemporary art hung on the wall.

She tested the door handle. It turned easily in her hand. Easing the door open, she slipped inside, quietly closed it behind her, and then crossed the room to the bedroom doorway.

From here, she had a clear view of the men. Their backs were toward her. Two of the men sat on the couch. The tall man perched on an ottoman.

The contact, the one called Najm, said, "We have to go back."

"No," said the one they had called Haddid. "We need to tell Zuabi what's happened. We don't know that the girl has anything, but we still have the information they wanted. Maybe Zuabi can arrange another trade."

Najm took another swig from his bottle. "We can't go to Zuabi without the information he needs. We must go back to Dizengoff."

"How can we do that?" the tall man said. "Haddid is right. The police are there, and by now they will have discovered the break-in."

"Maybe you should have thought of that before you killed the manager, Mansoor," Najm said.

49

Ganani crept closer to the doorway. The tall man whom Najm had called Mansoor froze.

Harah, shit, he had spotted her.

The man stood, shoving away the ottoman. He bolted toward her. Ganani leapt to her feet, pulled her gun, and fired.

Najm dropped his beer. The bottle shattered, and he launched himself toward her over the back of the couch.

The tall man clutched his belly and crumpled to the floor.

Fingers clamped down on her wrist. Najm smacked her elbow against the door jamb. A sharp pain caused her to loosen her grip, and he knocked the gun from her hand.

She swung her left leg and swept his feet out from under him. He landed with a crash but pulled her with him. She hit the floor hard and came up again, gasping for air.

He was back on his feet. He swung his fist, catching her jaw. Her head snapped hard to the side.

She punched his larynx. He clutched his throat and dropped to the floor.

With two men down, she picked up her gun and sought out the third. But he was gone.

Racing to the living room window, she watched as Haddid exited the front of the building. He looked up for a moment, a silhouette in the glare of the street lamp. Then, raising his arm as though waving good-bye, he disappeared into the darkness of al-Ajami. Chasing him was futile.

The tall man lay dead on the floor from the gunshot, his hands clutching his stomach, blood oozing through his fingers.

She walked over to Cline's contact and squatted beside him. "Your friend mentioned Zuabi."

She knew the name. He was head of the Palestine Liberation Committee, one of the main terrorist cells in Palestine.

Ganani pointed her gun at the man's head so he would under-stand the importance of answering her next question. "Where is the drive that Cline was to deliver to him?"

The Arab clutched his throat and gurgled. She had crushed his larynx. He was never going to answer.

Footsteps pounded on the stairs and a fist hammered the door. "Najm. Najm, are you okay? We heard shooting."

Her time was up.

Ganani snapped Najm's neck before checking the computer, the coffee table, and both men for the drives. Nothing.

"Najm!" shouted a voice. She heard the deadbolt slide. She could stand, fight, and continue to search the apartment, or she could leave the way she came in and find the man who got away. Or she could pay her own visit to the Americans.

Ganani sprinted to the bedroom, slipped through the double doors, and stepped onto the swaying metal balcony. Crawling toward the ledge, she heard cries as the bodies were discovered followed by feet pounding across the bedroom floor.

Quickly, she assessed the situation. It would take too long to work her way back along the ledge to the window. Besides, some-one had closed it. She couldn't know if they had locked it, so she had to assume that they had.

Scanning the alley for another escape route, she spotted a dumpster three stories down and to the left. It was heaped with large sacks of rubbish and likely a few rats and a broken bottle or two. It would have to do.

She anchored her feet on the ledge. The double doors behind her slid open. An old saying ran through her mind: *Ein somchim al ha'nes.* One should not rely on a miracle.

She promptly dismissed it, drew a deep breath, and jumped.

Chapter 12

Tom Daugherty, regional security officer for the Tel Aviv embassy, sat squeezed onto a small bench opposite the apartments. Jordan had spotted him waiting when she pulled up but kept him sitting while she wrestled her hair into a ponytail holder and clipped her cell phone onto her belt next to her holstered and clearly visible gun. Running her palms down the front of her Kevlar vest, she tugged at the hem and then crossed the street to join him. Behind him, the fountain towered like a silent behemoth at rest. The smell of olives suffused the night air. A minifleet of white Israeli patrol cars, blue lights flashing, formed a semicircle in front of the Zinah Dizengoff Apartments.

From the number of officers and the blue barricades cordoning off the entrance, clearly something catastrophic had occurred. The judge and his daughter were staying in these apartments, but it seemed like the attention was focused on the office. Which begged the question, why was she here?

"Enjoy your dinner?" Daugherty asked.

"What I had of it." She envisioned the half-serving of spaghetti with Bolognese sauce and the glass of Pinot Grigio she had shoved into the refrigerator.

His mouth twitched and then his face hardened into a craggy mask. "The apartment manager was murdered."

She heard footsteps behind her. "It's an ugly scene."

She recognized the voice. Dan Posner, her old boss. Keeping her emotions in check, Jordan turned. He looked the same as the last time she'd seen him. Smug and self-righteous.

"Dan." She held out her hand. He ignored it.

"Bet you're wondering why I'm here," Posner said, unbuttoning his signature G-man jacket and sticking his hands in his pockets. "Well, I've been reassigned to the secretary of state's advance security team."

She wanted to tell him that anyone else would have lost his job for what he pulled, but he still outranked her.

Daugherty chuckled. He seemed to be enjoying the exchange.

"Posner and I were having dinner ourselves when the call came through." He gestured to the seat beside him. Jordan shook her head and remained standing.

Posner shrugged and sat down beside Daugherty.

"The judge and his daughter were out," Daugherty said. "They got back, found the police here investigating a call on the manager, and found their apartment tossed." Daugherty jerked his head toward the apartment building, now cluttered with crime scene personnel. "You are now in charge of babysitting."

"The judge? You're not bringing him in?"

"Nope," Posner said. "I can't allow it. We don't have the room on the embassy grounds, and the advance team for the secretary of state's visit is taking up all the contracted embassy housing."

Daugherty tipped his head in concession. "Not only that, but the damn fool refuses to leave."

Jordan frowned in surprise. The judge was in trouble on foreign soil. Standard procedure called for providing an American citizen refuge at the embassy and helping him get home. The judge had told her earlier that his daughter, Lucy, needed two more weeks of medical treatments and that he intended to stay. But now things had changed. Surely he could see the only logical thing to do was to return to the States.

"Correct me if I'm wrong," Jordan said, "but if he's refusing to come in, he's not qualified for protection. The DSS only provides security for the embassy, foreign guests on U.S. soil, and U.S. government personnel on official business on foreign soil. We don't normally protect American travelers with their own private agendas."

Posner looked at Daugherty. "What did I tell you, Tom? Always 'by the book.'"

Jordan stiffened. They had protocols for a reason. If Posner had followed protocol that night in Denver, neither of them would be here now.

"This citizen's special," Daugherty said. "His ex-wife is Sarah Taylor."

"The junior senator from Colorado," she said, making sure he knew she had done her homework.

Daugherty nodded. "Turns out she's a good friend of Ambassador Linwood's."

Jordan drew a deep breath. "Crap."

Posner chuckled.

Daugherty cocked his head and cupped a large hand behind his ear. "Did you say something, Jordan?"

"That explains it, sir."

"You bet it does." Daugherty scribbled something in the notepad he carried and then pointed his pen at her. "You know, you still have a couple of years on department probation before your job is secure."

Jordan felt her mouth go dry. Why assign her this mission? She hadn't been in Israel long enough to receive her geographical orientation, much less her mission security briefing. There had to be a more senior ARSO he could assign. *Was this some kind of test?*

Her mind flashed to the night in Denver and the botched take-down. It hung in her memory as it became clear that Posner and Daugherty were old friends. Posner might not like the way the cards fell, but he had left her little choice but to tell the truth. He should've been fired. Lucky for him, he had friends in high places. He had been demoted and reassigned. She had been promoted and sent to Israel. Reward or a punishment? Right now, it was hard to say.

Posner's head bobbed. "You might also want to remember that sometimes this job forces you to color outside the lines."

"With the secretary of state's advance team on the ground, everyone else is assigned to priority duties," Daugherty said. "You're what I've got, Jordan. If you don't think you're ready . . ."

Posner scoffed. He was clearly expecting her to fail.

Jordan locked eyes with Daugherty. "I can handle the job, sir." If he thought anything different, he was sorely mistaken.

Daugherty grinned and wrote something more in his note-book. "Good to know."

Now for the question she would have known the answer to if she'd been formally briefed. "Will I have a team? In order to pro-vide adequate protection, I'll need some Marines."

Posner laughed. "Even with his connections, Taylor's a stretch on available resources."

Again, Jordan ignored him and looked to Daugherty for answers.

"I can afford ten Marines. Two guard details in rotating shifts."

"That's not nearly enough." She needed to fully assess the lay-out of the apartment building complex, but from what she could readily see, she would need at least twice that number. There were too many access points to the apartments and too many hours to cover. Hell, when Prince Harry had visited Colorado on a ski trip, there had been more than a hundred agents working the detail.

"It's the best I can do," Daugherty said.

"What about local help? Who's the embassy's local contact?"

"Detective Noah Weizman, Israeli police, Tel Aviv District." Daugherty gestured toward the office. "He's on scene."

He was the police detective who'd greeted her when she'd arrived on scene earlier that day.

"The lead on the sniper attack," she said.

"Then you already have a relationship." Daugherty uncurled himself from the bench. "I expect regular check-ins, Jordan. The first five Marines will report at twenty-two hundred hours. Better get some sleep between rotations."

"I'll do that, sir." She waited until Posner and Daugherty reached their car and then called out, "And I might even eat something."

Once they had pulled away, Jordan made her way toward the crime scene. The apartment manager had worked out of a storefront office on the bottom floor of a two-story building. Crime scene technicians packed the small room. Fingerprint experts worked the doorways and blinds, and yellow markers flagged footprints and evidence. Noah Weizman stood near the desk, where a photographer clicked photos of the carnage. The papers on the desk were covered in blood spatter, except for a thin void where someone had stood.

"I'd guess the murderer," Weizman said, barely glancing up. He gestured between the desk and the manager's body.

Jordan studied the scene. Based on the brutality, whoever had done this had killed with relish. "Any chance this was personal?"

"It's possible, but then why toss the judge's apartment?"

"So the killer was after the apartment number?" Jordan said.

"And the manager resisted." Weizman gestured and moved toward the back door to the office. "Daugherty tells me you are going to be the judge's minder."

Jordan followed. "Word gets around fast. Did he also tell you we have limited manpower?"

"No."

"Any chance for some help?"

"Not much." Weizman raised a latex-gloved hand to push back his hair and then caught himself. "We're stretched to the maximum."

"The peace talks." The secretary of state's visit had everyone stretched thin.

Weizman nodded. "Plus Judge Taylor is an American. My superiors will feel you should be forcing him home."

"Them and me both."

"So you agree that's best, and yet you are letting him stay." He offered a thin smile and fished a business card out of his pocket. "I'll see what I can do. No promises."

"Thanks." She slipped the card into her pocket before waving her hand at the crime scene. "Any idea who did this?"

"They left fingerprints everywhere, so I doubt it was our shooter from the square. She was careful and left no traces in the hotel. We'll run the prints through AFIS. With luck, we will get a hit. I'll let you know."

"Thanks again. Do you know where I can find the judge?"

"Across the garden, upstairs to your right. I left him with my partner, Gidon."

The automaton with attitude. Gidon Lotner seemed to have taken an immediate dislike to Jordan. The thought of having to deal with him now left a sour taste in her mouth.

Exiting through the back door, Jordan stopped on the stoop and took time to assess the security risks. The buildings were all two-story. The one with the manager's office abutted the sidewalk that surrounded Dizengoff Square. The two buildings in the rear shared a staircase and were accessible only through the garden and a locked doorway to the alley.

To her right, a path wound around the side of the building housing the office. Jordan followed it to the front sidewalk.

Mental note: post one guard here.

Continuing around the inside perimeter, she noted that the surrounding walls were easily climbable.

Post another guard at the back door of the office. From there, the sentry would have a clear view of anyone attempting to scale the garden walls and of the alley entrance for putting out trash. The back door of the adjoining bar stood open, and she wondered if the bar patrons ever used this area. She'd have to make the garden off limits to them.

Jordan crossed the garden and climbed the two flights of stairs backward, taking in the surroundings. A guard stationed outside the apartment door would have an unobstructed view of the area and, more importantly, a line of sight to the guards positioned at the path entrance and the office door. That left one guard for inside and one floater. It was doable, if everyone worked twelve-hour shifts.

Jordan turned and knocked. Detective Lotner answered, opening the door into a small room that functioned as a living area and kitchen. There was a short hallway on the right with three doors.

"Good, you're here to take over." The Israeli's thick accent slowed Jordan's processing of his English.

"Yes." Her delay in responding clearly annoyed him, and she switched to Hebrew, hoping he'd be easier to understand. "Where's the judge?"

"Putting the child to bed." He gestured toward the first door on the right.

"And the other two doors?"

"The judge's bedroom at the end. The bathroom in between." Lotner picked up a jacket draped across the easy chair and moved to leave. Jordan blocked his path.

"I need you to stay until the Marine contingent arrives," she said.

Lotner pushed her aside. "I need to rejoin my partner."

Jordan blocked the front door. "It's important you wait."

Lotner planted his feet and crossed his arms on his chest.

Jordan mirrored his stance, planning on waiting him out. She had no idea why this man was such a hard-ass. Maybe he disliked all Americans, or maybe he hated his job, or maybe he suffered from hemorrhoids. Whatever his problem was, it wasn't hers.

"They're on their way," Jordan said.

Finally, Lotner relented. "Fine."

Jordan nodded, stepped over to the living room window, and looked out into the alley two stories below. Checking the lock, she pulled the shade. "Did you conduct a sweep of the apartment?"

"Yes."

"Did you sweep for bugs?"

"I know how to do my job."

Not wanting to spar, Jordan glanced around at the disheveled room. "Any idea what they were looking for?"

"The judge."

This asshole needed to be taught some manners. "Inside the couch cushions?"

"Maybe they wanted to make a statement."

Chapter 13

Cradled in garbage, Ganani lay still for a moment. Then, with a groan and an effort that shot pain through her back, she turned over and pushed herself to her hands and knees. The bags beneath her rolled and pitched. She heard the clamor of feet on stairs and the shouts of men. From the corner of the trash bin, a rat bared its teeth at her, prepared to battle over its dinner. She shuddered and hauled herself to her feet.

Harah. Heaving herself over the metal edge of the dumpster, she dropped to the ground. The landing jarred her teeth and sent another shot of pain up her spine. The pashmina clinging to her shoulders stank of rotted fish, but she pulled it close to shield her face and fled into the darkness of al-Ajami.

The soles of her flats slipped on the loose dirt of the roadway, forcing her to slow her pace. She wove an intricate path through the alleyways, turning right here and left there, always aware of the shouts from the men in pursuit. Soon the voices faded away and the lights of Yafo welcomed her back.

People stared at her here, too. Not because she looked Israeli, she decided, but because she smelled. Ignoring the owner's protests that the toilets were for customers only, she limped through the nearest café and took refuge in the bathroom.

Her pashmina was ruined, the fine wool embedded with bits of food. A rent in the fabric split it nearly in two. She pitched it into the trash, splashed water over her face and arms, and blotted the stains from her clothes using a handful of wet paper towels. Finally, facing the mirror, she tousled her brown hair and fished the lip gloss out of her pocket. The tinge of red made her transformation complete. A marvel considering she smelled like spoiled *chraime*.

Exiting the bathroom, she purchased a cup of coffee and, likely to the café owner's relief, carried it outside to the patio. The night had cooled and, with help from the breeze off the water, the stench of the fish abated. Ganani sipped her coffee and pulled her cell phone from her pocket. She needed to call Brodsky.

The thought brought with it a stab of fear. He frightened her when little else did. Colonel Brodsky was not a man who tolerated errors, and she had made several.

The phone rang and she pictured him lifting the receiver. Tall and fit, with close-cropped hair, blue eyes, and a piercing insight, the colonel engendered fear. He would know she had failed.

"*Shalom,*" Ilya Brodsky said, his voice quiet yet fierce.

"It's Ganani."

She waited for him to secure the line. After a final click, he asked, "Has it been taken care of?"

"No." The truth was easiest when it came quickly.

Silence. Finally, he spoke. "Why not?"

She gave him a rundown of the events.

"And the Arab who got away?" Brodsky asked.

She chafed under his reproachful tone. She wasn't trained to make costly mistakes. Today, she'd made two, and Israel would pay the price for her failure. "I will find him."

"Does he have the information?"

Ganani didn't want to admit it. "I don't know for sure."

Again, there was a momentary silence. "If the mission is to succeed, we must have the information the Palestinians brought to trade."

"I am aware." Ganani tried wetting her lips, but her mouth was dry. She took a sip of the coffee and wondered how he'd react to her next idea. "Perhaps we should go to the detective in charge of the shooting investigation and—"

"No."

The word came strong. She knew that, from his vantage point, there were already enough rumors circulating about who fired the shots in Dizengoff Square.

Brodsky's next words solidified her thoughts. "There will be more to deal with once the police are called to al-Ajami."

She flashed back to the Palestinian's crushed larynx and the single shot to the tall man's head. More room for speculation. The thought made her self-conscious. She glanced around to see who besides the coffee shop owner would remember her. It was time to move on. She stood and started away from the table, but the motion caused static on the line. She stopped in the glare of a streetlamp for fear of losing the connection.

"For now," Brodsky said, "there are only rumors, nothing more. It is not your concern. Your job is to recover both of the USB drives. You must make sure nothing passes into the wrong hands. There is too much riding on your success."

She wondered at his meaning. Was he concerned about the mission, or was he suggesting there would be other rewards? "I understand, Colonel."

After he hung up, Ganani turned off her phone, slipped into the shadows of the building, and waited for the next bus to take her back into Tel Aviv. She studied the landscape, reassuring herself that no one showed her any overt interest. Now all she needed was a plan.

Chapter 14

Within fifteen minutes, a tap on the front door signaled the arrival of the Marines. Lotner left as four men and one woman dressed in military fatigues filed in.

"Master Gunnery Sergeant Prentice reporting for duty, ma'am."

Jordan smiled. The Marine who addressed her probably had ten years on her. Right now, she was glad for his experience.

"Master Guns, I need three of your men positioned outside securing the courtyard and door and two inside. One to secure the apartment, the other to act as a floater." Finding a piece of paper and pen, she drew a quick sketch of the garden. "I'm thinking we need guards here and here."

"Yes, ma'am." He sent three Marines outside, and then he and his man rechecked the apartment. She noted with approval that upon finishing their sweep, they'd taken up posts—one just inside the front door and the Master Guns to the right of Lucy's bedroom door, with a straight view down the hallway to Judge Taylor's room.

The door to Lucy's room opened.

"I think she's finally asleep." Judge Taylor said, quietly shutting the door to his daughter's bedroom. "What happens now?"

The judge looked taller than Jordan remembered. His sandy hair was disheveled. Yet despite the fatigue etched into his face, he seemed alert.

"We need to talk," she said. "I want to know why you're refusing to cooperate with the embassy. You do know the smart thing for you to do is go home?"

"I told you earlier," he said, "Lucy has two more weeks of treatment." He walked over and tried to make some order of the slashed cushions on the couch. "We'll need to get replacements for these."

Jordan wanted to know more about the "treatment," but right now she needed to put him at ease if she was going to get anywhere with him. "I'll arrange for a new couch. For right now, do you have any coffee makings in the apartment?"

"Sure." Taylor brushed past her, and she caught a whiff of cologne that she couldn't place but had to admit that she liked.

Sitting down in a kitchen chair, she watched him fill the coffee pot. He was handsome, sort of rugged looking—an Indiana Jones type. She put him in his early forties. Young for a federal judge. He was toned and fit and looked like a man accustomed to being in control of his life. The intent he put toward fixing the coffee showed he was less than comfortable with having them invade his home.

"Look, I'm asking questions because it's my job to protect you," Jordan said. "In order to do that, I need to identify the threat."

He set the package of coffee on the counter and half-turned toward her. "I didn't ask for your protection."

"No, but your ex-wife did. She's worried about her daughter."

"*Now* she's worried?" Taylor filled the bean grinder with beans. "Fuck her," he said, hitting the switch on the grinder.

Jordan glanced at the Marine by the front door. He kept his eyes forward.

Waiting until Taylor finished grinding and was knocking the grounds into the filter, she tried again. "Help me understand why you have to be here, Taylor. There are lots of doctors in the U.S."

He pulled two mugs from the cupboard and spoons from the drawer and set them on the table. "Not one like Alena."

"What makes her so special?"

"She's specially trained, and she's worked for us before." Taylor grabbed a carton of creamer and the sugar bowl.

"Do you mind telling me what's wrong with Lucy?"

When Jordan had asked earlier, after the shooting, he had deliberately changed the subject. This time, he turned away, poured two cups of coffee, and carried them back to the table. He set one in front of Jordan and then sat down and started doctoring his.

The seconds stretched.

Finally, he put down his spoon. "They diagnosed her with leukopenia."

Jordan wasn't familiar with the disease. "Is that like leukemia?"

"Just the opposite. It's when your white blood cell count is so low you have no resistance to anything." Taylor sat back.

Picking up on the cue, Jordan relaxed into her chair. If he wanted to tell her a story, she would be patient. The more information she had, the better.

"We were on Martha's Vineyard and Lucy complained about this wicked rash. The doctor thought maybe it was shingles. She'd had the chicken pox shot, but she was so young that he ordered more tests." Taylor sipped his coffee before cradling his mug. "Turned out, Lucy has very little resistance to any type of virus. The doctors told us if things got worse, they would have to put her in the hospital, in isolation, to protect her from infection. It wasn't the first time we'd been through this. We knew the doctors planned to play a game of wait and see. Wait and see if her blood counts continued to drop. Wait and see." He swirled his coffee. "I knew from experience that we had to act fast."

"She's been sick before?"

"No. My son. Ethan." His face clouded over. "He was diagnosed with the same damn thing, at about the same age. That's when we found Alena."

Jordan didn't know he had a son. Taylor continued before she could ask about him.

"Alena's an alternative therapist." Taylor set his coffee on the table and pulled his chair closer. "An expert in blood disorders."

"Alternative?" The word left a bad taste in Jordan's mouth. "Is she a homeopath?"

"No. She's an energy healer."

Jordan wasn't sure she heard him right. It must have registered on her face.

"I know, it sounds nuts, but Alena heals by manipulating the body's natural energy flow. She takes a negative flow, the energy making someone sick, and then changes it into a positive flow, making sure it circulates in the body correctly."

"You say she was specifically trained to do this?"

He nodded. "She holds a doctor of sciences degree from the Kyiv Medical Institute of the Ukrainian Association of Folk Medicine. It's an accredited university."

Jordan worked on her poker face. "So she's Russian. That explains a few things."

"You've heard of this type of treatment?"

"I was born in Russia. My father was born in Ukraine, when it was still part of the Soviet Union. My grandparents were big believers in this type of healing. I don't know much about it." She paused. "How did you end up connecting with her?"

"My ex-wife was the one who discovered her. A friend of Sarah's recommended her. I was against it. Totally convinced Alena was a quack."

"But you went."

"Fear trumped skepticism," he said. "My son was really sick." He shook his head. "You wouldn't have believed the scene. Alena was staying in this multilevel tract home on the outskirts of Denver.

66

We knocked on the door, and this man answered. He had a thick Russian accent and asked us to follow him into the basement."

"She didn't work out of an office?"

"She was visiting. The house was right out of the seventies. The basement walls were dingy, orange shag carpeting covered the floor. There was a small twin bed in the corner, and the man told Ethan to lie down."

"And you let him?"

"I admit, I wondered what the hell Sarah had gotten us into. I was ready to bail. Until Alena entered the room. That's when everything changed. She has this ethereal quality about her."

"She was attractive," Jordan said, trying to understand how an ex–Navy SEAL and federal court judge could be so easily bewitched.

Even the Marines were paying attention now.

"It's not what you think," Taylor said.

Jordan looked away and took a sip of her coffee. "What happened next?"

"Alena stood over Ethan, her hands open, her palms down. Then she skimmed her hands through the air about four inches above his body. When she finished, she turned, told us he had a blood disorder that needed immediate treatment."

"But she already knew that."

Taylor's jawline stiffened. He didn't like her pointing out the flaws in his reasoning.

"We hadn't told her, or anyone connected to her, anything about his condition," he said. "She told us that for five thousand dollars she could cure him. That it would take about five weeks."

"And you agreed?"

"Sarah wanted to try, so I went along. Ethan was really sick."

Jordan worked on keeping an open mind. "Did she pinpoint the cause of his condition?"

"No more than the doctors at Children's Hospital. She explained that Ethan's immune system was suppressed. While he could build antibodies to fight off disease, his body treated the antibodies like a virus. Instead of stoking his white blood cell count, his antibodies turned on themselves, killing each other and destroying any resistance he had to illness."

"So you went with Alena," said Jordan.

Taylor nodded. "He had three weeks of treatment, and he was better by the time we got in to see the specialist. The doctor said there was nothing wrong with him. He acknowledged the previous blood work and admitted, based on the reports, that he had given Ethan low odds for survival. He labeled it a 'spontaneous recovery' and gave no credence to Alena."

"How is your son doing now?"

Taylor seemed to steel himself. "He's dead."

Jordan didn't know what to say. "But you said he was cured."

"Alena wanted to keep treating Ethan," Taylor said, his voice heavy with anger. "She said he wasn't out of the woods yet and needed more treatment. Sarah refused. She was under pressure from some of the members on her senate committee to denounce the alternative therapy. They felt it was sending the wrong message. She became convinced the specialist was right—that Ethan got better of his own accord and that we had been duped. Two years later, the condition returned. Before we had time to react, Ethan was gone."

The pain made the lines in his face deepen. Jordan wished she could do something to smooth them out. "I'm sorry."

He nodded and stood. Picking up the coffee mugs, he carried them to the sink. "My marriage ended soon after that. If it weren't for Sarah stopping the treatments, my son would still be alive."

He couldn't know that for sure, Jordan thought, but she was beginning to understand. "And now Lucy has the same condition."

"Possibly worse," he said, turning on the faucet. "The doctors at Children's were talking about bone marrow transplants."

Jordan understood science, but bioenergy treatments? That was a little too out there for her. She picked up the creamer and sugar bowl and carried them to the counter.

"Instead, you brought her here?"

Taylor looked over. "My ex-wife wanted Lucy in a hospital in the States, but I put my foot down. This time we're doing it my way."

It required permission from both parents for minors to travel outside the United States. "How did you get your ex-wife to agree?"

"It was Lucy. She convinced her to sign the papers. It's one of the main reasons we have to stay."

"What's that?"

"Faith. It's a powerful tool. Lucy told Sarah that she believed."

"And you have faith, too? Enough to stay, even though your lives may be in danger?"

Taylor set a clean mug upside down in the dish drainer and turned to face Jordan.

"I know one thing, Agent Jordan." His hands gripped the edge of the counter, his eyes asking for understanding. "I'm not going to lose another child."

Chapter 15

Haddid fled through the streets of al-Ajami. Sweat beaded on his brow and soaked his shirt while slow-motion frames of what had happened clicked through his mind.

Mansoor advancing toward the intruder.

Najm diving over the back of the couch.

The woman, draped in her black pashmina, pulling a gun and firing.

He had snatched Najm's ID pass and the USB drive off the table. Then he turned and ran, leaving his friends to die.

Haddid assured himself that he had done what he had to do. He was no match for the woman. He had a family to think of, a son to raise.

From the street, he had glanced back at the balcony window. The woman was framed in the light. She had to be some type of professional, either government or private contractor. What other woman could have so easily dispatched Mansoor and Najm? If he had stayed to fight, he would also be dead.

His legs ached from the run, but he forced himself to hurry along. Every noise in the street caused his stomach to lurch. A footfall brought his head around. A chuckle made it snap the other way. He wove in and out of the alleyways in the direction of Yaffa, his own footsteps crunching the gravel causing him alarm. The woman would track him. His only hope lay in getting the USB drive in his pocket to Palestine.

Catching the ninety-two bus north, he sat in the back, his head down, his body trembling. He had escaped the woman, but now he sat alone, surrounded by Jews.

Fuck them. Anger burned beneath his skin and he snapped his head up, staring down a Hasid in his black felt hat. His gaze panned the seats in front of him. He sensed the fear and curiosity from the Jews, and he wanted to yell at them. He wanted nothing different from what they wanted—a house, safety for his family, food for his table, an education for his children. Now his best friend lay dead in a pool of blood, and instead of avenging his death, Haddid ran.

At the Tel Aviv Central Bus Station, he turned his back on the Jews and switched to the 872 express bus to Netanya. From there, it was a short way to Tūlkarm and the border crossing, where just hours earlier Mansoor had spoken with so much conviction. Haddid had not agreed with him on everything, but he had loved Mansoor like a brother. To bring word of his death and news of their failure to Zuabi left Haddid full of sadness and fear.

The crowds on the bus diminished until Haddid was the last one off. Shrouded in darkness and chilled by the night air caressing his damp shirt, he walked along the ditch toward the checkpoint. With Mansoor, Muatab, and Najm in paradise, he alone was left to face Zuabi. The thought caused his skin to tighten. Zuabi waited in Balata for Mansoor and Haddid to bring him the means for exacting revenge against the infidels who murdered his niece. As the leader of the Palestine Liberation Committee, he could have sent anyone. He had chosen them, and they had failed. Zuabi was not a man known for his patience and understanding.

Haddid stared at the coils of barbed wire that stretched forever beside the ditch. Two hundred meters ahead, he spotted four guards gathered in conversation around a fire pit at the checkpoint. To his left, an olive tree marked the entrance to the workers' crossing. The moonless night afforded ample cover as he trod the earth toward Palestine. Haddid found his stride. Then suddenly one of the guards straightened and peered in his direction.

"*Hacah!*" Silence!

Haddid stopped midstride and held his breath. Had they seen him?

"What do you hear?" demanded a second guard.

The first soldier turned and shouldered his rifle.

Haddid dropped to a crouch. His chest ached from lack of air. The dogs in the guards' compound barked and lunged at their chains.

"Turn them loose," said the second guard.

"*Lo,*" yelled another. "What if it's a pack of wolves? They would just kill the hounds."

"What do you suggest?"

The first soldier clipped a leash on the largest canine. "Let's take a walk."

The soldiers, rifles shouldered, each took a dog. They shined their flashlights along the road.

Haddid's lungs screamed for air. He was ten meters off the road and in plain sight. Exhaling softly, he drew a deep breath. He could see where the path ended in Taibeh, the dirt ending at a sidewalk. Another fifty meters and it rounded the corner of the building in front of where his car was parked. It may as well have been two hundred.

Haddid listened to the guards' footsteps crunch on the gravel road. Staying low, he matched their steps, masking his stride, sliding into the thorny bushes beside the beaten path. The brambles tore at this skin and clothes. More than once, he was forced to stop and pray.

A beam of light flickered near where he had stood on the path.

"There's nothing here," said one of the soldiers.

Haddid heard the clang of a dog lunging against a leash. A sharp bark. His heart hammered near this throat and he folded himself into a ball on the ground.

"Maybe it is an animal," said another soldier.

A flashlight beam skated across the branches above Haddid's head. He pressed himself harder against the ground and watched the light play on the soldiers' boots.

"There's nothing," said a soldier. "Do you have a smoke?"

A lighter flashed and the men turned away, yanking on the dogs. Haddid lay still. Sweat dripped from his forehead to the ground, creating a small rivulet in the sand. As the soldiers retreated to their post, Haddid rose and ran along the path. The sidewalk offered no cover, and he listened for the soldiers to set their dogs on him.

There came no command.

Once around the corner of the building and safely home in Palestine, Haddid slowed to catch his breath.

His car was parked where he had left it, and he drove the back roads into Nablus. The city, once known as the soap capital of Palestine, was now best known as the focal point of the second *intifada*, a battleground between the Israel Defense Forces, or the IDF, and the Palestinians. Haddid doused his headlights and kept his eyes open for IDF patrols. The last thing he wanted was another encounter.

Turning down the road toward the Balata Refugee Camp, he slowed. People simmered under the flat-top roofs of the buildings, constructed mostly of concrete. To be classified as a refugee, one had only to be descended from refugees. Haddid didn't believe Zuabi belonged here, but the camp provided a base for the resistance. The number living in the occupied areas had grown to more than four million. People who once defied permanent relocation had lost all hope of returning home, and anger over their displacement bred an environment ripe for rebellion.

For someone like Zuabi, there existed a surplus of jihadists in Balata. A man like Haddid, one who believed peace might be the answer, stood in the minority. In Balata, such a man brought danger to his family and friends.

Haddid wanted to turn toward home, but going there only postponed the inevitable. Instead, he turned toward Zuabi's camp. To exact his revenge, the PLC leader needed the information from Cline's contact—something Haddid could not deliver. But he could give Zuabi the USB drive Najm had planned to trade and, if necessary, tell him where he could find the American. Haddid prayed to Allah that it would be enough to buy goodwill for himself and his family.

Zuabi's camp was a two-story, cinder-block apartment next to a small grocery store in the center of Balata. Two windows barred with decorative iron flanked a front door covered in barbed-wire graffiti. Haddid parked a block away, with two tires on the makeshift sidewalk to leave room for cars to pass on the packed dirt road.

He checked the street before climbing out of his car and walked slowly to Zuabi's door. He tapped once, twice, and then again more loudly. Voices shouted from the back of the house. He heard footsteps in the entry. An eye appeared at the peephole, and then the door swung inward. A young woman gestured for Haddid to enter and pointed him toward the back.

Zuabi sat at a table surrounded by a group of his senior officers. They were men to be feared and respected.

"You're back," Zuabi said, standing to offer a cursory greeting. "Where's Mansoor?"

"We need to talk, Abdul."

"Then talk." Zuabi did not keep secrets.

The men all waited to hear what he had to say. Haddid stared at his shoes. "Mansoor is dead."

"What?" The shouts of the men echoed around the room.

Haddid looked up to see Zuabi gesturing for quiet. "That can't be."

"They are all dead. Muatab and Najm, too," said Haddid. "There was an ambush."

Zuabi sank into his chair. Mansoor had been his right hand. He had been like a son. Haddid could see Zuabi was taking the news hard.

"I am sorry, Abdul." Haddid related the details of the day, citing Najm's mistakes and describing the woman to the best of his ability. He glossed over the information about the girl and her father.

"You're telling me you don't have the information?" Zuabi's voice rose with each syllable, until he was shouting. "The information is lost?"

"We thought we had recovered it," Haddid dug in his pocket and produced the USB drive from Najm's house. "I have this, *Za'im*," leader, he said, hopeful that addressing him as such might lessen Zuabi's anger. "It's the information that Najm had. At least they didn't get this."

Zuabi turned the small drive in his hand. "'Like you've gone, like you've come back,'" he said, quoting an old Arab proverb that spoke of going on a mission and returning empty-handed. The faces around Haddid bobbed in agreement.

"Except three of our brothers are dead," someone said.

Haddid felt perspiration gather on his upper lip.

"Tell me about this American and his daughter," Zuabi asked.

Haddid looked down at his feet. He hated it when fear betrayed him. Haddid understood the consequences of crossing Zuabi, and he knew what Zuabi was capable of if he told him he might have seen a USB drive in the trash in the girl's room and had not recovered it.

"We searched their apartment and found nothing," said Haddid.

The Palestinian leader brightened. "Then it is possible one of them still has it on their person."

Fixed under Zuabi's cold stare, Haddid wiped away the sweat beading on his lip. "I suppose it is possible."

"Praise Allah! He has blessed us with opportunity." He turned in a tight circle and then stopped and pressed a hand firmly on Haddid's shoulder. "Go back to Tel Aviv, *Ib'ni*. Whatever happens this time, don't come back empty-handed."

Haddid's heart pounded. Zuabi had called him *my son* and entrusted him with the mission. It was the last thing he wanted. "Me? You want me to go?"

"Who better? You know where they live and what they look like. You are the one who has three deaths to avenge. I only have one." He curled his lip into a sneer and tilted his head as if to see Haddid better. "They will be watching for something to happen, so you must be very careful this time. Choose three others to go along. Any three you like." Zuabi gestured around the room. "Bargain, trade, or steal, but don't return with nothing again."

Chapter 16

Jordan's phone woke her in the middle of the night. "Jordan."

"It's Detective Weizman."

Her first thought was that something had happened to the judge and Lucy, but if something had happened at the Dizengoff Apartments, she would be getting a call from the Marines or Daugherty.

"Is everything all right?" Sitting on the edge of her bed, she fumbled with the light.

"That depends. I'm standing at a crime scene I think may be tied to the shooting in Dizengoff Square. I thought you might want to come take a look."

She glanced at the clock. It was 1:30 a.m. "What makes you think the crimes are connected?"

"I have two twentysomethings—one an Israeli Arab, the other a Palestinian—killed very efficiently. Witnesses claim they saw a woman fleeing the building."

"Our shooter?"

"Possibly."

*

It took Jordan thirty minutes to get to the address Weizman had given her on Rumman Street in al-Ajami. She turned into the neighborhood, headlights skimming the run-down buildings and illuminating brightly colored graffiti on most of the outside walls. Men still loitered in packs, near doorways streaming pale light onto hardened earth. There was a notable paucity of women and children. Except for the washboarded dirt roads and the Middle Eastern faces, it reminded her of places she had driven in D.C., places where even the cats ran in pairs.

Her skin crawled under the hard, hostile stares that followed her progress through the streets. She checked to make sure her doors were locked and tried imagining how the people who lived here felt.

Safe? Doubtful.

Desperate? Likely.

Resentful? Rhetorical, plus it seemed like an understatement. The Palestinians who lived in al-Ajami had been driven out of their homes, pushed from the finer neighborhoods to the north and west and discarded in squalor. It was exactly what had happened to the Jews throughout Europe. How many times did history have to repeat itself?

The five-story apartment building was easy to spot when she turned onto the correct street. A number of police cars with flashing blue lights fanned out across the entrance. With a tentative glance at the growing crowd, she bundled her hair into a ponytail and made a mental note to carry a scarf in her car in the future that she could use to cover her head. Locking the car, she pulled on her Kevlar vest before braving the throng of men who had come out to gawk and throw taunts at the Israelis manning the yellow crime scene tape.

"*Ana aasifah*," excuse me, she said in Arabic, trying to be respectful as she pushed her way through. Reaching the cordoned-off area, she flashed her ID for a guard. The officer scrutinized her credentials.

"Let her go up," a man yelled. Jordan looked up to see Gidon Lotner walking toward them. "Detective Weizman expects her."

The officer handed back her ID, and Jordan dipped her head in thanks.

"Are you leaving?" she asked Lotner.

"The crime scene technicians are here. Unlike some, I have no interest in working outside of my purview."

Jordan figured she was the intended target of that dig. No way was she taking the bait. "Have a good night, Detective."

Turning her back on the man, Jordan headed for the building. At the entrance, she slowed and made a mental assessment of the hall and the stairwell. The turquoise paint was chipping, and most surfaces were covered in dark graffiti that spewed hatred for the Jews. When she reached the third-floor landing, Weizman greeted her.

"Come in."

Cool air flowed from the apartment into the hallway.

"Air conditioner?"

"It's a good thing," Weizman said, "Otherwise the smell would be driving us out." He pointed to the bodies lying on the floor. "That one is Najm Tibi. He rents the place. This one is Mansoor Rahman. Both are known associates of the PLC."

Jordan took in the furnishings—the Persian carpets, the over-stuffed couch and ottoman, the state-of-the-art TV and stereo equipment. "Tibi lived well."

"Don't let the outside of these buildings fool you. Inside, many of the Arabs live like sheiks." Weizman consulted his notes. "He worked in the maintenance department of GG&B Engineering in Haifa."

Jordan looked at Weizman. "That's quite a commute."

He shrugged. "An hour tops. A lot of people drive that far to work every day."

They did where Jordan grew up, also. In fact, some drove farther. "What kind of engineering?"

"Agricultural planning and infrastructure, water, energy, and industrial engineering. According to their own press, GG&B is a billion-dollar international firm."

Squatting beside Tibi's body, Jordan ducked down to get a look at his face. "I've seen this man before."

"Where?" Weizman asked.

"He walked past me on the day of the shooting." She remembered the hairs on the back of her neck sending off warning signals.

"You're sure?"

"Positive. He ducked into the Postal Authority. There was something off about him. I almost followed him, but I went to find you instead."

"Do you recognize his friend?" Weizman pointed at the other body. Tall, thin, and brown-skinned, his face was turned toward her, his arms tucked beneath him in a futile attempt to staunch the blood.

"He doesn't look familiar." She studied his clothes and the stipple of brown. "Did you notice the blood spatter on his shirt?"

"I imagine forensics will tie him to the murder of Ofer Federman at the Dizengoff Apartments. Here." He tossed her a brown wallet. Inside were his ID card, some money, and a picture of him with another man wearing a *hattah*, or Palestinian scarf. Jordan turned the picture over. On the back was written a series of thirteen numbers.

"Do you see the mark on his neck?" Weizman asked.

The bright red mark at the base of his Adam's apple stood out so anyone could have seen it.

"She crushed his larynx."

"A difficult feat, indicative of training. We know she left through the bedroom." Weizman signaled for Jordan to follow him, leading her through the apartment to a pair of sliding-glass doors. Outside, a narrow metal balcony hung precariously from the side of the building. "If you look, you can see where the bolts separated from the plaster. The marks are fresh. The question is, how did she get into the apartment? There is no fire escape to climb up."

"Maybe she was already inside, waiting here for Tibi and his friend to come home." Jordan pulled a flashlight off her belt and checked out the damage to the metal balcony. It hung at an angle, attached by only one rusted bar. Directing the light to the walls on either side, she played the beam along the steep plaster until she hit a shallow ledge about six inches below.

"Check this out, Detective."

Weizman poked his head out beside hers and she danced the light beam along the ledge, stopping where a chip had been broken away and white plaster gleamed. Beyond the chip was the stairwell window.

"I'd say she climbed along here." Jordan pulled her head back inside. "Has anyone dusted the balcony for prints?"

Weizman turned to a crime scene tech.

The tech shook his head. "Not yet."

"Get it done," Weizman ordered.

Jordan headed for the front door and was halfway through the apartment when Weizman caught up to her.

"Where are you going, Agent Jordan?"

"To check out the stairwell." She kept moving until she reached the third-floor window. "She had to have gotten onto the ledge through here." Jordan pulled a pair of latex gloves from her jacket pocket and donned them before she carefully gripped the window handle and pulled up. The window slid open easily. Climbing up on the sill, she studied the window track. Touching her finger to the sash, she jumped down and showed Weizman the tip of her glove.

"Lip gloss," said Jordan. "She used lip gloss to grease the skids."

"So she came up the stairs, climbed out this window, and made her way along the side of the building to the balcony?"

"That would my theory," Jordan said. Bending over, she stuck her head back out of the window and studied the ledge. Taking in the angle of the balcony, she guessed it would have been impossible for the assassin to have backtracked this way. She tracked from the lower edge of the balcony platform to the ground, pulled her head inside, pushed past Weizman, and took the stairs two at a time to the ground floor.

"Where are we going now?" he asked, dogging her heels.

"Just follow."

At the ground floor, Jordan turned toward the alley entrance and shoved open the door. Looking in both directions, she spotted two men smoking cigarettes at the end of the building. Otherwise, the alley was empty.

"We should wait for one of my officers," Weizman said.

"We'll be fine." Jordan wasn't worried about two men. Across the alley, a deserted lot stretched to another rise of broken-down apartments. There wasn't a sign of anyone else in sight.

"What are we looking for?" Weizman asked, following her outside.

Jordan stopped in front of the dumpster.

Weizman checked out the metal bin and then shined his flashlight up toward the balcony. "Ah, I see what you're thinking."

"It would've made for a soft landing."

"Softer than the ground, anyway." He cupped his hands around his mouth and shouted upward. "Hey, Akim!"

The crime scene tech stuck his head out the window. "*Ken.*"

"Cordon off this dumpster. We'll need to take prints and search the contents."

"Why?"

"In case our suspect dropped something."

While Weizman talked with Akim, Jordan let her senses take the night's pulse. The warm air vibrated with the song of the cicadas, like the angry rhythm of a guitar strum. She wondered if it always felt like this here.

"Why was she here?" Jordan mused, walking the perimeter of the dumpster and stopping at a set of footprints.

"Excuse me?" said Weizman.

"She was here for a reason. What did she come for?"

"To kill the men."

"Because they killed the apartment manager and tossed the Taylors' apartment?" Jordan asked. "I doubt that. She could have killed them anywhere, but instead she tracked them here."

"Why?"

"Exactly," Jordan said. "We need to find this woman and find out what she knows."

Chapter 17

With fewer than four hours of sleep, Jordan parked in front of the Dizengoff Apartments and was surprised to see Detective Lotner pulling away. Flashing her credentials to the Marines on duty, she bounded up the stairs and into the Taylors' apartment. The Marine at the door let her in.

"Everything okay here?" she asked.

Taylor stood in the kitchen and looked at her over his shoulder. "Fine. Why do you ask?"

"I just saw the detective leave."

"He had a few follow-up questions," Taylor said. "He wanted to check to make sure things were secure, and he brought Lucy a game."

"That seems a little out of character."

"How so?"

"He doesn't seem the type, that's all. I get the feeling he doesn't really like Americans."

"He likes me," Lucy said, holding up a game board. "It's called *shachmat*. Do you know how to play?"

Chess. Jordan's father had taught her the game when she was a few years younger than Lucy. "Yes, I do."

"Will you play with me?" Lucy reached for a box under the coffee table. "I have to warn you. I'm very good."

"After breakfast," Taylor said, wielding a spatula in their direction. "Eggs or pancakes?"

Jordan realized he was speaking to her. "Coffee?"

"Coming right up."

Thirty minutes later, after feeding Lucy and putting the last dish back in the cupboard, Taylor excused himself.

"He's calling Mom back," Lucy said, retrieving the chess board and setting it up on the coffee table in the living room. "We'll have plenty of time to play."

Jordan watched as Lucy set up the pieces. The circles under her eyes looked darker today, her skin paler. Maybe the ex–Mrs. Taylor could talk some sense into the judge and get him to take Lucy home.

"I'll bet you miss your mom," Jordan said.

Lucy shrugged. "She can be a little smothery."

"That's a mom's job," Jordan said. "Why else would you just add an *s* to mother?" Still, she understood the feeling. She had been young when her mother, following her father's death, had brought her and her younger brother, Oleksander Jr., back to the States. Changing their last names to her maiden name, their mother had tucked them away in their grandparents' house outside of Denver and cocooned them from the world. If it hadn't been for her grandfather, a kind and intelligent man, Jordan might never have gotten away.

"I'm white," Lucy said, drawing Jordan back to the game. "I go first."

"Not so fast." Jordan picked up two pawns, one white, one black. Mixing them behind her back, she cupped one in each hand and extended her arms. "You pick."

Lucy eeny-meeny-miny-moed and then pointed to Jordan's left hand. "That one."

"White. Okay, you *do* go first." Jordan lowered herself into the easy chair. "Prepare to get beaten."

"That's big talk," Lucy said.

As they played, Jordan was surprised at how easily Lucy's mind processed the game, picking up on moves that hadn't been made and planning ahead. Standard moves didn't work against her either. When Jordan tried tricking Lucy into capturing the black bishop, leaving her open to capturing Lucy's queen, Lucy dodged and made an unexpected move with her knight.

"Smart," Jordan said. "But do you really think I'm going to let you pull off a knight's fork?"

Lucy looked confused.

"If I don't stop you, what's your next move?" Jordan asked.

Lucy pointed to the board. "My knight goes here."

"Ne3 plus."

"What?"

"Lucy, if you're going to become a master at chess, you need to learn the language." Running her finger along the edge of the board, Jordan could hear her father's voice in her ear. "Chessboards are numbered one to eight, starting on the white side. Sideways, the rows are lettered in lowercase, from *a* to *h*, starting on white's left."

Lucy concentrated on the board.

"You moved your bishop here, capital *B* for bishop to b8," Jordan said, pointing. Grabbing a pad and pen from the end table, she wrote, *Bb8*. "See?"

Lucy nodded.

"I expected you to capture my bishop with your rook, moving *R* for rook to b8." Jordan wrote, *Rxb8*. "The *x* stands for capture. Are you following me so far?"

Lucy nodded again.

"But you fooled me," Jordan said, "and played a *zwischenzug* by moving Nd5."

"What's the *N* stand for?"

"Knight. The *K* is already being used for the king."

Lucy scrunched up her face. "I *kinda* get it."

"Then tell me, if I don't stop you, what's your next move?"

Lucy got up on her knees, studied the board, and then pointed to a square.

"Ne3+," said Jordan, writing it on the pad at the same time. "The plus stands for check."

Lucy nodded but looked unsure.

Jordan laughed. "The point is, if I take your bishop, you're going to move your knight here, right? If I let you do that, what happens?"

"Your king is in check and you have to move him, and then I can capture your queen."

"Right. That's called a fork. You used one piece to put two of my pieces in jeopardy. It's called a knight's fork because you're using your knight to do it."

Lucy sat back on her heels. "But if I captured your bishop, you would have moved your queen there." She pointed again. "Then I would be in check and you would capture *my* bishop."

"She told you she was good," Taylor said.

Jordan glanced up. In the heat of the game, she hadn't heard him return.

Lucy leaned over the board. "You're going to pull a zwischen-thing too, aren't you?"

"A *zwischenzug*. Yes, I am. I'm moving my king to f2."

Jordan prevented the fork and the game continued, but Lucy had more tricks up her sleeve and won in ten more moves.

"Wanna play again?" she asked, resetting the board.

"How old did you say she was, Judge?" Jordan asked.

"Eleven."

"How many games have you played?"

"Six."

Jordan had been beaten by a preteen who had only just learned to play.

Taylor chuckled. "Ask her how many games she's won."

"Five," Lucy said. "I got beat my first one."

"Seriously?" Jordan said. Either the child was a chess prodigy or her opponents were letting her win. "One more."

"Game on." Lucy moved her pawn. Jordan countered and Lucy took her pawn *en passé*. The kid was a quick study. Fifteen moves later, she won again.

"I give." Jordan leaned back in her seat. *Damn.*

"Wanna play again?"

"What, and let you whip my butt a third time? No thanks."

Lucy sighed.

Jordan hated disappointing her. "How about tomorrow?"

Lucy brightened. "Pinky swear?" She held up her hand with her pinky crooked. Jordan hooked fingers and promised.

Lucy put away the pieces and the board and shoved the box back under the coffee table. Her skin looked pasty white except for two bright red circles dotting her cheeks. Jordan reached out and brushed her hand across Lucy's forehead. Her head felt warm. "Are you feeling okay?"

"I'm just tired." Lucy looked at her dad. "What time are we going to Alena's?"

"The usual, Luce." Taylor consulted his watch. "We have to leave in a little over an hour."

"Then I'm going to go lie down."

Jordan flashed what she hoped was an encouraging smile and pushed herself up from the chair. "And I need to hit the loo." She touched Taylor's arm. "Then we need to talk."

The night before, he had outlined their normal schedule for her. Every day, he and Lucy left in time to watch the fountain, walked to the doctor's office, and then walked back. That was not going to happen today. Jordan had floated the idea of bringing the doctor to Lucy, but the judge had nixed it outright. It might be worth another attempt at reasoning with him.

The whole thing with Dr. Petrenko seemed a little woo-woo to her, but after hearing the story about his son, Jordan understood his stubbornness. Besides, she couldn't force him to do anything. There was nothing official about this whole operation. The only reason she was here was because his ex-wife was friendly with the ambassador. She might be in charge of the detail, but the DSS was on precarious ground. The judge had never asked for protection.

At the sink, she flipped on the faucet, washed her hands, and then squeezed a dollop of toothpaste onto her finger and rubbed it vigorously against her teeth and gums. Regardless of what she advised, if Taylor insisted on taking Lucy to Petrenko's office, she needed to ensure them a safe trip.

Jordan sucked up a handful of water, rinsed her mouth, and spit into the bowl. Finger-combing her unruly curls, she smoothed her wrinkled white tee. From now on, she would carry essentials— deodorant, toothbrush, toothpaste, brush, hair-tie, and a change of underwear.

Back in the living area, Jordan found Taylor sitting at the kitchen table. She pulled up a chair.

"Is there any chance I can get you to change your mind?" she asked.

"We've been over this."

"I'm not suggesting you cancel. Just have her come here."

"I told you, she won't come."

"Why? What harm could there be in asking?"

Taylor squared off with Jordan. "She would just want to work on Lucy from there."

"From a distance? She can do that?" Jordan heard the skepticism in her voice. "How is that possible?"

"She finds her energy."

Jordan wondered if he realized how ridiculous that sounded. "If that's true, if she can do that, why not let her? Why not just stay here today? Or, for that matter, why not go back to the States where it's safer for you?"

"It's better if she treats Lucy in person."

"Seriously?"

"It's stronger."

The expression on his face said it all. This was a losing battle, and Jordan knew enough to surrender. "Fine."

A few minutes later, the Marine guard changed. Once new guards were positioned, Jordan spread out a map of Tel Aviv and called the new leader, Master Gunnery Sergeant Walker, over to the table. The night before, she had chosen their planned route. Now she laid it out for Taylor and the Master Gunny.

"One way there, another way back." There were plenty of options. The office was on Arlozoroff Street, one block east of Adam HaCohen. Because of all the one-way streets, the quickest, easiest, and most dangerous route was to take Dizengoff Street to Ibn Gevirol and then west on Arlozorov. Her plan was to cut south.

"I won't ride a bus," Lucy said. She was standing in the doorway to her bedroom. Jordan glanced over. Lucy's emotions were hard to read, but Jordan thought she detected fear in her eyes. Considering the circumstances, Jordan didn't blame her for being scared.

"No problem. We're going by car." Jordan said. "I've arranged for an unmarked vehicle to pick us up in the alley."

Taylor flashed a thumb's up. "Sounds like a plan."

Chapter 18

Ganani parked her car across the street from the Dizengoff Apartments and waited. With a clear view of the front of the building and the alley, she could see anyone coming or going. Knowing the Palestinian had left empty-handed, she was sure he would return, and she planned on being there to greet him.

Through Colonel Brodsky's back channels, she also knew that the USB drive with the information she needed hadn't turned up in al-Ajami. With luck, the Palestinian had it in his possession. Her sources identified him as Umar Haddid, a man with little tying him to the Palestine Liberation Committee except for his best friend, Mansoor Rahman, one of the men she had killed. Hopefully that was enough to drive him back.

An unmarked sedan pulled up in the alley at eleven sharp, and Ganani perked up. A Marine exited the vehicle and entered through the gate in the back fence. A block to the east, a driver in a green Subaru Forester started his engine and let it idle.

Ganani adjusted her side mirror and studied the vehicle. The Subaru's windows were illegally tinted a deep blackish-gray that repelled any attempt to see inside. The doors and fenders were streaked with dirt. A sign the vehicle had come from outside the city. There appeared to be three men in the car.

She considered leaving her car for a closer look, but common sense dictated that would also give Haddid an opportunity to identify her. Better to wait and watch.

The back alley gate opened again and the driver came back out. He checked the car, checked the alley, and then signaled to someone inside the fence. The DSS agent stepped out.

Ganani glanced down at the passenger seat at the dossier she had pulled that morning. The agent's name was Raisa Jordan. She was smart and well trained, not one to be underestimated.

Jordan hustled the American and his daughter into the backseat of the sedan before joining them. Another Marine followed, sitting shotgun.

Ganani watched as the sedan exited the alley and turned south. When it neared the corner, the Forester and its occupants fell in behind.

She hesitated only a second before she started her car and shifted it into gear.

Chapter 19

Everything ran like clockwork—the dash through the alley, the loading of vehicles. Now seated in backseat next to Taylor and Lucy, Jordan kept her eye on the road while PFC Donner drove and Corporal Price sat shotgun. Master Gunnery Sergeant Walker and one other Marine had gone ahead to scope out the situation and set up defense parameters. One guard had been left behind to cover the apartment.

Under Jordan's direction, Donner exited the hotel parking lot and headed south on Pinsker. Turning west on Bograshov, he drove straight to Ben Yehuda and turned right.

Jordan kept her attention on the cars around them, on the people on the streets, and on the windows of the buildings they approached and passed. It didn't take long for her to spot the black Hyundai one lane over. It tailed them as they crossed Gordon and stuck tight when they swung onto Jabotinsky.

Jordan tapped Donner on the shoulder. He nodded. He must have spotted it, too.

"Lucy," Jordan said, "I need you to bend over as far as you can and keep your head down." She gestured for Taylor to cover his daughter.

Taylor didn't panic, and he didn't argue. He pushed Lucy forward and covered her back.

Jordan pulled her gun from its holster as the car gained on them in the left lane. Glancing over at Taylor and Lucy, she sucked in a breath and waited for the car to pull even.

Donner slowed the sedan and the Hyundai shot even.

Jordan clicked off the safety on her gun.

A little old lady hunched over the wheel of the car while a boxer pup in the passenger seat barked frantically. Jordan puffed out her breath with a laugh. Lowering her gun, she patted the judge on the shoulder. "You can sit up now."

Taylor sat up as Lucy shifted and wiggled out from under her father's arm. Jordan felt a slight pang of guilt for scaring her. Still, better safe than sorry.

Two more right turns and Donner pulled up and parked in front of a small strip mall on Arlozoroff. Alena Petrenko's office was located in the basement. The ranch-style building had a wide, glassed-in entrance. A nail salon opened to the street on the left. On the right, a small convenience store served as a conduit into the mall.

Walker, wearing jeans, a T-shirt, and cowboy boots, loitered near the front entrance. Jordan could have spotted his buzz cut a mile away. So much for blending in.

Corporal Price joined Walker on the sidewalk. Taylor reached for the door handle, and Jordan placed her hand on his sleeve. "Hold on a minute. Let me check things out first."

She eyed the street for signs of trouble. If they were going to be ambushed, this was a logical place.

A black, unmarked car was parked in front of them. The Marine's ride. Across the street, a blue Nissan with two occupants, a man and a young boy, idled at the curb.

"The man's wife is in the salon," said Walker through the mic in Jordan's ear. "She's almost done."

A skinny kid smoking a cigarette scurried down the opposite sidewalk. There were no cars moving on the street and only a few parked in the next block—a silver Passat and a black Mazda.

"Any movement from the cars?"

"All's quiet. Harper's got a bead."

Gunnery Sergeant Harper was the detail's best marksman—markswoman. It made Jordan feel better knowing she was somewhere surveying the scene.

The sedan grew hot and stuffy and still Jordan waited. Her gaze traveled over the houses across the street, shifting from second-floor window to second-floor window. From the farthest one on the right, a glint of sunlight on metal caused her to plant her gaze.

"Harper?" she said.

Donner nodded.

"Okay, everyone wait here." Climbing out of the car, she signaled to Price. "You, come with me."

Jordan posted him outside the convenience store entrance and stepped through the doorway. Inside, it was crowded enough to stir feelings of claustrophobia. Shelves lined the walls, stocked floor to ceiling with everything from cigarettes to baklava. A *feenjan* pot bubbled on a hot plate on the counter diffusing the smell of Turkish coffee into the air.

A thin, dark-skinned man nodded at her from behind the counter and then turned his attention back to the pot. He pulled the *feenjan* free of the heat, barely in time to prevent it from boiling over, and poured the bitter liquid into two cups.

Jordan slipped down the aisle between the narrow shelves and the counter. Outside the door to the lobby, two men chattered loudly about how much time it was taking the shopkeeper to bring them their coffee and sweet cake. Reaching the mall entrance, she could see them seated at a small, glass-topped table in the lobby. They stopped speaking abruptly when she came through the door.

"He's pouring the coffee," she said in Hebrew. "It won't be long now."

They glanced at each other and then nodded, resuming their chatter.

Jordan quickly scanned the lobby. Except for the two men, it was empty. A cluster of three tables fashioned the small eating area, and what appeared to be offices ringed an open staircase. Aside from the store, only the beauty salon showed any activity. To the left, a corridor ran to the back of the building.

Jordan stepped back into the convenience store and signaled the corporal to enter. She waited for him to draw alongside and then spoke softly in English.

"Dr. Petrenko's office is downstairs. It looks like there's an exit at the end of that hallway." She pointed down the corridor that took a sharp left at the end of the hall. "Check it out."

"Yes, ma'am." The corporal took off down the corridor. A few minutes later, he climbed back up the stairs. "There's one door to the outside at the end of the hall. It's locked. The stairs to the roof are chained shut. I walked the stairs to the basement. Everything's secure. Most of the offices downstairs are empty."

A sense of fear fueled by adrenalin came and went. She hoped they hadn't missed something.

"Okay," she said. "Let's bring them in." Moving to the entrance, she pushed open the glass doors and spoke into her mic. "We're a go."

Chapter 20

Once Taylor and Lucy were inside the mall, Jordan ratcheted down a notch. The next big danger would be getting out and back to the apartment, which they would have to do in about an hour.

"Which office is it?" she asked, allowing Taylor to take point. He walked them down the stairs to an office on the right. Jordan stationed one guard at the top of the stairs and one by the door and then followed Taylor and his daughter in.

The waiting area was small and cramped, with sour-apple-green paint, four chairs, and a beat-up wooden desk. Three framed diplomas hung on the wall above the desk chair. In the back corner, a white door was closed.

"They'll come out." Taylor sat down beside Lucy. "They may have another client."

It wasn't long before a short, stocky man with spiked brown hair wearing khakis and a polo shirt stepped into the room. Better than most doctors' offices, thought Jordan. At least these guys were on time.

"*Shalom*, Ben," said the man. "Lucy."

"Yury." Taylor shook his hand. The man turned to Lucy and spoke in a thick Russian accent.

"And how are you feeling today?" he said with genuine interest.

Lucy moved closer to her dad. "Okay."

"*Nyet*, 'okay.' What kind of answer is this? Are you sick feeling? Does it ache in your head?"

Lucy looked up at her father.

"She ran a fever yesterday," said Taylor. "There was some trouble at Dizengoff."

"I read about it." Yury stared at Jordan, as if the trouble were her fault, and then looked toward the white door. A tall, angelic-looking woman with short-cropped, dark hair and nearly translucent skin glided into the room. Alena.

Foregoing introductions, the woman honed in on Lucy, tipping the child's chin upward and studying her eyes. The scrutiny came with a torrent of Russian that made Jordan chuckle.

Taylor looked at her. "What's so funny?"

"Something caused Lucy anxiety," Alena said in English. "It must be stopped."

"She said a lot more than that," Jordan said.

"What do you mean?" Taylor asked.

"She said you have a tendency to inflame things. That she spends a lot of time undoing the harm you've done." Jordan wasn't sure why she felt the need to translate so literally. She could see he looked hurt.

Yury looked surprised.

Alena threw up her hands. "I think you worry too much, that is all. It is normal for you to be worried, but the emotion transfers to Lucy."

Jordan held her hand out to Alena. "*Menya zavut* Raisa Jordan."

Alena stared hard at Jordan. "*Priyatna poznakomitysa*." It's a pleasure to meet you.

The woman gripped Jordan's hand. Jordan had to pull it away.

"You speak Russian very well," Alena said in Russian.

"Thank you. I was born there," Jordan answered in kind. "My father was Ukrainian."

"And his name?" asked Yury.

Jordan glanced between the couple. "Olek Ivanova."

Alena looked at Yury. "I took a class from Olek Ivanova."

"It must be a different Olek. My dad wasn't a teacher. He was a hockey player."

"Yes." Yury sounded excited. "The goalie for the national team."

"It was him I knew," Alena said. "He was ahead of me in school. He taught as a graduate student in one of my classes."

Jordan found that hard to believe. The doctor's diploma hung on the wall, and Jordan picked up the name. "At the Kyiv Medical Institute of the Ukrainian Association of Folk Medicine?"

"Yes." Alena nodded enthusiastically. "Your father was amazing."

Her father had been an intelligent man, and Jordan knew he had gone to college, but they had to be talking about someone else. Her father was a great hockey player, not a student of alternative medicine.

"Do you mind speaking in English?" Taylor said, clearly annoyed to be left out of the conversation.

Yury spoke in halting English. "We were just saying that Alena knew this woman's father. He was a Russian national treasure. A hockey player with very raw talent."

Jordan wanted to end this conversation. She wasn't comfortable with the direction it was going, and it wasn't the time for it. "I think we should get started here."

"Hold on," Taylor said. "I had forgotten you were from Russia."

"I mostly grew up in the States," Jordan said. "My father died when I was young."

"What happened to him?" Lucy asked.

Jordan tried to think of what to say. She didn't want to tell Lucy the truth—that he had been caught in the crossfire of a botched assassination attempt. The child had just experienced a shooting. "It was an accident. He was in the wrong place at the wrong time, that's all."

"*Nyet!* He was murdered," Alena said, lapsing back into Russian. "The KGB wanted him dead."

Jordan stared at Alena.

Taylor grabbed her elbow. "Is everything okay?"

Jordan yanked her arm free.

"Everything's fine," Jordan said before switching back into Russian. "Why do you say that, Dr. Petrenko?"

"Your father was much more than just a hockey player. He was part of the PSI program, until he married your mother."

Jordan had heard of the Russian, government-run program designed to study the use of psychic discovery in warfare and spying. At the end of the Cold War, the Russian PSI program had been working on their subjects' ability to physically control things with their minds. In the 1970s, the United States had created its own psychic program in response. Both were ridiculous failures.

"You're wrong," Jordan said.

Alena's expression softened. "You didn't know."

"Know what?"

Jordan must have raised her voice, because the office door swung open. The Marine guard stepped inside. "Everything okay, ma'am?"

She reverted to English. "Everything's fine. Hold your position."

The Marine glanced from Jordan to Taylor to Alena and then beat a hasty retreat. Jordan waited until the door clicked shut before reengaging with Alena. "Are you suggesting my father worked with spies?"

The doctor smiled.

"You are definitely mistaken. My agency would have picked up something like that in my background check." Information like that would have ended her career before it ever began.

Alena continued to smile. "Would they have? I can't say."

Taylor had tensed up and was looking annoyed.

"We need to talk more," Alena said. "But now I must see to Lucy."

Jordan nodded without actually agreeing. In her opinion, Alena Petrenko was nothing but a con artist who had convinced hundreds of people that she could cure their illnesses where Western medicine failed. Why should Jordan believe anything she had to say?

"I apologize for speaking with your friend in Russian," Alena said to Taylor before disappearing through the doorway.

Yury looped his arm around Lucy's shoulders. "Come, child. It's time."

Once the door was shut, Taylor turned on Jordan. "What was she saying to you?"

"Nothing."

"Bullshit."

"It was personal."

"You look a little shaken."

The last thing she wanted was her protectee worrying about her. "I'm fine."

Jordan ended the conversation by sitting down and picking up a magazine. She pretended to read while her mind wandered to an argument her mother and father had in the weeks preceding his death. The two of them were standing in their living room in St. Petersburg. Jordan was sitting on the stairs listening but not understanding. Her mother wanted to return to the United States, but her father insisted there was something he had to finish. Two weeks later, he was dead and buried, and she and her mother were on a flight to America.

Alena's allegations disturbed her. Jordan had survived the government's scrutiny of her Russian heritage, but there would be no surviving rumors—true or untrue—that her father was involved in the PSI program. The DSS rules were clear. There could be nothing in your past, or your family's past, that could be used against you. The slightest hint of something off raised questions of loyalty, and she already had Posner and Daugherty gunning for her.

Jordan glanced at her watch. Only five minutes had passed since Lucy had gone into the back room. Taylor had told her the appointment would last about an hour. No way could she sit still that long.

Putting down the magazine, Jordan slipped out of her chair. "I'm going outside to confer with the Marines about the plan for getting back to the apartment. Please stay here until I come and get you."

"Sure."

It bothered her that his tone was clipped. She had her hand on the doorknob before she turned back. "Taylor?"

He looked up.

"Thank you for letting it go," she said.

He narrowed his eyes. "No problem. Thank you."

"For what?"

He spread his arms so that they took in the waiting room.

Chapter 21

The cigarette smoke curled past the cracked window into the backseat and stung Haddid's eyes. He had no intention of saying a word. Zuabi may have allowed him to choose his companions, but he had also made recommendations no reasonable man could turn down. Haddid knew without a doubt that the three men in the car with him would not hesitate to kill him if he failed in this mission. Zuabi wanted the information Cline had offered for trade, and there wasn't a man among them willing to deny him.

Haddid looked out the window. All Zuabi cared about was revenge. It was not an emotion that Haddid understood, not even in connection with the deaths of his friends, but Zuabi embraced it. He had recently lost a niece, a young woman, who was like a daughter to him. She had been killed at the Lebanese embassy in Denver. And now Mansoor, a man who was like a son to Zuabi, was dead. Haddid knew he had upset Zuabi terribly by coming back empty-handed last night. It could not happen again. His leader wanted someone to pay.

"What do you see?" asked Fayez from behind the wheel.

Haddid ignored the smoke and focused his eyes on the front entrance to the mall. That's where the man and his daughter had entered.

"I'm speaking to you, Haddid."

"Yes, I know." Haddid stroked his chin and chose his words carefully. "I think that as long as the car remains parked where it is, we can assume that is where they will exit."

"What if there is another car?"

Haddid shifted his gaze to the back of Fayez's head. Was this some kind of test?

"From where we sit, we will see them drive away. Be patient, Fayez."

Basim, sitting in the passenger seat, leaned over to look at Haddid. "I say we go in through the back and surprise them." He grinned, craned his neck, and looked at the man sitting in the back beside Haddid. "What do you think, Yousif?"

Haddid turned. "Yes, what do you think, Yousif?"

If any of these men could be intimidated, it was this man, and it made him the most dangerous of the three. It would be impossible to know whose side he would take and on whose side he would remain.

"I think Basim is right. Let's go in through the back."

Fayez smiled at Haddid in the rearview mirror, his teeth flashing false-white against his deeply tanned skin. "We know there is only one soldier inside. Look," he jerked his head in the direction of the strip mall. "There's one at the front door and the driver in the car. Everyone is accounted for."

"Your count is off, Fayez." Haddid met each man's eyes. "There were five soldiers at the house. Only one was left behind. The one Marine came ahead with a woman soldier. Where is she now? Do you know?"

Haddid relished the doubt flickering in Fayez's eyes.

"He's right," said Yousif.

And so turned the tides.

Chapter 22

Jordan exited the office and bolted upstairs, as much for some fresh air as to check out the situation on the street.

"Everything good?" she asked Walker, who was standing near the front door.

He grinned. "I'd say we have company."

She scanned the street and her stomach knotted at the sight of a green car with three or four occupants parked on the approaching street. One block in the other direction, a black Volvo idled against the curb. It could be nothing.

"Any reason to be concerned?"

"PFC Donner took a stroll to check it out," he said. "There are four Arabs in the Forester. They've been there since you went inside."

"Harper?" Jordan hoped the radio mic picked up her voice. "Do you have eyes on the green car?"

"Negative, but I have a bead on the woman in the Volvo."

"You're sure it's a woman?" Jordan asked. Weizman had suspected a woman in both the shooting in Dizengoff Square and the murders in al-Ajami.

"Positive, ma'am."

"Tell me one of you have run the plates."

"Doing that now," Sergeant Donner said. He currently sat in the driver's seat of the parked sedan, pounding on a keyboard in his lap. "The Volvo's tags show it registered to one Batya Ruth, a resident of Tel Aviv. Everything about her appears to be in order. The Arab's car came back with plates registered to a company in Haifa."

Jordan had a gut feeling she knew which one. "GG&B Engineering?"

Sergeant Donner looked up. "How'd you know?"

"Call it an educated guess." Jordan brushed a stray curl away from her face and addressed the team through her mic. "Let's look alive, everyone. These might be our guys."

Four "Rogers" came back.

"Here's what we're going to do." Jordan was still unsure about a connection, but it was clear the front of the mall was under surveillance. She couldn't afford to take the chance. It could be nothing, or it could be everything. "Donner, find out everything you can about our friends on the corner and the woman in the black Volvo. Harper, keep an eye on her. I want to know if she sneezes." Jordan turned back toward the building and addressed Walker. "You keep an eye on the green Forester."

"Roger that." He smiled and popped his gum.

They were in trouble here. Things were escalating, and he was smiling and blowing bubbles. What about "fucked" did he not understand?

"Are you having fun?"

"Yes, ma'am. It's not every day I get to wear my boots and jeans to work."

"You're still a Marine, cowboy."

"Ten-four, ma'am."

"Keep your eyes open, Walker. We may be in for the next round of entertainment."

"I'm all over it, ma'am," he said.

Jordan nodded and tried her best to feign nonchalance as she reentered the building. Should she order a tactical pullout? Right now, all she had to go on were two suspicious vehicles and a gut that was on fire.

The doors closed behind her, and she glanced at the two old men still nursing their *feenjan*. The chance of a pullout leading to a firefight with casualties was high. But what were the options? The front was ripe for an ambush. If Donner brought the car around to the side, they would be picked up as soon as they turned on Y. Bin Nun or Ibn Gevirol. That left a backdoor retreat and a call for reinforcements. Time to uneven the odds in their favor.

Jordan turned on her cell phone and dialed Daugherty. Because there was no immediate embassy housing or safe house available, the judge and Lucy had been forced to stay in their apartment. Under the circumstances, and based on the judge's ex-wife's friendship with the ambassador, she was sure Daugherty would send in the cavalry.

She thought wrong. Daugherty turned her down flat, and she could hear Posner in the background egging him on.

"I don't care who the fuck he was married to," Daugherty said. "That asshole should have taken his kid and gone back to the States. Look, Jordan, the secretary of state arrives in two days, and you still haven't told me if Cline's murder is connected. Figure it out! Get the judge back to his apartment, lock his butt down, and get me some answers!"

Daugherty fumbled the phone.

"Rookie," he mumbled before clicking off. The word formed like it left a bad taste in his mouth, probably for Posner's benefit. The two were a pair of good ol' boys desperate to hold off their advancing age—and the advancement of the younger set. Not something she had time to worry about now.

Left with the local police as backup, Jordan dug Weizman's card out of her pocket and dialed the cell phone number scribbled on the back. He picked up on the fourth ring. Jordan quickly recapped the situation. "I need your help."

"How can you be certain there is even a threat?"

Honestly? "I can't. The woman may be tailing the Palestinians or early for a haircut. But a car with four Arabs registered to the company one of our murder victims worked for is too great a coincidence to ignore. I don't have the manpower to approach the cars without pulling Marines from the protection detail, leaving the judge and Lucy vulnerable."

"Stay put. I am ten minutes away."

Jordan hung up the phone and glanced at her watch. They could wait ten minutes.

The radio mic on her shoulder squawked.

"Agent Jordan?" Harper's voice sounded tentative.

"Yes."

"She's gone."

"What do you mean she's gone? I thought you had a bead on her."

"I did, but I heard someone in the hallway. I was distracted. Now the car is gone."

Jordan ran through the possibilities. The woman could have innocently stopped and then moved on. Or she might have realized they were watching and repositioned herself. The last scenario— that she moved into position for an attack—spurred Jordan to action.

"Okay, everyone—listen up. Harper, pack it up. Be ready to pick up Walker at the front door. Donner, you stay sharp and stay put."

Jordan took the steps to the basement two at a time. "Corporal Price, we need a back entrance, yesterday."

"There's only one. It's through one of the empty offices on the main floor."

"Which one?"

"I narrowed it down to two without kicking in doors."

"We have two options." Jordan pulled a map from her pocket. "We can hunker down and hope the cavalry arrives before the enemy, or we can vacate the building. We can't go out through the front or side doors. They're being watched. If we can locate the back exit and get an all-clear, we can move south on Weisel then cut over to Adam Hacohen on Yahalal. After that it's a straight shot south to Dizengoff."

The corporal nodded. "Smart. That puts us walking south against the traffic on a northbound one-way. Even if they catch on, it makes a snatch-and-grab nearly impossible. They'll have to circle around."

"Right," Jordan said. The problem was, it didn't prevent a kill shot.

Chapter 23

Jordan and the corporal kicked in two doors and located the back exit. They had inflicted some property damage. Jordan hoped Daugherty choked on the bill.

Pushing open the door, she checked the back alley. It looked deserted. She spoke into the radio. "I need an update."

"The two guys parked across the street just left with a girl from the salon," answered Walker. "No trouble. The dudes are still there. No movement."

"Any sign of the Volvo?" Jordan waited for the crackle.

"That's a negative," said Harper. "I think it's safe to say she headed down Y. Bin Nun."

Jordan wondered what the hell the woman was up to. Was she tailing the green car, or was she working in tandem with someone else? The Arabs had the front and side exits covered. Was the woman headed around to the back?

Jordan glanced at her watch. They had six minutes before Weizman arrived. A lot could happen in that amount of time. Logic said to stay put and wait. Instinct told her to run.

"We have to get out," Jordan said. "Now."

Walker, the commanding officer, agreed.

"Hold on!" She had an idea. "It's Taylor they're after, right?"

"Where are you going with this?" Walker asked.

"What if I send the corporal out as a decoy? We put him in Taylor's clothes. He keeps his head down and gets in the car with Donner. They drive off, and the four men follow."

"Won't they expect the kid to be with him?"

"Maybe they'll figure the kid stayed here."

"It might work." Walker sounded unsure, but Jordan figured it was worth a try.

"Even if they figure it out," she said, "timed correctly, the diversion might buy us a few minutes to get the judge out the back. We can reconvene at Dizengoff."

"That leaves you with only Harper and me."

"It's the best option we have." Once decided, Jordan sprinted back to Alena's office.

"Get Lucy," she said to Taylor. "We have to go." When he didn't respond, she barked, "Now!"

Taylor held his ground. "Alena's not finished."

"Yes, she is." Jordan pushed open the door to the back room. Taylor followed.

"Lucy, let's—" The scene inside caught her off guard, and she stopped midstride. Lucy lay on a small cot to the right of the door, her eyes closed. Alena sat in a chair across the room, turning and twisting her fingers. Yury stood behind a curtain that was strung across the back of the room, stubbing out a cigarette.

He pushed back the curtain. "What do you think you are doing?" he whispered. "You must not interrupt."

"We need to leave. There's no time to explain."

"Alena will finish shortly." Yury bullied her back toward the door.

Jordan stepped around him and took a step toward the cot. "She's finished now. Lucy, get up. We're going."

Lucy lay still, her gaze flitting back and forth between Jordan and Alena.

Alena stood and walked over to the girl. She placed her hand gently on Lucy's forehead and spoke softly. "Be careful with her. She is fragile and needs to rest. She will be running a fever. Give her nothing to bring it down. If her temperature climbs above thirty-eight degrees, call me. Immediately." The Russian picked up a bottle of water, pressed her palm firmly against the cap, and concentrated on the sloshing liquid. After a moment, she extended the water bottle toward Jordan. "Have her drink all of this within the next hour."

Jordan reached for the water. "Got it."

"*Nyet!*" Alena maintained her grip on the bottle. "It's important you do what I say."

Taylor took the bottle. "She'll drink it,"

Jordan reached out her hand and pulled Lucy to her feet. "Let's go." Pushing the child toward the door, she nodded to Alena and Yury. "You two, be careful."

Taylor started to apologize, but Jordan cut him off. "We need to move. You need to take off your clothes."

"What?"

"Do it. Trade clothes with the corporal."

The corporal was already stripped to his skivvies and holding his uniform. Taylor looked less than happy, but he complied. While he fumbled with the buttons on his shirt, she opened the door to the downstairs foyer and checked to make sure the hallway was clear.

"Hurry up," she said.

When the men were dressed, Jordan led them down the hall to the back stairs. She didn't want to scare Lucy, but Taylor needed to understand the danger he was in. "Listen to me, Taylor. We have company out front." She paused to let her words sink in. "We found a back door that doesn't appear to be guarded. We're going out through the alley to pick up our ride."

Jordan led the way through the lawyer's office and then checked her watch again.

Four minutes.

"The plan is to send the corporal out front disguised as you." Jordan jerked her head toward the Marine, who flashed a thumbs-up. Dressed in Taylor's clothes, he looked more like the judge than Jordan would have figured. They were close to the same height and had similar coloring. Taylor's shirt was tight and pulled across the corporal's chest, but if the corporal moved quickly and kept his head down, they stood a chance of pulling this off.

"The corporal will drive off with PFC Donner," Jordan said to Taylor. "Then Gunnery Sergeant Harper and the Master Gunny will head out in the second vehicle to pick us up. You, Lucy, and I are going to walk out through this door and start moving south against the traffic. Once Walker and Harper pick us up, we'll rendezvous back at the apartment."

Lucy clung to her father's hand.

Jordan bent down until she was nose to nose with the girl. "I get that you're scared, Lucy. We're going to protect you and your dad, but it's important that you listen to me and do exactly what I tell you to do."

"Back off," Taylor said.

Jordan straightened up and stared at Taylor. His expression indicated he was in charge of his daughter and would bridge no more interference. Her mind flitted back to Dizengoff. Cline dead in the square. The apartment manager slaughtered in his office. The two Arabs killed in al-Ajami. There were already four men dead on his account, and she was putting four more in danger—eight if she counted herself, Lucy, and the Petrenkos.

"It's important she understands," Jordan said.

Taylor waited a beat and then spoke to Lucy. "You stay right with me. We're going to follow Agent Jordan's lead."

Lucy sucked in her lower lip and nodded.

"Good. It's settled." Jordan gave a rundown to the Marines. "The corporal's coming out. Donner, watch for the men to follow. If they don't, then double back and cover the route. Walker and Harper, double back to Bloch." She traced the route on the map by memory. "Pick us up at the intersection of Weisel and Liberman."

Jordan turned to Taylor. "There are two suspect vehicles. We have eyes on one, a green Forester with four men inside. We lost track of the other, a black Volvo. The driver is a woman, possibly the same one who shot the Palestinian in Dizengoff Square and fired on you. We are going to walk out this door, turn to the left, and walk to the street. It is a northbound road. We will walk south. The Marines will pick us up one block down on the corner."

"Got it," Taylor said. Lucy nodded.

Jordan forced a smile. "It's going to be okay. Keep your eyes open. If you see anything out of the ordinary—*anything*—tell me."

Jordan was glad he didn't point out their failure in keeping tabs on the woman. No doubt she would hear enough of that once Daugherty got wind. She checked her watch again. Two minutes to backup if Weizman was punctual. A quick look told her the back alley still stood empty. Not that she expected to see the Volvo parked by the garbage cans, but she expected something. Her gut told her to keep moving.

"The corporal is in the car and they're moving. The green car has held position."

They hadn't taken the bait.

"Let's go," Jordan said, moving into the alley. Taylor kept Lucy behind him and stayed on her heels. There were a few parked cars, none of them the make or model they were looking for, all empty. Still, Jordan had a nagging feeling that something was off.

A squeal of brakes caught her attention. The black government sedan with Harper at the wheel turned into the alley and raced toward them at full speed.

"What the—?" She gestured for Taylor to get down and reached for her gun.

The radio on her shoulder squawked. "They're on our tail."

As the sedan squealed to a stop beside them, the Forester rounded the corner. The black Volvo headed straight toward it, careening up the street against traffic.

"Get in!" Jordan pushed Lucy into the backseat. Taylor followed.

"Go," Lucy shouted. "Go!"

"Get down!" Jordan yelled. "Keep her head down, Taylor."

A shot rang out and the Forester veered sharply right, slamming into a parked car. Jordan got a look at the man in the rear passenger seat, and then the Volvo swung around it and accelerated.

"What the hell happened?" Jordan shouted, as Harper wheeled out of the alley.

"Harper pulled up, and the next thing I knew, the dudes were behind us," Walker said. "I figured the best thing to do was get the three of you inside the car."

Why hadn't the Palestinians taken the bait? Jordan wondered. "Was it that obvious that the corporal wasn't Taylor?"

"He had me fooled," Harper said, careening into the street.

Positioning herself on her knees, Jordan faced the back window and pushed Lucy toward the floor. "Get down and don't get up until I say it's clear."

The Volvo screeched around the corner and then settled into a rhythm behind them. Jordan assessed the woman at the wheel. She had long, dark hair hanging around her shoulders and an intensity about her that commanded attention. This was a woman who wasn't used to losing.

Well, neither was Jordan.

The woman's hand came up. There was a flash of silver. Jordan leveled her gun. If this woman wanted to play, Jordan was game. "Turn left and then take the next right," she ordered.

"But that puts us into the neighborhoods," Harper said.

"That's right. Find a cul-de-sac."

Harper glanced at her in the rearview mirror. "Then we'll be trapped."

"Just do it." Jordan had a plan. Maybe not a good plan, but there was no way to shake this woman, and Jordan would be damned if she'd give up her charges. What they needed to do was capture her.

"Once we turn in to the cul-de-sac, I'm going to open the door and roll out. Taylor, you keep a tight hold on Lucy. Harper, the Volvo is going to come in behind you fast. Spin one-hundred-eighty degrees and face her."

"You want to play chicken?" Harper said.

"Hang on," said Walker.

"Are you going to jump out of the car?" Lucy said.

Jordan would have expected her to sound scared. Instead, the kid sounded excited. Jordan wondered if she was spiking a fever.

"Free to speak, ma'am?" Walker said.

"Yes."

"This is nuts."

Crazy or not, it was the only way she could see to end this and their best chance at getting some answers.

"Turn," she ordered.

The car veered sharply right. The driver's side wheels came off the pavement. Jordan threw open the door as the car settled back down with a thud. As the car swerved left, she launched herself out and tucked and rolled. She felt the pain and heard the squeal of the Volvo's tires as it followed the sedan into the cul-de-sac.

The government vehicle maneuvered 180 degrees, and the Volvo's brakes ground hard.

Jordan forced herself to her feet. Scrambling around behind the Volvo, she kept herself low. Two quick shots and the back tires went flat. Then, moving quickly alongside the car, she leveled her gun at the driver over the top of the driver's side mirror. "Hello."

The woman looked stunned. Throwing the car in reverse, she tried accelerating backward. The flat back tires slowed the vehicle's progress. Jordan shot out the front tires.

"Put your hands where I can see them."

The woman turned off her car and positioned her hands at ten and two on the wheel.

"She has a gun," Jordan said. "Somebody secure the weapon." Walker stepped forward.

"Cuff her hands, and watch out for her feet. I imagine she's very well trained."

"Bravo, Raisa Jordan," the woman said.

"You know my name." Somehow Jordan wasn't surprised.

"I know a lot about you. Perhaps more than your own government knows." Her statement had a chilling effect. Jordan's mind flashed to what Alena had revealed earlier. Jordan shook it off. The woman was toying with her, playing for time.

"What is it you want?" Jordan asked.

Her gaze flitted to the judge and Lucy, and then she locked eyes with Jordan. "You must have figured that out by now."

Jordan shook her head. "Not yet. But trust me, we will."

Chapter 24

Jordan paced the length of Weizman's office, a small, gray room with windows that faced out toward the highway. Outside the detective's door spread a maze of cubicles with desks and chairs, all painted the same drab gray as the carpet and manned by Israeli beat cops wearing navy slacks and light blue shirts.

Earlier, with no authority to arrest anyone, she had ordered the Marines to restrain the woman at the scene of the attack and waited for him to show up. In turn, he had hauled the woman in for questioning. Now, watching him pick his way across the squad room, she moved forward impatiently.

"The woman's clammed up," Weizman said, pushing her back and shutting the door behind him.

Jordan had expected her to ask for a lawyer. "Batya Ruth was the name on her registration," she said. "We couldn't find any more information on her."

"That's because it's a cover name. The woman is connected."

"What do you mean 'connected'?"

Weizman perched on the edge of a desk. "Her real name is Batya Ganani. She works for Shabak." The Hebrew and Arabic word for Shin Bet, the Israeli equivalent of the FBI.

"You're telling me she works for the Israeli government?"

Weizman nodded. "She asked to speak to Ilya Brodsky, who heads up a special antiterrorist unit. Colonel Brodsky has ordered her release."

"You're letting her go?"

Weizman threw up his hands. "Of course. She is an agent of the State of Israel."

"What about the attack on the judge and his daughter?" Jordan asked.

"Ganani claims she was tailing the Palestinians and realized they were planning an attack. She moved in to protect your flank. Shabak's stance is that you owe her an apology and a thank you."

"What about her involvement in the Dizengoff shooting? And al-Ajami? She must be the one you're looking for. Why else would she be tailing the Palestinians?"

Weizman shrugged. "I can't prove she's involved or that she did anything wrong if she was acting as an agent of the government. I have no reason to suspect Shabak of being involved in nefarious dealings."

"So you believe what she's telling you?"

Weizman smiled thinly. "If she had wanted to kill you or the judge, you would both be dead." He moved behind his desk, sat down, and gestured toward a chair. "Now I have some questions for you."

Jordan ignored the seat he offered. "What questions?"

"I need something to justify the discharge of U.S. weapons on Israeli soil and to explain why you shot out the tires of a Shabak agent and held her at gunpoint."

"Fuck."

He smiled again. "Did you draw your weapon because you were threatened?"

Jordan could see where this was headed. Moving forward, she planted both of her palms firmly on his desk. "Yes, Detective

Weizman. I heard a shot in the alley as we were leaving the doctor's office. I believe the Shabak agent shot out the front tire of a green Forester carrying four men who intended to ambush our transport. I drew my gun."

"Go back to the embassy, Agent Jordan." Weizman sat back, planting his elbows on the armrests of his chair, steepling his arms and tapping together his index fingers. "Take the judge and his daughter, put them under protective custody, and send them home."

"I can't do that."

Weizman sat up sharply. "Are you saying you have no power to force them into your embassy? With what's happened, the judge will not be so stupid as to refuse to protect his child."

"Maybe you can order your citizens around, Weizman, but we can't order Ben Taylor to do anything. He's an American here on legitimate business. He believes that the medical treatments Lucy receives are saving her life." Jordan made no attempt to mask her own skepticism. "We can't force him to leave. If I could, I would. How about you have him deported?"

Weizman cupped his chin in his hand and shook his head. "He has legal documents and, so far, he has done nothing wrong."

A door opened on the far side of the squad room, and Jordan turned as Batya Ganani stepped through the doorway. She glanced around until she spotted Jordan, and a faint grin spread across her face. She nodded slightly.

"Round one, Ganani," Jordan said.

"Excuse me?" said Weizman.

"It's an expression." She started for the door, but Weizman called her back.

"Hold up. I have something for you." The detective rummaged around in his desk drawer and then pulled out a small USB drive and pushed it toward Jordan. "It's a copy of one we found in the apartment at al-Ajami. I think you will find it interesting. It's full of American pop music. Maybe you can help me identify its owner?"

*

Haddid trembled. No one had died. Yousif had been wounded, but the rest of them had come through unscathed.

"Where did that crazy bitch in the Volvo come from?" asked Fayez. "Who the hell was she?"

They were sitting on the couch in the safe house, watching through the bedroom door as Basim doctored a moaning Yousif. He was lying across the bed and looked pale. The four of them had failed to fulfill their mission.

"She is the woman from Najm's house. She must be Shabak. I don't know."

Fayez raised his eyebrows. "If that's true, then why aren't we dead?"

It was a valid question. Plus, it would save Zuabi the trouble of killing them. Haddid shuddered to think how their leader would react to this latest news. There had to be some way of appeasing Zuabi without giving him the means to carry out his plan.

"Zuabi is going to be angry," said Fayez, as if reading Haddid's thoughts.

"It was beyond our control." Haddid feigned disappointment at their failure to capture the girl and her father. In truth, he was glad. She was only a child.

His thoughts drifted to his own son. Sami was younger than the girl but held the same innocence of youth. Children did not care about war. They did not care about politics. They did not care about race. They cared only about what their parents told them. About playing with their friends. About eating. His son was always hungry.

And his wife. What did she care about? She only wanted Haddid to go to work and come home. She wanted him to put a roof over their heads and food in their bellies. She hated the violence. She hated Zuabi. As the head of the Palestine Liberation Committee, he supported three things she opposed—Hamas, jihad, and racism. Haddid's beloved was convinced that one day it would be one of those three things that would bring death to Sami.

Haddid feared she was right. Zuabi was bent on revenge, and his view of the bigger picture was skewed. But these were not things he could share with his colleagues. If the others knew he rejoiced in their failure, there was not one among them that would hesitate to kill him.

"What are we to do now, Haddid?" asked Fayez.

Earlier, the man had treated him like he knew nothing, and now he wanted guidance? Why did he think Haddid had any answers?

"We wait," Haddid said. "We need to see what the father and daughter choose to do." It was possible that after this the man would take the girl inside the U.S. embassy. If he did, it was over.

Haddid closed his eyes and prayed to Allah. *Please, let the father use his brain.*

Chapter 25

The minute Jordan reached her car, she plugged the USB drive that Weizman had given her into the auxiliary player of her car. She found herself listening to Taylor Swift. Not the kind of music she expected a couple of Palestinian terrorists to gravitate toward. What was she missing?

Tumbling the facts into place, she listed what she knew.

One, Cline had to have been trading information via a USB drive.

Two, the Palestinians didn't have it. Why else would they have broken into the Taylors' apartment and tried to ambush them on the way back from Lucy's doctor's appointment?

Then she realized what Batya Ganani thought she had already figured out.

Jordan pulled the drive from the USB port and gripped it tightly. The Palestinians must believe one of the Taylors had picked up the drive in the square. That's why they had broken into the Dizengoff Apartments. But instead of finding the drive with the information they wanted, they'd come away with four gigs of Billboard's top one hundred. They weren't after the judge. They were after Lucy.

When their attempt to steal the drive failed, they had ambushed the transport on the way home from the doctor's office. Jordan didn't want to think about what came next.

Wheeling her car out of the police department headquarters, she made a beeline for Dizengoff Square. Parking on the street, she headed for the apartment, nodding to the Marine on duty in the courtyard and to the one posted on the stairs. Inside, she found Master Gunnery Sergeant Walker standing near the sofa, his weapon at the ready. When he recognized her, he lowered his gun.

"How is everyone?" she asked.

"Lucy went to take a nap. The judge headed to his room a few minutes ago. Are you here to keep me company?"

"No, I'm here because we found something." Jordan held up the small USB drive.

"What's on it?"

"Music."

"Lucy's?"

"That would be my guess."

"Lucy's what?" Taylor asked, emerging from the back room.

Jordan told him about their find. "Weizman gave me a copy. It was full of music. The kind of music an eleven-year-old girl listens to."

Taylor lifted it out of her hand while Jordan told them what happened at the police station.

"That chick was Shin Bet?" Walker said. "Jeez."

"What's important is that the Palestinians seem to think Lucy ended up with the information they want, and Shin Bet knew about it." Jordan turned to Taylor. "Has Lucy said anything to you about finding something that didn't belong to her?"

"No," Taylor said. "But then, she might not have realized what she had."

Jordan reached out and touched his arm. "We need to ask her."

"I want her to sleep. Let's look around first. Maybe check her purse?" He walked to the kitchen and snatched up a pink

Coach bag dangling off the back of a chair. "She carries everything in here."

He tossed the purse to Jordan and she sorted through its contents. A small compact with a mirror, lip gloss, gum, and a billfold with about ten dollars' worth of shekels and a picture of a beautiful blond woman standing on the steps of the National Mall.

"My ex-wife." Taylor turned the small USB drive in his fingers. "Where did you say this was found?"

"In the apartment of an Arab Israeli maintenance worker named Najm Tibi." Jordan closed the billfold and put it back in the purse. "He was found dead alongside another man, Mansoor Rahman, a known jihadist connected to the Palestine Liberation Committee."

Taylor's eyes grew alert. "The PLC is the group whose assets I froze."

Jordan zipped the purse shut. "This wasn't about retaliation. It was about whatever information they were looking to get."

She pointed to his hand. "That drive was found in the home of a terrorist involved in the murder of a U.S. Diplomatic Security Service special agent. Right now, I'm going on the assumption that this isn't about you. This is about a trade. I'd like to find out what they were trading before anyone else winds up dead. Are you okay with that?"

"When you put it that way . . . ," Taylor said.

"Great. Now what else would Lucy do with it?"

"It might be on her desk or stuck in a drawer. Or she might have thrown it away."

Jordan pushed herself up from the couch. "Let's ask her."

Taylor led the way to Lucy's room and gently pushed open the door. The hinge squeaked, but Lucy barely stirred. She was stretched out on the bed, her blond curls splayed across the pillow, her skin pale in the soft light seeping through the window curtains. Jordan couldn't help but notice the dark circles under her eyes and that her cheeks looked fiery red.

"She looks sick," Jordan said.

"The treatments are hard on her," Taylor said.

The bedroom looked like it had been tossed again. Extra pillows from the bed were strewn on the carpet, jewelry littered the white dresser top, and shoes were jumbled on the floor of the closet. Jordan scanned the room in grids and, noticing nothing, decided it was just the mess of a preteen.

Taylor picked his way across the bedroom, knelt beside Lucy's bed, and gently stroked her hair. "Luce?"

"Leave me alone." She pushed her father's hand away. She might have been eleven, but she woke up like the teenager she was going to be in a couple of years. Groaning, she rolled over and snuggled deeper into her pillow.

"Honey." Taylor jostled her shoulder. "We need to talk to you, Luce. Wake up."

"Go away!" She pushed at his hand pulled the pillow over her head.

"Lucy!" Taylor yanked the pillow away and settled his hand on her forehead. "She's burning up."

Lucy's eyes opened. "What are you doing in my room?"

"Agent Jordan needs to ask you some questions, honey."

"I'm sleeping."

Jordan turned to Walker, who stood near the door. "Can you go get a thermometer?"

"There's one in the bathroom." Taylor gripped his daughter's elbow and pulled her up in the bed. "You need to answer Agent Jordan's questions."

Lucy pouted and slumped back against the pillows in resignation. "What do you want to know?"

Jordan showed her the USB drive. "This is full of music I think belongs to you."

"That's not mine."

"The drive is a copy, but I think that the songs on it are yours."
Lucy held out her hand.

Jordan refused to relinquish the drive until she got some answers. "Lucy, I need to know whether you found another one like this."

"Yeah. What about it?"

"I need it," Jordan said. "I'll trade you for it."

Lucy rubbed her eyes, red and rheumy from fever. "Why? It doesn't work."

"What do you mean 'it doesn't work'?" Jordan asked.

Walker came back with the thermometer, and Taylor stuck it in Lucy's mouth. "Keep this under your tongue."

Lucy mumbled around the stick in her mouth. "It asked for a password when I plugged it in. I tried a couple of things, but I couldn't get it to open. I threw it away."

"When?" Jordan asked. "Where?"

"Over there." Lucy pointed toward the dresser.

Jordan unearthed a wastebasket from behind some discarded jeans, but it was empty.

"I emptied it this morning," said Taylor. "Before we left for Alena's."

"Is there a trash chute?" Jordan asked.

"I threw it in the dumpster in the alley."

Jordan headed for the door, stopping short beside Walker. "You let him go out in the alley?"

The Marine snapped to. "No, ma'am. Not me."

"Come with me."

"Dumpster diving?" Walker rubbed his hands together in mock excitement.

"He stays," Taylor called out from the bedroom. "I'll go with you."

Jordan turned around. She didn't want him outside. It was hard enough protecting them when they stayed indoors.

"What's Lucy's temperature?" she asked. The fever spots on the child's cheeks practically glowed.

"Thirty-seven."

Alena had told them to call if Lucy's fever reached thirty-eight.

Taylor shook down the thermometer and set it on the bedside table. "Go back to sleep, Luce."

The child rolled over and turned her face to the wall. Taylor followed Jordan into the living room. "I want to help. I need to do something. I got us into this mess. I need to help get us out."

To let him went against her better judgment. "I can't put you at risk, Taylor. Walker is—"

"Supposed to be watching my daughter."

"Supposed to be keeping you safe."

Determination hardened his face. "I can handle myself. Besides, we can cover a lot of trash in tandem."

Jordan tried to reason with him and then caved. She had no real authority over him, and he knew it.

"Okay," she said, "But I get to go first." Then, seeing the smirk on Walker's face, she told him to shut up.

Chapter 26

ive minutes later, Jordan squeezed through the gate into the alley and looked in both directions while Taylor waited obediently in the courtyard. The alley felt safe, even with its pockets of shadows. Unlike al-Ajami with its myriads of hostile observers, there wasn't a soul in sight.

The alley itself felt tight, hemmed in between the buildings. Across from the Dizengoff Apartments was a bank—dark, shuttered, and protected by a camera security system that rivaled the Pentagon's. *Safe.* Street lamps attached to the building walls winked on, pooling circles of light every ten or fifteen feet. The bulbs had all been replaced. At the far end of the alley, traffic moved steadily past the entrance. At the other end, the asphalt disappeared into dusk behind the hotel.

Knowing there were others who wanted to find the USB drive, Jordan kept her guard up. Whatever the information was, it had cost five people their lives. She had no intention of adding the judge or herself to the count.

Once she was certain they were alone, she signaled to Taylor to join her. "Let's be quick."

Jordan tossed him a pair of latex gloves, pulled on her own pair, and circled the dumpster looking for an easy mount. She failed to find one and had Taylor hoist her over the lip. Dropping into the trash bin, Jordan fought with her gag reflex. The dumpster was three-quarter's full and smelled of beer and vomit. Bar trash. The stench overwhelmed her.

Drawing a breath, she cautiously picked up a bag and heaved it over the side of the dumpster. One by one, she emptied the contents of the bin over the side. Taylor began opening bags, looking for signs of recognizable rubbish.

Once she conquered the odor, she fell into a rhythm, wrangling the slime and the grime. Then a movement to her right caused her to freeze.

"Chrrrrr." A reddish, squirrel-sized rat whipped around and bore its teeth. He chattered in his throat. He puffed up his body and whipped his tail back and forth.

"Crap!" She stood her ground, balancing on top of the shifting trash.

"Hey, I think I found something!" yelled Taylor.

"Perfect timing." Keeping her eye on the rat, Jordan backed cautiously toward the edge of the dumpster. Taylor held up the front page of a *New York Times*.

"English version, today's date."

Vaulting over the edge and barely missing the judge, she slammed the lid shut on the rat.

"The garbage police," she said, seeing his quizzical look. "Let's move inside the courtyard."

Taylor dragged the bag through the gate and dumped it onto the concrete sidewalk. Together they sifted through the contents.

Trash was a telling thing. It offered a microscopic view of a person's life. For example, Jordan learned that the Taylors ate a lot of ground beef, pasta, and sour cream. What better time than while digging through garbage to ask personal questions?

"That's a nice picture of your wife that Lucy carries around." Jordan said.

"Ex-wife," Taylor corrected.

"What really happened between you two?"

He hesitated, and Jordan thought for a moment that he wasn't going to answer.

"Like I said, she refused to let Alena treat Ethan."

"So you blame her for your son's death?"

Again, the beat of hesitation. Maybe this time she'd crossed the line.

"I tried to make it work. We went to counseling." He sat back on his heels. "Do you know that eighty percent of marriages can't survive the loss of a child? I thought ours would."

"Until . . . ?"

"Lucy got sick. I try not to blame her for Ethan, but I couldn't let it happen again. When I put my foot down about Lucy, Sarah left. She went for full custody, claiming that I was an unfit parent. That I was unstable." Agitated, he tossed aside an empty trash bag. "Can you believe that?"

Jordan wasn't sure what to think. Watching him with Lucy, she knew he had his daughter's best interests at heart. However, the treatment he sought from Alena bordered on witchcraft. Maybe it was time to change the subject.

"I can't believe we haven't found it yet."

"Back up, Agent Jordan. Are you telling me you have no opinion? I want to know if you think I'm crazy." He poured the contents of a used coffee filter into his hand and sifted through the old grounds.

"No. Maybe misguided. I think you're grasping at straws."

"Fair." He pitched a crushed milk carton to the side. "For a while, I questioned myself. Even now I know how it sounds, believing that an energy healer can effect a cure in a dying child. But she can."

She glanced over. "You have no doubts?"

Taylor shook his head. "Ethan's death was a life-altering moment. You know the ones. Something happens, life changes, and it will never be the same. Knowing that I could have done something to prevent that, that I can do something now, for Lucy . . ." He reached for another jumble of papers. "You're young. Have you ever had one of those moments?"

"It doesn't matter how old you are," Jordan said. Her thoughts flashed to a cold night in Russia. Her father's death meant moving from Russia to Colorado, from a loving family to her grandparent's house. She flashed back to a warm night in Denver, when Posner fired his gun. To Alena's revelations about her father. "I've actually had a few."

Taylor suddenly rocked back on his heels, a glint of silver in his gloved hand. Jordan's heart rate quickened.

"I think I found it!" he said.

*

Jordan assigned one of the Marines to reload the trash and headed inside with the judge. Pulling out Taylor's computer, they tried opening the contents of the USB drive with no luck. Lucy was right. It required a password to open. A password they didn't have.

"Even if you crack it, the contents are probably encrypted." Walker said. When Jordan turned to stare at him, he held up his hands. "I'm just saying."

Taking over for Cline, Jordan had gotten a feel for words he might use for a password. So far, they'd all failed. For all they knew, this wasn't even the right USB drive. She took another stab at it and came up empty. She turned to the Marine.

"What do you know about computers?" she asked.

Walker shrugged. "I took some computer science at MIT."

"Really?" Taylor sounded impressed. "How much computer science?"

"Four years. Then I found my real calling."

Jordan found it hard to believe he had thrown away a lucrative career in computers for the chance to stand guard at an embassy in Israel. The look on her face must have said as much.

"I lost my brother in Afghanistan a year ago."

A life-altering moment.

"Sorry," Taylor said.

Walker nodded.

Jordan shut the laptop. "We're done here."

"Looks like," Taylor said. "That leaves the tech boys at the embassy. They'll have toys that can crack it." He pushed away from the table. "I need to go check on Luce."

"Thanks for helping, Taylor."

"My pleasure. The sooner we crack that thing, the sooner my life gets back to normal."

Chapter 27

It was after 10:00 p.m. when she headed back to the embassy. The streets were empty, so she made good time. She hoped the tech squad was still working; otherwise, someone would be coming back in.

Pulling up to the small guard shack, she handed the U.S. Marine on duty her credentials. He studied them carefully and then waved her through.

Jordan pulled forward, maneuvering the sedan around the concrete median and a pile of materials being used in preparation for Thursday's secretary of state address. Two Bobcat tractors were parked near the compound walls, and a number of unmanned vehicles were scattered around the parking lot. Employee cars. People were working around the clock to be ready for the secretary's arrival. A good sign someone would be in the tech room.

Wheeling into a space near the DSS offices, Jordan slammed the sedan into park. Before climbing out, she switched off the headlights and allowed her eyes to adjust to the darkness. Other than the muted night-lights of the building's hallways, the only lit area was the consul general's building, which sat diagonally to the DSS offices.

Jordan wondered if the secretary appreciated how much work went into ensuring her safety. It was doubtful she had any idea.

Even with the training an agent like Jordan went through, from boot camp to gun handling to strategy and planning, personnel weren't always prepared. What had happened at Dr. Petrenko's office was a case in point.

She let her thoughts creep from Alena to her father, the Russian national hero who had been in the wrong place at the wrong time and paid the ultimate price.

Her father's legacy had been his exuberance. He loved Russia, then Jordan, her mother, and hockey—probably in that order. Even at age eleven, he had instilled in Jordan a belief that there was no point in doing something if it didn't evoke passion. He taught her right from wrong, how to tie her shoes, and to always tell the truth. She had served as a living example of his edicts from the day he died. If Alena Petrenko was right, was everything Jordan believed to be true based on lies?

Alena had confirmed one thing Jordan had thought for years—that her father was murdered. She never fully believed the official story, that he'd been killed in the crossfire of an assassination attempt on a prominent Russian businessman. No one had ever been arrested, and the uproar over the death of their hockey star kept anything else out of the Russian news. The case was closed quickly, with little investigation. Her father had died a hero.

Yet Jordan had always believed someone had orchestrated his death. That it wasn't a stray bullet but a deliberate shot that had taken his life. It was that conviction—that life-altering moment—that ultimately defined her future.

The bigger question was why anyone would want him dead. The answer could cost Jordan more than her childhood convictions. It could cost her a job.

Shoving away the thoughts, she pushed open the car door. Why was she entertaining the rantings of a psychic? As far as she was concerned, Alena Petrenko was a quack.

Jordan climbed out and swung the driver's side door shut. The sound shattered the still of the night. A softer click caused every hair on the back of her neck to stand up. Someone else was in the parking lot.

Nerves on high alert, she scanned her surroundings. The lot appeared exactly the same as when she'd entered it. There were no new vehicles. No one else had passed through the gates or entered or exited the building since she arrived. There was nothing to be frightened of, yet fear tightened her every muscle.

Moving toward the building, she took note of the shadows, of every rustle. Stress had a way of jangling her nerves, and she had been operating in overdrive the last couple of days. Once she was convinced the danger didn't lie between her parking space and the building, she allowed her gaze to stray to the darkened glass of the buildings across the street from the embassy entrance. From there, picking off a target in the parking lot would be child's play.

Reaching the side entrance, a Marine stepped out of the shadows.

"*Crap*, you scared the shit out of me," Jordan said.

"Sorry, ma'am. I need to see your credentials."

Jordan held up her badge.

The Marine studied it and then opened the door for her. The lights in the corridors were motion activated.

"Just extra precautions," the Marine said.

"No explanation needed. Thank you, soldier." She took comfort in his gaze on her backside as she walked down the hall to the elevator, but the discomfort returned in the muted hallway of the fourth floor. The tech offices were locked up tight. She would call from her office.

She took the stairs to the sixth floor, the click of her heels against the linoleum tap-dancing on the lining of her stomach. Once inside her office, she closed the door, flipped on the lights, and powered up her computer. Pulling up a list of embassy personnel, she called the head of the tech department.

"I need someone to crack a password on a USB drive, stat," she said, once he'd answered his phone.

"Can't it wait?" The fatigue in his voice drifted across the line.

"No. It's a matter of national security." The words sounded clichéd.

"Aren't they all?" he said. "I'll get someone to come back in, but it may take a bit. Give me your number. I'll have them call when they're in the building."

Jordan rattled off the numbers of both her desk phone and her cell phone. "As quick as you can."

"Sure."

Hanging up, she sat back in her desk chair and pulled the USB drive from her pocket. There was no telling how long the tech guys would take. Maybe she should try to crack the password again. Except how many times could she try before the data was permanently locked, or worse, wiped clean?

She could at least see what happened if it were plugged into an embassy computer. She slipped the drive into the port on the back of her laptop. Like earlier, another log-in request flashed up on the screen.

Jordan stared at the cursor flashing inside the small empty box until her vision blurred. Most people used something familiar, something they would remember—their birthday, their wife's or husband's birthday, an anniversary, a middle name. She could make a list for the tech. Maybe give him a jump start.

Pulling up Cline's dossier, she pulled every important date and name from the file. Then she turned her focus on the intended recipient, the PLC. Had Najm Tibi chosen the password, or their leader, Abdul Aleem Zuabi? There was no way to narrow it down.

"Having trouble?"

The voice gave her a chill.

Jordan looked up. Batya Ganani stood in the office doorway. "How did you get in here? How did you get past the guard?"

Ganani flashed a set of embassy credentials. "We're assisting with the protection detail for the secretary of state." She gestured toward Jordan's computer. "Did you get it open?"

Every nerve ending in Jordan's body sent out alarms. Pulling the USB drive from the computer, she jammed it into her pocket. Her left hand moved for the phone.

"Don't do that," Ganani said.

Jordan paused, her arm hanging in midair. She considered drawing her weapon, but that would only escalate things or get one or both of them killed. "What information is on the drive that has Shin Bet and the PLC willing to kill for it?"

"You haven't answered my question yet." Ganani said, gesturing toward Jordan's pocket. "Did you have any luck?"

"No, not yet."

"Do you mind if I try?"

Jordan laughed out loud. "There's not a chance in hell I'm letting you touch my computer or the USB drive."

Realizing she would get nothing out of Ganani, Jordan picked up the receiver and punched the auto dial for security on the desk phone. Ganani stepped forward and pushed down the switch hook.

"Give me the drive."

"Not a chance." Jordan stepped backward, her hand moving to the 9 mm on her belt. Ganani was quicker. She leveled her SIG Sauer at Jordan's chest. Jordan drew her hand away from her gun.

"You realize if you fire that weapon in here, the Marine guards will be all over you."

Ganani cupped her free hand, flashing the universal gimme sign. "Give me what I came for and I will go away."

Jordan had no intention of handing over the USB drive, but she also didn't relish getting shot. Slipping her hand into her pocket, her mind scrambled to find a way out.

Ganani tensed. "Move slowly."

Jordan adjusted her pace.

"What's on the drive?" she asked, drawing her hand slowly out of her pocket. "What was Cline trading away? You owe me that much."

"I don't owe you anything. My orders are simply to retrieve the information."

"But the files belong to the U.S."

"Do they? How do you know?"

"You know what I think?" Jordan said. "I think you have no idea what's on here." She held up the drive. "I think you're just following orders. You murdered three men and accosted an eleven-year-old child all because your boss told you to."

"I would not have hurt the child."

Jordan sidled around the edge of the desk until she was standing on Ganani's side. "Who was supposed to get this? Zuabi?"

Ganani shrugged. "Tibi was known to work for him, as well as others."

That confirmed Jordan's suspicions that Najm Tibi's loyalty went to the highest bidder. "Did you figure out he was working for the PLC before or after you killed him?"

Jordan could see it in Ganani's eyes that she was losing her patience.

Ganani pointed the gun at Jordan's chest. "Enough talking."

Jordan stopped moving. She harbored no doubts that Ganani would shoot her, and the agent had already proven her prowess at getting away. That left Jordan two choices. Hand it over or get close enough to disarm her.

"Despite your training, Agent Jordan, you need to believe me when I say, try anything and you're dead."

"I believe you. I just don't understand why you're willing to kill for what's on here. The information is safe with me. It won't end up in the wrong hands."

"Cline didn't seem to feel the same way."

"So he *was* passing off information."

"I'm done talking." Ganani reached and tried to grab the drive from Jordan's hand. "Give it to me, *now.*"

Jordan stepped backward and lifted her arms in surrender. Without a windup, she pitched the USB drive hard and fast at the Shin Bet agent's face.

Ganani flinched.

Jordan lunged at the same time, knocking Ganani to the floor. She dropped her weapon. It clanged to the floor just inches from her outstretched hand.

Ganani grunted and kicked, landing a blow square on Jordan's shoulder.

Forcing herself to move through the pain, Jordan rolled sideways and clambered to her feet.

Ganani stretched for her gun.

Jordan stomped down on the Shin Bet agent's wrist, resting all her weight on her foot. Ganani groaned, and Jordan kicked the weapon away. Pumped full of adrenalin, she couldn't stop herself from commenting.

"Is that all you've got?"

Ganani answered by wrapping a hand around Jordan's ankle and tugging her feet out from under her.

She landed flat on her back, her head bouncing off the tile floor. Small stars swam in her eyes, and she struggled for air. "You bitch."

Jordan lashed out with her own feet, her shoe connecting with Ganani's face. She heard the crunch of cartilage being displaced. Blood gushed.

Ganani's left hand flew to her face, but she kept moving for her gun.

Jordan's arm throbbed, but she had to get to there first. Planting her feet, she pushed hard and slid across the floor. She cringed as she banged into the desk. Reaching out, she knocked the SIG Sauer away and came up with her own 9 mm in hand. "Get up."

The Shin Bet agent sneered at her through streaming blood.

"I want to see your hands."

Ganani hesitated and then slowly raised her arms. Jordan climbed to her feet, secured the SIG Sauer, and then signaled for the Shin Bet agent to stand. "Now give me back the USB drive."

Ganani tried Jordan's trick, throwing it hard, but Jordan sidestepped. The drive hit the wall and dropped to the floor. Keeping her gun trained on Ganani, she bent down and retrieved it.

"For your nose," she said, reaching for the box of tissues on the window sill and tossing them across the desk.

"What now, Agent Jordan? Are you going to call in the Marines?" Jordan picked up the phone and dialed the RSO. Even with what happened to his good buddy Posner, Daugherty was her senior officer. She wasn't going to give him a reason to fire her.

"Daugherty."

Jordan identified herself and explained the situation.

"Do you have the USB drive?"

"In my hand. The tech guys are on the way in."

"Good. I know this woman's boss, Colonel Brodsky. He's a real hard-ass. You lock her up, Jordan, and she'll be out before you can get back to your office. Try talking to her. See what you can get out of her, then yank her credentials and have the MPs escort her off the premises."

"Are you coming in?"

"Not unless you can't handle this. I see no sense in adding my name to the mix when she complains to her boss and word gets back to the ambassador."

Daugherty was covering his ass.

"I'll take care of it, sir."

"Good work, Jordan," Daugherty said.

She hung up the receiver, wondering if he meant it. She smiled at Ganani. "According to my boss, you have a get-out-of-jail-free card. So how about I save you the hassle of having to call your boss and looking foolish again? I'll make you a deal. You tell me what I want to know and I'll let you go."

Ganani pitched a bloody tissue toward the wastebasket beside the desk and reached for another. "You have a good kick, Agent Jordan."

"Have a seat." She gestured toward a chair but kept her gun pointed at the agent. "Do we have a deal?"

Ganani sat down and pressed a clean tissue to her nose.

"I'll take that as a yes." Jordan moved around to her own chair. "So why don't you cut to the chase?"

"You are correct. I do not know what is on there. I do know Tibi and the others were securing information for Abdul Aleem Zuabi."

Jordan gripped the small drive in her hand. "Who are the others?"

Ganani turned her head away.

"There was one man with Tibi at the al-Ajami apartment," said Jordan. "A dead man. Are you saying someone else was there?"

Ganani nodded, wincing in pain.

"Did he get away? Did he take something?"

"He didn't get the information they were after. He may have gotten away with the information that Tibi planned to trade."

"Do you know who he is?"

"No, but I found him when he found you."

"He was one of the men at the doctor's office."

"Yes."

Jordan tried piecing it together. "Why borrow a dead man's car?"

"Because you don't have one of your own. These men walked across the border. They must have known that the car wasn't registered to Tibi and that it wouldn't have been reported missing yet. Do you know how many green Foresters there are in Israel? All they have to do is switch plates again, and they will still have transportation."

"What information do you think is on this drive? It must be pretty important."

"It doesn't matter," Ganani said.

"Of course it does."

"No," Ganani said. "It's only important that it never gets used."

"If you never find out what they're after, how do you stop them from trying again?"

"Timing."

"The peace talks."

"I think, for now."

Jordan tightened her fist on the USB drive in her hand. "It would seem you know quite a bit, Ganani."

"And you know everything I do." The Shin Bet agent pushed herself out of her chair.

"Stop right there," said Jordan.

"We had a deal. You have the drive, and you have beaten me twice. What more do you want?" She wore the same smirk she had in the Israel police station, and it ticked Jordan off.

"Give me your embassy pass."

Ganani took it off slowly and pushed it across the desk. "It will just be reissued."

"Not if I have anything to do with it."

Chapter 28

After the MPs picked up Ganani, Jordan got a call from the tech lab. She ran the stairs to the fourth floor, pounding out her frustration on the concrete steps. What the hell had Cline been up to?

The tech who'd come in handed her a form.

"I needed it yesterday," she said, looking around for a pen.

"Get in line." The tech plucked a pen from his pocket and handed it to her.

"How long before you'll know anything?" she asked, signing her name and handing everything over.

"Hopefully, sometime tomorrow. We'll call you."

"You're kidding. We need to know what's on there immediately."

"You and everybody else. Right now, we have every free hand setting up the IT network for the secretary's speech and visit. I'm just one person."

"You might be holding the key to who killed Steven Cline."

The tech scrubbed the side of his face with his hand. "Enough already. I'll move it to the front of the line. I will do my best to get you some answers, but *no* promises."

"You rock."

"Yeah?" The tech turned away. "Tell my mother."

*

After a quick trip home for a power nap and a shower, Jordan was back in the office by 6:00 a.m. Daugherty passed her doorway on his way in.

"You're here early," he said.

She stood and went after him in the hall. "I wanted to talk with you."

Daugherty jerked his head for her to follow him to his office. He made a beeline for the coffee machine. "Shoot."

While he started a pot of coffee, Jordan sat down in a chair by the desk. "I think Cline was trading state secrets."

"Want some?" he asked, grabbing some mugs out of the cupboard and cream from the small refrigerator. He poured himself a double of cream.

"You did hear what I said?" Jordan had expected more of a reaction. "Doesn't it bother you?"

He lifted the pot in her direction. She shook her head.

"It would bother me a lot if he'd actually succeeded. It appears he didn't." Daugherty carried his mug to his desk. "Now tell me again what happened, and this time I want details, starting with what happened at the doctor's office."

Jordan recapped the events, beginning with the attempt to kidnap Lucy, finding the USB drive, and Ganani's visit to her office.

"You took on a Shin Bet agent? You don't look too much worse for the wear."

"That's because I kicked her ass." Jordan rubbed her shoulder. "You should see Ganani. I think I broke her nose."

"Good job." Daugherty sounded impressed.

He should be. Jordan hadn't incapacitated the woman, but she'd done some damage.

"Now, from what I just heard," Daugherty said, refocusing on the matter at hand, "you think Cline is connected with some radical Jewish movement and was attempting to pass off encrypted DSS intel to some joker tied to the PLC?"

Put like that, her theory sounded farfetched.

"Sir, it's a fact that Cline, or at least his wife, has connections to people tied to some radical Jewish factions. Based on recent events, it seems clear his intent was to pass information to Najm Tibi. We won't know what until we crack the files."

Daugherty turned his chair and stared out the window. "Have you questioned his wife?"

"She's refusing to speak with anyone. She has her rabbi, Tiran Marzel, acting as her voice. He claims it violates her religious beliefs to speak to anyone outside her religious sect during this period of mourning." Jordan leaned forward, wishing she could see Daugherty's face, maybe read his expression. "Rabbi Marzel was once connected with Kach, a Jewish nationalist extremist group that operated out of the West Bank. He now leads a group of Neturei Karta living in Bnei Brak."

"Tell me about them." His voice sounded clipped, and he kept his back to her.

"The Neturei Karta is a group of ultra-Orthodox Litvish Jews—Haredis from the former Grand duchy of Lithuania." In the present day, the region included Belarus, Lithuania, Ukraine, and the northeastern Suwalki region of Poland.

"What's their philosophy?"

Having lived in Tel Aviv for nearly two years, Jordan was surprised he didn't know.

"The Neturei Karta opposes the political ideology of Zionism," she said. "In a nutshell, they believe that Jews are forbidden to have their own state until the coming of the Messiah." This made them a potential recruiting ground for anti-Israeli factions. "Marzel is a self-proclaimed follower of Rabbi Meir Kahane."

"I've heard the name. Refresh my memory."

"Kahane founded the Kach Party and supported the annexation of all the land occupied during the Six-Day War—the Sinai Peninsula, the Gaza Strip, the West Bank, East Jerusalem, and the Golan Heights—all of it. He also advocated the forced transfer of the four million Palestinians living there. Kach's main focus was to disrupt the peace process and oppose any steps taken to hand the land back to the Palestinians."

Daugherty swung his chair back around and set his coffee on the desk. "Correct me if I'm wrong, but didn't Kahane die?"

"Back in 1990, which is when his son formed a splinter group called Kahane Chai, or 'Kahane Lives.'"

"As I recall, the son died, too. Neither of these groups has been active for years."

"True." Kach and Kahane Chai still existed, but the groups had been banned from participating in Israeli politics for making threats against politicians. Ironically, now they refrained from violence in hopes the government would lift the ban and allow them to run members for political office. Jordan doubted it would happen.

Daugherty took a sip of his coffee. "I don't see the relevance."

"There was a third splinter group called Irgun Yehudi Lohem, or EYAL, better known as the Fighting Jewish Organization, formed by a man named Avishai Raviv. He's the man they believe planned and executed the assassination of Prime Minister Yitzhak Rabin. That's where Marzel comes in."

Raviv was alleged to be an agent of the Israeli Domestic Intelligence, better known as Shin Bet or Shabak. His original assignment was to gather information on right-wing extremists. Many believed Shin Bet established EYAL in order to spy on extremist groups. One of the most outspoken was Rabbi Tiran Marzel.

"And you think Rabbi Marzel partnered with Cline?"

"I think it's possible."

Daugherty tapped the side of his mug. "Tell me about this Tibi character."

"He seems to be more of an opportunist for hire than a true jihadist. All anyone has to do is look inside his apartment to see what he was about. Suffice it to say, he liked the finer things. Detective Weizman confirms it."

"What else do we know about him?"

"He was a maintenance worker at the GG&B Engineering headquarters in Haifa. He swept floors, mopped, cleaned blinds— that sort of thing."

"And he lived in Yafo, in al-Ajami?"

"It's not that uncommon. Some of the embassy employees commute from Haifa. It's all highway. An hour's drive, tops. A coveted position at GG&B would be worth the commute."

"For an Israeli Arab."

Stated like that, it sounded bigoted. Not exactly what she had meant.

"I mean for anyone," she said. "GG&B designed the National Water Carrier and is the go-to on all issues connected with water, energy resources, and waste management. They're in business for the long haul, pay top wages, give good benefits, and have lots of prestige." Jordan waited to see if he connected the dots the way she had. GG&B held the key.

"What's your theory, Jordan?"

He apparently wanted her to spell it out.

"The goal of these groups is to disrupt the peace process, right?"

Daugherty nodded.

"Maybe what they're doing is connected with the National Water Carrier?"

"No way," Daugherty said, dismissing the idea. "Israeli security is impeccable. Everyone here depends on the water, including the

Arabs. Terrorists have tried chemical spills, poisonings, bombings." He ticked the items off on his fingers. "You name it, it's been tried."

"What if they're planning something that's never been tried before?"

"Let's back up the truck. Consider what we have to go on. A maintenance worker and Cline, who you've loosely connected to a radical sect of Judaism . . ."

"His wife, Tamar's, connection to Neturei Karta is fact," Jordan said, trying to establish her case. "It's logical to assume her husband is also connected. If Cline had information for Tibi, then Tibi had something for Cline."

"I'll concede that it looks like Cline might have been radicalized, but it sounds like you're suggesting the Neturei Karta is in cahoots with the PLC."

"They share a common anti-Zionist belief. What's the old Arabic saying? 'I against my brother, my brothers and I against my cousins, then my cousins and I against strangers.'"

"That doesn't mean they've formed the Brotherhood of Anti-Israel." Daugherty picked up his mug. "Let's face it. There are plenty of Jews in this country that don't even talk to each other. How the fuck could enemies plan a covert op?"

"I'm not saying they've joined ranks. But they could both want something the other can provide. They could have separate agendas and still be facilitating each other's plans."

"You're sure it's not about money?"

"Positive. I checked Cline's bank records. There haven't been any unusual transactions."

"Maybe he has hidden accounts."

"None that I could find." She tapped her finger on his desk. "There's no evidence money was the motive, so it has to be about a cause, about beliefs. There's no way Cline would come away empty-handed."

Daugherty's mouth tightened. She couldn't tell if he was angry with Cline or angry with her because of the tack she was taking. It was time to press.

"I'd like to pay a visit to GG&B," she said.

"No." His answer came hard and fast.

"Sir, if I'm right, I'm convinced the information Tibi was trading came from GG&B."

"And if you're wrong?"

"We walk away."

"Jordan, what you have is a gut feeling and a boatload of conjecture. GG&B carries a fleet full of political clout. We're not riling them up without proof." Daugherty cupped his hands together. "Call Weizman. Let the local police investigate."

"Sir, the Palestinians may not have gotten what they came after, but what if these guys have a backup plan?"

"You bring me some proof, and I'll let you widen your investigation. Until then, we need to focus on protecting the secretary of state against the enemies we know."

"Damn right, we do," said Dan Posner, stepping into the office. "You find out anything useful, Agent Jordan?"

"Dan," Jordan said. Pushing herself out of the chair, she turned to Daugherty. "I'll check with the tech guys and see how close they are to having answers."

"Keep me informed," he said, waving Posner toward a chair. "Have a seat. Want some coffee?"

"Guess this means you're off babysitting detail," Posner said as she walked past him.

How much had Daugherty told him? "Not until we figure out what's going on."

"You better get to it, then." Posner plopped down in the seat she had vacated, as if squashing her like a bug.

The meeting was over.

Chapter 29

If Daugherty wanted proof that Cline had been trading information, Jordan intended to find it. Then maybe he would let her dig into Tibi's tenure at GG&B. Somehow the information Cline wanted and Tibi's work were connected.

Until then, she did have other options. She could still look at Najm Tibi's known associates. If only they knew whom the other person was in the al-Ajami apartment the night of the murders—the one that Ganani let get away. And there was Tamar Cline.

Maybe it was time to pay the grieving widow a personal visit.

Up until now, Rabbi Marzel had blocked all attempts to talk with her, claiming she was in *aninut*, or intense mourning. But she was also an American citizen, and her husband's death was a matter of national security. It didn't sit well with Jordan that the rabbi was blocking her investigation. They needed to know what Steven Cline had been doing the past week while he was supposed to have been stateside, who he had been associating with, and if there had been any changes in his normal routine.

Fitting with Haredi religious customs, Weizman had expedited the release of Cline's body for immediate burial. The funeral service was scheduled for 1:00 p.m., followed by the widow sitting Shiva.

Jewish custom allowed for friends and family to be at graveside and to then pay their respects to the bereaved at home. Jordan knew she might not be welcomed. But she was a colleague of Cline's, and maybe the widow would feel like talking.

Jordan opted not to check with Daugherty regarding her newest plan. Stopping off at her apartment to change into a dress, she found the mail piling up in the hallway, most of her stuff still in boxes, and every hemline in her closet two inches above appropriate funeral wear. She opted instead for a clean uniform and a dark silk scarf to cover her head.

She checked her appearance in the full-length mirror. She looked official, which was better than exposing her bare knees.

*

Tamar Cline lived in Bnei Brak, a dusty subdivision on the east side of Tel Aviv. According to the guide books, it was home to nearly two hundred thousand Haredi Jews. Poor and densely populated, it had begun as an agricultural community but had grown into one of Israel's largest cities. The community was close-knit. Its residents chose to keep to themselves and follow traditional practices, including dress codes and gender separation.

Jordan punched the address of Bnei Brak Cemetery into her GPS and followed its directions. Getting there wasn't difficult. The polished high-rises of Tel Aviv slipped into her rearview mirror, their places taken by two- and three-story buildings composed of white concrete. Laundry flapped from balconies, and contemporary Western dress morphed into the conservative costuming of the Haredi Jews.

Parking on the street, Jordan locked her gun in the glove box, buttoned her shirt to the neck, draped the scarf over her head, and headed into the burial ground. A crowd was gathered near an open grave on the far side—men gathered on the west, women to the east.

Tamar stood with the women. She was dressed in black from head to foot, her hair covered with a dark wig. Her daughter stood close. Tamar's young son stood with the men, close to the rabbi.

Jordan picked her way between the graves. Like other Jewish cemeteries, the plots of Bnei Brak consisted of a grave topped by a rectangular platform of poured concrete faced with stone tiles. The grave coverings rose two feet or more aboveground, with the name, date, and praises of the deceased inscribed on the top. In the case of some Holocaust survivors, the inscriptions were on the side. Jordan wondered why.

Aware of the stares of the gathering men and women, Jordan stopped beside a woman standing apart from the crowd. The woman fidgeted and tugged at her clothing, moving foot to foot as if she felt out of place. Dressed in Western-style clothing, Jordan marked her as Steven Cline's mother.

"*Sholem-aleykhem*," said Jordan.

"*Aleykhem-sholem*." The woman spoke in halting Yiddish. Her red-rimmed eyes and blotchy skin revealed her grief.

Jordan switched to English. "Are you Steven's mother?"

The woman looked surprised. "You're an American."

"I work for the DSS." Jordan didn't know what else to say. This woman's pain was going to intensify when she found out her son had died a traitor. Jordan wished she could find comforting words. "I'm very sorry for your loss."

The woman brightened. "You worked with Steven."

"Actually, I'm his replacement. I didn't personally know him, though I imagine others will be coming who did."

Mrs. Cline shared a sad smile. "I doubt it. Steven changed quite a bit after he married Tamar. He used to have lots of friends. Now there is no one but the Neturei Karta."

"I don't understand," Jordan said. She hoped her statement sounded benign. If his mother wanted to share information, Jordan intended to listen.

"Things were wonderful at first. She seemed happy to be out from under her strict rabbi, but Tamar comes from an ultra-Orthodox sect." Mrs. Cline grew quiet.

Jordan looked over at Tamar. She appeared to be insulated by Haredim. A glimpse of her face, among the others, showed a woman content in her element.

"It would seem she's reverted to her old ways."

"It happened when they moved to Tel Aviv."

Jordan remained quiet, hoping Cline's mother would volunteer more.

"It was Tamar who wanted to move to Bnei Brak. She was the one who sought out the Neturei Karta rabbi."

"Did Steven embrace the culture?" Jordan said. "I mean, he didn't dress like a Haredim. He didn't wear a beard or *peyos*, side-curls, or dark clothes."

"Only because of his job." Mrs. Cline leaned sideways toward Jordan. "He told me when he quit his job that he planned to commit himself to study of the Torah and could no longer in good conscience carry a gun."

"Because of the Neturei Karta?"

Mrs. Cline nodded, gesturing toward the rabbi and the men. "They are not just ultra-Orthodox. They are fanatics."

"In what way?"

"They believe in the biblical land of Jews and condemn the State of Israel and think it is their duty to defend a misguided position of authentic, unadulterated Judaism." Mrs. Cline's hatred came out through the tone of her voice and the stiffness of her body.

Jordan watched the men. Most talked quietly among themselves or prayed, though several men openly stared in their direction. The displeasure in their eyes caused the hairs on the back of her neck to rise. She reached for her scarf, ensuring it was properly arranged.

"When did you last speak with Steven, Mrs. Cline?"

"Less than a week ago."

The rabbi's voice breached any further questions. He began chanting the *Kaddish Yatom*, the mourner's prayer. The men joined in, then the women. The prayer was recited three times. Then the rabbi offered a short eulogy, followed by a friend of Steven's from the synagogue. At the end, each man rent his coat on the right side and then—using the back of a small, triangular-shaped spade—shoveled three spades of dirt into the grave. Steven's son tore his coat on the left side and then picked up a shovel.

Once the last man had thrown dirt and placed the spade back in the ground, the women moved forward.

Steven's mother leaned toward Jordan. "In Neturei Karta burials, the women wait for the men to finish before paying their respects at the grave. Non–*erlekhe Yidn*, nonvirtuous Jews, pay their respects last." She touched her chest. "Along with the *goyim*." She touched Jordan's sleeve.

Mrs. Cline started to move toward the grave and then turned back around. "I hope you are planning to come by the house."

Jordan nodded, thankful for the invitation.

She hung back while Tamar offered words of mourning and shoveled more dirt into the grave. Mrs. Cline went last. After all the women had dispersed, Jordan stepped up to the edge of the box. She looked down at the grave, at the plain wooden casket partially covered with dirt, and silently asked Steven Cline what the hell he'd been doing in Dizengoff Square.

Back at the car, Jordan debated what to do next. Part of her wanted to turn the car around and head back toward the Dizengoff Apartments. After witnessing Mrs. Cline's grief and the stoic acceptance of death from Tamar and the children, Jordan felt guilty about having come. She knew by the stares of the Haredim in attendance that her presence at graveside was seen as an intrusion. Then again, Mrs. Cline had invited her, and she still had questions for Tamar.

Jordan parked down the block from the Clines' house. Small, with a tiny yard, it sat midblock in a crowded subdivision. She pulled on the handbrake and watched as a steady stream of men and women entered and exited the house. The men strolled with importance, and every woman carried a covered dish.

Once the crowd appeared to have thinned, Jordan climbed out of her car. Retucking her shirttails and straightening her scarf, she locked the car and headed for the house. Out of respect, she kept her eyes averted as she passed a group of men standing in the front yard.

Inside the front door, a hallway led to a kitchen. Through an archway on the right, a group of men had gathered in the clean and sparsely furnished living room. Steven's mother hailed her from a smaller sitting room on the left, where she sat separated from the other women.

"You came," she said, her face lighting.

"Yes."

As Jordan spoke, Tamar Cline looked up from her chair near the front window. Turning, she whispered to the woman beside her. The woman intercepted Jordan halfway through the room.

"Tamar would like you to leave."

Jordan glanced behind her and then touched her fingers to her chest. "Me? I'm here at Mrs. Cline's invitation."

More Haredi women rose to their feet.

Tamar's spokeswoman said, "You are not welcome."

Mrs. Cline stepped forward. "Please, she is a colleague of Steven's. I invited her."

Tamar stood. "This is my home. You are a guest, but she is not wanted."

Mrs. Cline started to protest, but Jordan shook her head.

"*Hamakom y'nachem etkhem b'tokh sha'ar avelei tziyon viyrusha-layim*," Jordan said. The Omnipresent will comfort you among the mourners of Zion and Jerusalem. She had been to several Jewish funerals at home and knew it was the traditional thing to say to a mourner when taking your leave.

Mrs. Cline stepped forward. "I'll walk you out."

"There's no need." Jordan nodded her thanks and then turned and headed down the hallway for the door. Once in the hallway, she sensed the men from the living room closing ranks behind her.

"*Tamei*," one said. Unclean one.

"*Tamei*," said another, spitting at her as she reached the front steps of the house.

"Hey!" She considered confronting her harassers, but she didn't want to create more of a scene and kept walking. At the sound of her voice, the crowd of men in the yard turned. They took up the others' cry.

"*Lechi habaita!*" Go home, they yelled. One man picked up a large rock and pitched it in her direction. It clattered on the sidewalk near her feet.

Jordan's heart rate accelerated. Her breathing quickened. She stepped over the stone. "I'm leaving."

The second man to speak graveside broke free of the crowd. His dark eyes glowered at her from below the rim of his black hat. In his hands, he held a rock. "You are a disgrace. You dare to wear pants like a man. You come here and contaminate the house of Tamar Cline. You contaminate the streets of Bnei Brak. You deserve to be taught a lesson."

He heaved the stone. It struck Jordan in the back.

She winced and her hand instinctively went to where her holster should be. Then she remembered she had left her gun in the car.

Jordan picked up her pace. Clearing the yard, she figured the men would stop at the edge of the grass, but they followed her into the street.

The sedan was parked halfway down the block. She jogged toward the car, and the men followed, moving so swiftly the tails of their long black coats flared out behind them. Another stone was hurled, then another. Both missed. A fourth rock slammed into her ribs.

"*Tamei, lechi habaita,*" rose the chant.

Jordan broke into a run, clicking the unlock button on her key fob. Sliding into the driver's seat, she slammed and locked the door. A rock struck her window, fracturing the glass.

Starting the car, Jordan jammed it into gear and revved the engine.

The men swarmed the car, like flies on raw meat. Fists pounded on the windows. Another rock bounced off the glass, chipping the windshield.

"*Tamei!*"

Jordan bullied the car through the crowd. Once free, she looked in the rearview mirror. Men threw stones and cheered.

So much for the chance to talk to Tamar.

Chapter 30

Jordan backtracked through the streets of Bnei Brak, more aware of her surroundings now than she had been when following her GPS to the cemetery. She could see that she'd missed the signs pointing to the depth of the Neturei Karta fanaticism— the postings in the neighborhoods indicating which side of the street were for "men only," the ultraconservative dress of the women out walking. She had known the ultra-Orthodox were strict in their beliefs, but—except for some disapproving glances she had been given at the cemetery—there was no warning that she had offended anyone to the degree that they would stone her. She was wearing her uniform, for God's sake.

Pulling up in front of the Dizengoff Apartments, she parked the sedan in the shade. Her ribs ached as she climbed out of her car.

After retrieving her gun, she greeted the on-duty Marine at the backyard gate. Crossing the garden, she climbed the stairs to the apartment. Inside, she found Lucy and the judge playing a game of chess.

"Hey," she said.

"Oh, good. Now we can play a game," Lucy said.

Jordan walked over to the table. "You're playing with your father."

"Yeah, but he's not very good."

"She's right," Taylor said. "But you have homework to do."

"Aw, Dad."

Taylor pointed toward her room. "Go. When you're done, Agent Jordan will play. Right?"

Jordan returned his smile. "Right." After Lucy had disappeared into her room, she asked, "How is she doing?"

"Better today."

"That's good. I worry about her."

"Me, too. Here, have a seat." He stood and offered her his chair. Jordan sat, wincing as her muscles contracted against her ribs.

Taylor was quick to get a hand on her elbow. "What happened to you?"

She told him about the incident in Bnei Brak.

"Are you crazy?"

"I don't think so."

"You're damn lucky."

"Tell that to my cracked rib."

"There are certain places even other Jews avoid. Bnei Brak is one of them."

"Why?" Maybe he could shed some better light on the Neturei Karta.

"It's an ultra-Orthodox area with a radical faction. They are experiencing problems with what are being called 'modesty patrols,' composed of men targeting anyone they think violates their laws of Judaism."

"What laws?"

"Anyone not dressed modestly enough. Women who sit in the wrong seat on a bus or walk on the wrong side of the street."

"Those are religious edicts, not laws."

"In some areas, those laws are being enforced. Violators have been verbally harassed—or stoned."

Jordan felt anxious thinking about the stoning. She now knew she was lucky to escape with only a few bruises. "How many incidents are we talking about?"

"Several a month. Some are worse than others. In August, a group of Sikrikim poured acid on an eighteen-year-old girl because her skirt was too short."

Jordan remembered hearing about the Sikrikim, a splinter group of anti-Zionist Jews sometimes referred to as the Jewish Mafia. Many of its members had links to countries that were once part of the Soviet Union.

"Do they have ties to the Neturei Karta?"

"Loose ones," Taylor said. "At least according to the papers."

Jordan flashed back to the face of the mob leader—the friend of Steven's who had delivered the eulogy. "What happened to the men?"

"The police arrested one and put him in jail. The rest got off with a hand slap. Religious freedom is important here."

"It's important everywhere. But what about human rights?" Jordan braced her ribs with her arm, climbed out of her seat, and moved toward the kitchen. Taylor shadowed her.

"Religious rights come first here."

Jordan pondered that as she poured herself water. Turning, she leaned against the counter. "You know what I don't understand?"

"What?"

"How can a group of people who have been persecuted be so intolerant of each other's differences?"

"It happens everywhere."

"A shift of power and the persecuted become the persecutor."

Taylor moved her water to the kitchen table and pulled out a chair for her. "Since I've been here, I've been doing some reading. Do you know the two major challenges facing the Israeli population? They're not what you think."

"The Palestinian unrest and the growing tensions with the Muslim neighbors?" Jordan guessed.

"Wrong. First on the list are the ultra-Orthodox."

Jordan was surprised. "That seems more of regional issue, one that the government will eventually quash."

"Wrong again. They're having lots of children, and their numbers and power are growing. One of these days, there will be enough of them to vote their policies into law."

Jordan shivered at the thought. "What's the second challenge?"

"The *Aliyah,* the ascent or immigration of Eastern European Jews, mostly from the old Soviet Union, to the land of Israel."

"Hence the influx of Sikrikim?" Jordan remembered reading an article about the problems with the Russian immigrants. They came in droves, eating up monetary resources and bringing with them a high percentage of non-Jewish family members.

"You're talking about people like Alena and Yury Petrenko," she said.

"Speaking of Alena, I have some news," Taylor said. "I've been negotiating with my ex-wife."

"How did it go?" Jordan asked.

"Surprisingly well. For whatever reason, she's decided to back off. She's giving us the two weeks."

Chapter 31

Jordan checked with the tech squad on the status of the drive. They were working on it but hadn't been able to crack it yet. Returning to her office, she reported as much to Daugherty and then told him the senator had granted Judge Taylor and Lucy a reprieve.

He wasn't happy. She didn't care.

She didn't tell him about going to Bnei Brak. He was likely to hear about it at some point, but not from her. She let him think her soreness was due to the fight with Ganani. She was on the way home to take a long bath when Noah Weizman called.

"How would you like to ride up to Haifa with me in the morning?"

The invitation caught her off guard. She expected him to have questions about the Taylors or to have heard about the incident at Tamar Cline's home, not be asking her to go somewhere.

"What for?" she asked. The last thing she wanted to do was complicate matters.

"I'm meeting with Tibi's supervisor at GG&B. I thought you might be interested. Besides, the drive along the coast is beautiful. I can pick you up in front of your office."

At the mention of GG&B, Jordan's pulse quickened. Daugherty had made it abundantly clear that GG&B was off-limits. But the detective's requesting her presence changed everything.

If Daugherty saw her leaving with Weizman, it would raise questions. The less he knew at this point, the better. "How about in front of my apartment?"

"That works."

She gave him the address and then told him about Senator Taylor's about-face and her encounter with Batya Ganani.

There was dead silence before his voice came back, hard and cold. "That USB drive is evidence. You should have turned it over to me."

Jordan wasn't surprised by his anger. By diplomatic protocol, he led all matters of security outside the walls of the embassy. Technically, she should have asked his permission to dig through the dumpster.

"I'm informing you about it now," she said. "If the drive came from Cline, the contents could compromise U.S. national security."

"Or Israel's."

She didn't respond.

"Tell me about the man Ganani says got away," he said.

"She claims she couldn't ID him."

"I don't believe it. She has access to all the Shabak files. Trust me, by now she knows his name."

"Then ask her."

There was another silence. Then he said, "I'll pick you at eight a.m. sharp."

*

She was standing on the curb the next morning when Weizman pulled up. He reached across the passenger seat and flung open the door.

"Where's your partner?" she asked, climbing into the front seat.

"Doing reports."

Jordan tried to suppress her relief at the news Lotner wouldn't be coming.

"He likes you, too."

"Is it that obvious?" Jordan buckled her seatbelt, wondering when she'd become so transparent.

At first, it seemed as though Weizman was still angry with her over the USB drive, but his mood seemed to lighten as he turned the car out of the city and merged onto Highway 2, the four-lane road stretching along the coast to Haifa. On the left, sunlight sparkled off the flat waters of the Mediterranean Sea. On the right, olive trees and desert dirt splotched a flat landscape. The sun beat down from above, forcing the air conditioner to work overtime.

Grateful that the tension between them seemed to be gone, Jordan leaned back and enjoyed the cool air, soaking in the sights while Weizman played tour guide. He rattled off details as they traveled through one small town after another. After passing through the larger town of Netanya, they drove back into more scenic territory and he gestured expansively. "This is Caesarea."

Jordan had read about the area in the guide books, but she let him tell her what she already knew. He seemed to like showing off his country, and she was glad to establish some better rapport.

"It is now a national park." He pointed toward the sea. "But you can make out the ruins at the water's edge. The man-made harbor was built by Herod the Great."

She studied the square of the harbor and a stone structure that rose to its north. "It's beautiful."

Weizman nodded. "*Impressive* is the word that comes to my mind. This area has been controlled by many peoples over the years. At one time, it was held by the Romans, then the Byzantines, the Arabs, and the Crusaders. Even Pontius Pilate spent time here. Caesarea has a very turbulent history, much like Israel's."

"Except here you're talking thousands of years," she said.

"What do you mean?" His tone had shifted. It now bore an edge.

Too late to take back her observations, she plowed ahead. "Caesarea's unrest covers thousands of years. The State of Israel has only existed since 1947."

"Unless you are speaking of Eretz Yisrael," Weizman said. "Zion, the biblical land of Israel." She acquiesced with a nod, but he called her out. "You don't believe in the land of the Jews?"

Metaphorically, her shoes were already dirty. As a defined region, Eretz Yisrael included the current boundaries; the occupied territories; and parts of Jordan, Lebanon, and Syria. Over the past two-thousand-plus years, every country in the world had experienced shifting boundaries. Why should Israel be exempt?

"I know it's the preferred history," she answered. "The thing is, things change."

"Are you suggesting we accept what we have instead of going after what is rightfully ours?"

"I'm suggesting you've been given a second chance at a homeland. Maybe it's time to stop fighting and find a way to live with your neighbors."

Weizman's face hardened. "Most of us would prefer to live in peace, but Israel must also protect her rights and her people. We have no choice if we want to survive."

"There are always choices."

When he didn't respond, Jordan considered what to say next. If he believed what he was saying, then he believed Israel had biblical rights to Palestine. But she believed the Palestinians also had rights. Studying the dark tone of his skin, the scruff of beard under the sharp set of his jaw, she decided there was no point in fighting a losing battle.

"I'm sure there's a lot I don't understand," she said, hoping she had extended enough of an olive branch.

He glanced over at her. "Where do you stand on the peace talks?"

The question felt like a trap. She opted for diplomatic. "I like the idea of finding a common ground."

"But you don't believe it's possible."

"I think the odds are against it."

"Why?"

She twisted in her seat to face him. "Primarily because those brokering the peace are attempting to impose a Western-based compromise on Middle Eastern cultures. The inherent problems in that are obvious."

He downshifted and accelerated around a corner. "Go on."

"As Westerners, I think we tend to believe all societies have evolved to the point where adversaries can put aside cultural and religious differences and compromise enough to negotiate win-win solutions."

"Are you suggesting the Middle East hasn't evolved?" His anger was back. "Look at your own Congress."

"Touché. But that's not what I meant. It just seems like the peace brokers aren't in tune with how deep the differences run over here. In spite of how our politicians behave, Westerners are conditioned from birth to the idea of compromise. We practice it at home, at school, at work. I just don't think either the Israelites or the Palestinians can compromise on the land ownership and be happy with the end decision."

"Then hopefully Israel wins."

Jordan stared out the window at the sea. "In truth, I'm in the camp that believes the United Nations needs to take control of the holy sites and historical sites around the world. Make them world monuments and make everybody share."

"It would never work."

She turned back around. "Why not?"

"First, there's money. There is not an equal distribution of wealth in the world. Those nations who pay more for upkeep of the monuments would want more say over them."

"Good point."

"Second, there's purpose." He cornered the car again. "Many sites carry different meanings based on whatever your religion may be. What are important traditions and homage to some are sacrilegious to another." He presented a thin smile. "Need I go on?"

They had come full circle. "No, we're back to the concept of compromise."

They lapsed back into silence, though this time more amiable. Jordan settled back in her seat. Eventually the tranquility of the desert gave way to a bustling that signaled their arrival in Haifa.

Weizman navigated the busy city streets with ease, and before long, he pulled up in front of 53 HaMeginim Boulevard. The GG&B building was constructed of concrete and glass. Rising eight stories, it cast an imposing shadow over the street. Though she had never been in Haifa before, Jordan seemed to recognize the building. "Weizman—"

"We're late," he said, cutting her off and slamming the car into park. "The appointment was for nine-thirty."

He climbed out of the car, and she joined him on the sidewalk. "Detective Weizman, I—"

"Call me Noah. And remember, you are here as my guest. I do the talking."

She started to speak again, and he held up his hand. "I mean it." He started up the concrete steps. "Not a word. We have to be delicate in our approach. GG&B is an important company in Israel."

Now he sounded like Daugherty.

Jordan followed him into the lobby and then waited as he strode across the tiled foyer to the receptionist's desk.

"We are here to see Ester Cohen," he announced.

The young receptionist picked up the phone, spoke softly, and then nodded toward a row of chairs near the window. "Wait there."

Once they were seated in plastic chairs along the wall and waiting, Jordan tried again. "Noah."

"What?"

If her persistence annoyed him, well, too bad. "This building seems very familiar."

Weizman shrugged. "It's possible you've been in one like it. This is a government building, given to GG&B as part of their financial agreement. Israel takes plans they have already paid for, makes minor modifications, and then builds the same structure again and again. Recycling at its finest."

That might explain it. Jordan switched her focus to the task at hand. "Who is Ester Cohen?"

"She is the head of the maintenance department."

While Weizman scribbled into his pocket notebook, Jordan mapped the large, unadorned entry in her head. Filled with tile, plastic, metal, and glass, the waiting area reflected the stark reality of Israel. In the States, everything was plush and oversized. Here, the amenities were present; it was the element of comfort that was lacking. Everything seemed edgier in Israel—even the people.

She turned her head at the sound of the elevator and watched a dark-haired woman step out. She looked prim in her black skirt, white top, and sensible shoes. Her hair was coifed just so around her ears. She approached with her hand outstretched. "*Shalom.* I am Ester Cohen."

Weizman introduced Jordan first and then himself and explained in Hebrew why they were there.

Cohen seemed shocked to find out Najm Tibi was dead.

It seemed odd to Jordan that she hadn't been notified. She was, after all, the supervisor.

169

"What happened?" Cohen asked.

"He was murdered," said Weizman. "We notified the company president. He didn't inform you?"

"No." She shook her head and mustered her wits about her. "Najm was such a nice young man."

She also didn't seem to know the real Tibi.

"When was the last time you saw him?" Weizman asked.

"I don't usually interact with Najm. He works nights. He comes in Sunday through Thursday at nineteen hundred. But he had taken this week off to attend to some family business."

Weizman cleared his throat. "We suspect his murder is connected to the shooting of the U.S. embassy employee in Dizengoff Square."

"Najm involved in a murder? That's impossible." The woman's voice rose and her eyes grew dark. It was as if Weizman had called her firstborn child a bully. "Are you saying he killed someone?"

"No," Weizman said. "We will need to see his work space in order to get a sense of his daily routine."

"He doesn't—didn't have a space," replied Cohen. "He worked maintenance. He had a cart, but he shares—shared it with others." When Weizman remained silent, she grew restless and backpedaled. "Maintenance does have a communal station in the basement. I suppose I can show you that."

"Please," Weizman said.

Jordan smiled encouragingly. If Ester Cohen believed Tibi was a saint, who were they to burst her bubble? Not while they were seeking information, at least.

"This way, then." Cohen stopped to pick up visitor badges for both of them and led the way to the elevator. Swiping her employee ID through a card reader, she punched the button for the basement floor. "I really don't see the use in your coming."

"It may turn out to be a waste of our time," Weizman said. "I hope not."

DARK WATERS

Cohen stood with her back to the corner of the elevator, as if gaining strength from the walls at her back. "Just what is it you think he has done?"

"We're not sure he did anything. What we do know is that Najm is dead, and someone connected with a murder in Dizengoff killed him. We're looking for clues."

"Why would someone kill him? He is just a maintenance worker."

"Was he assigned to a specific floor?" Jordan asked. Weizman shot her a warning glance. So much for be seen and not heard.

"Yes. The executive offices." Cohen sucked in a sharp breath and covered her mouth with her hand.

"What is it?" Weizman asked.

Cohen shook her head.

Jordan glanced at Weizman. "Anything you think of might help."

"It's just . . . you don't think he was involved in some sort of corporate espionage, do you?"

Jordan tried the idea on for size and wondered how that dovetailed with Cline's involvement.

Weizman ignored her question. "Did he have computer access?"

The woman's face pinched, as though the thought was distasteful. "No. Only higher-up employees, like myself, have access to the network. Najm's key card allowed him entrance to the building. That's all."

Maybe Cline had been trading for access to GG&B.

Tailing Cohen and Weizman down the hall, Jordan surveyed the surroundings. Cameras were mounted in the corners near the doorways. Solid steel doors lined the corridor. Magnetic key cards were required to open them. Cohen swiped her card at the last door on the left.

"This is where the maintenance carts are stocked. In addition to supplies, there is a time clock in here and a small TV for when the workers take their breaks."

Jordan remembered the laptop in Tibi's apartment and wondered if he'd ever used it here. "Are employees allowed to bring in their own computers?"

The supervisor looked uncomfortable and shook her head. Jordan avoided eye contact with Weizman.

"No," Cohen said. "Najm and the others had no need for network access and had no time to sit around playing computer games. They were not even allowed to bring in iPods. No distractions. Just work."

Weizman picked up on Jordan's line of questioning. "Say he did want to gain access. How does GG&B control entry to the system?"

"I'm not at liberty to share that information," Cohen said. The woman was on full alert.

"We're only asking questions," Weizman said.

"I told you. There is no way for him to have gained access." Cohen's hands trembled. The idea frightened her. Was she worried she might be blamed if there was a breach?

"Let me rephrase. Who controls access?"

Cohen set her jaw. "It's controlled at the highest level."

"Which is . . . ?"

Cohen straightened her shoulders. "It is a C-level decision. It's up to the CEO and the COO. They decide who and the depth of access someone is given. For example, I am only allowed to view the maintenance records." The scrunch of her face showed that it pained her to admit the imposed limit. It took only seconds for the smug look to reemerge. "Najm had access to nothing."

"Didn't you tell us that Tibi had access to the executive level?" Jordan said.

Weizman shot her another look, but Jordan felt the point was worth making. Someone with computer savvy could hack into almost any system, provided he had access to a computer and enough time.

Cohen shifted her weight foot to foot. Now she turned toward the hallway. "There is nothing for you to learn here." Ushering them back into the hall, she checked to make sure the door was locked. "It is very sad about Najm. He was a good worker and a kind young man."

Jordan thought of the butchered Dizengoff Apartments manager and the attempt to kidnap Lucy. Najm was a real prince, all right.

Weizman blocked Cohen's retreat down the hall and jerked his head toward a door marked maintenance carts. To her obvious consternation, he ordered her to open the door and insisted on going over every inch of Tibi's maintenance cart. Standing to the side, arms crossed over her chest, Cohen watched while Jordan helped Weizman sift through bottles of floor cleaner, toilet bowl cleaner, soap, and hand towel refills. A feather duster, mop, and broom sprouted from the holder on the end. They found nothing unusual.

Finally, he called off the search. "Ms. Cohen, you've been a great help."

Cohen relaxed her shoulders and forced a smile.

"Now I'd like to see the executive floor," Weizman said.

"I can't allow that." For the second time, Cohen seemed scared.

Weizman rubbed his chin. Finally, he asked, "Then who can?"

Cohen bounced her gaze from ceiling to floor and wall to wall. There was no escape. She glared at Weizman. "Peter Graff, our COO. I'll see if he's available."

Weizman smiled. "Thank you."

Back in the lobby, Jordan pulled Weizman aside while Cohen placed the call upstairs. "That woman is terrified."

"She should be," Weizman said. "She stands to lose her job."

"Why? It isn't her fault her employee was a terrorist." Security appeared tight, and Jordan imagined there was an arduous employment screening process. "How can they fire her over something Tibi did?"

"She is head of the maintenance department."

Cohen was in a no-win position. She oversaw a staff of Israeli Arabs that probably didn't like her and that the other employees eyed with suspicion. No wonder she was reticent to call Graff.

Cohen spoke into the phone, handed the receiver to the receptionist, and walked toward them. "Mr. Graff is in a meeting. It may be a few minutes. Perhaps you'd rather come back?"

"Thank you," Weizman said. "We'll wait."

Twenty minutes later, the carpet was wearing from Weizman's pacing back and forth in the lobby, and Jordan's nerves were frayed.

"That is not helping, Noah. Will you please sit down?" The words had barely escaped her mouth when the elevator doors opened. Jordan stood up.

Two men stepped off the elevator. One she recognized as Peter Graff, COO of GG&B Engineering. His picture in the company brochure did him justice. Tall and lean, his black Armani suit draped his thin frame and spoke of money. His dark hair was gelled into place, his tan was perfect, and his shoes were polished: the quintessential executive of a billion-dollar company.

Then Jordan looked at the other man and her world tilted. She recognized him from her past.

Chapter 32

Haddid felt like a bird in the hand. Trapped.

After the shootout, he and the others had fled to the safe house. Yousif had been gravely injured. He still lived, but he needed a doctor. Fayez paced like a caged animal, each pivot ratcheting up Haddid's anxiety. Basim was on the phone, explaining the situation to Zuabi.

"Yes, *Za'im*."

Based on the high pitch of his voice, Haddid concluded that the conversation was not going well.

"The woman who was after the girl was the same woman that Haddid saw at Najm's house. They took her away in handcuffs, but mark my words, she is Shabak."

Haddid could hear Zuabi railing through the receiver.

"*Wuled el kakhbah!*" he shouted. Son of a bitch.

Basim bobbed his head up and down. "*Aasef, Za'im. Aasef!*"

Haddid thought it bad strategy for Basim to be apologizing. They were all being blamed.

"What is he saying?" Fayez said. "It is not our fault that a crazy woman charged in and ruined our plan."

"*Salaam, Za'im.*" Basim hung up the phone.

"So?" Fayez demanded. "What does he say?"

"He says that without the information, the mission is done."

Fayez ignited into a frenzy. "How can he expect us to find the USB drive with Marine guards watching the apartment and Shabak involved? What does he expect from us? Maybe they have already found it. If we take the girl, the wrath of the Americans will come down upon us. There is nothing more we can do."

"Zuabi doesn't care about your fear," Basim said. "He wants action."

Haddid watched as the tension between the two men escalated. He did nothing to stop it. With Allah's help, maybe they would kill each other.

"Are we supposed to blast our way in?" Fayez grabbed hold of Basim's sleeve. "Did you tell him we are a man short? Did you tell him that Yousif is dying?"

"Calm yourself, Fayez, and lower your voice!" Basim yanked his arm free and gestured toward the bedroom where their friend lay dying. "Zuabi wants us to prove our loyalty. He fears one of us may be playing both sides."

Haddid looked up and realized both men were staring at him. He swallowed, trying to control his fear. "You think it was me who sold out my brothers?"

"The Shabak agent let you walk away."

"I did not walk. I *ran*." Haddid looked from one to the other and placed his open hand on his heart. "I barely had time to escape with my life, and now I am back here with you to finish the job." Haddid forced himself to show strength. If they sensed any hesitation on his behalf, his wife and son would be in grave danger. "Whatever Zuabi wants is what we will get." He locked eyes with Basim and waited. At last, his cohort smiled.

"How are we going to get the information Zuabi wants?" Fayez asked. "We don't even know where to begin. We don't even know if the child has what Zuabi wants. How do we know the

Americans don't have it by now? Or worse, Shabak. There's no way the three of us can sneak past the guards and into that apartment. It is an impossible task."

"Enough!" Basim ordered. "Shut up, Fayez. You babble like a little girl." Basim stared toward the bedroom where Yousif lay injured. "Do you remember what Zuabi said as we left?"

"He said, 'Don't come back empty-handed,'" Haddid said, feeling a new fear niggling at the pit of his stomach. "What are you thinking, Basim?"

"We may not be able to get our hands on the child, but we have access to another bargaining chip."

Haddid's stomach churned like a washing machine. "What are you saying?"

"The girl goes to the office of Alena Petrenko."

"The doctor," Fayez said. "This means she is sick." He grinned, but then his smile faded. "Wait! How is this good?"

A wave of nausea enveloped Haddid. He didn't like the direction Basim was going with this.

"The doctor is not a normal type of physician. While you tended to Yousif, I did a little research," Basim held up his smartphone. "Dr. Petrenko has a website. On it, she describes herself as a 'bioenergy healer.' She claims she can cure patients by 'realigning their energy flow.'"

"She sounds like a lunatic Jew," Fayez said.

Basim grinned. "To me, she sounds like someone taking advantage of a man desperate to save his daughter. The question is, to what lengths will he go to save the only doctor he believes can cure her?"

"He will give everything," Haddid said, thinking of his own Sami. "Provided he has it to give. You understand he may not have what we want. If the Americans found the USB drive, there will be no more trades."

"There is one way to find out," Fayez said. "It is better than sitting around here waiting for Yousif to die, or for Zuabi to decide we are not to be trusted."

"Fine," Haddid said. "I will go." Then he could warn the doctor and buy himself time to figure a way out of this mess.

He started to rise when Basim cut him off. "No, Haddid. You have done enough. You will stay here with Yousif. Fayez and I will take care of this."

Chapter 33

Jordan stared at the Russian standing beside Peter Graff. Had he recognized her? She had changed a lot in nineteen years, but he had hardly changed at all. The decades had turned his blond hair white and softened his carriage, but his blue eyes still shone like freshly glazed ice, and his mouth curved in a smile that never moved past his lips.

The last time she had seen him, she had been six years old, standing over her father's casket, watching this man comfort her mother. Jordan remembered that when he knelt down to hug her, she had pulled back, and her mother had scolded her. Jordan had never expected to see him again and had never wanted to see him. But she had not forgotten him—would never forget him—and the shock of encountering him left her stunned.

The man shook hands with Graff and headed toward the door. Jordan tracked his movements until he disappeared from sight. Then she edged away from Weizman to stand near the large windows. The Russian walked down the steps toward a dark sedan at the curb. Her heart slammed against her sore ribs, adding to the pain of memories.

"I can't believe he beat us here," Weizman said.

"Who?"

"Ilya Brodsky. The man with Graff. He's Batya Ganani's boss."

179

"That's not possible."

Weizman frowned. "Jordan, are you okay?"

She shook her head to clear it. "I know that man. Twenty years ago he lived in Russia. I think he worked for the government."

"What are you talking about?" Weizman demanded.

Jordan gripped his arm. "Keep your voice down!"

The lobby was empty except for the four of them. Graff and the receptionist were engaged in conversation and fortunately didn't show any interest in Weizman and Jordan's discussion.

Jordan leaned in toward Weizman. "I'm telling you, that man is from St. Petersburg. He was a friend of my father's."

"You must be mistaken. Brodsky is from Ukraine. He's an Orthodox Jew. There is no way he ever worked for the Russians."

Jordan couldn't shake her memories. "I'm not wrong, Noah. He used to come to our house. My father introduced him to me as *Dyadya* Ilya—Uncle Ilya."

"Go on."

"He frightened me. My father explained that he was a very powerful man, named after a *bogatyr*, Ilya Muromets."

"What is a *bogatyr*?"

"It's a mythical Russian figure similar to the Western knight-errant. Muromets was considered the greatest *bogatyr*. He was known for his spiritual power, integrity, and dedication to his homeland. There are many Russian stories about his exploits."

"Muromets sounds like a positive role model."

"I think that's how *Dyadya* Ilya fancied himself." By Jordan's recollection, he laughed too loud and drank too much vodka. Her mother always seemed nervous when he was around.

He had come to their house two days before her father's death. Jordan had been reading in the living room when she heard her father arguing with him in the den. Creeping to the door, she peered inside to see her father seated on the sofa with Ilya, standing before him, yelling. He had told her father that he would never be allowed to leave Russia. Two days later, her father was dead.

The last time she saw Ilya had been at the cemetery. Her mother had wept in his arms. Moments later, he bent to Jordan's level, flashed a thin smile, and told her how sorry he was. She would never forget his cold, blue eyes—or her feeling that he had lied.

"Detective Weizman." This time it was Graff's voice that penetrated her thoughts. The sedan was no longer at the curb. Ilya Brodsky had disappeared into the bustle of Haifa.

The COO of GG&B crossed the lobby toward them, and Jordan did her best to concentrate.

Weizman plunged right in. "We have some questions regarding the death of Najm Tibi."

"Yes, yes," said Graff, "Terrible thing. Your office called." The COO shrugged. "I'm afraid Shin Bet beat you to it. I've just spent the last hour going over the files and computer records with Colonel Brodsky. We found nothing out of the ordinary."

Jordan tried making eye contact with Graff, but he kept his focus slightly off target.

"No suspicious activities?" Weizman asked.

"Not a thing." Graff sounded too casual. He was covering up something. "Tibi was exactly who he seemed to be. A maintenance man. There was nothing sinister going on."

"Then you wouldn't mind if we looked for ourselves," said Weizman.

This time, Graff made eye contact. "I'm afraid that isn't possible, Detective." His gaze flitted to Jordan. "This has moved beyond all our pay grades."

Weizman's expression hardened, but he remained silent.

Graff was an American, so Jordan tried the patriotic card. "This is an official investigation about a possible act of treason. Your government would appreciate your cooperation."

Graff sized her up. "I appreciate your concerns, but Colonel Brodsky assures me that he's handling this matter himself. If you have any questions, I suggest you speak with him. Now, if there's nothing more . . . ?"

Jordan was stymied by his lack of cooperation. When neither she nor Weizman spoke, the COO nodded and turned away. The tassels on his loafers bounced as he walked. Once the elevator doors had closed, Jordan spun on Weizman.

"Why would the colonel involve himself in this investigation? There must be something really important at stake."

"Yes. Israel's national security," Weizman said, heading for the exit. "Just like you are concerned about America's. If he's keeping something quiet, it's for a good reason."

Jordan trailed Weizman through the outside doors and down the steps. "So that's it? We just go back? Five people are dead."

Weizman hesitated slightly. "It is what it is."

"Can't you call someone and get a warrant? Somehow force Graff to let us in?"

Weizman reached the curb and turned. "That's not how it works in Israel."

"This is our investigation. Surely you can arrange a subpoena."

"Not now."

"You know as well as I do that Graff knows something. How can you let that go?"

Weizman moved around the cars. "Once Shabak takes over, it is out of my hands. I'll make an official request for answers, but for now, my hands are tied."

With their investigation into GG&B Engineering derailed, Jordan walked toward the car. Without Weizman, there would be no access to GG&B. Daugherty had ordered her to stay clear. If he found out she had disobeyed his orders, he might yank her off the case.

"What about going through back channels?" Jordan asked. She had no illusions about Brodsky sharing, but Weizman had to have contacts.

He depressed the car door opener, and the car beeped as the doors unlocked. "Shabak is not large on reciprocity. Their policy is 'need to know,' and only when it serves them."

That made sense. From her memories and the little she knew about Brodsky, he was a man who thrived on control. If only they could gain access to the information he wanted to hide.

"How much do you know about the colonel?" she asked.

"Brodsky?" Weizman buckled his seatbelt. "He is the son of Holocaust survivors, immigrated to Israel in the early nineties." Weizman inserted the key in the ignition. "He's an honorable man, a great asset, and loves this country. He has a big heart."

That didn't sound like the man she knew as a child. Even at six years old, Jordan had picked up on his lack of emotion. He didn't seem to care much for anything or anyone. He viewed her father as a catalyst, a means to an end, though he did have a soft spot for her mother.

"Do you know what the Russians thought of Israel?" she asked.

Weizman cranked the engine and shoved the car into gear. "Why do you keep insisting he was affiliated with their government?"

"Because I think I can prove it." Jordan pulled out her cell. There might be a picture.

A green light on her phone indicated she had a message. Swiping the screen, she discovered two missed calls from embassy phones and a voicemail message waiting. Something had happened.

Chapter 34

Ganani was seated in a café with a clear view of the Dizen-goff Apartments when her phone buzzed. She glanced at the caller ID and considered letting it go to voicemail, but she thought better of it. "*Shalom,* Colonel."

"We have another complication."

She sat up straighter. "What do you mean?"

"The doctor."

"What about her?" Ganani had a bad feeling. She took a quick survey of her surroundings to be sure no one was paying her special interest, picked up her coffee, and settled back in her chair. "She is scheduled to arrive at ten hundred hours, any moment now."

"Except that Judge Taylor has just received a phone call demanding the exchange of the USB drive for her life."

"How do you know this?"

"You are not my only asset, *krolik.*"

She hated it when he called her "rabbit." The endearment made her feel as if she were under the watchful eye of a snake. No doubt his intent. The fact that she allowed it to pass without comment sickened her. He was a sexist Russian pig. One day she would confront him.

Today she turned her attention back to the problem at hand. "What is it you want me to do?"

"Detective Weizman is in Haifa. I just left him at the GG&B Engineering building. Who is in charge on scene?"

Why did she think he already knew?

"His partner, Gidon Lotner, just arrived. He is inside with the judge and his daughter."

"Good." His satisfaction transmitted through the phone line. "I have spoken with the head of security at the American embassy. According to Special Agent Tom Daugherty, the judge telephoned him the moment he was contacted. Daugherty handed him the party line, 'that the United States does not negotiate with terrorists.' But since Dr. Petrenko is an Israeli, she is not the State Department's concern."

"She's ours." Ganani could see where this was going.

"I don't care so much about her, but we are in the business of identifying and capturing terrorists."

Ganani knew he was calling attention to her failure to identify the Palestinian that had gotten away.

"Colonel, we know the Americans have recovered the USB drive. It is my understanding that my presence here is just a precaution."

"Your mission has changed."

Ganani knew whatever he was about to ask her to do was outside her normal job parameters. She also knew she would do it.

"I spoke with Agent Daugherty and offered to help. He agreed to help us fake the exchange if we manage the cleanup."

Ganani's throat tightened. "Your plan is to let Judge Taylor deliver a USB drive with false intel into the hands of the Palestinians?"

"Yes."

"Have the Americans figured out what's on the original drive?"

"Not as far as Daugherty is admitting. Fortunately, he shares our interest in identifying and stopping those who turned his right-hand man. He also knows that, working together, the U.S. and Israel can help bring an end to the violence. The Americans will be looking out for the judge and overseeing the exchange. If they are lucky, the judge and the doctor will escape with their lives."

"And if they're unlucky?"

"Then they are unlucky."

Ganani wondered when the cause became more important than human lives, especially those who were innocent, those caught in a war not of their making. "What is my responsibility?"

"You are to make sure the drive ends up in the Palestinians' hands. Once they are away, you are to follow them. Secure the information that Cline was to receive. After that, kill them all."

Chapter 35

There were three voicemails waiting for Jordan. They signaled a problem. Before she could open the first one, her phone rang. Walker's name came up on the caller ID. She answered.

"We've got trouble," he said.

Jordan straightened in her seat, her brain running scenarios. "What's happened?"

"Alena Petrenko's been kidnapped."

He gave her the blow-by-blow. The doctor had never shown up. Instead, the judge received a call from someone claiming to be holding Alena Petrenko. While they were attempting to verify facts, Daugherty had called and asked for Jordan's ETA.

That explained the missed calls. "What did you tell him?"

"I told him you'd been delayed and were on your way." He paused. "You are on your way?"

"Thirty minutes." She glanced at Weizman.

He shook his head and mouthed, *forty-five*. He was on the phone, too.

"Forty-five minutes," she amended.

"Call Daugherty," Walker said. She noticed he left off the *ma'am*.

Hanging up, Jordan listened to her messages. One was from her boss, ordering her to call in immediately. "Shit."

When she tried calling, she got his voicemail.

"That was Gidon," Weizman said, closing his phone. He reached forward and flipped on the lights and siren. He had little to add to what she already knew, except for the fact that the plan appeared to be to exchange the information for the doctor.

"Daugherty would never negotiate."

"Apparently, he has already agreed." Weizman gunned the engine and shot into the passing lane. Cars peeled off to the right in front of them, and they hurtled toward Tel Aviv at 160 kilometers an hour. The desert blurred in the window behind Weizman's head.

It didn't make sense. The US policy was clear.

"Who will be doing the hand-off?"

"The judge."

"Daugherty is out of his mind."

"The judge is the one who gains from securing the doctor's release," Weizman said. "Maybe he talked his wife into exerting her influence."

"His *ex*-wife," Jordan said. "But that doesn't make sense. She thinks Alena Petrenko's a quack."

"Someone else, then. Someone with power."

"Ilya Brodsky," Jordan said, slamming her hand down on the armrest.

"The colonel has the power," Weizman said. "But what would he care about Alena Petrenko?"

"He cares about the information being exchanged. He sent Ganani to my office."

Racing toward Tel Aviv, Jordan found herself consumed with thoughts of conspiracies and a growing concern for the Taylors' well-being. Why would Daugherty strike an agreement with the head of a Shin Bet special terrorist unit to participate in an exchange to secure the release of an Israeli immigrant? Daugherty was red, white, and blue to the core. There had to be something more going on, something she wasn't privy to.

Maybe he was bucking for some promotion? Daugherty and Brodsky both stood to gain if the exchange went well. Daugherty would get credit for helping a U.S. ally. Brodsky would be a national hero for dismembering an active terrorist cell. And if the exchange was botched, both the DSS and Shin Bet could use Jordan as a scapegoat.

Turning the car onto Dizengoff Street, Weizman glanced over at Jordan. "You're awfully quiet."

"Just thinking," she said.

"You're going to have to tell Daugherty you went with me to GG&B."

"I'm sure he already knows."

Weizman pulled up in front of the Taylors' apartment building. "Tell Daugherty I insisted you accompany me—that I wanted your take on things." He reached across her and opened the passenger door. "I have to go to my office. Let me know what happens."

Crossing the courtyard, Jordan took the stairs to the second-floor apartment two at a time, not breaking stride until she reached the door. She knocked and the Marine granted her access. Just over the threshold, she stopped. The front room was crammed full of people—communication techs, policemen, the Marines. A man she'd never seen before claimed the starring role, directing the activity like a traffic cop. There was no sign of Lucy or the judge, but Daugherty and Batya Ganani stood in the kitchen talking.

"Glad you could join us," Daugherty said, speaking loudly enough that the room went silent.

Jordan refused to be intimidated. It wasn't as if being on the scene sooner would have changed anything.

She jerked her head toward Ganani. "What is she doing here?"

Ganani proffered a thin smile. Jordan enjoyed seeing that makeup couldn't completely cover the shiners caused by her kick to Ganani's nose.

"She's the Shin Bet agent in charge," Daugherty said. "She's running the operation."

Ganani held up a small, silver USB drive similar to the one Jordan had given to the tech geeks.

"Did they crack it?" Jordan asked Daugherty.

He nodded. "Cline had it loaded up with the secretary of state's visit itinerary, a map of the embassy guest residences, and detailed information about the security measures being taken."

"I knew it," she said. Jordan wanted to tell him "I told you so." She had pegged Cline as a traitor, even as Daugherty had doubted her. She had been right. "That's everything a terrorist would need to launch an attack on the embassy."

"And none of it's relevant anymore." Daugherty's voice carried a warning, but Jordan refused to back down.

"How does that make breaking with protocol acceptable?" she asked.

"That from the agent who ignored my orders?"

Ganani looked from Jordan to Daugherty and beat a hasty retreat.

"You're treading on thin ice, Jordan," Daugherty said. "Even though it's the policy of the United States not to negotiate with terrorists, Shin Bet views this as an opportunity to crack open a major terrorist cell. They've asked for our help."

"Doesn't that make us complicit?"

"Just because we provided some false information?" He let the words hang. "We've changed the secretary's schedule, tweaked the residence map, and changed up the security details. You're only job is to look out for the judge's safety."

"What does that mean?"

"The kidnappers have asked him to deliver the USB drive."

"Did you authorize that?"

190

"I actually had no say in the matter. It's up to the judge, and he told Ganani he's in."

Jordan gripped the edge of the counter. She couldn't help thinking about Lucy. "What if it goes badly?"

"Then it's on Brodsky."

The mention of his name notched up Jordan's discomfort level. "There has to be some other way. Sir," she added, reaching for the respectful, "why can't one of the Shin Bet agents make the trade?"

"The kidnappers asked for the judge, and he's insisting."

The idea of him putting himself in danger upset her. "He's not thinking clearly. He's my responsibility. It's my ass on the line if something happens to him. I'll talk to him."

"It's decided."

This was her case, and Daugherty, at Posner's prodding, had done nothing but undercut her at every turn. She had to assume it was payback.

"There are other options," she said. "What about good old detective work? Let's figure out who these guys are and launch a rescue operation."

"The clock is ticking, Jordan. We're running out of time," Daugherty said, scrubbing a hand over his close-cropped hair.

"If we can figure out what Cline was after in exchange, we'd have—"

Daugherty raised his hands and stopped her. "We've been over this, Jordan. We have to assume Cline did it for the money."

Except that there was no money trail. She had double- and triple-checked.

"I went to Steven Cline's funeral yesterday, and I learned a few things," Jordan said.

"You did *what*?" His voice rose. Anger discolored his face. "You went to his funeral?"

"That's not the point, Daugherty. What's important is that I can testify to the fact that Cline had aligned himself with the Neturei Karta." Jordan spoke quietly, hoping to deflect unwanted attention.

Daugherty kept chewing the bone. "Bnei Brak is off-limits to embassy personnel, except for official business."

"It *was* official business," she said, and Bnei Brak being off-limits was something she might have known if she'd been briefed by her RSO. Daugherty rubbed his face with a meaty hand. Jordan wondered if she'd pushed things too far.

"We're finished with this conversation, Jordan. The ship has sailed. We may never know what Cline was doing that day. Right now, our best plan of action is helping our allies get a bead on an active terrorist cell."

Ganani edged back into the kitchen. Private time was over.

Jordan directed her next question to the agent. "So what's the plan?"

Ganani stuffed her hands in the pockets of her black bomber jacket. "The judge hands off the drive in exchange for the doctor. We've embedded a tracking device. The team will make sure Judge Taylor and the doctor get back to Tel Aviv while I follow the kidnappers."

"How many are on the team?"

Before Ganani could answer, the door to Lucy's room opened and Taylor stepped out. Dark circles shadowed his eyes. Worry lines etched his face. Jordan had a sickening feeling that Lucy was getting worse.

Jordan moved toward Taylor. "How is she?"

"Sick. We need to move quickly." He shut the door softly.

"How sick?"

He pushed his hands through his hair and rubbed the back of his neck. "She's running a fever of one hundred four."

Jordan converted Fahrenheit to Celsius. Forty. They were told to call Petrenko if Lucy's temperature climbed above thirty-eight. "She needs to see a doctor."

Daugherty pulled out his phone. "I'll call the embassy physician."

"No!" Taylor stepped forward, his fists clenched. "We need to get Alena back. She's the only one who can help."

Jordan rested her hand on his sleeve and felt the bunched muscles under the soft cotton fabric. "Taylor, we have to do something to bring the fever down."

"No other doctor."

Jordan wished she could understand why he wouldn't seek help for his daughter. If he was worried that seeing a traditional physician would open the door for his ex-wife to swoop in, it was a risk he should be willing to take. This was about Lucy.

"A fever that high is dangerous," said Jordan.

"She needs Alena." His tone was firm. "Let's get this mission started."

Jordan hadn't known him long, but she knew that once he had made up his mind, there was no diverting him from this course. Still, they had to do something for Lucy. "First, what can we do to bring down the fever?"

Ganani looked bored and spread the map out on the table. "Why not give her some aspirin?"

"No medicine," Taylor said. "Alena specifically said no fever suppressants."

Of course she did. The more Jordan heard, the more Petrenko resembled a quack. Taylor's ex-wife was definitely onto something.

"What about a cool bath?" Jordan suggested.

"Great idea, Jordan." Daugherty had a couple of kids of his own. He knew the drill. He turned to Walker. "Draw a tepid bath, and let's get Lucy in it."

Walker headed down the hall and, within seconds, Jordan heard the gush of water hitting porcelain. Daugherty sent Taylor back to get Lucy.

Ganani looked up from the map. "When the terrorists call, we'll need him available."

Jordan's temper flared. "He shouldn't be involved in the first place."

"Drop it, Jordan. It's a done deal."

"You're like a mother hen," Ganani said. "I promise, I'll keep him safe. I have been instructed by Colonel Brodsky to make sure the exchange goes smoothly."

The reminder of Brodsky's involvement shattered Jordan's comfort level. There was no telling what they were walking into.

"I'd like it better if I had a grasp of the plan."

"Like I said, no one is going to get hurt," Ganani said. "The judge will hand off the information, then he and Dr. Petrenko will walk away. As soon as they're a safe distance, I'll move in and follow whoever makes the exchange."

"Shin Bet needs to know who's behind this and what they plan to do with the information," Daugherty said.

Ganani smoothed the creases on the map. "It's my assignment."

"You're not going in by yourself."

"I do my best work alone."

"That's a bad idea. Let me go with you," Jordan heard herself volunteer. "I can ensure the judge and Petrenko get away and help you track down the kidnappers."

"I don't need your help."

Jordan appealed to Daugherty. He shrugged.

"If Ganani doesn't want you tagging along, there's not much I can do."

Jordan could have predicted his response. But if she caved now, she might as well pack her bags for home. "Taylor is the one at risk. I should at least be there for the hand-off."

Daugherty cocked his head. "Not exactly 'by the book.'"

"And aiding and abetting a hostage negotiation and allowing a civilian to do the hand-off is?"

"Technically, we haven't negotiated anything. This is the Israelis' operation."

The official spin on things. Jordan had to work to clamp down her anger. Now wasn't the time to engage. For Taylor and Lucy's sake, she knew she couldn't afford to lose this round.

"Taylor and Lucy are my responsibility," she said. "The Marines can look after Lucy. I should be there if the judge is going to put himself in danger."

Daugherty's jaw muscle bunched. "I need to know you're good with what's going on here."

He twirled his finger to encompass the scene, and Jordan glanced around. The agents were busy with the com set up. Walker was still helping Taylor. What Daugherty really wanted to know was, could she stand behind the operation? So far, they had only facilitated access to some misinformation, and although it was unorthodox to use a civilian for the exchange, Taylor was insisting. What choice did she have?

Ganani and Daugherty both waited for her response.

"I need an answer, Jordan."

Jordan locked eyes with Daugherty. "I'm good."

He held her stare for a moment and then turned to Ganani. "Here's the deal. Agent Jordan is the DSS agent assigned to the protection of Taylor. In this case, I have to agree with her. It's in the best interests of both Taylor and the U.S. State Department that she remain involved."

Jordan was surprised he had backed her. Maybe he wasn't such a dick after all. Or maybe he hoped she would fall flat on her face. If she screwed this up, she knew he would send her home.

Ganani reached for her phone. "The colonel will not like this change in plans."

"You let me deal with Brodsky."

The agent's internal struggle flickered across her face before she nodded at Daugherty. "The ball is with you."

He nodded and turned to Jordan. "I do have a suggestion for you."

"Sir?"

He indicated her body from head to toe. "You better do something about your appearance. Maybe hide the hair."

Jordan glanced down at her outfit. The dark blue pants and light blue shirt screamed "federal agent." Unfortunately, her go-bag was in the trunk of her sedan at home.

"I'll have to send someone to my apartment."

"There's no time," Ganani said. Digging in her pocket, she produced a set of keys. "I have clothes in my car that should fit you. I'll be right back."

With the agent gone, Daugherty went to check on the com. Jordan checked on Lucy. She was out of the tub and standing on the bathmat, wrapped in an oversized towel.

"How are you doing?" Jordan asked, bending down to kid level. Lucy's skin had a grayish-white pallor.

"Her temperature broke," Taylor said. "I need to get her back to her room."

Jordan stepped aside as Taylor hefted Lucy into his arms and headed for the bedroom. After Lucy had put on a dry nightgown and climbed into bed, Jordan went in and sat down beside her.

"Jordan?" The girl's whisper barely rose above the rustling of the covers.

"Yes, honey?" The endearment popped out, surprising Jordan.

"Do you want to play chess?"

Jordan smiled. "Absolutely. Maybe later?"

"After I take a nap."

"Consider it a date."

Walker stuck his head in the door. "Ganani's back."

Jordan brushed a damp curl off Lucy's forehead. She was already asleep.

Ganani stood by the kitchen table talking with two of her team when Jordan walked up. Seeing her, the agent held out a small, black satchel. "I don't have a lot of choices, but you can make do."

Jordan went to the bathroom to change. Setting the small go-bag on the counter, she checked out the contents—a black pencil skirt; a long-sleeved, black, V-neck T-shirt; a black scarf; dark stockings; and a pair of three-inch heels.

The V-neck tee worked. The skirt and shoes both posed a problem, especially if she needed to run—or, for that matter, blend in. She thought of the stoning in Bnei Brak.

Stripping down to her panties and bra, she slipped on the tee. It fit well, curving over the swell of her breasts and clinging tight to her ribs. She pulled on the stockings and then the pencil skirt. As feared, it fit loose in the waist, tight across the knees, restricting her movement.

Fortunately, she was slightly shorter and thinner than Ganani. Hooking her fingers inside the waistband, Jordan rolled it once, twice, three times, until the hem was high enough to facilitate movement. Unfortunately, that caused the skirt's slit to ride up high on her thighs and point dramatically toward her butt. She untucked the T-shirt. It was the best she could do.

Gathering her hair, she bundled it into a low ponytail at the back of her neck and then draped her head with the dark scarf. Scarf on, she could pass for a Palestinian. Scarf off and around her waist, she could pass for a tourist.

Protocol required she keep her weapon in sight and securely holstered at all times, but screw that. Today, she and her gun were undercover. Using her belt, she fashioned a thigh holster and then practiced drawing her weapon. She fumbled her first two attempts, but in the words of either John Adams or Vince Lombardi, practice makes perfect. Trying again, she worked it until she could double-hand the stock, click off the safety, and faux-fire. She was good to go.

Walker whistled when she reentered the living room, and all heads turned. Jordan flipped him off.

Daugherty flagged her over to the kitchen counter.

"Have they called?"

She already knew the answer to her question. If they had called, someone would have knocked on the bathroom door.

"How the hell are you planning to run in that getup?" he asked, putting a voice to her fear.

"You'd be surprised how fast a girl can run in a dress," Jordan said.

"Nobody will be running anywhere," said Taylor from the living room couch. "I'm going in alone. The kidnappers made it clear. Any hint of a tail and the deal is off."

"All kidnappers say that," Jordan said. "They know the drill. We can't let you go in by yourself."

"Without Alena, Lucy dies. I can't afford to take any risks."

"And what if something happens to you? What would Lucy do?" Jordan asked. "I lost my father when I was six. No kid should have to go through that."

Daugherty stepped forward.

"It's nonnegotiable, Judge." It was the second time he had backed her that day.

Jordan walked over to where Taylor was sitting and sat down on the chair so they were at eye level. "Taylor, I promise. No one is going to do anything to jeopardize the exchange."

Taylor didn't look convinced. "If this goes south," he said, pointing at Jordan, "I'm holding you responsible."

Chapter 36

The apartment phone lines were tapped and every one wired by the time the kidnapper's second call came in. Jordan held the wireless receiver to her ear and looked over at the agent on com. On the third ring, he gave the go-ahead to answer.

"Keep him talking," Jordan told Taylor. "But don't freak if he hangs up. Most people think three minutes is the magic number for nailing a trace. In truth, unless you run into problems, it should only take seconds."

Taylor nodded and picked up. "Hello?"

"Do you have the USB drive we want?" The voice was deep, with a thick Middle Eastern accent.

"Yes."

Jordan looked for the signal that they'd nailed the trace.

"Where is Dr. Petrenko?" Taylor asked. "Is she okay?"

"You shut up. I am the one asking the questions."

Jordan honed in on the thick accent. Based on subtleties in pronunciation, she pegged the caller as Palestinian.

Ganani spoke softly into Jordan's ear. "He's from a village in the West Bank."

"Let me talk to her," Taylor said.

"She is fine, for now. You do what I tell you, and she will stay fine."

Jordan looked at the agent on the com tracker. They should have a location by now. The agent shook his head.

That meant the caller had to be using some type of GPS jammer, forcing the techs to triangulate the trace off of cell phone towers. Triangulation extended the trace time anywhere from two to five minutes to never. As the tech scrambled to pinpoint the caller's location, Jordan signaled Taylor to keep talking.

"I want to talk to her."

"I told you—"

"Listen, you let me talk to her or the deal's off."

Silence followed.

Taylor looked at Jordan, the anger in his eyes keeping concern at bay. Suddenly, Dr. Petrenko's voice came over the line—weak, but it was definitely her.

"Pazhalsta, pomogitse." Please, help me. Then Alena cried out and the Arab was back.

"Now you will do what I say?"

"I'm listening," Taylor said.

"Do you know the Mosque of Omar?"

"In Jerusalem?"

Ganani flipped over the map on the table.

"No, in Bethlehem."

Ganani pointed to a spot maybe five kilometers south and to the west of the Old City.

Jordan ticked through her memory banks, accessing what little she knew about Bethlehem. It was the site of the Church of the Nativity, the birthplace of Jesus, and administered jointly by the Roman Catholics, Greek Orthodox, and Armenian Apostolic authorities.

"Take a bus or taxi and go to Manger Square. Stand near the entrance to the Mosque of Omar. It's across the square from the church. Be there by two o'clock."

Jordan checked her watch. It was noon.

"How will I know you?" Taylor asked.

"You won't. I will know you."

Jordan glanced at the com tech. They still didn't have the trace. She signaled Taylor to keep talking.

"Let me speak to Alena again."

Silence.

"I need to ask her about my daughter."

The caller clicked off.

The judge slammed down the receiver. "Tell me you got that."

Jordan looked at the tech. He shook his head.

"We narrowed the location to somewhere in Jabel Mukaber," he said, pulling off his earphones. "Somewhere in Sheikh Sa'ad. That's as close as I could get."

Jordan looked for the town on the map. "Where is Sheikh Sa'ad? I don't see it marked."

"Here." Ganani pointed to a spot south of Jerusalem and east of Bethlehem. "It is in this section of Jabel Mukaber, now part of the West Bank. The security fence divides it from the rest of the city."

Jordan had heard of communities broken by the fence—family members separated, populations severed from the basic necessities of school, jobs, and medical care. Palestinians often referred to it as the "Annexation Fence," because it wandered off the Green Line, sectioning away large pieces of their agricultural land.

"Is the village accessible to Bethlehem?" she asked, picking up a pencil and circling the area on the map. "The checkpoint into Israel is marked 'foot traffic only.'"

"That's correct," Ganani said. "No cars can pass the Jabel Mukaber checkpoint. Cars pass here, at Al Sawahra Al Sharqia." She moved her finger on the map and pointed to an area within spitting distance of Jordan. "It's a terrible road, and the bridge is just fixed."

Jordan traced a finger along a small white line connecting Sheikh Sa'ad and Bethlehem. "What about this road?"

"It's nothing more than a deer path, mostly used for walking."

"But is it drivable?" Jordan asked.

"Maybe in a Jeep or a Humvee."

"The Forester is a four-wheel-drive vehicle." The room fell silent. Jordan looked at Ganani. "How far would it be from Bethlehem by car?"

"A few kilometers as the crow flies, but it could take hours based on the road conditions."

"Then why choose Bethlehem as the meeting place?"

"What difference does it make?" Taylor asked. "Let's roll. We're wasting time."

"The more we know about these guys the better," Jordan said. "We need to figure out how they're moving the doctor."

"Not through the checkpoint," Ganani said. "First, there's the matter of ID. Everyone must carry a card. Even if they forged a card that worked, all the doctor would have to do is call attention to herself in front of the guards."

Jordan knew that all Israelis and Palestinians over the age of sixteen carried identification. She had seen examples in the embassy. The Israeli ID card denoted Israeli citizenship categorized by religion—Israeli Jew, Israeli Arab, Israeli Christian. Blue cards denoted Palestinians of Jerusalem citizenship. Orange cards documented permanent residents of the occupied territories. By military law, Palestinians were not allowed to enter Israel without correct ID or an individual permit, and Israeli citizens were not allowed in certain Palestinian cities at all. So how had they gotten the doctor into Sheikh Sa'ad?

"The best chance for Alena is to do what we're told," Taylor said.

"The best chance for Alena is if we're prepared," Jordan said. "The fact they're holed up in Sheikh Sa'ad with difficult access to the exchange point suggests a personal connection to the town. They're planning to either bring her with them to Bethlehem or leave her in Sheikh Sa'ad for safekeeping. What happens if we have to follow them?"

"No one follows but me," Ganani said.

"I'm done here," Taylor said. "I'm going to check on Lucy before we leave." He pushed past Jordan and headed for Lucy's bedroom. Jordan moved over behind the com tech.

"Are you one-hundred percent sure of the location?"

"These are the cell towers that the call routed through." He tapped several points, causing ripples on the computer screen. "Based on the triangulation pattern, the man on the phone was here." He tapped the same spot on the map that Ganani had.

"What if we try an ownership check on the houses in the area?" Jordan said. "Check for known associates of Najm Tibi. Maybe we can narrow the search."

"Check for an Umar Haddid," said Ganani.

"The man from al-Ajami?" Jordan asked.

Ganani nodded.

Weizman had been right. She *had* come up with a name— one she had chosen not to share until now. "You might also check for the dead man, Mansoor Rahman," Jordan said, scribbling the names on a pad. "Any more names?"

Daugherty, who had been standing quietly in the kitchen, now spoke up. "That's in Area B, so there will be some Israeli settlers. I can check for Steven's associates."

Then Jordan thought of something else.

"Are there any checkpoints into Bethlehem crossable without documentation?" She figured it was doubtful, but they needed to consider everything.

"No," Ganani said.

The com tech disagreed. "There's one."

"Where?" Jordan moved back behind him.

He touched the screen at a spot near Bethlehem. "Beit Jala. It's a one-way entrance. Anyone can pass into Bethlehem there. Cars, taxis, and buses are waved through. There is no Palestinian check. But without proper ID, no one comes back."

"Which means your boys found themselves a route from Bethlehem to Sheikh Sa'ad." Daugherty nodded at Jordan, his lips pressed together in a thin line.

Ganani turned to Jordan, resting a hip on the edge of the table. "There is something you must know. Bethlehem is designated Area A, which means the city is controlled by the Palestinian Authority. Only the IDF can operate there, and even then, rarely."

"What about Shin Bet?"

"Our motto is 'Defends and Shall Not Be Seen.' Technically, we are allowed, but with this, we're dark."

"Meaning totally unsupported?"

"If something goes wrong and any of us are caught, we will not admit to being Shin Bet."

"What she's telling you, Jordan, is that you're on your own if this goes bad. Neither the Israelis nor the Americans can afford a political shitstorm right now."

"Hamas would love to make an example of us," Ganani said.

"Now is the time to rethink," Daugherty said. "Lines have been drawn in the sand, but you can still back out."

"I'm good," Jordan said.

Twenty minutes later, the team had come up with a plan. With no way of knowing who might be watching, Taylor would catch the 12:50 p.m. bus to Jerusalem and debark in front of the Yaffa Gate. He would then catch a number twenty-one bus to Bethlehem. Two team members would follow, ensuring that Taylor reached his destination and wasn't diverted along the route. Jordan and Ganani would go directly to Manger Square.

When Taylor was ready to go, Ganani handed him the USB drive. Daugherty cupped a hand on his shoulder. "Remember, Judge, you're there to deliver the drive. It's not your job to be heroic. Leave that to the agents."

"I'll do whatever it takes to save Alena."

"Just do what you're told," Jordan said. "Go to the mosque and give them the information. But no matter what they say, do not leave or go anywhere with them. We don't want to end up with two captives instead of one."

"What if they don't have Alena?"

"Then I'll find her," Ganani said. "Let's go."

Taylor adjusted his earpiece. "You don't inspire a lot of confidence."

Ganani glared at him. "That's because this is dangerous for everyone."

"I won't leave there without Alena."

Jordan stepped in between them.

"Getting her back is what it's all about, Taylor." She felt guilty as soon as the words left her mouth. She knew as well as anyone that this wasn't about bringing Alena Petrenko home. This was about identifying and destroying a terrorist cell. At best, Alena was a bonus. At worst, she was expendable.

Chapter 37

anani insisted on driving, and Jordan didn't argue. The Shin
Bet agent knew the roads to Bethlehem, and Jordan wanted
the time to bring herself up to speed on their destination. And, as
much as she hated to admit it, Jordan needed her as an ally.

Unfortunately, Ganani drove fast and jerky, yanking the wheel
sharply at the start of each turn. The constant motion made it hard
for Jordan to read. To subdue her queasiness, she alternated between
watching the scenery and plowing through the State Department
file on Israel that Daugherty had handed her on the way out the
door—the briefing file she should have received the day she arrived.

The landscape looked just as described. Alpine vegetation
blanketed the countryside. Intermittent settlements of white limestone and concrete terraced the hardscrabble hillsides between Tel
Aviv and Jerusalem. The settlements, nestled among the trees and
rocks, created miniature strongholds. The minimalist construc-
tion suited the militaristic society.

Near what she estimated to be the halfway mark, she spotted a
small fortress perched on a hillside covered in pines.

"Is that Latrun?" she asked. If so, the distance to Jerusalem
was less than she had thought.

"Yes." Ganani took a curve at high speed, causing Jordan to
reach for the chicken bar. "What do you know of Latrun?"

"Only what I've read," Jordan said. "Very little."

"It's a very historic place. It has been the site of many battles going back to biblical times. Its location gave it strategic value. It's where Joshua prayed for God to make the sun stand still so he could finish defeating the Amorites."

The Shin Bet agent knew her history. Jordan knew few specifics about Israel's ancient past. The reading she'd done covered mainly the current diplomatic events, the U.S. embassy's history, and the background information on some embassy personnel. Her rudimentary knowledge of the country's past and its religious sites came from high school and college history classes.

She flipped through the pages of the file to the section on Bethlehem, stopping at a picture of Manger Square. The Church of the Nativity stood at one end, the Mosque of Omar at the other. Between them stretched a large, paved square. The main entrance to the church, the Door of Humility, was small and squat, forcing even short people to stoop. The building looked old, uneven, and plain. Another picture showed two bell towers. The caption indicated they were part of the Armenian monastery and not the church.

"What can you tell me about Bethlehem?" Jordan asked.

"It's in Palestine. In 2002, during Operation Defensive Shield, when we were rounding up militants, the Palestinians laid siege on the city. Dozens of wanted militants barricaded themselves inside the church for thirty-nine days."

Jordan remembered watching the drama unfold on national television: the newsreels of Israeli tanks in Manger Square, the guns pointed at the Door of Humility. Eight Palestinians died from sniper fire, one Armenian monk was injured, and seventy-seven thousand dollars' worth of damage was done to the church. The remaining militants were exiled—either to Gaza or to Europe.

"If my memory serves," Jordan said, "the pope wasn't too happy."

"No, he wasn't."

Jordan understood the Israelis' desire to round up the militants. They were behind the series of suicide bombings that had killed hundreds of Israeli citizens. What she didn't tell Ganani was that she also empathized with the Palestinians. The issues weren't so cut-and-dried. On the surface, the conflict was about land ownership and possession being nine-tenths of the law. But it seemed more complicated than that.

"Are you reading or skimming that?"

Jordan skimmed through the last few pages of the section. "Reading."

Ganani nodded. "They say you're a genius."

"Who's 'they'?" Jordan knew she was smart, but she didn't think of herself as exceptional.

"You graduated top of your class. You speak four or five languages."

"Where did you get that? From the Shin Bet dossier on 'Raisa Jordan'?"

"Is it true?"

"I speak five languages fluently," Jordan said, qualifying her answer.

Ganani flashed a thin smile. "I'm sure you've done your own checking on me."

"'I like to know who I'm working with,'" Jordan said, quoting a line from *The Peacemaker*.

Ganani pointed to the file in Jordan's hands. "What did you learn about Bethlehem?"

"Not much of importance for this trip. The population is 25,266 per the 2007 census report. The name means 'house of bread' in Hebrew and 'house of meat' in Arabic. The traditional art is mother-of-pearl carvings."

"You're right. Useless." Ganani reached between her seat and console and pulled out a small, spiral-bound booklet. "This is more technical information on our destination. You may learn something worthwhile to know."

Jordan skimmed the booklet. It was a biased accounting of the occupied territories but gave a thorough overview of the current tensions in the area. Checking the index, she flipped to the section on Bethlehem. When she was done, she read the section on Sheikh Sa'ad.

A sudden shift in Ganani's driving signaled Jordan to look up.

"We are approaching the three hundred checkpoint to Bethlehem." Ganani took the book and put it away.

The checkpoint consisted of one manned guard station serving both traffic lanes. Red-and-white-striped bar gates blocked both the north- and southbound sides of the road. To the east and west, thirty-foot fences stretched away, one capped by a manned observation tower. The layout reminded Jordan of a maximum-security prison entrance, with one major difference—the cage-like pedestrian passageways stretching along the barrier wall for those coming and going on foot.

Beyond the wall, the city of Bethlehem capped a hillside rising in the distance. Buildings bunched together on its peak resembled a woven *kippah* perched on a man's head. Constructed of local stone, the buildings shone golden in the afternoon sun.

Ganani pulled into the vehicle queue. Checkpoint guards checked the IDs and travel papers for the car ahead. Then the bar swung up and down, and it was their turn. Ganani eased the car forward.

"*Dai*," stop. An Israeli soldier stepped up to the window.

Ganani flashed her credentials. Jordan reached for her passport and embassy ID, but the soldier stepped back and waved them through.

Ganani kept watch in her rearview mirror. "We will be there in a few minutes. Do you know the layout of Manger Square?"

"From pictures and tourist maps."

"The more in sync we are, the better our chance of saving the doctor and keeping the judge safe."

Jordan smiled. Ganani was using her own logic against her.

"Point taken," she said. "The main square is shaped like a large rectangle, with a smaller adjacent square to the southeast. The plaza is designated for pedestrians only, with a large number of benches and fountains throughout. There are numerous cafés, restaurants, and souvenir shops around the perimeter, with the town hall and tourist information offices close to the mosque."

"We can expect security," Ganani said. "Mostly at the entrances to the church. There will be a few Palestinian Authority guards, and maybe a few Bethlehem police officers. If they get suspicious, you can never know what they will do."

"They're manageable."

Ganani glanced sideways. "How do you think we should proceed?"

"I'm just along for the ride, remember?" Jordan's authority ended before they had crossed through the checkpoint.

"Taylor is your man."

Jordan decided this was Ganani's way of shedding the blame if something went wrong.

"Fine," she said. "Park as close to the mosque as you can, but somewhere with an easy exit. We'll find a bench with a direct line of sight to the building and pretend we're friends visiting the square. The *hijabs* should protect our identities. Do you speak Arabic?"

"Yes."

"Good."

"How will you get the judge and Petrenko away from the square?"

Jordan figured now was not the time to tell her that her plan was to stick with Ganani and send Taylor and Alena with the other agents.

"According to the map, the square has multiple exits," Jordan said. "We're coming in on Manger Road, which turns into Shepard, right?" Jordan looked to Ganani for confirmation. The multiple names for every road made being specific harder.

Ganani nodded.

"Paul VI comes in on the north side," Jordan said. "Milk Grotto runs east along the south side. Anatren, which becomes Kanah, runs south of the adjacent square. There are others, but those are the major routes. We'll use whichever works best to get us out of the area fast."

"You remembered all that from the file?"

"No, I studied the map before we left."

Ganani grinned. "Still, that's a very good memory."

"Not bad, though it works better for some things than others."

"We're here." Ganani slowed as they neared the main bus station to the north of the square. A group of Western tourists walking half-on, half-off the sidewalk slowed their progress.

Jordan spotted their turn coming up. "Take a right at the next street."

Ganani flipped on her turn signal and juiced the gas. She beat the tourists to the intersection but nearly sideswiped a white BMW at the curb, drawing an obscene gesture from the driver. Jordan averted her gaze and lifted her hand to cover her face. Even with the *hijabs*, she didn't want to take any chances that someone might recognize them later.

"It's possible to get on the roof," Ganani said.

"That leaves us too far from Taylor. We need to stay on the ground and stay close." Jordan couldn't shake the feeling that the men they were dealing with had only one agenda in mind—get the USB drive and go. Witnesses were a liability.

Ganani's response was to tighten her hands on the wheel.

"You do what you want," Jordan said, trying to relieve the tension. "I'm staying on the ground."

"I'll go with you."

Jordan fiddled with the listening device in her ear. "Time to go live."

She pressed the button on the communication transmitter hooked near her waist and resisted the urge to dip her chin and speak directly into the dot microphone attached to the inside of her tee. "Com, are you there?"

"Here." The tech's voice blasted through the receiver. Jordan quickly adjusted the volume on the transmitter.

"What's Taylor's time of arrival?"

"He's approaching the Beit Jala checkpoint."

"Are there eyes on him?"

"Negative. He is in the twenty-one bus, ahead of the car. He will be at the station in five minutes. Gidon Lotner is monitoring his frequency."

Jordan turned to Ganani. "What's Detective Lotner doing on this job?"

"He and Weizman both," Ganani said. "Two of our men were called off because of a bombing in Gaza. We're short-staffed, and the detectives were willing to help."

"When did this happen?"

"We agreed on the swap while you were changing."

"And you didn't think to mention it?" Jordan's bullshit meter was on high alert. This was feeling more and more like a setup to her.

"I didn't think it mattered."

She would ask more questions later. For now, she refocused her attention on the job.

Jordan heard static, and then com broke through. "Are you in position?"

"Almost," she answered.

Jordan wondered how Taylor was holding up. He was on edge, determined to do whatever it took to get Alena Petrenko back. He had been fitted with a static mike, tuned to a different frequency than the one on which they were talking. It transmitted continually, avoiding the need for him to cue the transmitter hidden under his shirt collar. The idea was to make it more difficult for the kidnappers to detect the com device. It also meant Taylor couldn't manipulate the situation and prevent them from hearing everything the kidnappers said in the event the men arrived without Petrenko. It made him angry at first, being left out of the loop, but the second channel offered the agents more options. And once the team switched to his frequency, Taylor would hear everything that they said, too.

"Com, we need a signal for switching to a private channel," she said.

"Does the judge speak Hebrew?"

"Not much." At least not much she was aware of.

"Then let's use the code word *tsara*." Trouble.

"I'm switching over to Taylor now."

Jordan turned the dial on the transmitter and was instantly assaulted by the chatter of tourists through Taylor's com device. Many spoke English. They all seemed excited to be nearing their destination. Lotner's voice cut through, updating Taylor on everyone's whereabouts.

As Jordan listened to his monotone, she calculated the distance from the bus stop to the entrance of Manger Square. Three, maybe four blocks—approximately one-third of a mile. The cars in front of them moved forward, and a Palestinian boy of about nine signaled Ganani to pull the car into the next vacant parking spot. The Shin Bet agent shook her head and pointed to a spot on the curb nearer the exit. They weren't likely to be boxed in there.

The boy ushered them into the space. Ganani asked him to point to the nearest public bathrooms and then tipped him well.

Reaching across Jordan, she pulled a blue *hijab* out of the glove box. "Let's start there."

Keeping her head down, Jordan pulled her scarf over her head and followed Ganani across the square. Without her head covered, she would draw attention. She didn't want anyone remembering her.

At the tourist information office, she noted the clerk seated inside behind a window pasted with flyers of events, the prayer schedule for the mosque, and the hours of access to the Church of the Nativity. Scooting past, she ducked into the restroom. Once inside the bathroom stall, she straightened her black *hijab*, tucking in the stray tendrils of hair curling around her face.

"Ready?" Ganani asked.

"Ready." Jordan scanned the square as they exited the restroom and made their way slowly toward the mosque. She could see why the kidnappers had chosen the square. It teemed with people. Young boys kicked soccer balls around the fountains and benches while tourists of all ethnicities queued up in front of the Door of Humility or window-shopped the jewelry and tchotchke stores. Young Arabs, men in Western clothing, and women wearing *hijabs* strolled along the marble pavers.

"Let's sit here," Jordan said, gesturing toward a bench about fifty feet from the front steps of the mosque. She spoke in Arabic so anyone overhearing them would think they were local.

Ganani followed Jordan's lead. "I agree. This gives us a very good view."

Scoping out the loiterers, Jordan didn't see anyone she recognized. "I think we beat them to the meeting place."

"Will you recognize them?" Ganani asked.

"I'll recognize Alena. And if the men who are holding her are the same ones involved in the car chase, I got a decent look at two of them. I'm more concerned they might recognize me."

"Keep your head down and you will be fine," Ganani said. Through the earbud, Jordan heard the bus driver announcing the stop at Manger Square. Tires squealed, air brakes hissed, and then came the chatter of passengers disembarking. She pushed the transmitter button to raise Lotner on the radio, when a young couple settled onto a facing bench. He wore jeans and a T-shirt, and like Jordan and Ganani, the woman wore a *hijab*. Probably a local couple taking a late lunch break, but Jordan didn't want to take chances.

Ganani noticed them, too, and pointed at the Church of the Nativity and offered commentary on the tourists in line. Jordan feigned interest.

The young couple displayed no special awareness of them, but there was still a real danger of exposure. Jordan engaged in Ganani's patter but kept an eye on the crowd filtering into the square. No familiar faces leapt out. Then the radio squawked in Jordan's ear, and Weizman's voice cut through. "Gidon and I have circled around to enter the square from the east. The judge will arrive from the west."

Jordan turned away from the couple and answered. "We are in position near the fountain across from the mosque."

Turning back, Jordan found the local girl watching her with mild curiosity.

Ganani leaned toward Jordan and said, "We may have to move."

The radio clicked back to the noise of the tourists and Jordan studied the crowd pushing into Manger Square. Ganani tapped her hand, a look of concern on her face. The young couple appeared to be watching them more intently.

"It seems our friend is running late," Jordan said out loud, hoping to deflect suspicion. "They have done a wonderful job with the square renovation."

Ganani and Jordan again practiced the idle chatter of friendship, talking about how much they liked the pedestrian walkway that had replaced the roadway and parking lot, the marble slabs that now paved the way from the Mosque of Omar to the Church of the Nativity, the rows of trees that provided shade for hand-hewn benches, and the water that spewed from fountains made of solid cubic stones. Eventually, the couple grew bored and their attention shifted.

Jordan kept her guard up, tracking the crowd in her peripheral vision. Only the Western tourists wore shorts, so she tossed them from the mix. Most of the other men, regardless of ethnicity, were similarly dressed, wearing jeans or khakis, T-shirts, and ball caps. A few wore *tazcats*—the predecessor of the skull cap. Fewer still wore *keffiyehs*, head scarfs, and not just the checkered ones Arafat made popular. Some were made of contemporary cloth. One or two older men wore *jallabiyehs*, flowing robes perfect for concealing a weapon.

Most of the Western women wore skintight jeans or leggings and short-sleeved tees with scarves at the ready around their necks. By comparison, Jordan's outfit looked almost conservative. The Arab women added *hijabs*, with a few wearing *jilbābs*, the large baggy overgarments that covered everything.

Finally, Jordan spotted the judge hugging the storefronts on the far west side, making his way toward the mosque. He moved quickly and then stopped halfway to scan the square.

What the hell was he doing? Looking for them?

Jordan wondered if she dared communicate with Taylor. She would have to speak in English. The young couple seemed thoroughly engrossed in each other, so she pushed the transmitter button. "Keep moving."

Ganani relayed Taylor's location to the rest of the team. "Look at the Maish tree in front of the olive wood store. It is still loaded with fruit."

Taylor looked up. If he wasn't aware he had been spotted before, he knew it now.

The couple across from them shifted in their seats, drawing Jordan's attention. They remained engrossed in each other but seemed more aware of their surroundings again. The noise rose and fell around them. Jordan spoke to Ganani in Arabic about the fountains and their special marble with the blue veins.

Lotner's voice cut through in English. "Everyone is in place. Move into position."

Taylor nodded almost imperceptibly.

"Do you know what causes the veins in the marble?" Ganani asked in Arabic, and Jordan wondered if she had missed something. The couple didn't seem to be paying them any heed.

"Graphite." Jordan tried picking up on whatever it was Ganani had seen. "The color variations of marble are caused by impurities in the soil—things like clay, silt, sand, iron oxides or chert, fossils from ancient times—working their way into the limestone. The variations depend on where the marble is mined."

"You remember that from the guide books?"

"No. Freshman year geology."

"What else do you remember?" Ganani asked.

"Nothing."

Taylor was now moving toward them. Jordan's focus was so intent all sound faded away until she heard only the slap of his shoes against the marble. His eyes flickered in their direction. Neither Jordan nor Ganani acknowledged him.

Jordan noticed his breath kept time with his footsteps. She felt the rustle of a breeze as he passed, heard the tinkling of the fountain, and smelled the tang of citrus and spice. Taylor's cologne or someone's cooking? She couldn't be sure.

Shifting in her seat, she watched from the corner of her eye as he climbed the steps to the mosque. He stopped at the top of the short flight of stairs and turned in a tight circle, his head held high, his gaze sweeping the square.

Weizman and Lotner entered the square to his right, Weizman moving straight forward while Lotner veered off and settled into the shadows of the police station.

Taylor's voice rose above the noise of the square. "Alena!"

Off to his left, two men half-carried Dr. Petrenko between them.

"Keep your voice down!" said the man nearest to Taylor. Short, with a stocky build and thick head of black hair, he looked like one of a dozen Palestinian men in the square. He wore khaki pants, a Banksy "Get Out While You Can" T-shirt, and Nike tennis shoes. He dropped Alena's arm and positioned himself between the mosque and the exit.

He glanced around. "Did you come alone?"

Jordan heard him clearly through Taylor's com. His was the voice of the man on the phone.

Taylor ignored him and moved toward the doctor. "Alena, are you okay?"

The man stepped sideways, blocking his route. "I asked you a question."

Taylor looked down on the man. "What have you done to her?"

"Answer my question. Did you bring the USB drive?"

"Answer him, Taylor," Jordan whispered, moving to the edge of her seat. The best way to get them to release Petrenko was to make the trade.

Ganani stirred beside her.

Jordan kept her eyes on Taylor and waited for him to speak. Whatever happened now, right here, determined all their fates.

"I came alone," Taylor said.

Hearing the anger in his voice, Jordan could only imagine the control it took for him to keep himself in check.

"Do you have the drive?"

"Right here." Sunlight flashed off the silver in his hand. "Let her go and it's all yours."

For her part, Alena remained unresponsive. She stood on her own two feet, but her head wobbled on her neck and her eyes appeared heavy. She had to be drugged.

"Ganani." Jordan turned, wanting the agent to flank the kidnappers, but the Shin Bet agent had disappeared. A quick scan of the square only turned up the young couple making their way toward a clump of Palestinian Authority security officers standing near the Door of Humility.

Jordan pushed the transmitter button. "*Tsara*."

She repeated the code and then moved the dial on her transmitter one click and waited for someone to respond.

Nothing.

She tried again.

Still nothing. She was on her own, and she needed to get closer.

Pulling a brochure out of her pocket, Jordan pretended to study the text, moving forward until she stood parallel to the doctor and the Palestinian who gripped her arm. He was taller, thinner, and more agitated than his accomplice. A look of paranoia distorted his face, and his eyes flitted in all directions. He gripped Alena's elbow with one hand, the other buried deep in his pocket.

She depressed the transmitter button and tried raising the com tech again. This time, an answering squawk nipped her ear.

"Where is Detective Weizman?"

"At the northeast corner of the mosque."

Jordan studied the building's façade until she found his form silhouetted by sunlight.

"Got him. Now track down Agent Ganani."

"We thought she was with you."

Was being the operative word. "I turned around and she was gone."

"Is it possible she went to high ground?" came the tech's response.

Jordan scanned the rooftops, catching the flicker of a shadow along the edge of the monastery roof. She watched for a few seconds, then, seeing nothing more, allowed her gaze to wander back to the square. The young couple from the bench had reached the Palestinian officers. They gestured in the direction of the mosque, and two of the policeman broke ranks.

Jordan depressed the transmitter button. "We're about to have unwanted company—my eight o'clock. Notify the team."

"Consider it done," said the tech.

Jordan switched the com back to Taylor's channel.

"Here." Taylor held out the drive but jerked it back when the man in the Banksy T-shirt reached for it. "Have your man sit her on the bench and walk away."

The short man gestured to the taller one, who shuffled Alena to the bench, dumped her unceremoniously, and stepped a few feet back.

Taylor held out the drive. The short man snatched it out of his hand and the two kidnappers moved swiftly across the marble toward the west-side exit. Taylor raced toward Petrenko.

She slumped sideways before he reached her, as a shot rang out in the square.

Chaos erupted. Some people dropped to the ground; others ran. Everywhere people were screaming. Jordan pulled her gun from under her skirt and bolted for Taylor and Alena.

He had dropped to his knees on the marble stones, pulling Alena with him, just before a second shot drilled a divot into the side of the mosque.

"Stay down!" Jordan helped Taylor drag Alena behind a large, square planter that was home to a tall palm tree. He knelt beside the doctor, his hands checking for a pulse. She lay on the stone, limp, with her hands flopped open and her eyes rolled up in her head.

Jordan took a quick inventory. Two shots fired, two shots missed, both of them aimed at Alena Petrenko. Someone wanted the doctor dead.

Chapter 38

Jordan tried scanning the rooftops.

Another shot was fired, chipping the top of the planter where Alena's head had been just seconds before. The trajectory told Jordan the shot was taken from one of the buildings of the Church of the Nativity.

"*Tawaqqafa!*" Cease! Stop! The police officers were closing in, guns drawn. A fourth shot ricocheted off the stones, forcing them to veer away.

Weizman materialized beside Jordan. "Come on!" he yelled. "Let's go!"

He grabbed Taylor's arm and stood up. The fifth shot fired caught Weizman in the back of the head, snapping his head back then flinging him forward to the ground. Jordan was beside him in seconds, rolling him over. His eyes were open, fixed, and a large exit wound gaped from the middle of his forehead.

"Jordan!" Taylor shook her arm, snapping her out of her stupor. "He's gone."

As an agent, she had seen dead people before, but she'd never seen anyone die. One moment he was there, telling her what she should do. The next moment he was gone. And they would all be joining him soon if she didn't pull it together.

"What about Alena?" she asked.

"She's still alive. We have to get out of here."

"Grab her arm." Jordan hooked her elbow under one of Alena's armpits. Taylor did the same. "Go for the road on the count of three. One . . . two . . ." On three, Jordan started running, firing her weapon into the air at the same time. The crowd panicked. She and Taylor bolted toward Paul VI, the street to the north of the mosque, dragging Petrenko with them. Behind them, the PAS officers scattered, the crowd hindering their forward progress. It opened a window.

"Keep moving!" Jordan ordered.

An officer broke free of the mob. "*Tawaqqafa!*"

"Go, go!" she yelled.

They ducked around the corner of the mosque and ran along the road. Alena started coming around and struggled against them.

"Where to?" Taylor asked, plowing their way through a crush of men headed to the square to see what the commotion was all about. Others behind them followed in their wake.

"Just keep moving."

Another shot rang out from Manger Square. Another surge of panic stirred the crowd. Ganani, Lotner, or a random shooter? All that mattered was that the chaos slowed down the officers behind them.

If Jordan remembered correctly, Paul VI was the main north-south artery into Bethlehem. The road intersected with Derech Hevron, skirted Rachel's Tomb, and then joined with Sderot Manger. The three hundred checkpoint lay just beyond. They could take one of the roads that branched off and try to find refuge in one of the churches, but it could also make them easy to track.

"Turn into the *souq*!" Jordan yelled. "Into the market!" It was their best chance, and hopefully it was packed with tourists at this time of day. "One more block, on the left."

The Bethlehem *souq* filled a small square between two main roads, Paul VI and Milk Grotto. Small souvenir shops in tented stalls created a maze where vendors hawked gold jewelry, olive wood carvings, handmade soap, and beautiful embroidery. For the tourist wanting a bargain, the *souq* was the place to go.

Jordan moved into the lead as they entered the market and slowed the pace as they wound deeper into the square. Reholstering her gun, she called com on the radio again.

"Have you found Ganani or Lotner?"

Neither of them had checked in.

Jordan switched channels back, this time hearing the chaos of the square and Taylor's hard breathing through the open com.

The people in the market seemed oblivious to what was going on up the street. The buildings surrounding the smaller square muffled the sound of street traffic and must have blocked out the gunfire, too.

Reaching the center of the square, Jordan pulled up short in front of a small shop selling T-shirts.

"Do you have any money?" she asked Taylor.

He dug in his pockets and came up with one hundred shekels. Jordan snatched them out of his hand.

"Keep moving," she said. "Take Alena and find a bench somewhere along the south wall. Wait for me there."

Whatever the kidnappers had given the doctor seemed to be wearing off. She nodded at Jordan's instructions. Taylor draped her arm around his shoulders, wrapped his arm around her back and propelled her forward into the marketplace.

Jordan rummaged through the selection of T-shirts, grabbing a blue one for herself and a bright red one for the doctor.

"May I help you?" asked the shopkeeper.

Jordan asked him how much.

"Eighty shekels."

Jordan paid him and then waited for him to pick up another customer before slipping between a row of embroidered *jilbābs* and stripping the *hijab* from her head. Shaking out her hair, she pulled off Ganani's black tee and wriggled into the T-shirt stamped "Bethlehem: The Holy Land," with a wreathed circle depicting the four major holy sites of the city on the front. Tying the *hijab* around her waist, she moved through the stall and exited on the far side. The shopkeeper spotted her leaving and pointed to the red T-shirt in her hand.

"Forty shekels."

"I've already paid," she said, starting to walk away.

The shopkeeper raised his voice. "Forty shekels."

"I told you—" she stopped herself short, realizing she was creating a scene. Digging in her pocket produced the change from Taylor's hundred. "All I have are twenty. Will you take twenty shekels?"

"No. Forty shekels."

"I need the T-shirt." She held out the money. He grabbed for the shirt.

"Is something wrong here?" said a voice. Jordan turned to find a Bethlehem policeman stepping in to referee.

"I already paid for this shirt once," she said. "Now he wants me to pay him again."

The shopkeeper spoke in Arabic. He told the policemen that she was trying to steal the shirt and had offered him twenty shekels.

"Why would you offer to pay him again if you had already paid?" The policeman narrowed his eyes at her. "Do you have a receipt?"

"No, he didn't give me one." Jordan forced herself to stay calm. He clearly hadn't come from the square, but she couldn't afford for the situation to escalate. Taylor and Alena were waiting for her, and then there was the matter of her gun.

"Forget it." Jordan tossed the red shirt back onto the pile of T-shirts and started to walk away.

The shopkeeper let loose with another tirade about how the shirt was damaged, dirty now, and how she had to pay.

"Wait!" the policeman ordered.

Jordan stopped, feeling the awkward press of the leather holster against her thigh. Turning, she spotted a PAS officer entering the square, causing a whisper about a shooting in the square to move through the market like wind rustling through the leaves of a copse.

"If you don't have the money, I must assume you planned on stealing the shirt. You will need to come with me." The policeman reached for her arm.

They had passed the moment of reasoning, and Jordan was debating what to do next—run for it or pull her gun—when Taylor's voice boomed in her ear.

"There you are. What's taking so long?"

Jordan pointed at the shopkeeper. "This man is accusing me of trying to steal a shirt."

Taylor stepped forward, looming over the shopkeeper. "You know that's not true. She asked me for the money while you were standing right there. I watched her hand it to you. Are you trying to cheat your customers, the tourists who visit here?"

"No, no." The shopkeeper waved his hands wildly. "I remember now." He picked up the shirt and shoved it into Jordan's hands. "Take it. Just take it and go."

When the policeman turned to argue with the shopkeeper, Jordan and Taylor ducked away. They cut over two aisles and then doubled back to where Taylor had left Alena sitting on a bench in the shade.

"Thank you for helping me back there," Jordan said.

"It was a good thing I could hear what was going on." He tapped his earbud.

Jordan sat down on the bench next to the doctor. "How are you feeling?"

"Sick. Weak," said Alena. "But I'm better than I was."

Taylor, who'd been keeping watch, suddenly moved over beside them. "There are PAS officers moving through the crowd. We need to move."

Jordan handed Dr. Petrenko the red T-shirt. "Put this on." Standing, she pulled Taylor aside. "We need to separate."

"What do you mean?"

"I'm the one they're looking for," Jordan said. "Hopefully, they won't recognize me. They saw three of us come in here. I want you and Alena to go out the back. Pretend you're an American couple and your wife is sick. Take a cab. I'll meet you back at the bus station in ten minutes."

"Wait. What are you going to do?"

"I'll head back the way we came in and hope I don't run into that policeman again."

A rumble traveled through the crowd behind them, and Jordan snapped her head around. "That's our cue. Go. Keep the radio on."

Taylor helped Alena to her feet, and the two of them disappeared into the throng of tourists. Once Jordan could no longer see her red shirt or Taylor's head above the crowd, she moved to the far aisle and walked back west along the stalls. Within moments, the PAS officers appeared.

"*Imshy,*" go, ordered the man in charge. The captain signaled his men to fan out and then stood on his toes and looked over the heads of the tourists. His gaze tripped as it flitted over Jordan. She looked down, feeling his eyes linger before moving past.

"They are not here," he said, speaking into his radio in Arabic. "We've lost them. You are sure no one has fled out the back?"

The answer was no, and Jordan didn't eavesdrop on the rest of the conversation. Whomever he spoke to had not apprehended Taylor and Alena.

Moving quickly toward the street, she spotted a different officer guarding the entrance to the *souq*. Whoever had coined the phrase "the best defense is a good offense" had it right. It was time to engage the enemy. Jordan approached the officer.

"Which way to Manger Square?" She spoke loudly in English. He grimaced and then stepped to the side and pointed up the street that she and Taylor had carried Petrenko down earlier.

"However, the square is closed," said the officer. "There has been trouble there. You must go around."

"What kind of trouble?"

"Nevermind that."

"I need to catch a bus."

He waffled on his position and then pointed back toward the mosque. "There is an alleyway to the left, just beyond the entrance to the square. You may go that way."

She murmured a thank you and slithered past him, swishing her hips slightly as she moved away.

Reaching the entrance of the square, Jordan slowed. A black body bag lay on the ground where Weizman's body had been, with one or two small cones marking nearby areas on the ground. A small contingent of officers huddled around, arguing about the trajectory of the fatal shot.

One of the policemen pointed toward the upper floors of the Armenian monastery.

"Hey." Another of the Palestinians had spotted her. "Move along. This is police business."

"Sorry," Jordan said, turning away.

"Stupid American."

Jordan took a last look at the bag. It could have been any one of them lying there. The gunman had appeared to be targeting Alena Petrenko. The way Weizman stood up, he must have thought so, too. The shot had caught him in his third eye. It was no mistake. Someone had wanted him dead, same as Alena. The question was, who?

Chapter 39

It took Jordan close to five minutes to reach the bus station. She had called Daugherty en route and brought him up to speed. He informed her that until a new foreign police liaison was assigned, he was ordering all DSS operations and investigations to be stopped. He assured her that the Marines would provide protection for the judge and Lucy until arrangements could be made for a new safe house location. She was to report to his office immediately upon her return.

She asked what would happen to Weizman's body. Daugherty didn't know.

By the time Jordan reached the car, only Ganani remained, seated in the driver's seat.

"Lotner showed up a few minutes ago," Ganani said as Jordan climbed into the passenger seat. "He had been trapped on the other side of the square after the shooting. He has taken Taylor and Petrenko and headed for the three hundred checkpoint."

Jordan hoped they would beat the BOLO for "persons of interest" that was likely already issued. "How was he doing?"

"Lotner?" Ganani looked over. "He was angry, but he was capable of doing his job."

Jordan hit the com transmitter one more time. "Let us know when Lotner crosses the border."

The silence stretched as they waited for confirmation. The heat inside the car pressed down. Even Ganani looked wilted. Jordan rolled down the window and instantly regretted doing so. The smell of bus exhaust and the noise from the busy terminal assaulted her senses.

"What happens now?" she asked.

"I go after the kidnappers." Ganani turned the key and fired up the vehicle.

"I meant in regards to Noah Weizman's body and what happened in the square." Jordan still entertained the theory that the detective was a possible target. She watched Ganani's reactions closely. The Shin Bet agent hadn't divulged her location during the rescue. For all Jordan knew, Ganani had been at the other end of the gun.

"Brodsky has arranged for an IDF patrol to collect the body, and he's done his best to shut down all communication avenues."

"Meaning what?"

"Meaning the officials won't be giving out any details. We can't stop the underground chatter, but we can slow down the dissemination of information." Ganani reached over and flipped on the air conditioning.

When the cool air hit her face, Jordan rolled up her window. The changes at the embassy would be more direct.

The com crackled and Lotner's voice signaled an end to the mission. "We've cleared the checkpoint. I will drop my passengers off at the Dizengoff Apartments in approximately forty minutes."

The com went dead and Jordan pulled the receiver from her ear. "What's next here?"

"You take the bus and go back," Ganani said.

"No. I'm staying with you."

"Somehow I knew you would say that." Ganani shoved her smartphone into Jordan's hands. "Then be useful. Navigate. The green dot on the screen is where the kidnappers are."

Jordan blew up the map on the screen to find the best route connecting them to the road the two men had taken—the white route to Sheikh Sa'ad.

"It's not much of a road."

Ganani pointed to a yellow roadway marked on the map. "We will take the road toward Ubeidiya. The road to Sheikh Sa'ad branches off here. We will go past and make a quick stop in Bayt Sahur before doubling back."

Jordan's thoughts were still back at the square. "Who do you think was shooting?"

"Are you wondering if it was me?"

"The thought crossed my mind, but I couldn't figure out a motive."

"Well, it wasn't," Ganani said, pulling the car into traffic. "I went to get in front of those involved in the hostage exchange, just in case they didn't release Dr. Petrenko and tried to escape. Maybe one of the other men came with them, and killing her was part of the plan."

Jordan didn't buy the idea. The kidnappers wouldn't have. "Turn here."

She concentrated on navigating until they hit the outskirts of Bethlehem. There the road opened up, making conversation more possible.

"What I can't figure out is who would want both Alena and Weizman dead," Jordan said. "Who gains from both deaths?"

"Why are you so sure that it wasn't a coincidence?"

Jordan detailed the cluster of shots aimed at Alena and the single shot that had dropped the detective. If she knew secrets about Ilya Brodsky, secrets like the ones she knew about Jordan's father, Brodsky might have wanted her dead. But what did he gain by facilitating Weizman's execution?

"Are you paying attention?" Ganani asked, slowing as she approached a curvy set of highways. "We are near where the road to Sheikh Sa'ad turns off."

Jordan watched for the road, marked by a faint, dashed, white line on the map. It was the only one between where they were and where they were headed. When they passed, it looked like a sheep trail at best. "We're going to need a different car."

"That's why we're stopping in the next town. I have already made arrangements."

Ganani must have made them before leaving Tel Aviv, thought Jordan, knowing all along that this was how it would end.

A few meters later, at the edge of Bayt Sahur, Ganani swung left into a small, middle-class neighborhood. She swerved around a group of young boys playing soccer in the street. Jordan braced against the door, holding herself in her seat.

One of the boys cursed, driving the ball into the passenger-side door. Ganani glared into the rearview mirror and cursed back.

Jordan grinned. "It might be the Israeli license plate or the fact you're a woman driving. Or maybe it's because you're a scary driver."

Ganani refused the bait. "Do you still have your *hijab*?"

Jordan pointed to the cloth knotted around her waist.

"Put it on, and take off the sticky T-shirt."

Jordan looked down at her tourist-shop acquisition. "I think you're looking for the word 'tacky.'"

"Whatever." Ganani slowed as she reached a town center where the traffic grew heavy. Skirting the main square, she turned off to the east and wound slowly through one of the neighborhoods. "Where we're going, it would be wise for us to appear Palestinian."

"We might need different license plates."

Ganani glared. Jordan wasn't going to argue. She gestured at her shirt. "I left your T-shirt in the market. This is all I have."

"You owe me a shirt." Ganani reached into the back seat, grabbed another black top off of the seat and pitched it at Jordan. She wriggled out of the tourist tee, and pulled on the new top.

"Explain something to me, will you, Ganani?" Jordan said. "Why are two women, traveling alone, taking the risk of driving cross-country through the desert? Why not just go through the checkpoints? We could have been in Sheikh Sa'ad by now, waiting to intercept them when they arrive."

"What makes you think they would show themselves if we'd done that? The Palestinians are crafty people. They will have someone watching the gate. It's my hope they don't have someone watching the road."

"What happens after we find them?" No matter how well trained, the two of them would have difficulty staging an attack in the middle of a known terrorist hotspot.

"We'll follow them back to whoever they're working for."

"Abdul Aleem Zuabi," Jordan said.

"That's what I believe."

"And what if they don't lead us to where you want to go?"

"We may be forced to neutralize them."

Ganani's matter-of-factness and her euphemism for murder soured Jordan's already tepid enthusiasm for this venture. Wadding up the tourist tee, she tossed it onto the floor in the back and covered her hair with the *hijab*. "Have you ever had the feeling that something was off, Ganani? Because that's the feeling I have right now. We're missing something."

"Like what?"

"We think we know what the Palestinians plan to do with the information Cline provided, but are we sure? And what about what Najm Tibi had for Cline?"

"Brodsky has that on my to-do list."

Jordan figured that if the two of them were going to work together, it was time to come clean. She could only guess how the Shin Bet agent might react. Ganani was being manipulated by someone who wasn't who he presented himself to be. Like Jordan, she followed orders. Unlike Jordan, she didn't do things by the book. She flitted along the edges of right and wrong. Maybe she already knew.

"You need to know something about Ilya Brodsky."

Ganani looked over.

"He's altered his history."

Ganani expression registered confusion. "What are you saying?"

Jordan chose her words carefully. "I met him years ago, when I was a child. I'm certain he worked for the Russian government."

She wondered when her suspicions had become fact in her mind. Perhaps with Alena's revelations? She had no real proof. Ganani jerked the wheel and the car swerved. Jordan planted one hand on the dashboard.

"It's the truth. If Brodsky thought Alena Petrenko could identify him, he would have had no choice but to eliminate her."

Ganani appeared unfazed. "If what you say is true, then why are you still alive? Wouldn't he want you dead, too?"

"I don't think he recognized me. Twenty years makes a difference. I was six then. I've changed. He looks the same, just older."

Ganani came up on a curve too fast. She hit the brakes. The car skidded around the corner. Jordan stomped on the passenger floorboards and grabbed for the chicken bar.

"Maybe you should slow down."

"I've got this," Ganani said, but she accelerated less through the flat.

"Assume that I'm right. If Brodsky wanted the doctor dead, could his reach have extended to Bethlehem?"

Ganani spoke after a moment. "Yes."

"I can tell you doubt my theory."

"Sometimes the things we come to believe distort our memory."

Jordan tipped her head. "And sometimes they dictate our actions."

Ganani changed gears and floored the accelerator. Her body language said she'd sustained a direct hit. Her words pushed them back to the operation at hand.

"For now, we must focus our attention on the mission."

"And just hope we're not being played." Jordan pulled down the visor and used the mirror to finish tucking her hair up into the *hijab* before turning her attention to the roads. In most American cities, the streets operated on a grid system. In Israel, the streets created ribbons of cracked asphalt that wound snake-like through crowded neighborhoods and barren desert. Where the roads intersected, they often changed names going from east to west or north to south. It took concentration to navigate.

After several blocks, Ganani turned down a road with four- and five-story apartment buildings, their roofs dotted with satellite dishes. Three blocks later, the scene changed. A makeshift camp spread across a barren plot of land the size of a football field covered with lean-tos constructed of plywood walls, white tarps, and corrugated metal roofs. It was there that Ganani pulled over and parked, leaving Jordan sitting alone in the car—an expensive Volvo—smack-dab in the heart of enemy territory.

Chapter 40

Ganani was hurrying up the walk toward the contact's residence when her phone vibrated. She glanced at the caller ID. Brodsky's number flashed on the screen. She ignored the call. The idea that he might be playing her didn't sit well, but she couldn't get it out of her mind. Over the past four years, how many people had she killed on his command? Ten? Twenty?

Stripping off her sunglasses, Ganani pinched the bridge of her nose. Three days ago she had attempted to facilitate Steven Cline's trade of U.S. classified information on Brodsky's orders. He believed Cline to be working with a group of Palestinian terrorists, a cell Shabak needed to dismantle to protect the State of Israel. Now, with an Israeli police detective dead, Ganani wondered whether or not anything Brodsky told her was true.

Her phone vibrated again. She had to answer. She wanted to pick up and demand the truth. Was Jordan's information accurate? If so, why was Brodsky in Israel, and whose interests did he have at heart? But challenging him would not bring answers. It would only put her job, and possibly her life, in jeopardy.

Ganani answered her phone. *"Shalom."*

"At last. Update your status. Tell me, where are you now?"

She sensed he already knew, but how much information had he been given? If what Jordan told her was true, Brodsky had just

ordered the attempted assassination of Alena Petrenko and possibly the murder of Noah Weizman. If so, his mole would have
reported by now.

"Judge Taylor is on his way back to Tel Aviv with Alena
Petrenko and the Israeli detective, Gidon Lotner."

"Are you in pursuit of the terrorists?"

"Yes."

"Are you traveling alone?"

She wanted to avoid speaking of Jordan. If the colonel was
who the DSS agent thought, it was only a matter of time before
he identified her, and there was no telling what he would do with
that information. "No."

"Is it the woman from the U.S. embassy?" The colonel had put
two and two together, or he'd been informed.

"Yes."

"You must not be swayed by the American, Batya. Your mission is to dispose of the terrorist threat. It's imperative you make
that happen." He paused, and Ganani felt the weight of his words.
"Americans tend to be soft. You cannot let this woman stop you from
fulfilling your duty. Do you understand what I am telling you?"

She understood. If Jordan got in the way, he wanted her
eliminated.

"Do you hear me, Batya?"

"It may not be that easy."

"You'll find a way, *krolik*."

She felt the bile worming its way up her throat. "Yes, Colonel
Brodsky. I understand."

Chapter 41

Jordan leaned on the car. When Ganani materialized around the side of the building, she pushed to her feet. "That was quick."

"I told you to wait in the car."

"The heat drove me onto the sidewalk. That and the spectators." A group of young teenage boys had gathered on the corner.

Ganani pointed to the car. "Lock it."

Jordan punched the button on the key fob and tossed her the keys. "Where's the new ride?"

"This way." Ganani headed along a cracked sidewalk sprouting weeds. Jordan felt dozens of eyes on them, but other than the soccer boys, no one appeared to be watching. Rows of windows shone black in the sun.

"What are we looking for?"

"That." Ganani pointed at the scarred shell of a Toyota 4Runner. "He made me promise to take good care of it. It's his only transportation."

Jordan eyed the rust on the bumper and the dents in the fenders and stifled a laugh. Ganani opened the driver's side door and then reached across to unlock the passenger side.

"He'll be lucky if you never trade back," Jordan said, climbing up into the passenger seat and reading the odometer: 350K-plus kilometers. There was no backseat, just rusted floorboards, and a jagged crack marred the windshield.

Ganani slotted the key into the ignition and ground the Toyota into gear. She adjusted the rearview mirror, pulled away from the curb, and backtracked through the neighborhood.

"How conspicuous are we going to be, driving this vehicle on the road to Sheikh Sa'ad?"

"We will be noticed, but it's not unusual for a Muslim woman to drive in the West Bank. Thankfully, we are not going to Gaza."

Ganani turned the car west on the main road. A few minutes later, Jordan spotted the turn. A half a kilometer ahead, a road fashioned out of two gravel ruts cut away from the main highway and slithered into the Judean wilderness.

The western part of the region was known as the Khirbat az Zu'rurah. In the distance, small hills rose like miniature sand dunes. Plumes of dust spiraled upward along the horizon, marking the travel of people or vehicles kicking up dirt as they moved along. Jordan looked to see if they had enough gas. The only establishment between where they were and Sheikh Sa'ad was Mar Saba, a monastery that dated to 483 AD. After that, they would hit the Nahal Darga, the largest wadi in the northern Judean Desert, though it was well past the season when water flowed through it.

"It's twenty kilometers to Sheikh Sa'ad," Ganani said.

"How long do you figure it will take us to drive? Four hours?"

Ganani grinned. "I'll get us there in half the time." The car jounced, yanking the wheel from her hands. "Maybe a little bit more."

Jordan glanced up at the sky. No clouds. That meant no rain to muddy the track and no respite from the sun. The grass and earth showed variation in colors of brown, darker shades reaching into the shadows of higher ground. She checked for service on her cell phone. No bars. It was an ideal spot for someone to disappear. She checked the transmitter beacon on Ganani's phone. No green dot.

"We've lost them." Jordan held up the screen.

"We know where they're headed."

They stuck to the main road, ignoring several faint four-wheel-drive tracks that headed off into the desert. The blue dome of Mar Saba rose in the distance. Up ahead, a small group of Bedouins crowded the side of the road. Several women trudged along on the edge of the road, the hems of their dark blue *thobes* dragging in the dirt. One carried a child. The men rode camels and led the entourage. They glared at the car as it passed, and Jordan dropped her gaze to the floorboards. No point in antagonizing the locals.

A few kilometers ahead, they reached the edge of the Nahal Darga. The road disappeared off the edge of a steep incline, and Ganani stopped.

"It looks steep." Jordan opened the passenger's side door and got out. The ground was cracked from heat, and the earth crumbled and broke away at the edge of the embankment. The road angled sharply across the steep incline, straightening out at the bottom of the dry riverbed before climbing out the other side.

"It looks drivable," Ganani said.

Jordan shielded her eyes and squinted toward the horizon. In the distance, a car headed away and kicked up dust.

"That car made it," Ganani said.

Side-slipping the car into the wadi, both Ganani and Jordan leaned in toward the bank, as if the redistribution of weight would anchor their car to the hillside. Reaching the bottom, they bounced through the dry bed and spun their way up the other side, picking up speed once they were back on flat ground. They passed a few more travelers winding along the road, but most were lost in their own journeys and showed little interest in them.

They reached the outskirts of Sheikh Sa'ad as the sun dipped toward the horizon. Built on a hillside, the town was a morass of concrete homes and apartment buildings set along winding dirt roads and home to approximately fifteen hundred men, women, and children—half of them Israeli Arab citizens holding blue cards, half of them Palestinians, and nearly all of them descended from one of five Bedouin families. Narrow streets with SUVs parked on either side made navigation difficult.

Turning the 4Runner up the first street she came to, Ganani ground the stick into low gear and crawled the vehicle toward the top of the hill.

"We need to be watchful," she said. "The men we hunt are not our only enemies here."

"Care to elaborate?"

Ganani braked for a group of grade school children crossing the street. "This area is known for its terrorist factions. That is the reason for the placement of the fence."

As the Toyota inched forward, Jordan studied the streets and alleyways. The town reminded her of most communities in the late afternoon. Children played outside in the streets while women prepared dinner behind half-opened windows. From the west, the sun cast a warm, inviting light onto concrete sidewalks and packed earth.

"It looks so peaceful."

Ganani looked at Jordan as if she were a child in need of edification. "There are things that go on here the guidebooks don't tell you."

*

Several false starts and four streets later, Jordan pinpointed the signal inside a three-story concrete building that appeared to be broken into several apartments. It was decided that Ganani would stay with the car while Jordan cased the building. Ganani would circle around and park on the next block with a view of the front.

Jordan got out and walked steadily toward the structure. She could hear voices through the open windows. A child squealed. A woman laughed. Climbing the stoop, she opened the front door and conducted a quick recon of the foyer, turning up twelve mailboxes.

"*Amkin ana asa'idk?*" May I help you?

Jordan turned around to find a woman standing in the doorway. She wore a Western suit and a brightly colored *hijab* and carried a briefcase. In her arms, she cradled a stack of papers with childlike writing. A teacher?

"I am looking for my cousin," Jordan said. "We call him Al-Ta'boul." The stocky one. "For all I know, he may be skinny by now. I haven't seen him in years." She described the leader of the kidnappers to the woman, hoping it would be enough and that she wouldn't ask for his real name.

The woman smiled and bobbed her head. "Yes, I know him. Basim. He lives on the main floor, in the back. Apartment four."

"*Shukran.*" Thank you. Jordan dipped her head.

"*Afwan.*"

Jordan moved down the hallway in the direction the woman had pointed. The corridor was narrow and dim. Two lights hanging from the ceiling cast deep shadows into the corners. Four doors lined either side of the hallway. On the back wall, a fifth door was armed with an emergency alarm. Jordan assumed it led outside, but the alarm meant that opening the door was out of the question. She and Ganani would be forced to enter from the front or through a window.

Jordan listened until the woman in the entryway moved, her footsteps receding as she climbed the stairs, and then Jordan turned back, noticing a camera in the corner of the hallway. There was another in the entryway beside the front door. Instinctively, Jordan reached up and felt the edges of the *hijab*, glad she had taken care to tuck in every stray curl. Whoever watched the tapes would only see a woman dressed in black.

By the time she exited the building, the sun had dropped low on the horizon. Cars lined both sides of the hard-packed dirt road. Most were covered in thick layers of dust, signaling they hadn't been driven in quite some time. The street had emptied, the children called inside. Timing was of the essence, and the time was now. For all they knew, the men could already have transmitted the information from the USB drive to Zuabi. Their chances of finding out what Cline had been after were dwindling. That was the whole reason she was here. The whole reason she had put her career on the line to come on this mission.

Jordan stayed in the shadows and performed a quick recon of the perimeter. Windows cut into the structure on all three levels—large in the main living areas, smaller in the bedrooms and bathrooms. Moving cautiously past the windows, Jordan worked her way around to the back of the building. When she reached the quadrant for apartment four, she stopped. The back window was dark, but she pressed close, listening for voices.

Draped with dark curtains, the window was cracked one inch. Someone lay on a bed shoved against the far wall. She thought she heard arguing from the front room. Three voices. There had been four men involved in the attack at Petrenko's office. Two of them had been in Manger Square.

Hoping for a better vantage point, she moved around the corner and surprised a young boy poking a stick in a hole in the narrow, unplanted flowerbed that ran the length of the building. Time to abort the recon.

She brushed past the child, sensing him watching as she crossed the street and headed toward the 4Runner. Rather than draw attention to the car, she walked past, turned at the next corner, and looked back. The boy was gone.

Ganani picked her up in the next block.

"Did you see the boy?" Jordan asked, climbing into the vehicle. "He looked about nine or ten."

"I saw him. He went inside the apartment building."

"Damn."

"What's wrong?"

"He saw me come from behind the building."

Ganani drove around the block and parked where they had a view of the building and both of the cross streets. She stared through the windshield, eyes narrowed, jaw clenched, with a determined, hard line to her mouth. Finally, Ganani reached for the door handle.

"Let's go," she said. "If he tells someone and we don't move quickly, the mission is over."

Jordan's hand shot out and she grabbed Ganani's sleeve. "Wait! What's the plan?"

"To stop the boy from giving us away."

"Let's stay in the car and watch for a moment. If he told someone, we'll know soon enough. They'll come looking. Meanwhile, how do you propose we get into the apartment?"

Ganani jerked her arm away but stayed in the car. "What did you learn inside?"

Jordan recounted her conversation with the woman in the entryway, explained the layout, and told her about the cameras and about the arguing she had heard while circling the building.

"The only way in besides the front door is through a window in the back," Jordan said. "It's open a crack. We might be able to force it open enough to climb in through there. If necessary, we can use the emergency exit as an escape."

"Good. Here's what we'll do. You go through the front and knock on the door to apartment four. Say you are looking for your cousin. I will climb through the back window and we will have them trapped in between."

"What happens if they resist?"

"Then we will shoot them."

"That's apt to draw some unwanted attention."

"That would be unfortunate." Ganani reached for the door handle again.

Jordan glanced at her watch. "Let's give it ten more minutes."

"By then, the sun will have set and we will be without light."

"Exactly. It's our best window of opportunity. At the call to evening prayers, many of the residents will go to the mosque. There will be less chance of interference, less chance of discovery. If our targets go, it gives us an opportunity to get inside and be waiting when they return. If they don't, it gives us an emptier building to operate in."

Ganani slumped back in her seat. "I should have thought of it myself."

Time dragged for the next ten minutes. Then, exactly on schedule, the *muezzin*'s voice echoed across Sheikh Sa'ad. "Hasten to prayer. Hasten to prayer."

Immediately, the front doors of the buildings opened and people poured into the streets. Four families exited the apartment building where the terrorists were holed up, including the boy who spotted her.

"That's the boy," Jordan said. "The woman beside him is the one I spoke with in the hall."

Sliding down in their seats, Jordan and Ganani waited for the streets to empty. Two minutes after the start of *Maghrib* prayers, Jordan opened the passenger's side door. Ganani joined her on the sidewalk.

"I'll tap three times on the emergency exit door," Ganani said. "After that, I will climb through the window. That will be your signal to knock."

Jordan nodded, and Ganani moved away up the sidewalk. Jordan watched her make for the back of the building and then counted to ten and crossed the street. Drawing near to the front of the building, she could hear voices raised in prayer through open windows. Not everyone had gone to the mosque. She hadn't seen either man from the square come out. She wasn't sure she would have recognized the other two. She hadn't gotten a good look at any of them. That meant they had to assume there were still four men inside apartment four.

Climbing the steps to the apartment building, Jordan took stock of the street. There was no sign of anyone watching. The light had faded, leaving the city drenched in shades of gray. The low rumble of praying voices stirred the air.

Stepping into the foyer, she kept her head down and moved quickly into the hallway. Stark light from the hanging bulb illuminated sharp corner edges. Frayed carpet beneath her feet muffled her footsteps.

Once she reached the doors in the back, she waited. She began to wonder if Ganani had been forced to abort when three short taps rattled the emergency door.

Game on.

Jordan moved to the door of apartment four and knocked. She heard a shuffling from inside and then the door opened a crack. A short, gold-colored chain kept it from swinging free. The face peering out looked familiar. Not one of the men from Manger Square, but one from the ambush at Alena's office.

"What do you want?" he asked.

"I am looking for my cousin," she answered.

The man's eyes narrowed, then widened.

Shit. She'd been made. It took all Jordan's restraint to keep her hands from checking her *hijab*.

"Who is it, Haddid?"

Jordan recognized the second voice as the one from the phone, the one from the square.

"It's nobody, Basim," said the one called Haddid. His head twitched, motioning in the direction of the hall. Was he signaling her to leave? "It's just a woman at the wrong door."

A strangled cry from inside drew his attention. Ganani appeared in the back hallway. Basim shouted.

The one called Haddid started to close the door. Jordan slammed her shoulder into the wood. The chain caught, popped, and the door flew open. Haddid fell backward, while momentum carried her into the room.

Jordan drew her gun and trained it on the young Arab sprawled on the floor. "Stay down."

A man materialized from the back room and grabbed Ganani around the neck. Jordan caught the glint of a blade in Ganani's hand. The agent swung her arm up and back. A spray of blood and the man collapsed to the floor.

"Close the door," Ganani said, the dripping knife still in her hand. The man who had gripped Alena Petrenko's elbow in the square lay on the floor, clutching his throat, blood pulsing from between his fingers. Fear shone in his eyes.

Jordan pushed the door shut and threw the deadbolt.

"You fucking bitch!" shouted a man in the kitchen. The other man from the square. He launched himself at Ganani, his face contorted in rage. In spite of his size, he was quick and knocked her backward. She sprawled onto the floor of the narrow hallway leading to the back of the apartment, dropping the knife. Pinning her arms to the wood with his knees, he smashed his fist into her face. Blood spurted from her nose. Ganani grunted and bucked. The man rode her like a cowboy, his hands circling her neck.

Moving outside of Haddid's reach, Jordan turned and trained her gun on Ganani's assailant. "Stop!"

He ignored her. Ganani clutched at his fingers, trying to loosen his grip. He just squeezed tighter, lifting her head and smashing it into the floor.

"Basim," Haddid shouted, starting to move.

Jordan shifted the gun and Haddid froze. Then, turning the gun back on Basim, Ganani's assailant, Jordan took aim and fired.

The bullet impacted with his head. Blood from the exit wound spattered the walls and the floor. Basim's body jerked, arched back, and belly-flopped on top of Ganani.

Haddid lunged at Jordan and grabbed for her weapon. Catching the movement out of her peripheral vision, she sidestepped and brought her arm up into his nose. He dropped to the floor, grabbing her ankle and yanking her down. Her elbow slammed into the floor, sending a jolt of pain up through her arm. The gun, jarred from her hand, slid across the kitchen tiles.

Haddid's fingers, still clamped around her ankle, dug into her flesh. Jordan exhaled loudly and kicked. Haddid dodged the blow. Crawling forward, he stretched for the gun.

Jordan scrambled to her feet. She stomped down on his hand as he reached forward. He cried out but kept moving forward, closing his other hand on the butt of the gun.

Jordan levied a kick to his groin. So much for civility.

Haddid screamed and released the weapon. He curled into a fetal position, his hands covering his balls.

Jordan snatched up her gun, verified the room was clear, and went to help Ganani. She had managed to push Basim's body aside and sat propped up against the doorjamb, blood dampening her dark shirt.

"I was doing fine," she said, gesturing toward the dead man on the floor. "You could have killed me with that shot."

"But I didn't." Jordan holstered her weapon.

Blood spattered the side of Ganani's face, and blood ran from her nose. She used her sleeve to stem the flow and pointed with her other hand. "You were the one who wanted to interrogate the terrorists. This man can no longer talk."

"And you're alive."

Ganani leaned her head back against the wall. "Three are down. These two, and there is a man in the bedroom. He was dead when I came through the window."

"All we need is one alive."

Haddid groaned and Jordan moved toward the kitchen, searching the drawers for duct tape or cord. She found only mouse droppings and a dingy washcloth. Wetting it under the faucet, she checked the cupboards. All bare. The counters were covered with soiled dishes.

Walking back across the room, she shoved the rag into Ganani's hand. "Here."

The agent nodded her thanks and pressed the cloth to her nose.

Jordan's eyes cut to Basim's corpse and the jagged hole in the side of his head. His skull had shattered where the bullet tore through. Shreds of brain, blood, and skin clung to the hallway baseboard. Jordan felt her stomach clench. Crossing back to the kitchen, she puked in the sink.

"The first one's the hardest," said Ganani.

"How did you know?"

The agent shrugged. "You may have saved my life. Thank you."

Jordan wiped her mouth with the back of her hand. "We still have to get out of here. Someone will have heard the shot."

"They're used to violence," Ganani said. "We have more time than you think."

At that moment, footsteps pounded on the stairs and shouts echoed in the hallway.

"So I was wrong." Ganani pushed herself to her feet.

"We'll go out the back." Jordan grabbed Haddid's arm and helped him to his feet. "If you want to survive, don't try anything and keep your voice low."

"Don't worry," he said. "I will help you."

Ganani scoffed. "That is why you made for the gun."

"I was afraid she would shoot me."

"Shut up," Jordan said. "Follow her."

Ganani squeezed past Basim's body, then Haddid, then Jordan. They reached the opened window at the end of the hall about the same time pounding shook the front door.

"Basim? Fayez? Is everything okay?" yelled a man. "We heard a gunshot. Open the door!"

Jordan pointed at Haddid. "Can you handle him?"

"Yes. Why?"

"I'm going out first. I'm the only one who's not injured, and we need to block the emergency exit."

Clambering over the windowsill, Jordan dropped to the ground and searched for something she could use to wedge under the door handle. She needed a stick. But you needed trees to have sticks, and trees needed water to grow, so sticks were in short supply.

The noise inside was escalating. More voices in the hallway shouted Basim's name. The pounding on the door increased.

Glad for the darkness, Jordan dashed for the side of the building. She passed the spot where the boy had been digging in the garden and moved swiftly along the side of the building. She stuck to the shadows, squinting in the low light, searching the ground until she found it—the stick the boy had been drawing with. It lay under a lone olive tree near the front door.

Snatching it up, she raced back to find Ganani and Haddid, both outside. She heard the splintering of wood and the shouts of the men as they discovered the bodies.

"Close the window," Jordan yelled. She tried jamming the stick under the emergency door handle. It was too long.

"Here, let me." Haddid grabbed the stick and stomped on it with his foot, cracking it in two. He took the longest section and stuck it under the door handle. Jordan grabbed the smaller piece and wedged it into place between the window casing and the frame. It was long and slipped sideways as a hand slapped the glass and a face appeared. The man slipped his fingers beneath the window. Jordan pushed the stick up as he yanked on the window. The stick bowed but held.

"Go to the back," the man yelled. "They are getting away."

"Let's move," Jordan said. "Now!"

Ganani headed for the street, but Jordan stopped her. "We'll never make it to the car."

"We can make it to my car," Haddid said.

Jordan and Ganani both looked at the man. He dangled a set of keys in his hand.

"Let's kill him now," Ganani said.

"No!" Haddid said. "I told you. I want to help. We must go this way." He gestured toward the side of the building that bordered the next lot and a hedge. The other side of the building was bare to the street and provided no cover.

"We should head to the crossing on foot," Ganani said. "We can't pass the checkpoint by car anyway."

"And we can't outrun a mob," Jordan said. "We can cross on foot once we get there. You *can* get us past the Israeli guards?"

"Yes, of course."

Haddid's car was parked halfway down the street that ran parallel to the front of the building. The three of them moved swiftly, Haddid wincing with each step. The biggest challenge would be beating the vigilantes to the sidewalk.

It didn't happen. They were halfway along the side of the house when Jordan heard the front door crash open.

"Circle around!" yelled one man. "Circle around!"

The three of them dove into the hedge of Palestine buckthorn that created a fence between the apartment building and the property next door—Haddid first, Ganani second, and Jordan in the rear. She pushed through just before the mob reached the side yard.

"Say one word and you are dead," Ganani whispered into Haddid's ear.

"I would not like that," he said.

The man leading the mob slowed and shined his flashlight into the brush. Jordan froze. Her arms stung from the scratches, but she remained still—a chameleon in natural camouflage.

"Hurry," another man yelled.

The flashlight beam played across the bush above Ganani's head. The man moved in, spotted her, and opened his mouth to yell. Ganani's arm shot out and she slit his throat. Deadly and silent, she killed two more men the same way as they rounded the building, while Jordan and Haddid crawled through the hedge and made for the street. Jordan heard a siren in the distance.

"Go," yelled Ganani. "The police will only draw more attention."

Haddid tugged at her sleeve. "She's right. We must go—now."

Under the cover of the buckthorn, they reached the sidewalk. Jordan checked in both directions. "It's clear."

Haddid pressed the keys to the car into her hand. "Take these. I can throw them off your trail."

"No, you're coming with me. I have questions for you."

"The fact that I am alive and my friends are dead makes me suspect. If I stay here, Zuabi will never trust me again. I might as well be dead. If you take me as your prisoner, I will become a martyr to the cause, and my family will be safe. I will meet you near the crossing."

Ganani joined them at the sidewalk, picking up on the tail end of his speech. "We cannot trust him. He will turn against us."

Haddid looked over his shoulder. "You must hurry. They are going to come." He pushed Jordan toward the sidewalk. "Wait for me at the turnstile. I give my word to Allah. I will be there."

Jordan hesitated. Haddid had sent mixed signals. At first, in the apartment, he seemed to want to protect her. But then he had gone for her gun. Was he trying to save his own neck, or was it possible he really did want to help?

"Okay," Jordan said. "At the turnstile."

Jordan held Ganani back as Haddid pushed into the yard and hobbled toward the rear of the building. She heard him shout, telling the men to head down the street toward the mosque.

As their footsteps faded, Jordan and Ganani ran for the car.

"We need to move fast," Ganani said. "The police will be here any moment."

"I'll drive. You navigate."

Ganani climbed into the passenger's seat and Jordan headed for the driver's side door. Reaching for the handle, she found herself pinned in a beam of light.

She turned, expecting to see an officer. Instead, it was the ten-year-old boy. In one hand, he held a high-powered flashlight, pinning her in the beam. In the other hand, he held a stick, which he pointed and pretended to shoot.

Chapter 42

Jordan stood frozen, trapped in the beam of the flashlight.

"Get in," Ganani shouted. "Put it in gear."

Jordan slid into the driver's seat. "He's only a boy."

"Pretending to be a Palestinian fighter." Ganani watched for the reinforcements she knew would come. Taking the keys from Jordan's hand, she stuck them in the ignition. "Do you want to die?"

"No."

"Then start the car."

Jordan turned the key and ground the car into first. "Which way do I go?"

"Turn right at the next street and go up the hill to the top. We have to go back the other way, a little more than two kilometers. It's across the city, and only certain roads will work. Can you see the Dome of the Rock?"

"No, but I'll keep my eyes out for it."

Ganani felt the car accelerate and was impressed with the speed with which Jordan threaded the vehicle through the narrow streets. The American could drive.

"There's no one behind us—yet," Jordan said.

"Trust me, they will come."

"Do you think Haddid will meet us there?"

Ganani coughed out a laugh. "Are you crazy? He took the chance to escape."

"He didn't give us away," Jordan pointed out. "He seemed to feel he was in danger here. We need to know what information he has."

"Perhaps you should have considered that before letting him go."

"He saved our lives."

"He won't be there." Ganani twisted in her seat, trying to keep an eye on the road behind them. A blue flashing light appeared in the side mirror. Ganani could see the police car closing the gap behind them. "Time is up. Drive faster."

"We're about maxed out here."

"Drive faster!"

Jordan goosed the gas and the car leaped forward. In front of them, cars lined either side of the street. She threaded them like a needle. "Are you sure the checkpoint is open?"

"It's open." Ganani remembered how angry she'd been when a judge in Jerusalem ordered the Sheikh Sa'ad checkpoint to be manned twenty-four hours a day. She had thought him soft at the time, caving into Palestinian demands. Now she silently whispered his praises. His action may have just saved their lives.

The checkpoint was nothing more than a fence with a built-in, eight-foot-tall turnstile that one passed through to get into Jabel Mukaber. The roadway that used to pass cars was blocked by a ten-foot line of barbed wire and a row of three-foot-tall cement posts. By day, the checkpoint bustled with a full contingent of IDF soldiers. Now there were only two soldiers present—one male and one female.

Jordan skidded the car to a stop near the turnstile.

The soldiers raised their weapons. One stepped forward.

"Halt," he shouted in Hebrew.

Ganani jumped out of the car holding up her ID.

"Halt!" The woman soldier stepped to the fence and signaled Ganani to move closer.

"I am Shabak." Ganani glanced over her shoulder. The sirens were getting louder, the blue lights closer. "Come here, Jordan."

The female soldier waffled her aim. She pointed her rifle first at Jordan, then back at Ganani. Had their roles been reversed, she being the soldier and the soldier her, she would have been dead by now. Keeping her ID aloft, Ganani moved around the car, pushing Jordan toward the gate. "You must let us pass."

Jordan pushed back. "What about Haddid?"

"Forget him." Flashing lights filled the wide area near the turnstile. The sirens hurt her ears. "They are almost upon us."

"Wait!" Jordan yelled. "There he is."

Ganani glanced in the direction Jordan pointed. Haddid was limping toward them along a narrow footpath. Jordan met him and, for show, yanked his arms behind him like a prisoner.

"Step forward," the male soldier ordered. He reached through a slit in the fence and grabbed Ganani's credentials. "I will check these. You wait here."

Ganani heard the slide of tires. "You do that and we're dead. Take us through and you can call it in after that."

The Palestinians shouted as they poured from their cars.

Ganani heard the sound of guns being readied. The soldier turned back.

"Hurry." The soldier signaled for Ganani to move forward and for Jordan and Haddid to stop. "You cannot enter."

"She is an American agent," Ganani said, ushering Jordan into the turnstile ahead of her. "He is our prisoner."

"Stop," shouted a voice behind them.

"Let her pass!" Ganani ordered.

The soldier relinquished his ground and Jordan swept through. Ganani waited until she heard the click of the turnstile resetting, and shoved Haddid forward. "You're next."

A Palestinian Authority officer broke from the crowd and rushed forward. "Do not let them pass."

Ganani turned back. The Israeli soldier raised his weapon at the mob surging forward. Jordan had taken custody of Haddid and was moving him away from the guard shack. The woman soldier was calling for reinforcements.

Someone seized her arm.

Then Ganani heard the click of the turnstile. Twisting free, she shoved hard against the rotating gate. It spun, and she was through.

*

It took several hours to sort out the situation at the checkpoint. The Palestinians retreated in the face of the IDF tank patrol, but by the time Jordan and Ganani had filled out all the reports, it was 1:00 a.m.

Jordan was surprised when Lotner showed up to drive them back to Tel Aviv, and even more surprised when Ganani agreed to interrogate Haddid at the Israeli Tel Aviv District offices of the Israeli police.

The police station was practically empty. Most of the officers were home in bed or assisting with security preparations for the U.S. secretary of state's arrival later that day. A sergeant at the desk had glanced up and waved them through. Now they were situated in a stark interrogation room. Haddid faced Jordan across the interrogation table, his hands cupped around a glass of water. Lotner and Ganani leaned against the pale gray walls, bookends on either side of the two-way mirror. Jordan wondered who was watching through the glass. She hadn't called Daugherty. She wasn't ready to answer his questions yet.

"What is your full name?" Jordan asked.

"Umar Haddid."

"What exactly was the plan?"

Haddid appeared to hold nothing back. He started at the beginning: crossing the border with his friend Mansoor at Tūlkarm.

At the mention of the town, Lotner moved toward the door. "I'll be back."

Jordan nodded. It was important he pass along the information about the porosity of the Tūlkarm crossing. Securing the Green Line was not an easy task.

"Go on," she said. "Why did you come to Tel Aviv? What were you after?"

Haddid explained how the American had contacted Najm Tibi. "He wanted him to bring him some information from his place of work and offered to make an exchange. At first, they were going to use the Internet, but the American grew more and more afraid. He was convinced his keystrokes were being tracked. Najm suggested he use an Internet café, but the American insisted on making the exchange in person." Haddid paused, took a sip of water, and then set the glass back on the table. "He was right to be worried."

Jordan thought about that. Brodsky had known about the exchange. He had ordered Ganani to be there.

"Do you know what they were trading?"

"Only that Najm had information the American wanted. In exchange, he was to give Najm specifics about the U.S. secretary of state's visit."

That much was true.

Haddid reached out his shackled hands. Jordan hadn't thought it necessary, but Ganani had insisted. "You have to believe me," he said. "I never wanted any part in all this. If I had refused, my family would have been in danger. They may still be in danger."

"From Zuabi? He is the one behind all this, right?"

Haddid looked straight at the mirror and nodded.

He only confirmed what they already suspected. Jordan stared blankly at the file in front of her. "Do you know what Zuabi plans to do with the information?"

"No, only that it's personal."

Jordan looked up. "How is killing the secretary of state personal?"

Haddid looked surprised. "The secretary is not the target."

Jordan leaned across the table toward him. "Why else would he want information about the secretary's visit?"

"It is the man that Zuabi is after."

"What man?"

"The man he blames for killing his niece. She died in an ambush in Denver, Colorado."

Suddenly the pieces fell into place. Jordan got to her feet. They were protecting the wrong person. Zuabi was going after Posner. "When are they planning the attack?"

Haddid shrugged. "I told you. I don't know any details."

Jordan was halfway to the door when Haddid spoke out. "This is a minor thing compared with what the American and his associates had planned."

Jordan turned back around. "You just said you didn't know anything about that."

"I don't know the specifics. But it's something big, very big. It's something that will impact all of Palestine, all of Israel. Zuabi was preparing for an apocalypse."

"Then we're fortunate the exchange never happened." Jordan headed for the door again. She needed to contact Daugherty and make Posner aware that they were coming for him.

"There are other ways to get information," Haddid said.

His pronouncement stopped her cold. Cline was after information from Tibi's place of work, from GG&B. Brodsky had sent Ganani to Dizengoff Square to oversee the exchange. He had commandeered the investigation, stonewalling them at GG&B. But why? What was the end game? And were her suspicions enough to force Daugherty to listen?

"Wait here."

Haddid jangled his chains in response.

Jordan tapped for the guard and stepped into the hallway. Ganani followed her into the hall.

"I know what you're thinking, but Brodsky would not do something to harm Israel," Ganani said. "He may be ruthless and calculating, but he is a Jew."

"Maybe, but how far would he go to further a cause?"

Ganani wet her lips but kept her mouth closed.

"Exactly," Jordan said. "Does he know Haddid is here?"

"Yes. Agents are on the way here to pick him up."

"You called him."

"What else could I do? The soldiers at the border checked my credentials. He knew that three of us crossed the border."

Gutted by Ganani's confession, Jordan fell silent. If Brodsky got his hands on Haddid, the Palestinian was as good as dead.

"We need to get Haddid out of here," Jordan said. "You know what will happen if we don't."

"You would trust the Palestinian over Brodsky?"

"Yes," Jordan said, but she could tell Ganani still wasn't convinced. "Steven Cline was a radical. He and his wife were tied into a group that believes in uniting Israel as written in the Old Testament. By our own admission, Brodsky wanted the information that Najm Tibi was handing off to Cline. Knowing that Brodsky was once part of the Russian government, how sure are you of his motives?"

Again, Ganani didn't respond.

Jordan shook her head. "You realize that Brodsky has implicated you in his plans. If I am right, if Haddid's right, then you will share the blame for what happens. Unless you do something to stop it by helping me now."

Before Ganani could answer, Lotner approached from his office, looking pleased with himself. "Thanks to our friend, we have plugged the leak at the border."

"Good," Jordan said. "Now I need to ask you for a favor. I need to take Haddid with me, back to the embassy."

"That is not going to happen."

Jordan considered appealing to him about the danger Haddid was in, but Gidon didn't seem the type to care. She needed to contact Daugherty. "Who is the new Israel PD liaison assigned to the U.S. embassy? Have they appointed one?"

"Yes. I am your new liaison." He smiled and then excused himself when someone signaled to him from the front.

Jordan watched him walk away and then turned to Ganani. "This isn't good. Lotner is very by-the-book."

It was a funny assessment coming from her, but recent experience had altered her thinking.

"What do you expect me to do?" Ganani said.

"Take Haddid into your custody. Tell him you have orders to deliver him to Brodsky."

"What if he checks with the colonel?"

"Haddid can help us identify the men who want to harm one of our agents, and he can help me convince Daugherty that something far worse is coming. If we wait too much longer, Haddid dies and there is no one left who can corroborate either threat. No one left to help exonerate you. Are you with me?"

Chapter 43

Ganani jerked her head toward the security checkpoint at the front entrance. "Those men Lotner is talking to . . . they are some of our agents."

"If we're going to do something, it has to be now," Jordan said.

Together, they stepped back into the interrogation room.

"Haddid, I need you to listen to me." Jordan turned off the recorder on the table and leaned in close to his ear. "Things are complicated. We are not sure who we can trust. For your safety, we need to move you somewhere else."

Haddid looked alarmed. "You are kidnapping me?"

"We are moving you. I need you to follow my lead and do what I say."

Ganani took a key from her pocket, unlocked Haddid's hand-cuffs, and then recuffed his hands behind his back. "I'm not taking any chances."

"We're going to go out the back entrance and through the underground parking garage," Jordan said.

"What car will we use?" Ganani asked.

"We're going to have to take one." Jordan wasn't sure she could hotwire a car, but being out on the street was better than turning Haddid over to Brodsky's men.

"Let me go first," Ganani said. "I can talk to the agents and buy you some time."

Jordan stood at the window of the interrogation room and watched her cross the bullpen. Ganani reached Lotner at the same time the last agent was clearing security. This would be the true test of whether or not she could trust the Shin Bet agent. Ganani wormed her way through the men before turning around and engaging them in conversation, forcing their backs to the big room. That was her cue.

Jordan opened the door and gestured to the guard stationed outside. "The prisoner needs to use the bathroom."

The guard moved to take charge, but Jordan pushed herself between him and Haddid. "I'll escort him."

The guard pointed her to the back of the room.

Shepherding Haddid in front of her, she spoke softly. "I'll turn around when we reach the bathroom to make sure the guard hasn't followed. On my signal, we'll move down the hall and out the back door. If we run into anyone along the way, you let me do the talking."

Jordan stole a glance behind her at the door to the bathroom. The guard was watching Ganani. Everyone was watching Ganani. She was reenacting the scene at the Sheikh Sa'ad crossing.

Jordan pushed Haddid into the hallway. "Go."

The two of them sprinted for the back door. Once through the parking garage and at the exit to the street, Jordan took out her keys and uncuffed Haddid's hands. "I'm trusting you not to run."

"You have my word."

"This way." She steered him down the street. When they were half a block away, a car screeched to a stop at the curb beside them. Jordan's hand moved to her gun. The passenger car door flew open and Ganani leaned from the driver's seat.

"Get in."

Jordan ushered Haddid into the backseat of a standard-issue cop car. A screen protected the front seat from the back, and the child security locks were engaged.

Jordan slid into the passenger seat. "How did you get the car?"

"I borrowed the keys."

Jordan pulled out her phone and punched a one on her speed dial. Daugherty answered on the first ring.

"Where the fuck are you?" he asked. "Lotner called me and said you were picked up at the border with Batya Ganani. What the hell were you doing there?"

"There isn't time to explain. I have reason to believe—"

"I don't give a flying donkey what you believe, Jordan. But you better know this. You're headed stateside on the next transport after this clusterfuck."

"Sir—"

"I don't want to hear your lame-ass excuses. An Israeli policeman is dead, and I have the ambassador and the director breathing down my neck, wanting to know what happened out there and why we were using the judge for an exchange."

Jordan stiffened. "That was your call, sir."

"You ran the operation. You're the one with the answers." His voice sounded cold. He had turned on her, just like she knew he would.

"Ultimately, Jordan, you are responsible for reporting on what happened out there. Now answer the question. Where the fuck are you?"

Daugherty had ridden roughshod over her since her arrival in Israel. He and Posner. She had followed his orders and now he had set her up to take the fall.

But there was no way in hell she was going to let that happen.

"Sir, I need you to listen to me. I have knowledge of two credible threats."

"Bullshit."

Jordan soldiered on. "One against Dan Posner and one against the State of Israel."

She hoped the mention of Posner's name would grab Daugherty's attention. The silence on the phone made her think for a moment that the line had gone dead.

"Sir?"

"What is it with you and your conspiracy theories, Jordan?"

The question was rhetorical. She didn't answer.

"Where did you get this intel?"

Jordan wondered how much to say over a nonsecure line. She turned and stared out the window at the empty streets of Tel Aviv. "We captured one of the terrorists, sir."

"And he volunteered all this? Or maybe your Shin Bet buddy helped you coerce it out of him."

Jordan could picture the wheels turning in his head.

"Where is this terrorist now?"

Jordan stared out at the backdrop of the city slipping past the car window as she considered how to respond. Lights flickered on in the buildings as the city awoke. A taxi passed. A pedestrian walked a dog. She realized that if Daugherty got his hands on Haddid, the Palestinian was just as dead. Brodsky would demand that Daugherty hand him over, and Daugherty would comply.

Ganani turned to look at Jordan. "What is he saying?"

Jordan shook her head slightly.

Daugherty started in again. "Did it ever occur to you that your prisoner is lying? It's classic. He's got you focusing your attention somewhere other than where it belongs."

"I believe he's telling the truth."

"I want to talk to this fellow myself. We need to make sure he's telling the truth."

If Jordan had learned one thing in the past few days, it was that sometimes you had to improvise to get the job done. She looked back at Haddid. "I can't bring him in, sir."

Ganani threw her a sharp look.

"Why not?" Daugherty asked.

"The prisoner has already been taken into Shin Bet custody."

Ganani's mouth twitched into a smile. Haddid's gaze bounced to Jordan through the rearview mirror. She didn't know him well enough to read his expression.

"Great," Daugherty said. "Let him be their problem. All that's left now is to pull the guard detail at the Taylor apartment."

His comment caught Jordan off guard. "We can't pull the detail."

"It's over, Jordan. The terrorists are all dead or in custody. Taylor and his kid are no longer targets. We could use the man-power. I'll call off the Marines. You get your ass home." With that, Daugherty hung up.

Jordan looked at her phone. Ganani looked at her expectantly.

"The plan has changed." Jordan filled her in on Daugherty's half of the conversation while their prisoner listened. "We can't risk handing Haddid over to anyone at the embassy. And I don't know that Daugherty will warn Posner."

"What do we do now? Your boss ordered you to bring in the operation, and I've put my career on the line." Ganani's foot tapped the brake. "Maybe it's time to turn around."

In Jordan's mind, the implications were clear. She could let Ganani take Haddid in and maybe salvage her job. After what happened in Manger Square, Jordan's career with the DSS was all but over. If she was lucky, she would be reassigned to a desk job checking license plates. Or sent to some remote location, some-place nobody else would willingly go, to protect someone nobody had ever heard of.

Thinking about it was enough to kick-start a plan. She had worked hard for this job, and she'd be damned if Daugherty was going to prevent her from doing it right.

"Drive to Dizengoff Square," she said.

Ganani continued to slow down. "Why there?"

"We need to get Haddid off the street and get word to Posner to watch his back. Taylor can help with that." Jordan strategized as she spoke. She knew that she couldn't get through to Posner except through Daugherty, who considered her off the reservation. But Taylor's ex-wife was a friend of the ambassador's. Taylor could deliver a message.

"After that?"

Jordan decided to deliver the message straight. "We're going to hack into GG&B's computers and find out what Tibi took."

Ganani stared hard at her hands on wheel. "Do we have an alternative?"

"Do you have a better idea?" Jordan glanced back at Haddid. "We're running out of time."

The car began to accelerate.

Jordan lay her head back against the seat. "I'll take that as a yes."

Chapter 44

They rode the rest of the way to Zinah Dizengoff Square in silence. Once in sight of the apartments, Jordan gestured toward the motel across the street. "Park over there."

Ganani angled into a spot with a view.

Jordan started to get out, and the Shin Bet agent reached for the door handle.

"I am going with you," she said.

"You need to stay here with Haddid. Let me scope out the situation."

Ganani rolled down the window and slouched low in her seat. "Five minutes."

Jordan held up her phone. "If I don't call, get Haddid out of here."

"To where?"

"Somewhere," Jordan said. "Anywhere."

Keeping to the shadows, Jordan skirted the square, showing herself in pools of light from the street lamps only. Not a soul stirred on Dizengoff Street. She saw a flash of car lights two blocks up, but the vehicle turned in the other direction. Then her phone vibrated in her pocket. She checked the display. Walker.

"Hello?"

"What's the word, boss?"

Jordan stopped short of the garden gate. There was no sign of the Marine guard. "Did Daugherty call?"

"Yes. He ordered us to pull up roots."

"Did you?"

"I sent everyone else packing. I'm still here, because Taylor arranged it with Daugherty to have me stay."

"For how long?"

"The next seventy-two hours, during which time he can arrange for private bodyguards."

Jordan swung open the gate to the garden. "Have Taylor meet me outside at the back door of the bar in two minutes."

"Covert ops?" Then, when she didn't answer, "Oorah."

*

Jordan watched Taylor exit the apartment. She sat deep in the shadows, perched on the edge of a wrought iron bench in the garden—the one the bar patrons used when smoking outside. From there, she had a good view of the fenced-in courtyard, the entrances, and the other apartments. The bar was locked up tight, and the only building unit with any visible lights belonged to Taylor and Lucy.

"I take it you've heard," Jordan said, when Taylor slid onto the bench beside her.

"That the guard has been pulled? Yes. Got that news."

"Are you okay with it?"

"No. I'm worried about Lucy."

"How is she doing?"

"She's red-hot with fever. Alena helped her as much as she could in the state she was in. Alena's in the hospital for now and expected to be home on Sunday."

"Just be glad she's not dead," Jordan said.

"It easily could have gone that way." Taylor scrubbed a hand through his hair. "Meanwhile, the last thing I want right now is to have to watch my own back."

"I hear you have until Monday." Jordan glanced down at her watch. She'd burned two minutes. Taylor leaned forward, knees on his elbows, and cupped his head in his hands.

"Your boss referred me to a private protection agency. After throwing my ex-wife's name around, I finally convinced him to let me keep one guard for another seventy-two hours."

"That's great."

Taylor sat up. "You seem to be taking this well."

"I'm just glad he left you with a guard. After everything that happened, who knows whether Zuabi or his men will come after you again. I'd rather we didn't find out the hard way." Jordan rubbed her eyes, aware that the strain of the day was catching up to her. It made sense to give Taylor four days. Shabbat began in fewer than twenty-four hours. Arranging for a private bodyguard between now and Sunday could prove impossible, even in Tel Aviv.

"At least Daugherty's done one thing right."

Taylor must have picked up on her stress. He sat up straighter. "What haven't you told me?"

Was she that easy to read?

Jordan scanned the perimeter of the courtyard. Her watch said three-and-a-half minutes were gone. It was time to man up.

"Batya Ganani is across the street waiting for my call. She has one of the terrorists with her, a man named Haddid. We freed him from custody tonight. By now, the Israeli police and Shin Bet are looking for him, and for us. The DSS wants a chance to talk to him, too."

Taylor was fully alert. "Why did you spring him?"

"Haddid saved my life tonight. And based on what he's telling us, there is a large-scale terrorist attack about to take place in Israel."

"Can he prove it?"

"No, but we think we can duplicate the information Najm Tibi was passing to Steven Cline. We know it was pulled from a secured computer at the GG&B offices in Haifa. If we can access the computer, we may be able to obtain the data and figure out its intended use." Jordan looked over to make sure Taylor was following.

"Can you get to it?"

"That's the million-dollar question." She was down to one minute. "We also have another problem." With time running out, Jordan quickly explained Zuabi's plan to eliminate Dan Posner. "This is where you come in. We need you to deliver a message."

"That's it?"

Jordan moved sideways, bumping shoulders with Taylor. "That's it, unless you can hack a computer."

Chapter 45

Twenty minutes later, Jordan called an impromptu powwow in Taylor's living room. Dawn was cracking the horizon, painting the sky and apartment walls in colors of orange and purple. Haddid was tied to a chair at the kitchen table. Lucy was still in bed.

"Is she doing any better?" Jordan asked when Taylor emerged from her bedroom. She imagined the girl as she'd last seen her, cheeks burning red with fever.

"Her temperature is still high, but it's coming down. She seems stable, for now." Taylor said it matter-of-factly, as though treating someone from your hospital bed was a normal thing. Funny how it now fit within her definition of "normal." A few days ago, Jordan would have deemed him crazy.

"So what is the plan?" he asked, sitting down on the couch and completing the circle that included Jordan, himself, Walker, and Ganani. "I'm ready to nail the bastards who killed Weizman."

Ganani stared at him. "They're already dead."

By the expression on his face, Taylor was looking for payback, and her assessment wasn't what he wanted to hear.

"I have a more important job for you," Jordan said. "We need your help getting to Posner." She sketched out the plan that had formed in her head. "Your ex-wife is a close friend of Ambassador Linwood's wife, right?"

"Yes, Sarah and Tracy Linwood met in college. Both members of the Young Republicans."

"Do you think she'd agree to see you?"

"Hell, yes. Tracy would love nothing more than to tell me face-to-face what an asshole I am."

"Who is Dan Posner?" Walker asked.

Jordan fit the pieces together for him. "He was my previous boss. He oversaw a raid in Denver, where Abdul Aleem Zuabi's niece was killed. Posner now heads up the secretary's guard detail. He'll be at the visiting guest residence tomorrow. Today," she amended, acknowledging the morning light sifting through the window shades. "The secretary arrives at ten a.m."

"You're sure this Zuabi dude's not targeting the secretary of state?" Walker said.

"He's planning a revenge killing," Jordan said. "The secretary of state's death would be a bonus."

Ganani picked a pen up off the table, pointing at various objects with it like an experienced marksman. "How do they know where Posner will be if the information we gave them was false?"

"The itineraries were switched—the scheduled visits, times, routes of travel—but the protection detail doesn't change. Posner's still assigned to be at the embassy residence."

Taylor stretched his arm along the back of the couch. "That's still a lot of territory to cover, and they won't know where he'll be exactly."

"Unless someone is feeding them information." Jordan had her suspicions that there was a mole among them. "Whoever shot Weizman in the square yesterday knew what they were doing. That was a planned attack."

They all looked at each other.

"There's too much ground to cover to find one man," Ganani said.

He was a glory hound, thought Jordan. "He'll stick close to the action."

"So requesting an audience with the ambassador's wife puts me in proximity to the target."

"Right," said Jordan. "I can get us through the gate. I just don't know what will happen once Daugherty discovers I'm on the grounds. He may have issued orders for the Marines in the guard shack to report or detain me."

"None of this helps us identify the attacker," Walker said.

Haddid scooted the kitchen chair, causing it to squeal against the tile. "I can identify Zuabi's man."

They all swiveled their heads to stare at him.

He jumped the chair again, moving it closer to the couch. "I'm the only one among you who can. I know Zuabi. He does not have enough men for a full-scale attack. He will have someone on the inside, a worker who can pass the gate."

Jordan knew it made sense. "Someone who's been there long enough to have smuggled in a weapon."

Haddid nodded. "Najm was not the only Israeli Arab willing to help with the cause."

Jordan locked eyes with the Palestinian, but she couldn't read him. She considered the idea that he might want to protect the insider, but that seemed uncomfortably close to Daugherty's way of thinking. "Why would you help us?"

"I have a son and a wife. If I do not act, I fear my son will grow up knowing only hatred and war. That he will become a man like Zuabi—a man who cares not what happens to others as long as he can exact his revenge. If I do not act, I fear my wife will not like the man I am destined to become."

Walker was the first to speak. "The dude makes sense."

Taylor nodded in agreement.

"He's playing us," Ganani said. "How can you not see it?"

"And I think he's telling the truth," Jordan said. That made it three to one.

The U.S. embassy employed lots of local workers, lots of Israeli Arabs. Profiling discrimination accounted for overly zealous background checks on anyone of Muslim faith—searches for known associates, prior convictions—but the recent attack on the U.S. embassy in Kabul attested to the fact that it was always possible for someone to slip through the cracks.

Ganani set down the pen. "Are you saying this worker could pass back and forth through the gate?"

This time, they all turned to Jordan. "Yes" wasn't the answer any of them was looking for, but it was all she had.

"Only the ambassador, a few key personnel, and the security detail live on the embassy grounds. Everyone else comes and goes every day." She considered the ramifications. It was dawn. The workers were already arriving. She could hear the clock ticking. "If Haddid can identify the assassin, it's worth the risk to put him on site."

"And if this is a game?" Ganani said.

Jordan shrugged. "Then you can shoot him."

Within twenty minutes, they had cobbled together a plan, knowing full well they might have already lost their advantage. Taylor and Jordan would time their arrival at the embassy for the hour before the secretary of state's arrival. Ganani would take Haddid to a vantage point across the street from the embassy entrance.

While Ganani gathered equipment for a stakeout, Taylor went to check on Lucy and Walker assembled a makeshift command center in the kitchen consisting of an HP laptop, an iPhone, and a set of Tel Aviv maps taped to the kitchen cupboards.

With Jordan watching over his shoulder, Walker logged onto Taylor's computer. Within minutes, he had hacked the tenant log of one of the tall buildings across the street from the U.S. embassy and located an empty suite on the fourth floor with a great view of the guardhouse.

"You can see the main entrance and parts of both main parking areas from here." Walker pulled up the site on Google Earth and showed Ganani and Jordan a view of the building. Swiveling the icon, he showed them a view of the embassy grounds. It must have been quiet the day the footage was shot. There was one guard on duty and an empty parking lot. Today would be different. The secretary of state was due to arrive in less than five hours. Today there would be a full guard and security contingent, along with the press, the political pundits, and some who simply liked the hoopla.

"If Haddid identifies the insider, can you shoot him from here?" Jordan asked.

Ganani nodded. "As long as he's either entering the grounds or on the west side of the buildings."

The stakeout location secured, Ganani departed with Haddid. She would check in once the observation point had been established. Knowing that she and Taylor had two hours to wait, Jordan pulled a chair up to the kitchen table and watched Walker do his thing. "What do you think our chances are of hacking into GG&B's computers?"

"With this state-of-the-art setup, how could I miss?" Walker waved his hand across the assembly of gadgets. "The truth? Don't hold your breath. My only chance is to remote access my computer. I have some gadgets and apps that can help, but GG&B's security is tight. If I can get through, and that's a big if, it could take me hours. At least if we don't want to be noticed."

Two hours later, Ganani and Haddid were holed up across the street from the U.S. embassy. By the last check-in, Haddid had not spotted any of Abdul Aleem Zuabi's known associates and GG&B remained unscathed.

Walker arched his back and stretched. "Their security is iron-clad. If I had better equipment . . ." He let his words taper off.

"What about the embassy's?" She and Taylor were headed in that direction. "How friendly are you with the geek squad?"

"Not friendly enough to be granted access to their equipment, but I'm sure as hell not getting anywhere here." Walker shoved the mouse and an arrow scurried across screen. "If I could get into the embassy tech room, I might be able to make some headway. But then there's Lucy. She can't stay here alone."

They needed a babysitter. Someone Lucy would be comfortable with and who liked Lucy. Someone they could trust. Jordan ticked through the possibilities in her head. Finally, only one name remained.

Chapter 46

Gidon Lotner arrived in twenty minutes, his sour expression saying it all. Dispensing with any formalities, he cut straight to the chase.

"You're asking me to babysit Lucy? The answer is no. Now tell me what you've done with my prisoner."

"He's in the hands of Shin Bet." It wasn't a lie, but Jordan didn't think he'd approve of their plan any more than Weizman would have. They would be ordered to come in, and there was too much at stake.

"We need you to stand guard," Jordan said in English for the benefit of Taylor and Walker. She hoped Lotner would find the "guard" terminology more palatable. "Walker and I need to escort the judge to the U.S. embassy."

"Why me? Why can't you take the girl with you?" Lotner asked.

"Because she's sick and sound asleep in her bed," Jordan answered. "Because she likes you, and you like her. You taught her to play chess."

"She's no longer in danger."

Those were close to Daugherty's words.

"We don't know what Zuabi's men will do in retaliation for what happened yesterday. We cannot just hire a babysitter and put someone else in danger." Jordan could tell he was waffling. "We need your help, Detective. You're the only one we can trust."

"Is she feeling better?" Lotner asked, a sign he'd surrendered.

"A little," Taylor said. "She'll feel much better when she sees you're here. Someone she can play chess with."

They left ten minutes later, promising to be back in under an hour. Walker drove, Taylor rode shotgun, and Jordan sat in the backseat. From Dizengoff Square, the grounds were just over one kilometer away: walkable if you didn't need a getaway car. Jordan kept a vigil. She had no way of knowing whether Brodsky or Zuabi had eyes on them.

"Do you think this will work?" Walker asked, driving along Pinsker, through a neighborhood that had seen better times. The question seemed posed to either of them. Taylor took the bait.

"Damn sure. The ambassador's wife was a bridesmaid at my wedding. She begged Sarah not to marry me. She'd do anything to help my ex get Lucy back to the States."

Jordan listened, peering out the windows and studying the faces of the people in the cars around them. The streets were clogged with morning traffic. Like rush hour in the States, most of the drivers were talking on cell phones, some singing along with their radios, others shushing children in the backseat. People blanketed the sidewalks, nearly half of them soldiers with guns. Funny, what had once been disconcerting now offered her a measure of reassurance.

Walker slowed at the turn onto Trumpeldor Street. Ankori High School sat on the southwest corner. Buses and cars converged to drop off young students, jamming traffic to a crawl. Except for the armed soldiers, it could have been any school in the United States. Teens behind the wheel honked. Teens on the sidewalks grouped into cliques. Parents waved and drove off. Jordan wondered how many of them knew about the secretary of state's arrival and how many were just citizens going about their day.

Clear of the high school, traffic thinned and ran free to HaYar-kon Street. Nearing the embassy gate, Jordan glanced up at the two large buildings next to the Isrotel Tower, where Ganani and Haddid were waiting, focused on the gate. As predicted, the embassy had doubled the guard. The parking lot looked full.

"State your business." A tall Marine stuck out his hand for their credentials.

"We're headed into the office," Walker said.

The guard looked in the car, took a moment longer than normal to study the documents in his hand, and then handed back their papers and waved them through. The first hurdle cleared, Jordan allowed herself another glance at the building across the street. She caught a flash of light in an upstairs window, carelessness on the part of the Shin Bet agent. Jordan pulled out her cell phone and hit speed dial for Ganani. The phone rang and rang.

"Did either of you see that?" Jordan asked, looking to see if any of the guards had noticed.

The only Marines in sight were busy searching the next car in line. The driver stood to the side, his attention fixated on the activity surrounding his vehicle. Finally, the guards waved him back to his car. When he reached the door, he turned.

A jolt of adrenalin pulled Jordan up in her seat. She recognized the man. She had seen him before in Sheikh Sa'ad. Short, with a wide face, he had been walking to the mosque with his family. He was the father of the boy who had been playing with the stick.

*

Ganani checked her phone when it vibrated a second time. The colonel. She had already disregarded three calls from him, but she couldn't ignore him much longer or he might start to suspect that she was up to something.

"I have to take this," she said, lowering the butt of her rifle to the table.

Haddid turned toward her, pulling the binoculars away from his face. Sun caused the lenses to mirror.

"Idiot," she said, snatching the glasses from his hand. "Who are you signaling?"

Haddid frowned. "No one."

She stared hard at the Palestinian. He sat with his hands on his knees, his back straight. Not defiant, but not afraid. She shoved him aside and moved to the window.

"That's Jordan and the judge who just passed the guardhouse."

Haddid pressed toward the glass. Jordan's sedan pulled forward. The duty soldiers turned their attention to the next in line. There appeared to be no problems, no unusual movement on the grounds. After a moment, the guards waved the next car through. No one paid any attention to the building where the two of them hid. The Americans felt secure in their protection detail.

The phone vibrated again. Ganani handed the binoculars back to Haddid.

"I must answer this call. Understand something: any sound puts us in danger."

With barely a nod, Haddid resumed his vigil.

Ganani punched the connect button. "Yes?"

"Where have you been, *krolik*?" Brodsky demanded. "How many times have I called?"

Ganani registered the anger in his voice and the use of the nickname.

"The prisoner escaped," she said. "The police and I have been tracking him down."

"He escaped?" Brodsky's bellow forced Ganani to pull the phone away from her ear.

"How did this happen?" he asked. "There were agents en route."

"They did not arrive in time." A lie depended on details. Too much embellishment or not enough signaled a fib. Ganani opted for simplicity. "The Palestinian must have been helped."

"By who?"

"The DSS agent believes there is a mole."

The colonel's lack of response erased any doubts in her mind. He knew of the mole. For the moment, she had chosen the correct camp.

"Can she identify this person?"

"I am not certain who she thinks it is."

"But you must have ideas, *krolik*. Don't forget, it's me you are talking to."

"I have no ideas."

The colonel's silence stretched until Ganani felt uncomfortable. She knew better than to expose herself and waited for him to break.

"Find the terrorist," he said. "Then kill him."

Ganani waited in silence, sensing he wasn't finished.

"If you wish to continue to work in the field, *krolik*, I fear you need some additional training."

The hair on the back of her neck stood at attention.

"What type of training?" she asked.

"The kind that helps you remember to answer your phone."

Chapter 47

Jordan bounced her hands off of Walker's headrest. "In the car behind us, the white Renault. The driver is from Sheikh Sa'ad."

Walker hit the brakes and their car lurched to a stop. Throwing it into reverse, he powered backward toward the vehicle.

The driver jumped into his car and accelerated, pulling sharply to the right.

Walker skid the car to a stop. Shifting gears, he cranked the wheel hard and hit the gas. The car surged forward before he slammed on the brakes to avoid hitting a beige car that had pulled into their path. Jordan lurched forward, catching hard against the seatbelt.

Hitting the horn, Walker shifted back into reverse and spewed gravel as he snaked backward. Once he had enough clearance, he stopped and ground the transmission into first gear.

Jordan kept her eyes on the man from Sheikh Sa'ad and listened for the shot. If Haddid had identified him, Ganani would take him out.

The Renault sped through the parking lot. No shot came.

Unclipping her seatbelt, Jordan leapt from the car and started running.

"Halt!" A sharp whistle from behind stopped her cold. She turned. Two Marines who had been lounging in the shade of the guardhouse ran toward her, weapons drawn.

Jordan reached for her badge.

"Keep your hands where I can see them," the lead Marine yelled.

"We have a terrorist on the grounds," she said. "He's getting away."

If she moved, Jordan knew the Marine would shoot her.

"Turn around." The Marine advanced, signaling her back toward the car. The second Marine already had Walker and Taylor spread eagle across the hood.

"I'm DSS," Jordan said. "Check my credentials."

"Confiscate her weapon," the Marine ordered, snatching her badge from her outstretched hand. He studied the shield.

By now, a crowd was gathering and the Renault had disappeared. Not wanting to spark a panic, Jordan spoke, keeping her voice low. "The man who came through the gate behind us, the one in the Renault—he is a terrorist. He is headed to the secretary of state's quarters."

"What did she say?" asked the Marine overseeing the others.

The soldier with her credentials suddenly shouldered his weapon and snapped to attention. "Ma'am, Special Agent Jordan, ma'am."

Jordan took back her gun and snatched her badge from his hand. "Notify Daugherty that we have a situation, and notify the secretary of state's convoy to pull up and wait for orders."

"It's too late, ma'am," said the first Marine. "She arrived early, nearly a half-hour ago."

Walker jumped back into the car and cranked the engine. Taylor slid into the passenger seat. Jordan climbed into the back and rolled down her window. "Get a warning to Dan Posner. Tell him there's a man on site who is gunning for him."

Walker goosed the gas, and her words were taken by air. Speeding across the parking lot, she kept her eyes on the cars, searching for any sign. She spotted at least five similar vehicles in the lot. Walker pulled up behind the guest residence and locked up the brakes.

"Where the fuck did he go?" Jordan yelled, out of the car before Walker had ground to a stop. Then she spotted the car ten feet away, abandoned, the driver's side door standing open.

Jordan started forward and then stopped. "Do you think there's a bomb?"

"Possibly," Walker answered.

"Taylor, stay in the car." Jordan scanned area. There was no sign of the suspect. Several Secret Service agents wearing black suits and dark shades approached, guns drawn. The Marines held their ground in front of the doors. The mood was high alert.

A female agent advanced. "This is a restricted area."

Jordan flashed her badge. "Where did the man who was driving this car go?"

"Inside. He works in the residence."

"Which door?" Walker asked.

"I didn't see where he went."

"Can you reach Dan Posner?" asked Jordan.

"He should be on com."

"Get a message to him. Tell him someone's gunning for him. And get someone out here to check out this car. It might be rigged." Jordan shouted to Walker. "Head to the front and alert the security detail. Secure all the exits. I'll take the back." Then, heading for the side entrance, she shouted back to Taylor. "Get Daugherty on the line! Make sure he knows what's happened and that someone warns Posner."

Jordan broke into a jog. If she knew Posner, he'd be upstairs, in the air conditioning, as up close and personal with the secretary of state as he could get. The agent assigned to the side door nodded as Jordan flashed her credentials.

"Did a man enter here in the last few minutes?" she asked.

"More than one. They all had passes."

"I'm looking for one in particular." She gave the description.

"He just came through."

Jordan drew her gun. "Call for backup."

Counting to two, she pushed open the door. The entrance led into a stairwell, and she quickly cleared the area. Approaching the door to the main floor, she stayed clear of the window and signaled the agent behind her that she was going to open the door. He took a stance. She counted down three on her fingers.

The hallway was empty.

"Do you know where Dan Posner is stationed?" she asked.

"Upstairs, outside the secretary's suite."

"Can you raise him on the com?"

The DSS agent spoke into his mic, listened, and shook his head. "He's not answering, but Daugherty did. He says to wait for backup."

Posner would be dead if they waited. For all she knew, he was already dead. "There isn't time. Tell Daugherty I'm going in."

Bounding up the stairs, she fished out her badge and waved it across the fire door glass. No shots rang out, so she ventured a look through the window.

The door opened into a hallway leading to a wide landing at the top of the main stairs. Contrary to Israeli utilitarian style, this floor of the residence bore soft, beige Berber carpet and Putnam ivory-colored walls—textures and a palette more suited to American tastes.

Jordan traveled the floor layout from memory. The secretary's suite was through an entrance to the left, off of the large foyer. Halfway down the hallway on the right were two doors: one to a maid's closet and the other to a small office. No agents were visible.

Yanking open the fire door, she stepped into the hall. Without the filter of glass, the light in the corridor seemed sharper, edgier.

Voices traveled up from the lower floor, the insurgency not yet registered by the agents stationed out front.

Gun ready, Jordan pressed her back to the wall and moved swiftly down the hallway. The carpet deadened the sound of her footsteps, giving her the element of surprise.

Nearing the landing, she spotted Posner and the other agent posted to the upstairs foyer kneeling against the far wall. The man from Sheikh Sa'ad stood with his back to her.

From this vantage point, Jordan could see that Posner looked scared. He had his fingers laced behind his head and a "please don't kill me" look in his eyes.

"Tell me your name, infidel." The Arab cracked Posner's jaw with the butt of his gun. The man had found his target and didn't even know it.

"Who wants to know?" Posner said.

"I do." The Arab hit him again. "It is my honor to die here today, but I want to know who I take with me."

"Up yours."

With the third strike, Jordan heard teeth shatter. Blood spurted from Posner's mouth. From the stairwell came the sound of a door buckling. Agents had breached the outside side door.

Shouting ensued. Footsteps hammered up the stairs.

The terrorist's finger tightened on the trigger of his gun. Jordan's mind flashed to Jabel Mukaber, where she had killed the man attacking Ganani. She had the same shot here. She could kill the Palestinian, but it meant the possibility of killing Posner. Not such a tough decision this time.

Posner's eyes widened. The terrorist moved left as Jordan squeezed off a round. The bullet hit the drywall inches above Posner's head.

The Arab turned and fired. Jordan flattened herself to the wall.

She moved to return fire when a shot echoed in the foyer. A red spot bloomed on Posner's shoulder. Shock marred his features.

The second agent lunged forward to tackle the Palestinian. He dodged sideways, and the agent sprawled on the floor. The Palestinian pressed his gun to the back of the agent's head, and Jordan squeezed off another round.

The bullet winged the man from Sheikh Sa'ad. He grabbed his arm and then fired wildly in her direction. She returned fire, and he threw himself through the doorway of the secretary's residence. Posner lunged for the man and missed, sprawling across the carpet and blocking Jordan's path.

"Your mission is over," Jordan shouted in Arabic.

"I may have failed Zuabi," the man said, his voice traveling down the hallway to the secretary of state's residence. "But with Allah's blessing, no one can stop that which is yet to come. May the people of Israel shrivel like grapes in the sun."

Posner hadn't moved. Footsteps banged up the stairs, and then Daugherty was behind her, his bulky frame casting a wide shadow across the carpet. "Where is he, Jordan?"

She gestured toward the guest residence.

Together, they grabbed Posner by the feet and dragged him to the side. He was still breathing. She rolled him over. A hole in his chest bubbled with blood. Posner gasped for air. Jordan pressed her hand over the hole and tried to staunch the bleeding.

"We need a medic!" she shouted. Posner writhed in pain.

"Leave him!" Daugherty yelled.

She struggled with the choice, but it was the job. An agent put his life on the line for those he had sworn to protect. Posner knew the score.

More footsteps and suddenly Taylor appeared beside her. He was supposed to be in the car.

"What are you doing here?" she asked.

"I'm helping." He scooped his hands beneath hers, taking over with Posner. "I've got this."

Jordan scrambled to her feet and took up position with Daugherty on either side of the entryway to the private residence.

"Ready?" he asked.

She nodded.

"Let's go then, on the count of three."

Chapter 48

Ganani turned back toward the stakeout and knew immediately that something had happened while she'd been talking to Brodsky. Haddid stood at the window, his nose pressed close to the glass.

"What's going on?" she asked.

"Zuabi's man was in the car behind them. He drove past. Now the main problem is there." Haddid pointed toward the guest residency.

Ganani traced his line of sight. She was too far away for any shot accuracy. If this was a normal operation, she would be shutting things down.

"Agent Jordan should have called," Haddid said.

"She may be busy." Ganani checked her phone. Two calls, both while she was dealing with the colonel. She reached for her gun bag. The GPS tracking in her phone was disabled, but she was sure Brodsky would have traced their call. "We need to move from here."

"Why?" asked Haddid.

"By now, they know where we are. The enemy seems always to be one step ahead. We cannot take the chance anyone finds us here. Besides, we missed our opportunity."

Haddid looked at her, incredulous. "Only a handful of you know where we are, and yet you want to run. You don't trust your own team?"

Ganani's hand stroked the stock of her gun. She picked it up and shoved it into its bag. "I don't trust anyone."

*

Jordan entered the hallway first. Following the jihadist proved easy. A blood smear on the beige carpet led to the right. One of her shots had hit its mark.

She tried remembering the apartment layout. The bedroom suite was to the right. The office was to the left. A row of floor-to-ceiling columns separated the living room, dining area, and kitchen from a walkway that stretched the length of the apartment. Somewhere inside was the secretary of state.

"Federal agents!" she yelled. Daugherty followed her through the doorway. Walker came on his heels.

Jordan pointed to the blood trail on the carpet and gestured that she would take the bedroom. Daugherty moved forward into the large main area and signaled Walker to move left.

Moving quickly along the backside of the columns, Jordan made her way toward the bedroom. The door stood ajar.

A woman screamed. A man shouted. Jordan sprinted down the hallway.

A shot exploded.

Reaching the door, Jordan could see an agent down. Pressing her back to the doorframe, she stepped over his legs and swiveled to find the secretary of state staring down the barrel of a gun.

"Stop or I kill her," said the man from Sheikh Sa'ad.

Jordan stopped.

The Palestinian stared at her through the mirror over the dresser. Sweat beaded on his forehead, and he looked pasty beneath the natural dark of his skin. Blood soaked his shirt near his abdomen.

Terror contorted the secretary's face.

"Put your gun down," the Palestinian ordered.

"That's not going to happen," Jordan said. "Not while you have a weapon pointed at the secretary. Why don't you put your gun down and let me get you some help?"

"I will kill her."

"That's what I'm afraid of." Jordan didn't hesitate. She pulled the trigger.

A surprised look crossed the man's face. A red spot bloomed on the back of his head. Blood and brains spattered the secretary's travel suit, the ornate mirror, and the cherrywood dresser. The Palestinian stumbled and fell. The secretary dropped to the floor.

Jordan stepped forward and kicked his gun away. The man was dead. Quickly, she moved to the secretary, who cowered beside the bed. "Are you okay?"

The secretary's hand was on her heart, and she sagged against the wall.

"Madam secretary?" Daugherty pushed past Jordan, followed by a crowd of agents. "Someone get a medic."

Jordan allowed the chaos to surge past and then backed toward the door. Stepping over the dead Palestinian, she froze. All the training in the world could not have prepared her for the wave of guilt that washed over her. He was the second man she had killed in the past twenty-four hours. It didn't matter that he considered himself a soldier or that he acted the part of the enemy. He was a husband, a father.

She felt a hand on her arm.

"We need to go," Walker said.

Jordan turned away, stuffing the feelings deep. She knew they would resurface, but for now she needed to stay in control. She backtracked toward the residence entrance. Walker fell in behind.

"Where are we headed?" he asked.

"Anywhere off the embassy grounds." If they stayed, it wouldn't take long for the Secret Service to isolate them and lock down personnel. They would be debriefed and the rest of their impromptu operation terminated.

At the entrance to the residence apartment, they found Taylor watching two medics crouching over Posner.

"How's he doing?" Jordan asked.

Taylor shrugged. "Badly. He's got a hole in his chest."

She heard Posner wheeze, saw the bubbling blood, and knew his lung had collapsed.

"Jordan." Daugherty's voice boomed through the doorway behind her. "What the hell is going on?"

She quashed the desire to flee. "There isn't time to explain, sir."

"Make time." Daugherty stepped around the medics, and they moved into the back hallway. While Taylor and Walker listened, she gave him the condensed version. She told the truth, omitting only a few of the details. She let him believe Haddid had escaped and didn't tell him what she knew about Brodsky's past. She did tell him about Brodsky's connection to GG&B.

Daugherty worked his jaw muscle. "If you're right, something big is about to happen."

Jordan nodded.

"If you're wrong—"

"I'm not."

"They're going to want to talk with you." Daugherty jerked his head at the Secret Service agents gathering on the other side of Taylor and the medics. "If you're going to walk out of here, you need to do it now."

Jordan stared at her boss. "I have your permission to go?"

"I can't protect you. And I don't want to know anything about what you're planning or where you're going."

Jordan knew he was hedging his bets. If she was right and able to stop whatever was about to go down, he would come out the hero. If she screwed up, he could make her the scapegoat.

"It's called 'plausible deniability.'"

Jordan looked back at the medics working on Posner. "I hope he makes it, sir."

"You and me both."

Taylor gripped her shoulders. "We need to go."

They took the back stairs to the parking lot. The agents in sight were clustered near the front entrance. Walker had beaten them to the car.

"Get in." Walker fired up the engine. "We'll go out the back gate. There'll be less traffic and fewer guards. With luck, the Secret Service hasn't locked down the grounds."

Jordan slid into the passenger seat, stared down at the blood on her hands, and struggled to get her emotions in check.

Walker threw the car into gear. "Where to?"

"Let's take Taylor back to the Dizengoff Apartments. Maybe he and Lucy can get away before someone's dispatched to pick them up. I'm sure Daugherty will try to hold them off."

They were approaching the back gate, and Walker slowed the car. "Right now, we may have bigger fish to fry."

Jordan watched a guard walk toward the car, his gun drawn, and realized she was covered in blood. Tucking her hands up into her sleeves, she crossed her arms over the front of her shirt.

"I need you to turn around and park the car," the guard ordered. "We're on lockdown. No one is being allowed on or off embassy grounds."

"She's the ARSO," Walker said.

"I don't care if she's the secretary herself. My orders are to stop everyone."

"I'm on it." Walker tossed a salute before stepping on the gas.

The sedan shot forward, knocking the Marine guard off balance. The soldier scrambled to his feet and shouldered his rifle, a bullet striking the back fender.

"Give me your phones," Walker said, careening around the next corner.

Jordan pulled hers from her pocket and handed it over. Taylor refused. "I have to make a call first."

Walker pitched his phone and Jordan's out the window, while Taylor dialed. With sirens echoing in the street behind him, Walker took one side street, then another, until it was clear they had lost the tail. Jordan could hear Taylor murmuring in the background, leaving a message, telling Lucy that he'd be home soon and not to worry.

"Dizengoff's out," Walker said. "That's the first place they'll look."

"Why isn't Lucy answering her phone?" The stress in Taylor's voice jarred Jordan into action.

"Let me borrow your phone. I'll send Ganani over there."

*

Ganani knocked on the door of the Taylors' apartment. No one answered. She knocked a second time and then forced the door. Entering with caution, she and Haddid went room to room, looking for signs of disturbance, finding none. Lucy's computer sat on her desk, and her pink Coach handbag hung on the spoke of her chair. The TV was in its hutch. The apartment was empty, but more so than if someone had stepped out for a walk. It seemed deserted, as if no one had been there for hours. There was no lingering heat from the stove, the faucets were at room temperature, and the sink was dry.

"There are no signs of a break in," Haddid said. "It looks like they went out."

Ganani agreed. It didn't make her feel any better. Her gut told her something was wrong. She signaled for Haddid to take a seat on the couch. Keeping him in her line of sight, she stepped out on the stair landing and called the colonel. He answered on the third ring.

"Where have you been, *krolik*?"

"I've been tracking the Palestinian, as you requested." It was not the first time she had lied. She wondered how much information he had and who was feeding it to him. Right now, her bet was on Gidon Lotner.

"Did you find him?"

If she was correct, Lotner would have told him that the prisoner was with Jordan.

"No," she said. "He is with the DSS agent, and she is missing."

She could sense his satisfaction with her answer.

"Where are you now?" he asked.

Ganani was sure he knew that, too.

"At the Taylors' apartment. The girl and Lotner are missing. I'm worried that something may have happened to them."

"What makes you so sure anything has happened?"

"The girl's pink purse is here. She never goes anywhere without it."

The silence stretched. Finally, he spoke, his tone stern. "They are not your concern."

"Someone needs to wait and verify that they return. That or notify the Americans and the Israeli police."

"That's not your job, Batya. Your job is to follow orders. It is time you come in. I'll expect to see you within the hour."

Knowing it would do no good to argue, she acquiesced. Then, hanging up, she walked to the kitchen and set her phone on the counter. "We must go, Haddid. He will send agents for me, for us. Perhaps he already has."

Haddid pushed up from his seat. "What do we do now?"

"First? We need to buy a new phone."

Ten minutes later, as the fountain kicked to life, raining down fire and water behind her, Ganani dialed Taylor's phone number from a burner phone and got Jordan on the line.

"Lucy's gone. There's no sign of her or Lotner. No note, no indication of where they might be. I think Brodsky knew."

"Do you have another phone?" Jordan asked.

"Yes."

"Give me the number," said Jordan.

Ganani rattled off the digits. "What now?"

"Ditch the phone," said Jordan, "And meet us in Caesarea at two o'clock."

Chapter 49

Taylor's fingers dug into Jordan's shoulder. "What's going on? Where is Lucy?"

Jordan turned to face him, trying to stay positive. "She's not at the apartment, but according to Ganani, nothing's been disturbed. There's no reason to believe that she and Lotner didn't just go out for a bit. Maybe they went to a movie. Or maybe he had to go into his office and he took her with him."

She watched as he struggled to keep his emotions in check, and then she told Walker to head north.

They stopped to get gas on the outskirts of Tel Aviv. She and Taylor stayed in the car while Walker disconnected the DSS radio. He disposed of it in the store dumpster and then went inside, coming back with five burner phones, three bottles of water, and three granola bars. Within the hour, they were pulling into the parking lot near the Roman ruins, the same ruins that had prompted her discussion with Weizman about Eretz Yisrael, the biblical land of Israel. Jordan was convinced it was this idea that drove Brodsky. The question was whether Lotner believed in it strongly enough to be acting as Brodsky's mole.

Ganani was leaning against the fender of a beat-up sedan when they pulled up. Haddid sat captive in the backseat.

Ganani pointed to the blood on Jordan's hands. "What happened?"

While Taylor and Walker gave her the lowdown, Jordan walked down to the Mediterranean and rinsed her hands. Posner's blood liquefied, swirling in the tide, making purple ripples in the blue water. When the last remnants ebbed away, she stood and wiped her hands dry on her pant legs.

The ruins stretched in front of her, a reminder of all the battles fought for this land, of all the blood spilled. To what end? This country had never known peace. She doubted it ever would. The differences and resentments among its people ran deep. Their lives became a commodity of war. Today, one agent had paid the ultimate price, while Posner hovered on the brink.

She had shot the perpetrator, a man manipulated into seeking revenge for the death of someone he didn't know in order to stand for a cause. She thought of her father and wondered how she was any different. She had made this about Brodsky—about her questions about her father and his killer and her desire to see the person she believed murdered him burn in hell. But this was about more than that. This was about stopping a power-hungry man from derailing a chance at peace. To do that, they needed to figure out exactly what he had planned.

Jordan turned away from the water. When she reached the cars, Ganani pushed to her feet.

"We move to plan B," Jordan said. "But first, what the hell happened back there? Why didn't Haddid raise the alarm when the Palestinian came through the gate?"

Ganani looked away. "He didn't see the man drive up."

"Why not? He was watching the guard shack, wasn't he?"

"He was watching."

From the expression on Ganani's face, Jordan knew something had gone wrong. "Tell us what happened."

"The colonel kept calling, and I had to answer." Ganani's tone was defensive. "I told Haddid to be silent when I picked up. He was distracted for a moment."

"Distracted?" Walker stepped forward. "Your moment cost one agent his life and may have cost Posner's his."

Jordan had heard enough. Stepping forward, she opened the back door of the sedan and motioned for Haddid to get out.

Ganani moved to block her. "That man is a prisoner."

Jordan waved her off. "He saved our lives in Jabel Mukaber. We need him as part of this team."

Everyone looked skeptical, even Haddid. He climbed out into the desert sun and eyed her warily.

"You told me that Najm Tibi was to supply information for a major terrorist attack," she said.

"That's right."

"What else do you know?"

"I have told you everything I know. I have no knowledge of who is planning the attack. I don't know where it will happen or how. I only know that it will set Israel and Palestine back for many years in the future." He kept his eyes on the ground, his hands jammed into his pockets.

Jordan gestured at his body. "Your posture says you're lying. What aren't you telling us? Now is not the time to be stupid."

He shifted and looked away, as though weighing his options. When he looked back, his eyes held a conviction she hadn't seen there before. "In my things, the ones you took at the police station, there is an ID."

The police guards had searched him and bagged his possessions. Jordan turned to Ganani. "Do you have the envelope with his effects in the car?"

The Shin Bet agent leaned inside the front seat and produced a manila envelope from the glove box. Jordan rummaged through the contents and pulled out a white plastic card.

"That belonged to Najm," Haddid said. "I grabbed it when I left the apartment, along with a USB drive with the information he had to trade."

Ganani stepped toward him. "What happened to the USB drive?"

Haddid stepped back until he bumped up against the fender. "I gave it to Zuabi in order to save myself and my family. I could do nothing else."

Jordan figured they had all been in his situation sometime in the past.

"We all have to answer to someone," she said, studying the card. Tibi's picture adorned a corner on one side. The other side had "GG&B" inscribed in raised letters in the same color as the plastic. A thrill of excitement coursed through her. It was a key card, like the one Ester Cohen had used for access at GG&B. It was their ticket into the building.

Chapter 50

As night settled in around the buildings that housed the GG&B Engineering offices, Jordan sat still in the passenger seat and watched the security guard finish his rounds. Walker and Haddid were slumped down in their seats. The night was quiet except for the sound of an occasional car passing on the street. The smell of oranges and olives sweetened the air.

"How much longer do we wait?" Haddid asked.

Jordan pulled her hair back into a ponytail. "We go when the guard is done with his rounds."

Several hours ago, Taylor and Ganani had headed to Tel Aviv to see what they could find out about Lucy and pick up supplies. It took every bit of Jordan's willpower not to call Taylor for an update. She knew he vacillated between scrubbing the mission and finding Lucy and seeing this through to the end. She could only pray they had gotten a lead on Lucy's whereabouts. Jordan was supposed to call at twenty-hundred hours. By then, Taylor and Ganani should have ferreted out what information they could and collected the items the team might need—packs, Camelbacks for drinking water, night vision goggles, extra ammo, new com devices, and ropes.

Jordan, Walker, and Haddid had spent the same time planning a break-in at GG&B's offices to find out what Tibi had stolen.

They had stopped in Haifa and purchased dark T-shirts and pants, solid footwear, and black gloves and masks. Jordan had sketched a diagram of the building from memory, noting the location of the maintenance area where the cleaning carts were kept and the location of the executive offices.

Thirty minutes after their arrival on site, the GG&B offices had closed for the night. The employee entrance was positioned on the street side of the building. The security offices faced the alley. Once the building had emptied, two guards had taken turns walking rounds every twenty minutes. One guard took approximately five minutes to check the outside doors and windows, while the other stayed behind to watch the cameras. So far, neither of the guards had gone inside.

At one point, both guards had jumped up and walked their rounds together. Jordan assumed they'd been put on alert.

Now the guard walking rounds came around the building and jiggled the lock on the front door. He scanned the street, his gaze flitting over their nondescript sedan. Then he headed back toward the alley.

"Okay, guys." Jordan slapped Walker's shoulder. "It's go time. The pass key should get us inside. Head for the stairwell. I don't know about the cameras there. Hopefully the guards will believe we are the cleaning crew arriving early. If they come and check, Haddid does the talking."

"What if the pass key has been disabled?" Haddid asked.

"Then we'll have to break in, which will likely trigger an alarm system, and there's no way to know if the guards will have backup. Let's all pray the pass key works."

As the guard disappeared around the corner, Walker's hand moved to the door handle. "Ready?"

Jordan pulled a *hijab* over her head. Looking the part of the cleaning crew was easy for Haddid and somewhat easy for Jordan.

Not so easy for Walker. Tall, light-haired, and buff, he oozed Marine. Unfortunately, he was also the one who possessed the crucial element. He was the only one with the know-how to hack the computer system.

The three of them climbed out of the car. Haddid reached the front door first. He looked straight up at the camera and then swiped the pass key.

It didn't work. Jordan felt the first tremor of fear.

Haddid frowned, turned it around, and swiped it again. This time the red light clicked to green and the door opened.

Walker and Jordan followed him inside. They climbed the short riser of stairs leading to the large waiting area with the tall windows looking out on the street, passed the reception desk, and turned the corner to the bank of elevators and the stair access.

While Haddid headed to the basement for a cleaning cart, Jordan and Walker climbed to the fourth floor. Inside the stairwell, they were tracked by security cameras on every landing.

"Here goes." Walker tried the handle on the door leading onto the fourth floor, but it didn't budge. He pointed to a box on the wall. "We need the pass key."

"Then let's hope Haddid figures out to open the door." This would be the first real test of Haddid's dedication to the mission. If he didn't open the door for them, they would be trapped: sitting ducks for the security guards.

Walker leaned against the wall and Jordan settled in beside him. She grew aware of the heat of his body, the smell of his new T-shirt, and the cold concrete at her back. "I guess the seventy-two-hour deal is shot."

"Yep," Walker agreed. "Maybe they'll believe I was in hot pursuit. Or that you had me at gunpoint."

"It'll never fly." Unless somehow he could leverage Taylor's being with them as an excuse. She wondered again about Lucy. If

Lotner returned with her, then she and Ganani had him figured out wrong. That would mean they still had a mole to uncover. Either situation was horrible.

Suddenly, Walker bent forward and pressed his ear to the door. "I hear someone."

Jordan flattened herself against the wall. Walker took a fighting stance two steps down facing the door.

It swung inward.

Haddid's face popped into view. "Ready?"

Jordan moved quickly. "Did you have any trouble?"

"None."

"Peter Graff is the COO. His office should be two doors down on the left." She led the way. The door was keyed. "Can either of you pick a lock?"

Haddid positioned the cleaning cart to block the view of the security camera while Walker knelt down and jimmied the door with a pen knife. Jordan grabbed the vacuum and located a plug.

"Got it." Walker moved inside the office. "No cameras in here."

Jordan pretended to vacuum, leaving the machine turned off so she could hear but pushing it back and forth for effect. "Haddid, close the blinds. Leave the door open."

She heard the computer power up and Walker typing on the keyboard.

"There's some high-tech security."

"Can you hack it?"

"Patience."

Haddid came outside and grabbed a spray bottle and rag off the cart. "I can see the entrance to the security office from the window. So far, no one has shown any alarm about us being here. I'll signal when the guard starts his rounds."

"I'm in," Walker said.

Abandoning the vacuum, Jordan headed into the office and leaned in over his shoulder as he scrolled through the files.

"Here we go." Walker pointed at the screen. "Based on the dates and time of access, it looks like he was interested in the maintenance files. He kept going back to a particular folder." He made a few clicks on the keyboard. "He was most interested in the Sapir Pumping Station files. His last day at work, he printed out a blueprint."

"What is the Sapir Pumping Station?" Jordan asked.

"It is the original pumping station of the National Water Carrier," Haddid said. "It's located on the northwestern shore of the Sea of Galilee."

"Why make it a target?"

Walker tapped a few more keys and brought up some information. "Maybe because the Sapir Pumping Station supplies nearly eighty percent of the drinking water to Israel and the occupied territories."

Jordan scanned the document. "If the plan is to destroy the pumps, Israel will be brought to her knees."

"Why would they harm their own people?" Walker asked.

"Eretz Yisrael. Cline had connections to the radical Jewish group the Neturei Karta, which has ties the Sikrikim, a group known for its violent acts. The Sikrikim feels persecuted by secular majority in Israel, and neither group believes the State of Israel has the right to exist until the coming of the Messiah and the joining of all of the lands defined in the bible as Israel's. That includes the current boundaries; the occupied territories; and parts of Jordan, Lebanon, and Syria."

"They want to start a war," Haddid said. "Without the pump, Israel will have no choice but to divert water from the Jordan River."

Walker sat back in the chair. "And you think Cline is . . . was behind this?"

"I think Brodsky is behind it. He used Cline like he used Ganani. Though I'm not convinced it's because he's a religious zealot. Still, what better way to retake the land?" Jordan pushed Walker back to the keyboard. "Can you save a copy of the blueprint?"

"I can send it to an e-mail account."

"Do it. How about printing the file?" She looked around for a printer. "Blueprints tend to run large. Do you see a printer?"

He clicked a few keys. "It says I can send the file to a printer. They must have a printer room somewhere."

"We have to go." Haddid turned away from the window. "The guard is starting his rounds and bringing the other guard with him."

"Walker, can you find a company blueprint?" Jordan asked. "It should have the printer room marked."

He worked through the file directory with Jordan leaning over his shoulder.

"Try the security folder. There." She pointed at a folder marked "office layout." He popped open a file with a markup of the rooms.

"It's on the second floor. Two doors down on the right from the elevator."

"Send it," she said.

"We have to go." Haddid grabbed up the cleaning supplies. "They are coming inside."

The faint bang of an outside door sounded.

Walker powered off the computer. "It should be at the printer."

"The two of you take the stairs." Haddid pressed the key card into Jordan's hand. "I'll take the cart down in the elevator and return it to the basement."

Jordan shook her head. "We should stick together."

Haddid loaded the vacuum onto the cart. "I'm what they expect in a maintenance worker. I'll tell them I was instructed to clean up a mess in the boss's office. Now go."

The elevator button dinged on a lower floor.

Walker held the door to the stairwell open. "They saw us on camera. They're going to ask about your helpers."

"I'll tell them we finished and that I sent you home."

"You'll need this for the elevator." Jordan pressed the key card into his hand. She and Walker would have to pick the locks to get out.

Haddid refused to take the card. "From the main floor, yes, but not from inside. But you will need it to access the second floor."

The light above the elevator signaled the car had reached the floor. Haddid shoved them into the stairwell. "Go, quickly. We need to stop this plan. It is not only the Jews who will suffer. Everyone will pay."

The elevator doors started to open, and Walker gently allowed the door to click shut. Jordan listened as Haddid talked to the guard.

"Go up," Jordan mouthed, pointing to the stairs.

Walker soundlessly climbed to the next landing, Jordan close on his heels. She froze as the door below them opened and the guard's voice echoed through the stairwell.

"Hey," he called out in Hebrew. "Are you in here?"

There was a pause. Then Jordan heard the static of his radio.

"The cleaner says he sent his helpers downstairs. Watch for them. I'm going to check out things up here, then escort him down."

Jordan held her breath until the door to the fourth floor closed. "Let's go. Second floor."

Swiping the key card on the second-floor door, Jordan pushed it open. The copy room door was two doors down from the elevator bank on the opposite side. Walker swiped open the lock as the elevator door rang.

"Shit," Jordan whispered. "They must be checking each floor."

Jordan dove into the room. Walker followed. Neither one could close the copy room door.

"What the . . . ," the guard said. Jordan heard him key his radio. "Did you check to make sure all the doors on second were shut?"

"Yes."

Jordan's heart pounded. He was coming to check.

The light from the hallway crossed the floor in geometric patterns, altered by the shadow of the guard. Jordan signaled Walker to get out of sight and wedged herself behind a large printer near the door. The guard swung the door inward, gun drawn. He flipped on the lights and Jordan shrank into the printer's shadow.

His radio crackled.

"Is there a problem?" came a voice.

"The door to the copy room was left open. I'm checking it now."

He walked forward until Jordan could see his silhouette. Reaching down, he messed with one of the printers.

Static. "Do you need me to come up?"

"No. One of the printers is on. The paper seems to be jammed."

Static. "Leave it."

"If you say so." The guard turned and Jordan shrank farther into the shadows. He walked back to the door and flipped off the light but stayed in the doorway. Did he sense their presence? Finally, he swung the door shut. Once it latched, he rattled it and Jordan stretched out her legs.

Walker jumped to his feet and raced to the printer. Clearing the jam, he checked the controls. "Let's hope it's in memory."

"Wait." Jordan held up her hand, stopping him from punching the button to print. She walked over and pressed her ear to the door. When she heard the elevator close, she signaled a go. The machine fired up. It took a few seconds to spit out an 11 × 17-inch copy of the Sapir Pumping Station blueprint. Jordan folded it up and stuffed it into her back pocket.

Quickly they made their way to the stairwell. They headed down, their footsteps loud on the metal stairs. Reaching the first floor, Jordan eased open the door. The reception area was empty. "It's clear."

With Walker on her heels, she made a dash for the exit. Footsteps caused her to duck behind the reception desk. Walker slid in behind her. A guard climbed the short flight of stairs from the front door. Had he seen them? He stopped in front of the reception desk and keyed his radio.

"Did you just enter the stairwell?"

The radio crackled. "No."

The guard moved quickly. When he rounded the corner, Jordan jerked her head toward the exit. Staying low, Walker's hand on her back, they took the low rise soundlessly. The elevator dinged as she pushed open the outside door.

"Did you find them?"

"No. The stairwell is empty."

"That's impossible."

With a whisper of a click, she closed the door behind her and the two of them ran.

Chapter 51

Haddid was already waiting in the backseat when they reached the car.

Walker started the sedan and peeled out of the parking lot. "What happened?"

"They asked me some questions and then let me go."

"You got lucky," Walker said.

"I must look trustworthy, for an Arab."

Ignoring the banter, Jordan dug the burner phone out of the glove box. She was a few minutes early, but she dialed the number Ganani had given her. Taylor answered. From his tone, she knew immediately that Lucy was still missing.

"There's no sign of them," he said.

"Did you try the police station?" she asked.

"The sergeant at the desk says Lotner was off duty today."

"Did you check his home?"

"There's no sign of them there."

Jordan could hear the measure of control in his voice. How close he was to the edge, she could only guess.

"Ganani managed to tap the Shin Bet records on Lotner," he said. "It turns out his wife and Tamar Cline are close friends."

The link. A small one, but enough to finger Lotner as the mole. His feeding Brodsky information had allowed the colonel to stay one step ahead. But what was the end game? And which one of the two was feeding information to the Palestinians? The answers lay in the blueprints.

"Lotner won't hurt her, Taylor," Jordan said. "He needs her for when things go south." It surprised her how easy it was to fudge the truth. "The best bet for getting her back is to see this mission through to the end."

Ganani's voice broke through the line.

"Call us again in two hours," she said. The line went dead.

Jordan set the phone down on the seat beside her and pulled her knees up into a tight fetal position.

"What happened?" Walker asked. "Any word on Posner?"

Jordan shook her head. She'd forgotten to ask. "Lotner has taken Lucy."

The tears that had threatened before now spilled down her cheeks unchecked. She thought of her father and about her promise to herself to find out the truth about his death. She heard the oath she had taken to safeguard those in her care. She had failed on all counts. She squeezed her arms around her legs.

"Turn around," she said. "It's my job to find Lucy."

Haddid's hand connected with the back of the seat, jarring Jordan forward. "After what we have learned? You cannot waste time."

"Lucy is my responsibility," she said.

"What about your responsibility to the people who live here?"

"I work for the United States government. My duty is to the Americans I was sworn to protect, not to Israel, and not to Palestine."

Even as she said the words, Jordan knew she couldn't defend them. As much as she had a duty to the Taylors, she had a responsibility to the seven-million-plus people who would be affected by an attack on the water system. But knowing there were bigger things at stake didn't make ignoring her responsibility to the Taylors any easier.

"What you told him was right," Walker said. "They're not going to hurt her. She's the bargaining chip. They need her alive."

Jordan unfolded her body and swiped away her tears. Doing nothing wasn't an option.

"Maybe we can do something about both. Lucy might not have taken her purse, but what about her cell phone?" Jordan asked. "If she has it on her, can you trace it?"

"Maybe," Walker said, "if the phone's GPS is activated and I can get on a computer."

Two big ifs. Still, it was worth a try. "Let's find a coffeehouse."

Walker drove north out of Haifa. Thirty minutes later, they reached the main drag of Nahariya and found a twenty-four-hour café with Internet access. While Jordan and Haddid found a table, Walker parked the car on a side street just in case an APB had been issued on their plates.

Glancing around, Jordan took quick stock of the coffeehouse. The bar ran the length of the room in the back, mirrored and stocked with bottles full of a variety of flavorings. Small tables for two and four were spread evenly around the floor in front, most hosting a computer. Only two of the tables were occupied. At a table in the back, a young man with dreadlocks hunched over a laptop computer. Jordan could hear his earbuds humming from fifteen feet away. On the opposite side of the room, a young couple were more engrossed in each other than in their coffee.

Jordan selected a table toward the front, near the window and door, with a view of the street. Walker came in, ordered them coffee, and purchased a computer access card with one hour's worth of time.

"Here," he said, setting down a tray laden with three coffees, a variety of pastries, a bowl of creamers, and three types of sweeteners on the table. "Pick your poison."

Jordan chose a mug, doctored it with cream, and selected a raspberry Danish from the pile. She hadn't eaten since early in the day, and the warm liquid combined with the pastry calmed the pain in her stomach and helped clear her mind.

Pulling the blueprint from her pocket, she flattened it on the table while Walker logged in to the computer.

"What's Lucy's number?"

"I have no idea," she said.

"That makes it harder, but not impossible."

While Walker worked his magic, Jordan studied the layout of the pump station. The black-on-white drawings located the pumps, the walkways, the staircase, and the various rooms and their contents. Circled in the corner was a small schematic of the operation as a whole, and on the left was information about the equipment. Three-quarters of the main structure appeared to be underground, housing a computer room, two fifty-foot cranes, and three massive pumps in cistern-like structures. Several access tunnels, reachable from the surface, housed electrical lines, cables, and equipment.

"Okay, here we go," Walker said.

Jordan slid her chair around beside Walker's, dragging the blueprint with her. "You found her?"

"Hmm huh." He tapped a few keys and several targets appeared on the map. He tapped a few more keys until one target remained. "Unn uh."

"What do you mean?"

Walker tapped the screen, causing the image to liquefy. "The phone is at the apartment, Jordan. She must have left it behind. Sorry."

Jordan watched the map on the computer meld. Then the street names become legible again, and the red target marking Lucy's cell phone signal came into focus. It hovered over the Diz-engoff Apartments. As the image gelled, Jordan felt herself unraveling again. She had been assigned to keep Lucy and her father safe. Now the girl was in the hands of men who thought nothing of killing in order to further their own agenda.

Jordan's hands trembled, crumpling the edges of the blueprint.

"Don't let them succeed," Haddid said. "You must stay focused on the bigger picture."

His words hit their mark, cauterizing the fraying threads of her resolve. It was time to accept the fact that there was nothing more she could do. She was convinced Brodsky had manipulated Steven Cline, facilitated the assault on Posner, orchestrated Alena Petrenko's kidnapping, and engineered Lucy's disappearance. She refused to let him hurt anyone else. There was no way could she let him win. The only thing left to do was stop the attack on the Sapir Pumping Station.

Jordan smoothed the edges of the blueprint and focused her attention on the etched details of the drawings.

"The pump units are accessible only through panel doors located on top of the cisterns," she said. "The specs say the panels are automatically sealed when the pumps are running."

"Everyone knows this," Haddid said. "The government allows tours of Sapir."

"Let's check it out online." Walker hit a few keystrokes on the computer and then studied the screen. "Security appears to be tight."

Jordan looked at the blueprint. "What about one of the access tunnels?"

Walker shook his head. "We'd never get to them. According to the website, there are guards everywhere. The perimeter is surrounded by a wire fence topped with barbed wire and patrolled by soldiers twenty-four-seven. There is an aboveground pump, used as a backup system, housed in a concrete structure separate from the main building. But it's also guarded around the clock. I don't see how we're going to get in unless you plan to start shooting Israelis."

"How will Brodsky and his men get inside?" Haddid asked.

"Through the main entrance." Walker and Jordan spoke in unison.

"Think about it," Jordan said. "If you were a guard and a Shin Bet colonel wanted access to the pumps, what would you do?"

Haddid played with his coffee cup. "I'd let him pass. But once he has sabotaged the pumps, how does he plan to escape?"

"Through one of the tunnels," Jordan said, "or maybe out the front entrance. For all we know, his plan is to kill the guards."

"I doubt he'll even show up," Walker said. "There's nothing solid tying him to this operation. Just conjecture and circumstantial evidence. If he's the mastermind, he'll just send his goons to do his dirty work."

Jordan hoped Walker was wrong. She looked back at the plans. There had to be another way in—a way no one would consider. She turned the document, coming at the station from every angle, and found herself repeatedly drawn to the star-shaped apparatus marking the end of the submerged pipes. She turned the document again and then ran some calculations based on the specs.

"There."

Haddid and Walker stopped talking and looked at her.

"I just found our way in."

Chapter 52

Jordan placed the call to Taylor and Ganani at exactly two hours after the last one had disconnected. Again Taylor picked up.

"How are you holding up?" she asked.

"How do you think?"

"Did you contact Dr. Petrenko?" Jordan was sure he was nodding.

"Daugherty also made some calls. The police have Alena under guard."

Before Jordan could offer any reassurances, Ganani's voice cut over the line.

"What is the plan?"

Jordan told her about the Sapir Pumping Station blueprints. "I think I've found a way in. If we make a move now, we can be waiting for them when they attack."

"We have no idea when that will be," Ganani said.

"They know we're on to them. We'll be lucky if they haven't moved already."

"Tomorrow is Shabbos."

"What better time for a surprise attack?" Jordan waited for her words to sink in. "We'll need to gather a few supplies. Do you know a place near Tiberias where we can meet?"

"We can meet at the market."

"What about someone who will help?"

"I have a friend who runs the horticultural lab for the Kibbutz Ginosar. The kibbutz is north of town and owns the land adjacent to the pump station."

"Can we trust him?" Jordan asked.

"Her."

"We'll need access to a computer."

"I'll make a call."

Jordan hung up. While she waited for Ganani to call back, she placed one more call. To Daugherty. "You're hot, Jordan," he announced.

"How so?"

"You have every cop and every soldier in Israel looking for you and your friends. Detective Lotner has put out an APB for you and Ganani, and Colonel Brodsky called this afternoon to let me know he'd taken over on the Dizengoff shooting case."

"Sir, you can't trust either one of those men."

"Why not?"

She told him her theory that the two men were working together.

"It's all conjecture. Where's the proof?"

"Are you saying you won't help?"

"I'm saying I can't help, Jordan. Without something I can take to someone above me, my hands are tied."

*

The dive shops in Nahariya opened at 8:00 a.m. Looking rumpled from sleeping in the car, Jordan and Taylor purchased two sets of diving equipment—wet suits, small tanks, regulators, weights, masks, rubber-soled boots, strap fins, and wet packs. Accessories included dive lights, watches, knives, and wire cutters. Jordan paid with a government credit card. By the time anyone traced the charges, this would be over.

Their rendezvous point in Tiberias was a little over an hour's drive. The small city, also known as Kinneret, was nestled on the western shore of the Sea of Galilee, approximately twelve kilometers south of the Sapir Pumping Station. Ganani and Taylor were waiting at the outdoor market. Transferring the gear into Ganani's vehicle, they ditched Jordan's car in a corner of the crowded parking lot.

It was noon when they arrived at the entrance to the Kibbutz Ginosar. Sun lit up the orchards and dappled the lake. One of the largest growers of bananas, mangos, and avocados in the country, the kibbutz was a destination tourist resort, providing a view of Lake Kinneret to the west, the Karei Deshe Youth Hostel and some archeological ruins to the north, and the Sapir Pumping Station just beyond. At noon, almost everyone was at lunch or serving lunch. The timing was perfect for Ganani's friend to smuggle them in.

She left them with a spread of fruit, vegetables, and cheese in the one-story, sprawling nursery facility that housed the lab and sat on the northern edge of the kibbutz. While they ate, Jordan laid out the plan.

Ganani pushed back her plate. "You're crazy. We should ambush them on their way in."

"My plan will work." At least Jordan hoped it would. "We have no idea how many they'll bring, and it's our best chance for rescuing Lucy. Someone will know where she is."

Taylor rose and walked to the window. Jordan knew his thoughts were with his daughter, but at least he was here. He played a crucial role in the plan, and they needed to keep him onboard.

"It is a suicide mission," Ganani said.

"It's the only way." Jordan looked to Walker and Haddid for support. They'd been over it. There wasn't a better option.

"Jordan's right," Walker said. "It all comes down to the timing."

Ganani crossed to where the blueprints were spread out on a table. "Explain it to me again."

Jordan joined her, pointing to the end of the roadway leading to Sapir Pumping Station. "Haddid will be stationed here. He'll give you a heads up when he sees them approach, then provide you with backup."

Ganani looked like she'd swallowed a roach. "I don't need backup."

"I hope not." Jordan pointed to a spot across the road from the main entrance. "You will be here. This should give you clear vision of the guardhouse, the entrances to two of the access tunnels, and the doors leading into the main building. You want to avoid shooting anyone."

"Where is the fun?"

That evoked a chuckle from Taylor.

"Walker will be here, manning the computers," Jordan said. "He's the only one who can shut down the pumps. The files we accessed by e-mail gave us the override codes. He's already hacked the computers. Once he turns the motors off, the hatches on top of the cistern will unlock and we can get into the main room. On his command, Taylor and I will go up through the pipes in the lake. We'll have exactly three minutes. After that, the backup generators will kick in, relocking the hatches. It's all in the timing. The biggest danger is entering the pipe openings while the pumps are still running."

Ganani looked between Taylor and Jordan. "How long has it been since either of you have dived?"

"Five years for me," Taylor said, his back still to them.

"One," said Jordan.

"And you think you're ready for this?"

Taylor turned away from the window. "I'm good. This is who we have. I know my shit, and I trust Jordan knows hers."

Jordan nodded. "The pipes are five hundred thirty meters long. By all calculations, it will take us five minutes and forty seconds to swim."

"Maybe longer," Walker said. "It takes the average swimmer thirty seconds to swim a fifty-meter lap."

"And it's not like you're going to be in a pool." Ganani was clearly in the *this-idea-is-crazy* camp.

"Let's just agree that it's possible," Jordan said. "Based on the flow rate of the water being sucked into the pump, if we swim with the pump suction, we shave two minutes off our time."

"Approximately," said Walker.

Jordan glared at him.

"I'm just saying."

Jordan turned back to Ganani. "The diciest part is shutting down the pumps."

"If you can do that, why can't the colonel?" Ganani asked.

"It wouldn't do him any good." Taylor walked back to the table. "Shutting down the system is just a temporary measure."

Ganani looked to Walker for confirmation.

"The pumps have a fail-safe generator system that kicks on once the main power source is deactivated," Walker explained. "That's where I work my magic." He swiveled his chair away from the computer and locked his hands behind his head. "I stop the pumps before Jordan and Judge Taylor get all the way to the cistern."

"Or what?" Ganani asked.

"Or we get sucked into the impeller." Jordan was getting tired of the negativity. "Do you have a better idea? I'm open for suggestions."

Ganani didn't say anything.

"This is our best option, so let's get on with it." Jordan pointed back to the map. "On Walker's signal, Taylor and I will swim along the pipe to the entrance. It will take approximately seven minutes."

She dared Walker to contradict her. He surrendered, and she continued.

"There is a screen we'll have to cut off. Add another minute. At the eight-minute mark, we'll enter the pipe. Based on the calculations of the flow rate, exactly three minutes later, at the eleven-minute mark, Walker will shut down the motors. That leaves us with seventy meters to go. It should take one-and-a-half minutes to swim into the cistern and find the ladder, leaving us one-and-a-half minutes to get through the panel hatch before the generators kick in and the hatch relocks."

"And if you don't get through?" Ganani asked.

"You'll find us either shredded or hanging on the ladders when you come to rescue us," said Jordan.

"Do you have all the equipment you need?" Ganani asked.

"Yes."

Ganani's eyes met Jordan's and held. "You're sure this will work?"

"Not at all."

Chapter 53

Staring out at the black, glassy surface of Lake Kinneret, Jordan battled the nerves in her stomach. Night had fallen, and she and Taylor had been sitting in their diving gear at the edge of the water for the better part of an hour. Six meters to their left, a dry stone wall topped with barbed wire marked the southern boundary of the Sapir Pumping Station. To their right was a mango orchard.

"Anything yet?" Ganani's voice boomed through the earpiece wedged in Jordan's ear. She reached up and turned down the sound.

"Negative. You?"

"Nothing. Maybe I was right that they wouldn't do this on the Shabbos."

"Patience." Jordan was talking to herself as much as to Ganani. Why hadn't Brodsky's men made their move?

Taylor gave her a thumbs-up. He was as convinced as she was that the attack would come tonight. He was keeping his Navy SEAL head in the game.

The sound of youths enjoying the Shabbos at the Karei Deshe Youth Hostel drifted toward them from two hundred meters along the shore. Shabbat meant there was only a skeleton crew of guards on duty at the pump station. The moon was waning, a mere sliver in the sky. It was the perfect night to destroy a nation.

Three underground pumps had to be destroyed in order to incapacitate the pump station. If they damaged one pump, no one would notice the difference. If they damaged two pumps, the aboveground pump would kick in, fulfilling its purpose of covering breakdowns and malfunctions. Two downed pumps would affect the water supply, but Israel would have enough surplus water to survive. If all three underground pumps were destroyed, the nation would be brought to its knees.

One document she'd read had indicated that after a catastrophic failure, it could take as many as five years to get the pump station back up and running. During that time, the nation would be forced to depend on its desalination efforts and on the inadequate number of wells tapping the underground aquifers. Destroying the Sapir Pumping Station would derail the peace talks. Israel would never agree to sign an accord. Anyone who could read a map could see that. The underground aquifers were all located in the occupied territory. Surrendering the occupied territory meant surrendering control of the remaining water to the Palestinians.

What came next is what Jordan figured drove Brodsky and the Neturei Karta. Destroying the pumps meant Israel would be forced to divert water from the Jordan River—an act once perpetrated by their enemy and a precursor to the Six-Day War. This time, it would become the catalyst for reclaiming Eretz Yisrael. Jordan figured, if all went as planned, because of the deaths and the involvement of the Palestinians, including the attack on the U.S. secretary, the PLC would be blamed. Cline's death raised some questions, but not enough to prevent the allies from throwing in.

Jordan stretched to ward off the bone-deep weariness that threatened to overtake her. She hadn't slept in twenty-four hours. None of them had. Yet here they were. They knew how to get in, but they had no knowledge of the end game. They had to be prepared for anything.

They were all in position and ready. Haddid, the floater, was parked on approach. Ganani, the sniper, was perched in her nest. Walker, the computer whiz, was hunkered down in front of the computer back at base. And finally, Taylor and Jordan, the SEAL team, waited beside the south wall of the pumping station, ready to move on Walker's signal.

Jordan tugged at the collar of her wet suit and repositioned the small dive pack on her back. It held the oxygen tank, a wet bag with her gun, and extra ammunition. She stirred the water with the toes of her fins.

"They're coming," Haddid said. Jordan froze in position. "I see two SUVs moving up the road."

Headlights swept the grass one hundred meters behind Jordan and then swung to the left. Ganani confirmed the sighting.

"They're turning in through the gate," she said.

"Do you recognize anyone?" Jordan asked.

"Unknown." Ganani had dropped her voice to a stage whisper. "Driver and passengers are still in the cars."

Jordan heard one of the guards speak, followed by the rattle of chain links. She heard the crunch of gravel and, a few moments later, the slam of car doors.

"They've parked near the entrance to the building," Ganani said. "I count four."

"We have more traffic," Haddid said.

Dry grass rustled as Ganani moved position. "It's Lotner."

Taylor started to stand as a patrolling guard turned the bend near the water and moved up alongside the south fence. Jordan grabbed Taylor's arm and yanked him back to the ground.

"Lotner can tell us where Lucy is," he whispered.

"You can't help her if you get yourself killed."

Walker's voice came through the com. "On my mark."

Jordan wanted to shout "not yet," but now she didn't dare speak. She and Taylor pressed themselves close to the low wall and froze. The guard raised his flashlight, shining the light out across the open grass to the orchard.

"Go," Walker said.

Jordan started counting seconds in her head. She didn't dare look at her watch.

The guard standing above them swung the beam back and forth, settling the light on a small mango tree. He was waiting for something. Had he heard them speaking?

"I count three more men, plus Lotner," Ganani confirmed. "That makes eight."

"I'm headed your way, Ganani," said Haddid.

At the shouts of the men at the gate, the guard clicked the light off and hustled away. Jordan continued counting for ten seconds.

"Walker," she whispered. "Restart the count."

Forty-five, forty-six.

"Walker!" The stage whisper wasn't enough to raise him. They couldn't afford to lose their window. Reaching out, she tugged on Taylor's sleeve.

"Let's go." Jordan marked the time on her watch. "We have less than eight minutes to enter the pipe."

A gunshot stopped her at the water's edge. "Who fired?"

"Lotner," Ganani said. "The guard at the elevators picked up the phone, possibly to confirm his orders. Lotner shot him."

Jordan heard the retort of a rifle. The guard who had been by the dry wall fence dropped. Had he spotted them? Had Ganani shot him? Jordan didn't know if he was hit or hiding.

"We have to go now," she said, splashing into the water up to her knees.

"Do you see Lucy?" Taylor asked.

"No. She's not here," Ganani shouted. "Go. Now!"

Shouts from the youth hostel mixed with gunfire and the screams of men. Several of the Karei Deshe Youth Hostel guests started into the grass.

Taylor pulled the com device out of his ear.

"We're down to seven minutes before we have to enter the pipe," Jordan said, stuffing her own com device into the wet bag. Tightening the dive weights around her waist, she pulled on her mask and clamped the breathing apparatus into her mouth. Reaching back, she turned on her air.

The water felt cool as she slipped into the lake. The shore dropped off quickly, and she swam as fast as possible toward the pump station. After several meters, she reached the first pipe.

She looked back for Taylor and then checked her watch. Six minutes, forty-five seconds. Keeping her hands on the steel pipe casing, she dove and kicked toward the end of the pipe. The shore dropped off and she swam deeper and deeper. It took her a moment to remember her dive training. Breathe in through the mouth and out through the nose. She felt short of breath and battled an urge to swim for the surface. Treading water, she forced herself to breathe slowly and her heart rate to calm. She needed to keep her wits about her.

Taylor came up behind her. He gestured to make sure she was all right. She gave a thumbs-up, clicked on her dive light, and started moving again.

The pipe seemed to go on forever. She glanced at her watch periodically and felt fear start to grip her. At fifteen seconds, she felt the suction. The current grew stronger, dragging her toward the pipe. Fighting a wave of panic, she yanked her feet free of the rip and moved to the top of the pipe where the pull of the water wasn't as strong.

Jordan forced herself to calm down. There was no time to indulge her fears. She and Taylor were already behind schedule.

Pressing herself close to the steel to mitigate the strength of the suction, she crept forward until she reached the pipe opening. She motioned for Taylor to free the bolt cutter strapped to his back.

The giant grate covering the mouth of the pump was littered with trash from Lake Kinneret—diapers, bathing suit tops and bottoms, and cups and plates. It looked more like some kind of free-form modern art than a garbage trap. Taylor fit the blade of the cutter on the top wire, and Jordan tapped his shoulder and shook her head. She pointed down to the bottom. Unless they cut the grate loose from below and stripped it away, the suction would simply hold it in place.

Together, they tackled the wires. Taylor cut, and Jordan peeled. It took them a minute to push the grate free of the mouth of the pipe. They were forty-five seconds behind schedule.

Swinging herself into the mouth of the pipe, Jordan trusted that Taylor would follow. The suction grabbed her and dragged her inside. She banged her leg on the outside lip of the pipe and felt a sharp pain slice across her thigh.

The force of the water tumbled her forward. She banged her head, her elbows, and her knees. It was like being tossed around in a water slide. She struggled for position. In order to make maximum time, they needed to swim with the current. She had no idea how far along the pipe she was or how much time had elapsed. She had no idea how far behind her Taylor was. She just put her head down and swam.

Chapter 54

A vibration in the pipe signaled the pump shutoff. The suction stopped in a beat, and the swimming grew harder. Jordan started counting strokes. Her dive light made the water glow green around her. She couldn't see much. Twenty-five or thirty strokes later, a huge shape loomed ahead of her. The pump.

Jordan stopped swimming and floated forward through the knuckle where the pipe attached to the cistern. Casting her light about, she followed the curve of the round cistern until she spotted the rungs of the ladder. Grabbing a rung, she unclipped her dive weights, kicked off her fins, and started climbing.

About three-quarters of the way up, she reached the water level. She climbed higher and pressed her hands against the hatch cover on top of the cistern. The water lapped at her knees. Her watch cast an eerie glow. They had less than one minute before the generators kicked on.

She pushed against the concrete hatch.

Nothing. The cover was heavy—too heavy. Shrugging out of her pack, she secured it to the top rung of the ladder, turned off the air, spit out the regulator, and yanked off her mask. Climbing higher for better leverage, she tried moving the cistern lid again.

It didn't budge.

Shining her light back toward the water, she wondered what was taking Taylor so long. It was going to take both of them to open the lid of the cistern. Her leg ached. Blood oozed from a gash in her wetsuit. She remembered the diapers on the grate and couldn't help but think that she needed a tetanus booster.

Digging the com device out of the wet bag, she put it back in her ear and tried to raise Walker. Her voice ricocheted around the cistern.

No answer.

Muffled voices drifted in from somewhere. Possibly maintenance workers, possibly Brodsky's men.

Her watch now read thirty seconds.

Suddenly Taylor burst from the pipe into the cistern.

Jordan felt a slight vibration and heard a small hum. The power was coming back on. She waved her arm. He fumbled with his weight belt. The vibration grew. Finally, the belt dropped away and Taylor shot to the surface. She pointed to the hatch.

Together, they pushed against the concrete cover. It lifted slightly, but not enough to flip it off. Taylor climbed higher on the ladder and pressed his back to the lid. The hum grew louder and the sides of the cistern shuddered. Jordan climbed up a step, and they threw all their weight against the lid.

The hatch cover moved as the pump roared to life. Jordan fought the current tugging at her feet and climbed out on top of the cistern. Taylor heaved himself up.

Lying on top of the concrete cylinder, Jordan checked her timepiece again. According to her watch, they still had ten seconds.

A commotion on the main-floor catwalk caused her to look up. Four stories above her, she spotted Lotner leaning over a railing that protected a balcony running along the north wall. He was shouting at his men in Hebrew and pointing. His focus wasn't on her.

He was shouting instructions on where each one was to go.

Feet pounded on the stairs. The sound echoed off the walls of the underground chamber. Jordan reached back inside the cistern, pulled her gun from the wet bag, and slammed the magazine into place. Taylor shucked his gear and did the same. Jordan signaled him toward the edge of the cistern.

A row of ladder rungs provided a way down on one side, but that was the side where Brodsky's men were setting up. Jordan lay flat on her stomach and watched to see what would happen. A walkway ran north to south. On the right were the computer and crane controls; on the left were the cisterns. Three Israeli guards lay in a heap in the walkway. They appeared to be dead. Two men with Uzis stood guard at the first cistern. Another straddled the cistern lid, his back to Jordan and Taylor. With an Uzi slung across his back, he attached the crane hook onto the lid of the cistern and signaled to the crane operator to add tension. Then he gestured to someone in the computer room.

Jordan felt the pumps power down again. They had used their trick and manually overridden the generator system.

Footsteps from above indicated that another person was descending the stairs. That made six in the pump room and two upstairs with Lotner.

Jordan lifted her head. The last man down was holding what looked like a twelve-inch round metal canister—a bomb!

Taylor tapped her foot. She wondered if he felt as helpless as she did. From this distance, with the weapons they carried, there was little they could do. If they attracted any attention, Brodsky's men would have no trouble taking them out.

"Okay." The man on top of the cistern flashed a sign to the crane operator. He threw the wench switch and powered the lid free. The man with the bomb climbed halfway up the cistern ladder and handed the canister to the man on top. After prying a small panel off the side of the can, he punched a series of numbers on a keypad inside. Jordan didn't have a clear view, but she might be able to emulate the sequence, provided she could get close enough to disarm the bomb. The timer beeped once. The charge had been set. Sealing it up, he dropped it into the cistern.

"We're done. Lower the hatch," he yelled, circling his hand in the air.

Jordan had no way of knowing how much time had been programmed or if there was any way she and Taylor could stop the blast. At the very least, they needed to stop Brodsky's men from setting any more bombs.

Jordan pushed herself to her knees. She whispered to Taylor, "I'm going to jump across to the next cistern. You get a bead on the base. When the first man reaches the top, I'll take him out. You take out the two guards at the bottom."

Taylor nodded. "After that?"

"I'll take the crane operator. You take the guy in the computer room."

"What about the one going for the next bomb?"

"Take him out. Take them all out."

Jordan looked up at the railing spanning the main level. Lotner and three more guards were somewhere upstairs. So were Ganani and Haddid.

Blocking out the pain in her leg, Jordan concentrated on beating Brodsky's man to the top of the next cistern. "Ready?"

Taylor nodded. A group had congregated at the bottom of the cistern with the bomb, and they were synchronizing their watches. Jordan waited until the man climbed off the top of the first cistern and jumped to the floor.

As he jumped, she leapt, her toe catching the edge of the cistern. She belly flopped onto the concrete, the sting traveling outward along her nerves. She lay flat and waited to see if anyone had heard.

"What was that?" one of the men shouted.

"It was just me, jumping down."

She raised her head. Lotner leaned over the catwalk. Their eyes met.

"Idiots, they are on top of the cisterns!" He gestured to someone behind him and then pointed toward Jordan. "*Atsor!*" Stop!

Jordan scrambled to her feet. Racing to the edge of the concrete pillar, she shot the first man she saw. Taylor took out the second. A third man shouldered his rifle and Jordan felled him on the spot.

Taylor scrambled onto the ladder. Gunshots ripped the air. Two men with Uzis strafed the cisterns. Jordan rolled, chased by a smattering of gunfire. She heard Taylor yell.

Rolling off the backside of the cistern, Jordan caught the edge with her fingers. It was a two-story drop. What choice did she have? Sucking in a deep breath, she let herself fall. A jolt of pain shot up her ankle at landing. She moved sideways, forced herself to her feet, and hobbled into the protection of the cistern. Pressing her back to the concrete, she inched her way around to get a view of what was happening. Taylor was on the ground. She didn't know if he was hurt or just playing dead. A bullet had shattered the glass to the computer room, and a man lay crumpled over the control panel. Taylor had taken the shot. Two men were coming down the hallway. She could hear them talking. It was the man from the crane and the bomb carrier.

Jordan waited for them to get closer. Her 9 mm was no match for an Uzi.

By the way the men talked, she knew they thought she was down. They also didn't seem worried about Taylor. Either they didn't know he was there or they thought he was dead.

Jordan waited until they moved into sight and then stepped into the open. She fired one shot. Taylor fired the other. Both men dropped.

There was no time to confer. Lotner knew they were there, and he had three guards up top.

"Surrender now," Lotner yelled from upstairs, "and I'll see the girl lives!"

He must think she was stupid. If she surrendered, what would stop him from destroying the pumps and killing them all? She considered the options. Even if Lotner was exposed, their weapons lacked the range to take him out. On the other hand, his men could hit them from this distance with their eyes closed. Where the hell was Ganani?

Think! Five of his eight men lay on the ground. Their Uzis were in reach—*if* she could get to one of them without getting shot.

Holding her gun in her right hand, she crab-walked toward the bomb carrier.

"Be smart, Jordan. You don't want Lucy to die."

She didn't, but for all she knew, Lucy was already dead. And where was Taylor?

Jordan spotted him moving for the elevators. If she could keep Lotner distracted, maybe he could get to the upper level and take Lotner out. She scooted around the cistern and assessed the situation. Going for the bomb carrier's gun left her exposed. "I trusted you, Lotner."

"Your mistake. Now don't make another. I have no reason to kill Lucy, unless you give me one. Come out where I can see you, and I promise, when this is over, I'll let the girl go."

She wished she could blow the condescending smile off of his face. Unfortunately, if she came out blasting, his men would drill her full of holes. Footsteps on the metal stairway signaled that the three remaining men were descending. Headed to take her out, to finish planting the bombs, or both?

She figured his priority was on the explosives. The timer on the first bomb had established the clock, putting Lotner under his own time pressure. But if she allowed them to plant the rest of the bombs, she sentenced more than seven million people to suffering and war.

"Still there, Jordan? All it takes is a call from me to settle this one way or the other."

A boot banged against the cistern. A vibration traveled through the concrete. Someone was climbing the ladder on the other side. She needed to act quickly.

One man on the cistern meant another man in the computer room to shut down the pump. That left the last man to operate the crane.

Jordan shoved off the side of the cistern and slid out into the main aisle. Stripping the dead bomb carrier of his Uzi, she aimed the weapon at the man on the ladder and pulled the trigger. He fell, dropping a silver canister, which bounced on the concrete floor and rolled out of sight. The crane operator came out of the cab shooting, and Jordan fired another round. He fell backward off of the crane, his head bouncing off the concrete.

A bullet slammed into the cistern above her head and Jordan ducked for cover. Pressed tightly to the side of the pillar, she looked for the man in the computer room.

Not there.

A pounding resounded from upstairs. "Shabak. Open the doors."

Finally! The elevator sounded. Taylor had also reached the top floor.

"You have nowhere to go, Lotner!" she yelled. "If you're smart, you'll surrender."

The pounding on the doors had stopped. If Lotner had any intelligence, he was running by now. What happened to him was up to Ganani and Taylor. Her job now was to try to disarm the timer on the bomb. Jordan moved cautiously toward the first cistern.

"Don't do it, Jordan. Just stay where you are." Lotner stood on the top rise of the stairs with his finger on the "send" button of his phone.

"Who are you calling, Lotner? Brodsky? Did he send you to do his dirty work so he could keep his hands clean?"

"Shut up." The detective started descending the steps.

"I'm right, aren't I? It's him." Jordan kept her eyes and ears open. Lotner was likely buying more time for his last man standing. Two could play that game. Right now, Jordan was the threat keeping Lucy alive. Once they took her out, Lucy would be expendable.

Ganani stepped to the railing and leveled her gun at the police detective's head. "Lotner!"

He looked up and an explosion ripped the air.

The force of the blast threw Jordan backward. Small pieces of concrete, mixed with water, hailed down. It was like being in the fountain at Dizengoff Square. She covered her head with her arms and looked for Lotner. The stairs to the lower level dangled at an odd angle.

"Jordan!" Taylor stood beside Ganani at the railing.

Jordan waded through the debris until she could see them clearly. "Where's Lotner?"

"Find him," Taylor shouted.

The floor under Jordan's feet was slick with water and blood. The room smelled sickly sweet. Her hands were empty. She must have dropped the gun when she'd been thrown by the blast. Searching for the weapon, she spotted movement to her left.

The maintenance tunnels.

Lotner was limping down the tunnel.

"Give it up," Jordan said, stepping into the open and leveling a rifle his head. "Tell me where Lucy Taylor is."

He stood beside the gaping hole that was once the first cistern. Water lapped the edges of the broken slabs of concrete, the water level higher now that the remaining hole was clogged with debris. He no longer held a weapon, but he still had his thumb poised to send.

"Press that button and you're a dead man."

The elevator kicked into action. Lotner cocked his head to listen. They were down to seconds before Ganani and Taylor joined them.

"I'm a dead man either way." Lotner punched the button and pitched the phone toward the open cistern.

"He's in the tunnel," Jordan yelled, running for the cistern and the phone. The phone landed on a flat slab of concrete, and she could hear the ring. If she could reach it fast enough, disconnect the phone, and get the number he had dialed, maybe she could save Lucy yet.

Grabbing a handhold, Jordan jumped down to the rubble. The slabs shifted and rocked under her weight. She dropped to her hands and knees. Crawling over to the phone, she hit the disconnect button just as a voice said, *"Shalom."*

Jordan stared at the phone as the screen went dark. Had she been fast enough to save Lucy? Or was the call itself the signal to dispose of the child?

One final shot rang out, jarring Jordan from her trance. She stood on the unstable slab and looked toward the tunnel. Ganani walked toward her. Lotner lay sprawled on the tunnel's hard earth floor. Taylor reached down to help her out of the cistern.

Chapter 55

The Sapir Pumping Station had been locked down. Ganani was put in charge of the investigation. She'd been the highest-ranking officer on scene and she deserved it.

Haddid had disappeared. No one had seen him after he'd called out his last warning. Jordan liked to think he'd gone back to his wife and his son and that they were living happily ever after somewhere deep in Palestine, far from Zuabi's reach. If anyone deserved a fairy-tale ending, it was him.

Walker announced that he had six months left on his current tour, and then he was heading back to MIT. He might be the oldest one in his class, but he was convinced his talents could be used more effectively hacking into enemies' IT systems than standing guard at embassies. All he required was a little more training.

An hour after the attack, Lucy had been found sleeping on a bench outside a trendy café along Tel Aviv's iconic Sderot Rothschild Boulevard. The child couldn't remember anything that had happened. Doctors suggested that she had been drugged. Other than her memory loss and some dehydration, she appeared to be fine.

The number on Lotner's phone was traced to a high-rise apartment building at the corner of Allenby Street and Sderot Rothschild—a building where Brodsky occupied two thousand square feet on the twenty-third floor, northwest corner. Police were dispatched to the location and a burner phone had been fished out of the dumpsters.

"I'm telling you, Daugherty, he's our guy," Jordan said. They were sitting in his office. He was drinking coffee. She was doing her best not to pace.

"He's Shin Bet and you need proof to accuse someone."

"The evidence is all right there, sir. Brodsky knew about the plan from the start. Ganani will testify to that. He ordered her to be at Dizengoff Square for the initial hand-off."

"Circumstantial. He collects a lot of intel. Maybe he heard something was going down and assigned her to follow up."

"He ordered her to al-Ajami to pick up both drives. He sent her to my office, for God's sake."

"Again, circumstantial. He probably figured there was something on those drives that was a threat to the State of Israel. As it turns out, he was right."

Jordan leaned forward across Daugherty's desk. "Lotner was Brodsky's mole. The detective was feeding Brodsky information. Lotner kidnapped Lucy Taylor, and she was found near Brodsky's home. The burner phone was found in his apartment building's dumpster."

"Can someone corroborate your allegations?"

"You know that they're all dead."

"Jordan, anyone could have pitched that burner." Daugherty set down his coffee mug. "Did it ever occur to you that maybe Lotner was manipulating Brodsky? Lotner was the one with the connection to Cline. Their wives were good friends. Lotner was involved in the specifics of the investigation all along. What makes you so sure Lotner wasn't the mastermind?"

All the things I can't tell you, Jordan wanted to say. She wanted to divulge the information that Alena Petrenko had shared that day in her office, but that would only raise questions about Jordan's father and likely get her removed from her job. She had only told two people what she knew about Ilya Brodsky: Weizman and Ganani. And Weizman was dead.

"Ilya Brodsky is a patriot. You've got nothing against him but a lot of circumstantial evidence tied up by a gut feeling. Let it go, Jordan, for your own sake."

Was Daugherty right? Had her focus on Brodsky become a witch-hunt driven by threads of a past she was just beginning to unravel? There was no doubt in her mind that he had something to do with her father's murder, no doubt as to the veracity of his past ties to the KGB. But Daugherty *was* right. She had no tangible proof of Brodsky's involvement in the Sapir Pumping Station attack—just a burning in the pit of her stomach that reminded her he was evil.

"Look at it this way, Jordan. You're a hero. Enjoy it."

*

The next day, Jordan dropped by the hospital to check on both Posner and Lucy. Posner was out of danger but facing months of rehab. Lucy was there for observation and scheduled to go home the next day. Jordan found her sitting up in bed talking to her father and Alena.

"Hey," Taylor said when she walked in.

"Hey," Jordan said. He looked good. She handed Lucy some cut flowers. Taylor snatched them up and took hold of Jordan's elbow.

"Lucy, you stay here with Alena for a minute. Agent Jordan and I are going to go down to the kitchen and look for a vase."

"Will you bring back some ice cream?"

"Sure." Taylor steered Jordan into the hallway and led the way to a small room with some cabinets, several vending machines, and a refrigerator. He pushed the door closed and then pulled Jordan toward him, kissing her hard on the cheek. "Thank you for saving Lucy."

Jordan stepped back in surprise. "I really didn't do anything."

"If you hadn't stopped the phone call . . ."

"I'm not sure I did." Someone had been holding Lucy, and that person had gotten away. It didn't feel right to be praised. "I'm just glad she's okay. She is okay?"

"She's doing fine. It annoys her that she can't remember anything, but I think, at least in this case, it's better that way."

Jordan tended to agree. "I'm the one who should be thanking you—for putting your life on the line out there."

Taylor found a vase in the cupboard. Jordan arranged the flowers. When she was finished, she stepped back. "Done."

"Perfect," he said.

They found some ice cream cups in the freezer of the refrigerator and snagged a few spoons. On the walk back to the room, he reached over and held her hand. "You need to know we're going to be leaving at the end of the week."

"So soon?" She was surprised that it bothered her—surprised how much she liked holding his hand. "I thought Lucy had another two weeks of treatments."

"We have to cut it short because Alena is leaving. Sarah wants Lucy home."

"When is she leaving?"

He nodded. "In a couple of days."

"How will that affect Lucy?"

"I think she'll be okay. Alena plans on giving her extra treatments while she's here, and then she'll treat her from a distance." He let go of Jordan's hand, and she found that she missed the warmth.

"Is it because of what happened in Bethlehem?" she asked.

"I imagine so. You'll have to ask her." He held the hospital room door open for Jordan and then followed her in, brandishing the flowers with flourish. "Here you go, Luce."

"And here's the ice cream." Jordan set the four small containers on the bedside tray. "We brought chocolate."

"Yay," said Lucy.

Taylor smiled at Jordan. "Lucy and I want to have you over for dinner before we go."

Lucy handed Jordan a container and spoon. "Will you come?"

Perching on the edge of the bed, Jordan slipped an arm around the girl's shoulders. "I'd love to."

"Good, then I can beat you in chess."

They ate ice cream and chatted for a few minutes longer, and then Jordan stood up to leave. "I don't want to tire out the patient."

"We like the company," Taylor said, the crow's feet punctuating the smile in his eyes.

"Still."

Jordan said her good-byes, and then Alena offered to walk her to the elevator. In the lobby, she pulled her aside.

"I wanted to talk to you," she said in Russian, settling into a small alcove in the back of the waiting area. "Did Ben tell you that Yury and I are leaving?"

"He did, but he didn't say why."

"It's Brodsky," Alena replied. "The man is dangerous."

"Has he threatened you?" Jordan's question sounded stupid, even to her. "I'm working on proving his involvement in your kidnapping, in Lucy's abduction, and in the attack on the Sapir Pumping Station. He needs to be held accountable."

"*Nyet.*" Alena fingers dug into Jordan's wrist. "Promise me you will stop."

Jordan pulled her arm away and massaged her skin. "Why? That man deserves to be brought to justice."

Alena leaned forward to whisper, her soft, dark hair brushing against Jordan's cheek. "There are things you do not know, Raisa. Things about your mother and father. You must be careful. Promise me you will leave it."

"I can't make that promise." Jordan knew herself. She would never be happy until she learned the truth. She didn't understand why Alena didn't feel the same. "I want to know what his involvement is. I need to know the things you know."

"Have you heard of the old adage 'Be careful what you ask for'?"

"Regardless of the consequences, I intend to see justice served." Even if it meant living in fear, not just of losing her career, but for the family and friends and country she loved. She had sworn an oath to serve, and Brodsky had threatened the safety of people she had vowed to protect. "I'd like to set up a time to talk with you before you leave, Alena."

"You are so much your father's daughter." Alena reached up and touched the side of Jordan's face. "I'm sorry, there isn't time."

Jordan studied Alena's expression. "Or is it that you're not willing to talk to me about him?"

"As I said before, there are things you don't want to know."

That wasn't what she had asked. "If you are trying to deter me, trust me, it won't work. Olek Ivanova was my father. Good or bad, I have the right to know who he was as a man."

"Even if it tarnishes your impressions? You seem to idolize him."

"What could be so bad that you would keep me from knowing my father?" Jordan pushed up from the chair. "Whatever it is you don't want me to know, it won't stop me from seeking the truth. Nothing you say will convince me it's better to live with blinders."

"Then promise me something?" Alena waited for Jordan to nod. "Promise me you will always remember two things."

"Which are?"

"Remember that, no matter how close they once were, your father never, ever trusted the man you know as Brodsky."

"And the second thing?"

Alena looked grim. "Sometimes it is better to let the dead sleep."

Acknowledgments

It has been said that writing is a solitary endeavor, but there is always the backup team!

My forever love and gratitude to my family, especially Wes for his unflagging confidence and support and Mardee, Danielle, and Addie for helping me explore Israel and their boundless enthusiasm for this book. To my BFFs: Laura Ware for being the best cheerleader on the planet, Cynthia Harbert for the chants, Anne McHugh for the goose bumps, and Janet Chapman for campfires and boat rides.

A big thanks to Gayle Lynds and David Morrell for being terrific mentors. To Twist Phelan, who bled red ink all over my pages. To my critique partners, who listened, advised, and sometimes slaughtered my first drafts, especially Don Beckwith, Tom Farrell, Marlene Henderson, Tom Holliday, Chris Jorgensen, Jedeane MacDonald, Mike McClanahan, Bruce Most, Piers Peterson, Suzanne Proulx, and Laurie Walcott. To my friends at the Rocky Mountain Chapter of Mystery Writers of America and the WRW family, with a special shout-out to Roman White for his "Kill the Girl" campaign. And to my Think Tank pals: Kay Bergstrom, Carol Caverly, Chris J., Cheryl McGonigle, and Leslie O'Kane for their sage advice about the publishing world.

I would be remiss not to mention the experts who helped along the way: Dwayne from Remington; the S.W.A.T. guys, who at their request will remain nameless; and my dear friends Moshe and Sandra Kafri, who helped add to the color. Thanks to all the people of Israel and the West Bank who showed me their country and shared their struggles. A special debt to Peter Rubie, who is as much my friend as my agent; Matt Martz, who saw the thriller in my manuscript and helped me to bring it out; and Nike Power, his assistant and copy editor extraordinaire.

Last, my undying gratitude to Irena, whom I can never repay. Thank you for a most precious gift.